Nissim Ezekiel

the authorized biography

R Raj Rao

VISHWAKARMA
PUBLICATIONS **VP**®

Nissim Ezekiel
the authorized biography

1st Edition–published in Viking by Penguin Books India in 2000
2nd Edition (updated)–published by Vishwakarma Publications in Dec. 2016
© R Raj Rao

ISBN - 978-93-85665-49-3

Published by:
Vishwakarma Publications
283, Budhwar Peth, Near City Post, Pune- 411 002.
Phone No: (020) 24448989 / 20261157
Email: info@vpindia.co.in
Website: www.vpindia.co.in

Cover Design : Abhishek Darekar

Typeset and Layout : Chaitali Nachnekar (Vishwakarma Publications)

Contents

Preface V

I   The Saturday Oil-Man...1

II   'I Was Born Here and Belong'..............................17

III   Freedom at Midnight 38

IV   To Say Hello to the Queen..................................68

V   Jewish Wedding in Bombay 98

VI   Everyman in His Humour 130

VII   'I'm a Poet and I Know It' 149

VIII Flower Power... 176

IX   Hymns and Fancies 207

X   Verse, Versatility 245

XI   Padma Shri Shri Ezekiel.................................... 285

XII   Totem Pole 323

Appendix 378

Notes.. 389

Index.. 401

Preface

I began working on the authorized biography of Nissim Ezekiel in 1994. The idea of embarking on the project came to me a few years before that, when the National Book Trust, New Delhi, commissioned me to write a review essay on him, for their two-volume *Masterpieces of Indian Literature.*

I have known Nissim for almost twenty-five years, first as a teacher, then as a fellow-poet, and finally as a friend. He is one of the few teachers whose teaching I genuinely benefitted from, who sincerely contributed to my education. Like him, I am a hard-core Bombayite (NOT Mumbaikar, please note). As a Jew, he is a minority person; I too regard myself as a minority person in heterocentric (and heterosexist) India.

Yet, if I had to write a biography today, I would most probably choose to work on a gay author like Aubrey Menen, or a lesbian such as Suniti Namjoshi. Between 1994 and now, my own concerns have drastically changed, with gay activism being pretty high on my list of intellectual priorities. I no longer have time for the kind of 'ladies man' Nissim was!

I was also working against several odds. The most debilitating of these was Nissim's failing memory. I caught him in the nick of time, as it were. When I began my research, Nissim was still able to recall most of his early life for me. By the time I was finished, his memory had almost completely let him down. Things came to such a head that whenever I went to see him, I found he had copies of Bunny Reuben's *Monkeys on the Hill of God* stacked on his table, and he asked me every five minutes whether he had given me a copy of the book! I learned afterwards that he did this to nearly every other visitor who went to meet him.

Then, Nissim's family was uncooperative from the start. He often told me that they were, for some reason, opposed to the project. Under no circumstances did he want me to talk to his wife, Daisy, and son, Elkana.

He did not mind my talking to his daughter, Kavita, though. But when I approached her, she only promised to send me a reply to my questionnaire; in reality, the replies never arrived. Nissim's sister Asha (Lily) too turned down my request to be interviewed, saying it was 'too painful' for her to talk about her brother. Only Khorshed Wadia Ezekiel, wife of Nissim's late brother Joe, was friendly. An interview with her appears in the Appendix.

Nissim Ezekiel passed away on 9 January 2004. It was a year that would witness the death of two other major Indian English poets—Arun Kolatkar and Dom Moraes. Earlier, A. K. Ramanujan had passed away in Chicago in the United States of complications following surgery. Commentators lamented the phasing out of this first generation of post-independence Indian poets in English that could not be replaced by a less illustrious second generation of poets, made up of poets like Ranjit Hoskote and Menka Shivdasani, whom the first generation nurtured. Nissim's funeral was a low-key affair. Academic duties prevented me from attending his funeral in Bombay, but from what I gathered from friends who attended it, and from news reports in the press, not many friends and relatives were present at the funeral. It was as if the fame he had achieved as a poet had already been forgotten, or thought of as inconsequential. His five-year illness prior to his death contributed to his being obliterated from public memory. As such anthologies that appeared in the 1990s, edited by scholars like Arvind Krishna Mehrotra and Vilas Sarang, questioned his position as the first of a new wave of modernist poets in post-independence India. Not everyone agreed with this view, but it went a long way in reassessing Nissim's stature as a poet.

This biography is written from Nissim's point of view. It is subjective. I was not interested in cold, clinical objectivity, or a documentation merely of facts and statistics. I wanted to write about things the way Nissim remembered and interpreted them. I restricted my conversations and interviews to those people with whom I was comfortable. This biography is also the response of one writer to another. I haven't tried to mask my own subjectivity either.

The list of people I wish to thank is fairly long. I must begin with Nissim himself, who never resented the time he had to spend with me, Saturday after Saturday, answering my questions. He also gave me all the material on himself that he had in his possession. The late Khorshed

Wadia Ezekiel was of invaluable help; I shall never be able to thank her enough. Among Nissim's friends, I am especially indebted to Abraham Solomon, Adil Jussawalla, Gieve and Toni Patel, and Ranjit Hoskote for the exhaustive interviews they gave me. But there are many others who allowed me to interview them, and it will be ungracious on my part not to mention them and express my gratitude. They are: Rameshchandra Sirkar, Minakshi Raja, Vrinda Nabar, Tara Patel, Jerry Pinto, Ronita Torcato, Kavita Sahni, Gauri Deshpande, Victor Gaikwad, Freya Barua, Jessica Mahadevan and Anthony Burge. I am thankful to my mother, sister Anjanee and her husband John, and to my friends Rajendra and Rakesh for the emotional support they provided during the years I was busy with this book. Thanks are due to Girish and Anjali Patil of Cyberworld, and to their typists Saraswati and Vaishali, for helping me deal with my 'technophobia' and putting my manuscript on disc.

I am thankful to Satish Gore for painstakingly going through the proofs.

Above all, I am thankful to Vishal Soni of Vishwakarma Publications for bringing out the much-needed paperback edition of the book at a time when Nissim Ezekiel seems to be all but forgotten as a poet.

Pune
November 2016
Nissim Ezekiel

The Saturday Oil-Man

In the years that followed World War I, a pregnant woman once crossed the Mahim Creek of Bombay in a boat. From the boat she threw a coconut into the water. When she returned home, she wore a new sari, and new green bangles made of glass. Then she took part in a ceremony in which Elijah the Prophet was asked to give her a safe childbirth. After that there was dinner.

The woman's name was Diana. She was an amateur stage actress, married to Moses Ezekiel Talkar, and they were having their first baby, whom they would name Joe. There was a daughter who was born before Joe. However, she died soon after birth. Moses had seen Diana in a performance, fallen in love and proposed. No one knows for certain the significance of the ritual described above. But the Bene Israel, the community to which Moses and Diana belonged, widely believe it to bear a connection with the story of their ancestors' shipwreck two thousand years ago. Diana went on to have four more children, of whom two were boys and two girls. But she never crossed the Mahim Creek in a boat again, for the ritual was meant to be practised only during a woman's first pregnancy.

If this is a fictionalized, if dramatic, account of the birth of Diana's first surviving child, the facts are less colourful. Joe was actually born in Gwalior in the hinterland. Diana did not actually go through the ritual of travelling in a boat, throwing a coconut into the water, and wearing a new sari and glass bangles. For, this was the 20th century and people had become practical.

On 16 December 1924, Diana gave birth to her third child, a male once again. There was a wonderful symmetry in her deliveries, the way (in the case of her first three children) girl followed boy, and boy followed girl. Joe's birth had led the way for his brother's as far as ceremonies were concerned; so the naming and circumcision of Diana's second son were relatively simple affairs. Among the Bene Israel, both ceremonies usually take place on the eighth day after birth. Thus, ironically, it was on the eve of Christmas, 1924, that the child was named Nissim, which means 'justice' in Hebrew; he was carried to the Magen Hassidim Synagogue at Agripada for his circumcision, as Joe had been before him, by Diana's brother as was the custom. Diana herself did not remain present during the circumcision, but her husband and brother did.

Diana's parents lived in Bombay, but she studied in Pune. The child who came after Joe and preceded Nissim was Sarah, and the one that followed Nissim was Hannan. Lily came last. According to standard religious practice among the Bene Israel, it was on the twelfth day after birth that the newborn child was bathed and placed in a cradle for the first time. It was also on this day that it was taken to its maternal grandparents' home, along with its mother, and made to stay there at least till the day of the mother's 'purification'. This took place on the fortieth day of the birth of a male child, and on the eightieth day of the birth of a female child. The child's head was also shaved at this time.

In the case of the Ezekiels, there is no readily accessible family album containing pictures of those early days, by means of which we can establish whether the young Nissim's head was actually shaved on the fortieth day, and whether he was taken to Pune to meet his grandparents. Nissim himself feels it is possible that both things happened.

In order to understand the kind of life that the Ezekiels lived, and to see it in the right perspective, it is necessary to know something of the background of the Bene Israel in India. The words 'Bene Israel' would translate into English as 'Children of Israel'. The Bene Israel are regarded as one of the Lost Tribes of Israel. The most famous legend about the origins of the community is that they landed in southern Maharashtra, off the Konkan coast anywhere between 1600 to 2000 years ago, when their ship was wrecked in a storm. One theory is that they took to the sea in order to escape from Muslim persecution in Persia. Another is that it was a Greek ruler, Antiochus Epiphanes, who drove them out of North Palestine. The exact place of their arrival is the coastal village of Navgaon, very close to the modern beach resorts of Alibag and Kihim, frequented by Bombayites. It is believed that only fourteen people survived the shipwreck, half of these being men, the other half women. The dead were buried at Navgaon village in two 'elongated mounds' which may still be seen.

The survivors are said to have settled down in villages along the coast of Raigad district, one that this part of Maharashtra comprises, and in which no less a hero than Shivaji was coronated. They took to farming, and especially oil-pressing (or crushing seeds) for a living. They lost touch completely with people of their own faith elsewhere in the world; the only point of contact that remained was the Sabbath, which they observed on Saturdays. The oil-pressers among them came to be known as Saturday Oil-men or Shanwar Telis, the sect to which the Ezekiels belong. (Interestingly, there are in this region both Friday Oil-men or Shukrawar Telis and Monday Oil-men or Somwar Telis. The former are Muslims, the latter Hindu 'untouchables'.)

Other Bene Israel opened shops. However, to avoid rivalry, they were told by the local people not to sell what others were selling. The Shanwar Telis, too, were not allowed to charge a fee for their services, though they could sell the crushed seed to agriculturalists, which became their principal means of supporting themselves.

Much later, Nissim would refer to these origins in one of his most well-known poems, 'Background, Casually':

> My ancestors, among the castes,
> Were aliens crushing seed for bread
> (The hooded bullock made his rounds).

The Shanwar Telis were quick to assimilate local conditions. As the villages in which they spread themselves were mostly on the coast (though some were also inland), many of the native inhabitants were fishermen by profession. There were even inter-marriages between the Shanwar Telis and the Kolis, the traditional name by which the fishermen are known, although the Bene Israel were, on the whole, conservative about marrying outside the community. The native population, especially, requested them to avoid such marriages.

Like the upper-caste Hindus of the area, the Shanwar Telis adopted new surnames, based on the villages from which they came. Sometimes the Shanwar Telis even 'nativized' existing Jewish names, as for example, when they made the name Moses Mussaji. The word 'Talkar', which Nissim's father Moses Ezekiel added to his surname (but which he later dropped) is such an invention. However, according to Nissim, they are still registered at the Magen Hassidim Synagogue as Talkar. The village of Tal (sometimes spelt Thal), a few kilometres from Alibag, is the only place that the Ezekiels can rightfully call their 'native place'. On a Sunday morning in February 1995, while celebrating the birthday of a friend at Alibag, I visited Tal to gather first-hand impressions of the village. The bus ride from Alibag to Tal took twenty minutes. As we got off the highway and came to the road that leads to Tal, it became narrow and winding, full of zigzag turns. This was probably the very course through which Nissim, as a schoolboy, trekked to and from Alibag, during visits to the house of his paternal grandfather Haskelji Israel, who had fought in the Boer War of the 1880s, and would entertain his grandchildren with heroic stories. A variety of trees surrounded the road on either side, and among these we could identify coconut, palm, betelnut, banana, peepul and chickoo trees. The trees were so numerous that they provided a sylvan shade all along the three-kilometre route to Tal. Interspersed between the luxuriant foliage were houses that looked sparsely inhabited, and belonged to the well-to-do. Many of the fruit trees were, obviously, private holdings of the more affluent households. The architecture of these houses was modern, and they had a distinct, non-Hindu ambience, that reminded me of dwelling places in rural Goa. (Later, when we visited Kihim, I found that the settlements were very similar.)

The idyllic quality of the landscape was lost once we actually reached the village of Tal. Now we were smothered by nondescript shops through which the people uncomplainingly made their way. There were elections in the state of Maharashtra on that day, and the village was full of presiding policemen who went about in jeeps that raised a ton of dust. The sloping-roofed houses that looked rather like huts were clearly those of ordinary folk, and had none of the distinctiveness of houses on the village's outskirts. Possibly, one of these houses was the late Haskelji Israel's, the house in which Nissim's poem 'Night of the Scorpion' is set; it is based on what had once happened to his mother in the 1930s:

> The peasants came like swarms of flies
> and buzzed the Name of God a hundred times
> to paralyse the Evil One.

The Ranade High School, which we passed, was one of the area's more prominent landmarks. The sea air was damp on the skin. When we boarded the bus back to Alibag, it was full of spirited fisherwomen proud of their catch.

None of Nissim's immediate or distant relatives live in the village of Tal any more. However, the surname Talkar is by no means an uncommon one, and some of the most fascinating stories about the Bene Israel in Raigad concern the Talkars. According to one such story, which has been in existence for over two hundred years, Shelomo Abraham Talkar, a wealthy Shanwar Teli, was accused by the Peshwas of conspiring with the Muslim Nawabs of Janjira against them. They ordered that he be trampled to death by elephants. However, the elephant that was assigned the task of 'executing' Shelomo, instead of harming him, quietly picked him up in its trunk and placed him on its back. The stunned Peshwas took this as proof of Shelomo's innocence, revoked their order, and granted Shelomo not only a permanent position in their court, but also a jagir of village Gangli.

The Jews in India fall into three groups, the other two groups besides the Bene Israel being the Baghdadi (or Iraqi) Jews and the Cochin Jews. Of these, the Bene Israel have been in India for the longest time. The Baghdadi Jews and the Cochin Jews came afterwards, and their arrival is tied up historically with British imperialism in India. The Baghdadi Jews essentially came to India as a trading community in order to join their European Jewish counterparts in the East India Company at Surat, on the coast of Gujarat. Of course, it is also said that like the Bene Israel, they were compelled to come to India in order to escape the wrath of the Pasha kings in Iraq. The Cochin Jews are believed (by the Bene Israel) to have landed in India as late as the first half of the nineteenth century, though some Cochin Jews claim that they have been here for at least 500 years.

The relations between the three Jewish communities in India have, on the whole, been harmonious. But it took the Bene Israel some effort to convince the Cochin Jews that they were not the first to arrive in India (the Cochin Jews claimed that they had lived in India for hundreds of years and had come here much before the Bene Israel). If the Cochin Jews did not know of the existence of the Bene Israel, it was only because the latter were, until the nineteenth century, still living in villages with undeveloped means of communication, and had not begun emigrating to the cities.

All the three Jewish communities in India, but especially the Bene Israel, are somewhat distanced from Hebrew, the classical language of the Jews. The Cochin Jews seemed to know the language reasonably well when they began their 'missionary' activities in India in the nineteenth century, and part of their energies were directed at teaching it to the Bene Israel. This is proved by the fact that while there were almost no inscriptions in Hebrew on Bene Israel tombstones in the eighteenth century, there are several such inscriptions on tombstones belonging to the nineteenth century, in cemeteries at both Navgaon and Bombay. This, of course, was only as far as graveyards were concerned; the Cochin Jews did not succeed in making Hebrew a household language among the Bene Israel. In Nissim's own home, for example, although the prayers were said in Hebrew, neither he nor any of the members of his family knows enough Hebrew to be able to speak it. For most Bene Israel in India, it was Marathi that came to be their first language, or the nearest to what one may call their mother tongue. This is easily explained by their origins in coastal Maharashtra. However, as the region that they made their home covers a large area, and extends almost into the Konkan, some of them were equally well-versed in Konkani. The Ezekiels, too, knew Marathi and regarded it as one of their first languages, along with English. But their use of it was restricted to the domestic sphere. When Nissim would grow up and become a poet, one of his chief regrets in life would be that he did not know how to write poetry in Marathi. Partly he would attribute this to the fact that he went to an English-medium school, where even to speak a word of Marathi was forbidden. He would try to make up for this by attempting, occasionally, to translate a poem from Marathi (as he did, for example, the poems of Marathi poet Indira Sant with co-translator Vrinda Nabar). Then he would try to speak in Marathi to waiters, clerks and office boys. But the regret would remain, for throughout his life, Nissim would never manage to make much headway with Marathi. His younger brother Hannan, too, who would become a distinguished economist and journalist, and was for ten years the editor of the *Economic Times*, was nonetheless poor in Marathi, and would confine all his intellectual work to English.

No community in Hindu India, howsoever small, has been able to escape the debilitating effects of the caste system, and the Jews are no exception. Arguably, caste Hindus consider people of all other religions in India to be traitors, lower in status than even the 'untouchables', no matter what their origins. Often, they are unable to make a distinction between those religious communities that converted to other religions as a result of indoctrination (Christians, Muslims and Buddhists), and those that arrived here in their own right ages ago (Zoroastrians and Jews). What is especially unfortunate is that because of osmosis, minority religious communities also become casteist in their thinking, although there is no place for caste in their religion. It is easy to see how the Bene Israel have fallen prey to these prejudices. They were at the receiving end, both among the caste Hindus of coastal Maharashtra, as well as the Baghdadi and Cochin Jews, who must have regarded their traditional occupation of oil-pressing as unclean. Thus, in a way, they were considered to be the lowest of the low, and would have to put in a considerable effort to rise above their status.

When the Bene Israel emigrated to cities like Bombay in the second half of the nineteenth century, it became possible for them to slowly move away from their traditional occupations. Even before the shift took place, some of them had already given up oil-pressing and had become weavers and boatmen. It is not clear whether any of Nissim's own ancestors gave up oil-pressing and took to these other professions. But when in the early '50s a broke Nissim would earn his passage from England to India by scrubbing decks aboard the cargo ship in which he was travelling, it was as if he was especially equipped to do so by something in his genes. It was as if he was only doing what his ancestors must have done decades ago.

Once they arrived in the city, there were more professional choices available to the Bene Israel. Some of them became skilled carpenters, for whom there must have been considerable demand in British India. Others joined the British Bombay Native Army. Much later, this is probably how Nissim's grandfather Haskelji Israel found himself fighting in the Boer War; he was charting a course already explored by others in the community. In contrast, Nissim himself would grow up to be gentle and soft, with none of the ruggedness that one expects of soldiers, although he would develop a capacity to rough it out on journeys, beginning with that famous voyage from England to India on a cargo ship.

In the nineteenth century, there was further upward mobility among the Bene Israel. Caste-consciousness gradually came to be replaced by class-consciousness in the city, and many of them obtained 'white-collar' jobs. By the time we come to the twentieth century, the social gap between the Bene Israel and upper-caste Hindus on the one hand, and Cochin and Baghdadi Jews on the other, narrows down considerably, more so after Independence in 1947. Now it was relatively easy for them to take up 'respectable' jobs like teaching. When Nissim's grandfather Haskelji left the army, he became a teacher, and following his example, both Nissim's parents became teachers; and when the time would come for Nissim to decide on a career, he would give up more lucrative jobs in advertising and journalism, opting for a lecturership in a college.

With social mobility came a sense of cultural superiority. The new-found status of the Bene Israel prompted them to identify with upper-caste Hindus, particularly with regard to dietary habits. They made sure that they did not eat beef. They looked upon lower-caste Hindus like the Mahars and Mangs, who ate dead animals and birds for food (because they were cheaper), as unclean, and stopped employing them as servants in their homes. These beliefs were shared to a large extent by the Ezekiels, and made a part of their daily life. Nissim himself would become a vegetarian in his post-LSD years and, attribute it not only to the effects that the drug had on his mind, but also to reasons of health. He would advocate Indianness (or Hinduness) in poetry, and self-consciously employ it in his own verse, in an attempt to overcome his cultural and spiritual alienation from mainstream India. It wouldn't be far-fetched to suggest that, on the whole, he would want the world to see him as a Brahmin Jew.

Shirley Berry Isenberg, in her book *India's Bene Israel,* describes the average Bene Israel as having 'straight to wavy black hair, black or dark brown eyes, oval face, straight nose. Obesity was and remains rather rare among the Bene Israel. Skin colour can vary from very light to very dark brown, and the average height used to be from five to five and a half feet (but by the twentieth century they were on an average considerably taller).'[1]

Many of the above traits are present in Nissim. The wavy hair, the oval face, the light skin, are a very definite part of his personality today, and have always been so since his childhood. It is also true that he has never been obese, even in his middle years. His nose tends to be hooked rather than straight, or at least seems so from certain angles. Isenberg says that in the twentieth century, the Bene Israel were taller than they were earlier, and once again this applies to Nissim quite accurately: he is five feet seven-and-a-half inches tall. But he certainly doesn't resemble any of the Maharashtrian castes that Isenberg claims the Bene Israel do. Perhaps if it came to that, his younger brother Hannan could be said to pass off for a Maharashtrian (Hindu). Nissim is instead easily mistaken for a Parsi, and this gives credence to the view that the Bene Israel hailed originally from Persia, and were hounded out of their country by the Muslims.

My neighbour says, you are Parsi?
No, I say genially, acknowledging his interest, Zoroastrian.
He leaves the subject alone.
The train has stopped between stations.

('The Local')

In addition to the influence of the Cochin Jews, who, as pointed out earlier, played a sort of missionary role in the lives of the Bene Israel, there were also the Christian missionaries of the nineteenth century who were concerned with preventing them from identifying too closely with the local Hindu population. Both the Cochin Jews and the Christian missionaries were thus performing the role of teachers, and they later recruited some of the better-educated Bene Israel as fellow-teachers to help them advance their cause. This must have suited the Bene Israel, who were looking for ways to break away from their hereditary calling of oil-pressing. Inspired by the missionary activity of the Cochin Jews and the Christians, the Bene Israel would begin to rank teaching as higher than other 'white-collar' jobs, and in the next hundred years or so take to it in a big way. In our own day, teachers infiltrate the Bene Israel community in large numbers; and it isn't surprising that three generations of the Ezekiels should have thought of teaching as a more noble job than anything else they could possibly do.

More significantly, some Bene Israel became writers. The community began its creative career as artisans in the nineteenth century; but it was as early as the eighteenth century that the first Bene Israel folk poet, Elloji Nagawkar, is believed to have made his appearance. He was actually a singer of ballads. The nineteenth century saw the arrival of another folk poet-cum-singer, Robenji Isaji Nawgaonkar, who was born sometime in the 1830s. But the poems of both Nagawkar and Nawgaonkar were rendered orally, and are not available to us today. The first published work of literature by a Bene Israel Jew was *Gul and Sanobar*, which appeared in the year 1867. Its author was Bahais Joseph Talkar. This was followed, shortly afterwards, by a novel, *Bago Bahar*, by M.D. Talkar. Later, there was a highly-respected Bene Israel painter who also had the surname Talkar. Whether or not the Ezekiels are related to any of these Talkars is difficult to say; but given the likelihood, it is tempting to suggest that poetry was in Nissim's blood at the time of his birth.

Apart from creative writing, the latter half of the nineteenth century also witnessed a surfeit of 'ecclesiastical' writing by the Bene Israel. It is evident that this was the direct outcome of the religious education that they received. The Jewish community acquired its first Hebrew printing press in Bombay around this time. Later, it acquired another press in Pune. It also founded its own publication house, known as the Subodh Prakash Samaj, and brought out its own periodicals. Most of its books in Hebrew were prayer books; it is believed that in all, the community published 146 books in Hebrew, of which eighty-eight were by Baghdadi and fifty-eight by Bene Israel Jews. A considerable amount of time and energy was spent by the members of the community translating Jewish liturgical works into Marathi. Perhaps the most prolific writer in this respect was Joseph Ezekiel Rajpurkar, who published as many as twenty religious books between 1858 and the time of his death in 1905, of which some were originally written in Hebrew, others translated from Hebrew into Marathi.

Nissim would both continue and break away from this tradition of religious writing when he became, a writer. For one thing, he would not confine himself only to poetry, but would experiment with prose as well. He would begin his spiritual journey believing in religion, would then be drawn away from it, and would come back to it again. This would be reflected in his writing. The theme of religion would recur in many of his poems, and in the titles of some of his later collections of poetry. But he would never write a religious tract, or 'stoop' so low as to write anything that was preachy and propagandistic. His passion for his religion would be restricted to community work, and would never find direct expression in his writing.

When it came to family life, the Bene Israel were strongly influenced by the Hindus. Until the twentieth century, they lived in joint families, which comprised the father, mother, unmarried sons and daughters, married sons and their wives, and their children. In the twentieth century, city life must have compelled many of them to reject the joint family norm and opt for 'nuclear' families. Nissim's own family was never a joint family in the conventional sense of the term. In the '30s, when they lived in Readymoney Mansion near the Byculla bridge, the family consisted only of Nissim's parents, himself, and all his brothers and sisters. There were no grandparents living with them. However, in the '40s and '50s, after the weddings of Joe and Nissim, the two brothers' wives did for a short time become a part of their extended family. They had moved by then from Readymoney Mansion to The Retreat on Bellasis Road, not far from Bombay Central station. Although their apartment in The Retreat is fairly large, with many spacious rooms, Nissim remembers his mother partitioning off a part of an outer room for him and his wife Daisy soon after their wedding. The other part of the room was probably being occupied by other children in the family. This, of course, was only a temporary or a stopgap arrangement; eventually, Nissim and Daisy moved to Warden Road, a better locality.

The two sacred days in the year for the Bene Israel, as for Jews all over the world, are Rosh Hashanah and Yom Kippur. They occur every year during the months of September or October. Among the Jews, these days are sometimes referred to as the High Holidays. Rosh Hashanah is the New Year, on which the creation of the world with God as ruler is celebrated. The celebrations last for ten days, known as the Ten Days of Penitence. They end on Yom Kippur, or the Day of Atonement. In the old days, on Yom Kippur, the Bene Israel would bathe first with hot and then with cold water, and dress in white clothes. They would go to the synagogue making sure that they did not come into physical contact with non-Jews. (This notion of pollution by touch could probably be another of the destructive influences of Hinduism.) They would spread their handkerchiefs on the floor of the synagogue, kneel, and say: 'Blessed be the name of the glory of His kingdom for ever and ever.' Then they would lie prostrate with their faces on their handkerchiefs.

We know it for a fact that the Ezekiels themselves went through none of all this, except the customary visit to the synagogue on Yom Kippur. Moses perceived himself a scientist and a rationalist, and was against superstitious or ritualistic practices. Nissim would later justify his father's stand by pointing out that they were not the only family to ignore ceremonies associated with their religion: in their own day, a sizeable number of the rituals described in their holy books were dropped by members of the community, and only a few relatively uncomplicated (and practical) ones were retained as part of the heritage.

Traditionally, Saturday is the Sabbath day for the Jews. Certain Protestant groups, such as the Seventh Day Adventists, also observe Saturday as the day of rest, unlike most Christians who observe it on Sunday. On the other hand, to the Hindus, Saturday (or Shaniwar) is inauspicious and unholy, a day when work can only produce negative results. Saturday is thus of significance to both the Hindus and the Jews, albeit for different reasons. In the early days, when the Bene Israel first arrived in India, their close association with the Hindus and assimilation of Hindu cultural practices could have easily led to the belief that Saturdays were unlucky days. But they did not allow this to influence them. They continued to regard Saturday as the most holy and auspicious of all days of the week, and, as we have already seen, the Shanwar Telis even derived their name from the word 'Saturday'. Also, over the centuries, and particularly once they came to Bombay, where they took up full-time jobs, the Bene Israel could not exercise their choice when it came to observing Saturday as a day of rest. So they became realistic. This is one more instance of a traditional practice being relaxed and it corroborates Nissim's belief that there is something very rational about the Bene Israel psyche that enables members of the community to take an unsentimental view of religious dictates. Nissim himself would work as hard on Saturdays, as he would on other days of the week. Interestingly, when this biography was being researched, he had long sessions with me on Saturdays–my only days in Bombay–without any qualms.

As far as food was concerned, the Bene Israel were less unwilling to imitate the dietary habits of their Hindu (and Muslim) neighbours. Ellul, which occurs around August or September every year, became the month of fasting for them. During this time, they ate only one meal in the day, usually in the evening. (Saturday, the day of the Sabbath, was the only exception, when they ate both their meals.)

It is needless to say that the Ezekiels were not very strict about Ellul. Moses and Diana instilled the idea of a balanced diet in the minds of their children as they were growing up. There were scientific uses of fasting (as opposed to religious ones), and these were commendable. But Nissim and his brothers and sisters grew up on the idea of restraint in matters of food, which made any kind of fasting unnecessary. Nissim, for example, was very fond of sweets as a child (and continues to be so to this day). He could endlessly feast on puddings, cakes, chocolates and mithai. But his parents never let him indulge. They taught him the harmful effects that sweets could have on a person's health. Years later, when he grew up, this discipline would stand him in good stead.

Scientific as he was, Moses wanted all his children to be conscious of their health when they grew up. One of the things he was particularly against was the consumption of foods fried in ghee. In Nissim's case, all this would pay off. He would develop the habit of exercising daily, and would be drawn to all kinds of books on good health. He would learn to keep a check on the quantity of sugar in his tea, to avoid eating the yolk of eggs (though, later, when he would come to live alone at The Retreat, he would sometimes fry his own egg, disregarding his now dead father's advice), and to consume a small quantity of groundnuts, bought from roadside vendors every day. He would remember the foods recommended to him as a boy by his parents, and supplement his diet with dairy produce like milk, curds and lassi, although in later life he would cut down on milk after reading of its dangers. Similarly, he would regularly eat fruits like chickoos, bananas and mangoes, and drink fresh fruit juices before they became prohibitively expensive. But the most important item in his diet would be salads, made up of fresh vegetables, and these would become a must with every meal. As he would turn vegetarian after the age of forty-five, salads would assume a special significance for him. There is nothing very Jewish about all this: reason, rather than religion, would govern Nissim's concept of diet.

Like the Zoroastrians, the Bene Israel also associate certain kinds of underclothing with their religion. Among the Zoroastrians, the kasti and the sadra are worn by all members of the community, and this has become one of the symbolic ways in which a Parsi in India distinguishes himself from others. The Bene Israel wear the tzizit, which is a sort of garment with fringes at the corners. It may be thought of as the equivalent of the kasti and the sadra, just as Ellul is the Jewish equivalent of the Muslim Ramzan.

Nissim's undergarments would always be secular, the standard vests and briefs manufactured by numerous firms in India dealing in hosiery, and advertised widely on television, radio and in the press, or sold on the pavements. He would never wear the tzitzit, which is associated with orthodox Jewish values. As in matters of food, in matters of clothing too he would develop his own logic, as he grew from a toddler into a boy and a boy into a man. In his youth he would take some pains over his dress, particularly when he would travel abroad; in his old age it would all disappear. Ever since I got to know him as a poet and a teacher, in the mid-'70s, I would always notice an ascetic streak in his attire. He would usually wear light-coloured bush shirts and dark trousers, and the pattern would never change. The bush shirts would never be printed ones, nor would they be tucked in. Occasionally, he would wear a kurta, made of hand-woven khadi, but would switch back the next day to light bush shirt and dark trousers. These would probably have been purchased at inexpensive 'readymade' garment stores in Bombay, or would sometimes be presents from friends and relatives. Rarely would they be made-to-order clothes stitched by tailors. Nissim would do little to maintain his wardrobe. As a boy, his mother would attend to his clothes, wash and iron them regularly, or get them laundered by servants. Later on, it would be his wife Daisy. But when, in his mid-fifties, he would start living by himself, there would be a marked neglect in his appearance. His clothes would remain unwashed for days, till friends would complain that they stank. Often a button would drop off from his shirt, and he would do nothing to replace it. Moses would bequeath the gift of reason to his son, and Nissim would learn to rationalize his predicament, and ask his many 'critics' what difference it made if he dressed shabbily. In a recent interview, the journalist Behram Contractor has compared him to a boarding-school boy, out of his mother's care.[2] There is also the possibility that he would come to have a certain image of the poet in his mind's eye, dishevelled and all, and would fancy himself living up to it. Nissim himself would be aware that he was badly dressed and noticed by people; in that sense, his dressing would be self-conscious. As late as November 1994, when he would be asked in an interview how important looks and general appearance were to him, he would answer, predictably, that they were not at all important, and that 'I'm afraid my family feels that I go to the other extreme . . . of not caring enough about clothes and shoes.'[3]

Some religious customs can be so quaint, that rather than giving them up, the more imaginative members of the community may think of manipulating them and turning them to their advantage. One such ceremony among the Bene Israel seems to be, surely, the Hath Boshi or kissing-the-hand ceremony, which is so evocatively described by Isenberg in her book that one cannot excel her. According to her, during this ceremony, which was practised at the end of all synagogue services, 'a senior person, thumbs uppermost, approached a junior, took the junior's hand in both of his/her own hands, while the junior placed his/her remaining hand on the outside of the hand of the senior; then both released hands and immediately, putting the tips of their respective fingers to their mouths, kissed their own fingertips; then they proceeded to repeat the process with another person until the entire congregation (if possible) had thus greeted each other.'[4]

Isenberg tells us further that the kiss in question was sometimes referred to as 'The Kiss of Peace'. She compares it to a similar (though not identical) custom among the Christians and the Zoroastrians, though the Christians went a step further and kissed each other on the cheek! But whether it's the cheeks or the fingers, the 'physicality' of the practice cannot be overlooked.

It is inappropriate to try and guess, at this stage, how many people Nissim would kiss in his lifetime, although an attempt towards this will be made in later chapters. But no matter what the number, the reasons were certainly not religious! One of his favourite anecdotes in old age would be about a certain woman who would rhyme his name with the words 'kiss him'. Nissim would sing to friends whenever he was in a good mood:

Nissim, Nissim,
I want to
Kiss him.

Perhaps some of the friends to whom he sang (many or most of who were women) would take this to be a pass he was making. But kissing would be as important to Nissim in poetry as in life. Here is his own version of Hath Boshi, to be found in 'Nudes 1978', one of his most erotic sequences of poems:

'You haven't learnt to kiss', she said,
'open your mouth a little, yes,
that's the way.' I was quite ashamed
but quick to learn-or so I thought.
'Is this all you want, you funny boy?'
I waited, and my wanton friend
displayed her body, turned around,
her laughter filled my basement room.
'Did you enjoy it? No? You have
to love the other person, then you do.
Never mind, you love my breasts, thighs,
buttocks, don't you? Of course you do.
It's O.K., you know, and I love
your body too, though you're hardly
my cup of tea.'

While the Ezekiels disregarded most of the rituals associated with their religion, or at any rate modified them to suit their convenience, one of the rituals that the boys of the household went through was the Bar Mitzvah, that marks a male child's passage into manhood, and is celebrated during his thirteenth year: there is something of a paradox here, because the Bar Mitzvah is a ceremony that, traditionally, was not observed by the Bene Israel in India in large numbers. In the twentieth century, its importance increased slightly, and some Bene Israel synagogues, particularly in Bombay, began conducting it; but it was still practised by relatively few in the community.

Nissim recalls that Joe, Hannan and he all went through the ceremony in their thirteenth year. In Nissim's case, the year would have been 1937. However, the boys were not taken to the Magen Hassidim Synagogue at Agripada, where they had been circumcised, although this was the synagogue where most Bar Mitzvah ceremonies were solemnized. Instead, they were taken to the Rodef Shalom Synagogue, situated near the Victoria Gardens. This synagogue, housed in a building formerly known as Mathilda House, was run by the Jewish Religious Union and was founded in 1925, a year after Nissim's birth. The Jewish Religious Union was liberal and progressive in its thinking, and attracted broad-minded Jews like Moses, who preferred to shorten their prayers and sometimes even say them in English rather than in Hebrew. Many years later, when Nissim would no longer be the son but become a father, he would take his only son, Elkana, to this very synagogue in Bombay for his Bar Mitzvah.

'I Was Born Here and Belong'

There is a plaque near Jerusalem, situated at the Tomb of the Matriarch Rachel, by the side of which is a small well. A reference in it is made to the city of Bombay. The inscription on the plaque is in Hebrew, and the year in which it was written is AD 5625 according to the Jewish calendar (September AD 1864 to September AD 1865). The inscription, when translated into English, reads as follows:

> The construction of this well was made possible through a donation from the esteemed, our brothers the Bene Israel, who are living in the city of Bombay, may the Lord protect it well! In honour of the whole assembly of the community of Israel, [through those] who came to bow over the gravestone at the burial place of our Mother Rachel. May her memory protect us. Amen.

Given in the year 5625, according to the Jewish calendar.[1]

The inscription confirms something we already know: that by the middle of the nineteenth century, there was a steady exodus of the Bene Israel from their coastal villages to the island city of Bombay. The Bene Israel were among the earliest beneficiaries of the British Indian Government policy to develop Bombay as a modern city. That was on account of its fine natural harbour. The government itself took its cue from the East India Company that had begun the process almost two centuries earlier. This was also the time when a transition was being made from Surat, as the centre of affairs, to Bombay, and the Bene Israel made the most of it. Even the capital of western India was shifted from Surat to Bombay, which came to be known as the Bombay Presidency. While Surat was already home to the Parsis, and the Bene Israel would have faced some resistance had they attempted to establish themselves there, Bombay was relatively unoccupied, unspoiled territory. Besides, Bombay was in close geographical proximity to the Alibag region where the Bene Israel had lived for centuries. Doubtless, all this was advantageous to them.

The entire process of emigration to Bombay was concentrated, and seems to have occurred over a short period of time. While records show that in the year 1739 hardly any Bene Israel had settled in Bombay, by 1785 they had acquired their third cemetery in the city. By 1796 they were already building their first synagogue.

Of course, the Bene Israel were not the only 'minorities' to move to Bombay. Others, such as the Cochin and Baghdadi Jews, as well as the Parsis from Gujarat, simultaneously began arriving in the city, making for cross-cultural interaction. It was the mood of the time, the advent of the modern industrial age. Bombay was coming to be the very symbol of industrialization and modernity, as opposed to the places from which these people hailed, with associations of feudalism and agriculture. In a way, it is ironic that it is Bombay that should have come to acquire such an image, that it should have been bestowed with such an honour, so to speak, for the early history of the city reveals it to be a veritable backwater. It was only a fishing village and a tiny island. Its name, Maha Amba, derived from the Hindu goddess Bhavani, and corrupted later to Mumbai, then Bombay, was anything but secular. Yet Bombay had a liberating influence that enabled the Bene Israel to move away from oil-pressing, a job they were 'destined' to do, and explore other, more creative possibilities. Thus it was in Bombay that 'the Bene Israel for the first time developed into a substantial, vigorous community.'[2] A community that had for centuries stayed content toiling for a living, suddenly became exposed to religion, education and culture in a significant way.

Like any other Bene Israel of his day, Haskelji Israel too had aspirations. He wanted to empower himself by joining the tide and migrating to Bombay. But his restlessness could get him only as far as the Boer War, which struck him as a way of leaving the village. This was before the turn of the century, by which time almost everyone who had wanted to leave their village and opt for a new life in the city, had done so already. But Bombay was one place Haskelji Israel did not succeed in going to. It is difficult to say why he did not make it there. He couldn't have lacked the spirit of adventure, having fought in the Boer War. Perhaps the war had exhausted him, and the practical difficulties of shifting base, particularly when the shift is from village to city, put him off completely. The result was that after his war stint, Haskelji Israel returned to Tal and settled down to a quiet life, teaching in a school.

But somewhere, deep in his psyche, the aspiration to go to Bombay remained. He fulfilled it vicariously by sending his children to the city for their college education. This was how his son Moses graduated in science, and became a man of strong scientific and urban attitudes. Haskelji Israel did not encourage Moses or his other children to return to Tal after finishing their studies. He realized that they had better lives awaiting them in Bombay. Even the thought of his own impending old age and loneliness did not make him change his mind, and ask his children to return.

Thus it was that Nissim Ezekiel was born in Bombay. Moses and Diana lived in a chawl off the Byculla bridge, where the birth took place. Nissim recalls that the house was situated in a narrow side lane in the area, which abounds in lanes and chawls. However, his memory fails him when it comes to identifying the building. During the course of my research, I took him to the Byculla Bridge by taxi one afternoon, and we walked through three or four crowded lanes before giving up: clearly, locating the house of his birth was a task beyond him, although as a boy, his parents must have at some stage pointed out the place to him, especially as it isn't far from The Retreat on Bellasis Road, where they eventually came to live. But the house is real, and it exists, and is probably being occupied by someone who doesn't know that a poet was once born here, way back in the '20s. Possibly it is on props, under the care of the Bombay Municipal Corporation, and alternatively, there is also the chance of its having collapsed during one of the many monsoons. But it is here that he was born.

The description of the house and its location give us a clear indication of the economic status of Moses and Diana in those early years after their wedding. They were not well-off; in future years, Nissim would often refer to his parents as 'poor'. This substantiates his claim that he was delivered at home, not in a nursing home or hospital, which his parents may have found expensive, though there is no means by which we can verify the claim. Yet, if Diana went through some of the religious rituals associated with the birth of children, it proves that they were not hard-pressed for money, for all such ceremonies usually entail some expense.

This is not to undermine their hardships, or to suggest that they had no financial difficulties. Something that provides a clue here is the fact that Diana took up a school teaching job early in life, even before she was through with the birth of her children. These are usually years when mothers, if they can afford it, want to stay at home and supervise the raising of their children. Moses had by then obtained a lecturer's job at Wilson College, but teaching jobs were not well-paid, and his salary wouldn't have been decent enough to support a wife and five children. That Diana should thus supplement the family income by herself going to work, would have been considered a welcome gesture. Of course, there is the other side of the story, which is that Diana was doing whatever she was out of choice. She was educated, she did not want to waste her talents, and was teaching because she loved it.

The school in which Diana taught was actually a sort of municipal school to which children from relatively unaffluent homes went. It occupied a part of the Tiphereth Israel Synagogue, situated at 92 Clarke Road–Jacob Circle. But the school was not really connected with the synagogue-it was merely its tenant! The children admitted to the school were not necessarily Jewish.

Nissim's own comments shed useful light on the socio-economic status of his parents in the '20s and '30s. When quizzed on the subject, he admits that while the environment in which they lived was not high middle class, it was not poor either. They may have started out in a chawl, but gradually moved into apartments of different kinds, with at least three to five rooms, where they paid rents up to as much as Rs 35 per month. They were much better off than many of Nissim's boyhood friends, who lived in chawls and even slums. Their status may also be determined by the fact that they always owned a radio, though never a tape recorder until much later.

Moses was a lecturer in Botany and Zoology at Wilson College, Chowpatty. He would commute every day from Byculla to Chowpatty and back by tram, changing trams at Khada Parsi Square, near Nagpada. He was an enthusiastic and dedicated teacher who taught for love of the subject, and not merely to earn his living. Because he loved his subject and loved teaching, he would regularly organize field trips for his students to the Victoria Gardens nearby. The young Nissim, in his growing-up years, would sometimes accompany Moses on these visits. In an unconscious way, all that Moses said and explained to him during those visits, must have been responsible for the intellectual curiosity that is one of Nissim's chief personality attributes today.

Yet, for all this, Nissim was more attached to his mother than to his father. (When he tells me this, he hastens to add that it must not be taken as an adverse comment on his father.) Nissim had no reason to dislike his father, for although he was strict at home in the positive sense of the word, he was never authoritarian in his dealings with his children.

By the beginning of the '30s, Nissim was at school. To start with, it was not the Antonio D'Souza High School facing the Byculla Bridge, to which he would be admitted later, but a smaller school run by Christian missionaries, known as the Convent of Jesus and Mary. The family had moved into a building called Readymoney Mansion in the same locality as the school, close, once again, to the Byculla bridge. (Both the school and the home were a passing phase in Nissim's life; they did not have a quality of permanence.) Nissim would climb down from the third floor, on which their flat was situated, and walk to the school by himself. It was an early exercise in self-dependence, crossing busy thoroughfares without adult help, unlike the children of the rich who are either driven to school in cars, or at least escorted by ayahs and servants. It was a training that would stand him in good stead all through his life.

In 1934, Nissim obtained admission to the Antonio D'Souza High School. Although cosmopolitan, it was a part of the Gloria Church, and was even referred to sometimes as the Gloria Church School. The students admitted to that school belonged to all the major communities–Hindu, Muslim and Christian. Nissim was admitted to the third standard (of those days), having completed standards one and two at his previous school.

At the school, Nissim was not particularly shy. He got on well with his classmates. The Hindi film 'showman', Raj Kapoor, was in his class, and Nissim and he were friendly. Nissim recalls that eventually, when Raj Kapoor failed his matriculation exams, his father Prithviraj Kapoor came to the school and tried to persuade the principal to pass him. Raj Kapoor wasn't a good student at school. And yet Nissim once lost a school prize to him, because he was, after all, Raj Kapoor. Nissim was very disappointed. He also remembers that Raj Kapoor was something of a prankster at school–he mimicked his teachers and made fun of them. Many years later, Nissim and Raj Kapoor found themselves together on a flight, and to Nissim's horror, Raj Kapoor announced to all passengers at the top of his voice that Nissim was a poet!

These were also years when Nissim's sexual nature was rapidly developing, tending to make him high on Eros.

From the third to the seventh standard, that is, between 1934 and '40, Nissim took part in all games played in school. These included cricket, football, hockey and basketball. But he remembers that he wasn't really good at games. One of his continuous regrets as a schoolboy was that he was never able to represent his class in any of the games it played at local competitions. In sports, too, while he invariably took part in events such as the hundred-metre race, high jump and long jump, he never won prizes. In races he was often the last to arrive, and this was a great source of frustration to him.

Realizing that sports and games were not his forte, the boy turned to the arts, and attempted to take part in dramatics. But here too he didn't succeed. He would forget his lines while on stage, and the people in the auditorium, mostly fellow-pupils and their parents, and of course the staff of the school, would, he remembers, burst out laughing.

The result was that having tasted so much failure during his impressionable years, Nissim grew up with a sense of failure, which he retains even now, and which manifests itself as a lack of confidence. Looking back on his life, he says he has a long history of failures on which he could perhaps write an entire book! The sense of failure that he first experienced at school was carried by him into college, university, and the world at large. So much so, he is convinced, that if ever he writes his autobiography, he will call it 'A Thousand Failures'!

Of the various failures that he talks about, many of which will be discussed in the chapters to come, the one that strikes me most is his inability to act on the stage. While there is no direct connection between acting and writing, and the history of drama has shown us that there are many playwrights who wouldn't have necessarily made successful actors, I am tempted to link up his clumsiness on stage with his failure to later write workable plays. In a way, his 'Very Indian Poems in English' have come to have greater dramatic potential than most of his plays, but then these are not theatre; when it comes to dramatics, Nissim simply doesn't know how to proceed. However, a critical discussion of Nissim's plays will be taken up at the appropriate time; suffice it to say here that in school he did not make much headway with drama as an extracurricular activity.

There was no one in Antonio D'Souza High School, teacher or fellow-student, whom Nissim would regard as an anchor in his life. Real companionship came from home, from the family. Nissim's relationship with all his brothers and sisters, Joe, Hannan, Sarah and Lily was 'broadly normal', even though there were petty differences, common among brothers and sisters. What made them true friends was that temperamentally they were more or less the same, with the introspective habits inculcated in them by their parents. They were all voracious readers, something for which their father, Moses, and mother, Diana, were undoubtedly responsible. They would bring home books of various kinds (science, literature, the classics) from libraries, and insist that their children should read them. They would even discuss their reading with them. It was Moses and Diana, more than anyone else, who were an anchor in the lives of the Ezekiel children.

The constant supervision and guidance of their parents also helped the children to shape their personalities. Nissim identifies one of his personality traits as this feeling, the assumption, that if someone could do something, say, win a hockey match, produce a play, or learn a new language, he could too. His father, who naturally, had the highest ambitions for his children, must have instilled it in him. But what Moses probably failed to realize as many parents tend to, is that by encouraging children to overreach themselves, they are also exposing them to the dangers of psychological damage. Not that Nissim suffered from psychological damage; but one wonders whether the 'sense of failure', which has become such an integral part of his mental make-up, is one of its symptoms. Reflecting on it, Nissim said to me: 'This way I tried almost everything under the sun. I now regret it–the feeling that I could do everything.., unlike people, who from childhood know they're good in some things, and not good in other things.'

There is little else that Nissim regrets about this childhood. Life was peaceful at home, with no more than the usual conflicts between parents and children, brothers and sisters. There were no major illnesses that afflicted the children, say chickenpox or smallpox. Moses and Diana were very careful about the food and water that their children consumed. Nissim calls it their 'convictions'. Nor did any of the children have an unpleasant temper. It is not as if Nissim never lost his temper, but it was comparatively rare for him to do so. If he was angry with someone, he was more inclined to withdraw from the scene rather than explode in the person's presence. However, he frequently suffered from headaches, even as a boy, and they were so severe that he would remain absent from school. The ailment stayed with him until much later, when it was 'miraculously' cured. Perhaps it was these headaches, coupled of course with the 'prevention is better than cure' attitude of his parents, that caused him to take a keen interest in issues related to health, and carefully read whatever he came across. This habit stood him in good stead in later life, when he was able to diagnose his own illnesses, especially minor ones, and rarely needed to visit a doctor.

The Antonio D'Souza High School used to have a five-day week. But like some schools run by the Jesuits, notably the St. Xavier's High School in Bombay's Metro cinema area, it observed Thursday as its weekly holiday, instead of Saturday. The other holiday, of course, was Sunday. On Thursdays, Nissim would sometimes accompany his mother to her school, and sit in her classes to watch her teach. He enjoyed Diana's classes much more than he did most of his own, but he was obviously being partial towards his mother here.

It was probably on Thursdays and Sundays, and in his summer and winter vacations, when, like all other children, he found himself with a lot of time on his hands and did not quite known how to spend it, that Nissim first began to write. Putting together the various statements he has made over the years, we may conclude that he wrote his first complete poem in 1936, at the age of twelve. However, in the interview with Behram Contractor, he suggests that he wrote his first poem when he was barely nine or ten years old.[3] This seems less likely than his earlier accounts. In a previous interview with the critic and academic John B. Beston, Nissim has stated that he actually started out writing fairy tales in imitation of what he read, and then graduated to poetry, around the age of twelve.[4] This seems much more plausible.

Nissim's parents knew that he wrote poetry, though nothing in his personality then made them suspect that he would grow up to be a poet. Among his teachers at Antonio D'Souza High School, he remembers one Mr Abraham who read and taught poetry extremely well,[5] while others generally encouraged him to write, and read poetry aloud. But the story of how his first poem was received in his own class is well known, and has often been told by him. There was this woman teacher, who was shown the poem by one of Nissim's classmates, to whom he first recited it, and the teacher exclaimed: 'Ah, ha, listen all of you, we have a poet in the class.' The remark had its effect. Nissim says: 'I decided at that moment, whatever happens, I am going to write poetry, good bad or indifferent.'[6]

Unfortunately, we have today neither the poem, nor the name of the teacher, that were responsible for shaping the course of Indian English poetry!

Naturally, Nissim's favourite subject throughout his school life was English. He responded well to the poems of Wordsworth, Keats, Shelley,

Byron and Tennyson, whom they had on the syllabus. Better at any rate, than most of his other class-fellows. 'All of them studied poetry as part of the school curriculum, but not out of a special love for it,' he told Tara Patel in an interview.[7] But he feels that just because he wrote poetry and had a fondness for it, it was generally assumed that he was weak in science and had a distaste for the subject. He certainly did not have a distaste for science. As pointed out earlier, he was by nature curious about everything that informs our lives; besides, his father was a man of science, and some of his love of the subject was a direct legacy of his father. It is true, though, that in his exams he didn't do very well in science subjects. In this context, he once admitted in an article: 'As a schoolboy, I loved science without being able to master it. . . I made up for it by doing a lot of "mugging" and passed the necessary examinations. But I've never been able to grasp the elements of any science. At the same time, I did not question the value of science as knowledge. It was not, for me, a mere examination "subject" . . . I regretted then and I regret now my inability to understand how science really functions, its methods and its discoveries.'[8]

In this way, Nissim pulled through school life and reached his final year, at the end of which he took his matriculation exams. It was 1941, and he was less than seventeen. Matriculation, in those days, was standard seven in Antonio D'Souza High School; in some schools it was standard eight. And Nissim did well.

Sometime between 1944 and 1947, Diana resigned from the school where she taught, and set up her own nursery school at Umerkhadi in south-central Bombay. Long before she actually started this school, she had begun attending special classes for prospective kindergarten teachers. Kindergarten was of primary interest to her. The main reason for her decision to start out on her own seems to have been her dissatisfaction with the system of education as it then existed. One of the things that irked her was the tendency among teachers to inflict corporal punishment on their students, no matter how young they were. Diana strongly believed that children should not be beaten. She never beat her own children at home, and in her school, physical punishment of any kind was ruled out. Nissim found himself in agreement with his mother. He had witnessed (though not experienced) beatings in Antonio D'Souza High School, and they always bewildered him. The Ezekiels were like Tagore here, idealists. Tagore too had set up his own school at Bolpur in West Bengal, which he called Shantiniketan or the Abode of Peace, because he was disillusioned with the way teachers in regular schools taught their pupils, and especially because he was opposed to the way they 'assaulted' them physically.

Around the year Nissim finished his schooling, the Ezekiels changed their residence. They now moved into an apartment that was part of a colony of bungalows, known as The Retreat. It was the perfect name for a poet's house, and as fate would have it, Nissim would always return to it, to live first with other members of the family, and then by himself. The Retreat is located on Bellasis Road, the road that connects Bombay Central station to Nagpada. It is almost opposite the Alexandra cinema, which is a gateway to Bombay's red-light district close by. Shuklaji Street, one of the city's most infamous streets, is only a stone's throw from The Retreat. But the ambience inside the housing complex, once entered, has little to do with the notoriety outside. The people who live here are 'decent', well-to-do middle-class people, many of them belonging to minority religious communities,

The bungalows in The Retreat were first constructed by the British in 1896 for their administrative personnel. Even before Independence, they were taken over by the Parsis, and then the Muslims. There are only four apartments in each one-storeyed block, with the result that they are very spacious by contemporary standards. In today's terminology, the house being occupied by Nissim would be described as a two-bedroom hall with twin entrances (although he now uses only one of them). When the Ezekiels moved in, they paid a monthly rent of Rs 47. Today, because of the Rent Control Act, rents have remained low, and Nissim pays a mere Rs 226 per month as rent, in an area that would be regarded by businessmen and property developers as a prime location. There have been, in fact, moves to demolish the bungalows and construct high-rises in their place, but luckily these have so far come to nothing. However, Nissim is apprehensive that this may someday happen, and then he will be compelled to find accommodation in far-off places like Borivli, much against his will.

Apart from the years he spent in the Warden Road area after his marriage, first in a one-room ground floor apartment with a garden at Mazda Mansion, and then at Kala Niketan where his wife Daisy presently lives, Nissim has always been located in the Bombay Central-Byculla belt right from his childhood. This is clearly a sort of Jewish quarter of the city, and his preference for it indicates that for all his cosmopolitanism, it is with the people of his own community that he feels most secure.

Landmarks connected with their social and cultural life often determine the importance of a place to members of a community. Bellasis Road, Clare Road and Kamathipura, not far off, are known for the Jewish cemeteries and synagogues situated there. Discussing the phenomenon, Shirley Berry Isenberg actually speaks of a Bene Israel communal neighbourhood in Bombay, and informs us that the original neighbourhood was located where the Byculla, Nagpada, Mazgaon and Umerkhadi sections of Bombay meet, making all the residents in those days within walking distance of each other.[9] In fact, Isenberg lists the Bene Israel neighbourhoods of Bombay in the order that people of the community favoured them. We find Mandvi, Dongri, Umerkhadi, Mazgaon, Byculla and Nagpada topping the list, followed by Jacob Circle, Parel, Dadar, Matunga and Mahim. Bandra, Khar, Kurla, Santa Cruz, Kalina, Vile Pane and Andheri come at the end.

When Nissim and Daisy decided to settle down on Warden Road, which is a much more 'aristocratic' locality than any of those mentioned above, it may have been on account of a desire to be upwardly mobile, like some 'wealthy and successful' Bene Israel, who bought houses in areas as expensive as Malabar Hill and Colaba. Daisy liked their flat in Mazda Mansion because it was on the ground floor, and there was a garden in the front, giving it the look of a cottage. At heart, however, Nissim is unostentatious, and even while he lived on Warden Road, his lifestyle was at odds with a conventional Warden Road lifestyle. To provide just one example in support of this contention, Nissim and Daisy never owned a car, and though he claims that this was because both of them attempted, and failed, to successfully learn driving (failure again!), the truth is that he was never really seized by the desire to possess. It was left to his son, Elkana, much later in the '90s, to take to driving, in a car he would be provided with while working for a corporate firm in a managerial capacity. Nissim agrees with my view, and admits that in those days, as today, he didn't see the need to spend money on buying things. If he had extra money at any given time, he would prefer to spend it on charity. He usually travelled third (now second) class on local and upcountry trains. He rarely used taxis, a habit that has stayed with him to the present day. It was only in his retired life that, for a while, he bought a first-class season ticket to commute from Bombay Central to Churchgate; that, on the insistence of Elkana.

Interestingly, the roads in Bombay that have been named after well-known Bene Israel men are anywhere but in the areas inhabited by them. Except for Israel Mohalla in Mandvi, the roads are far away from residential places. Dr E. Moses Road, that connects Worli Naka to the Mahalakshmi railway station, and runs parallel to the race course, is not a residential area. Similarly, Samuel Street and Issaji Street are in downtown Bombay, in the heart of the central business district.

A sense of roots and belonging is perhaps essential to every poet, because in the last analysis, it gives him the terms of reference for his writing. Nissim's roots are in Bombay; Bombay is the city where he belongs. He was born in Bombay, has always lived here, and always came back to Bombay, wherever he went. The longest time he was away from Bombay was between 1948 and 1952, when he was in England. But even before he went to England, he decided that Bombay was his home, and once in England, he made up his mind to return to Bombay and spend the rest of his life here. Nissim's years in England coincided with the time the Jews in India started emigrating on a large scale to the newly-formed nation of Israel (from 1949 onwards). Though he took interest in this development, he rejected the Zionist notion that Israel was the Promised Land to which all the Jews of the world must return. This is because he thought of himself as an Indian.

When Nissim was in England, he was able to view his life in India objectively. He realized that Bombay was the one place where he felt completely at ease, even though there were many things about the city of which he was critical. In England, he was also seeing Indians of the diaspora for the first time. He felt they were under an illusion that they would do better in the West. He could never share their optimism; he was somehow never 'sold on the idea' that one could be successful in a Western country. Indians who find work abroad, do not have a sense of belonging to any place, he recently said to Neema Kamdar in an interview.[10]

The idea expressed earlier, that in Bombay Nissim was most comfortable in a Jewish neighbourhood, rather than anywhere else in the city, is borne out by his admission that there were large parts of Bombay which he didn't know or relate to. In this, he includes working-class Bombay. What he did believe in, of course, was the idea of a neighbourhood, which for him mainly comprised Byculla where he grew up. To this he also adds Warden Road, where he lived for a while, and Churchgate, where he worked. However, he doesn't see this relation to a specific local reality as narrowness, for he feels it is only the starting point from which one can extend one's sphere of interest to the whole country. In this context, he says he has never felt alienated anywhere in India, though he regards himself a Bombayite. In other words, he has no complexes. This might even seem contradictory to his claim that he doesn't know large parts of Bombay, like the labour areas–strange for a man who regards Byculla and Bombay Central as his familiar neighbourhood! No, he doesn't even attribute his preference for Bombay to the fact that it is a cosmopolitan city that has room for minorities. He accepts his minoritism as given, and says that as far as he is concerned, he relates to people on the basis of their attitudes and values. But he agrees that Bombay is a haven to minorities for principally this reason (its cosmopolitan character), and points out that this is also true of cities like London and New York.

Nissim strongly feels that the reasons why people grow attached to places, and begin to like them, are emotional. 'If I spent the first twenty-five years of my life in my village in Tal, I may have felt something towards if for just that reason,' he said, implying it had nothing to do with the relative backwardness of Tal, or the progressiveness of Bombay.

When he made the 'crucial decision' of his life to settle in Bombay, he was aware of all the odds. 'A hundred relevant questions came to mind,' he says. Some of these were his own; others were asked by people who knew him. Most questions had to do with the stereotypical issue of rural versus urban life. But Nissim knew there were positive sides to life in a city. He has always loved Bombay's variety and multiplicity, which add up to authentic experience. So when people dismissively refer to Bombay (and Bombayites) as 'Westernized', he feels they're prejudiced. 'May be they're revolting against their own Westernization,' he says, using pop-psychology as a trope. He himself has never experienced any guilt on this score, because he has always been interested in what he calls 'multiple expressions of human culture.' Moreover, he is opposed to generalizations.

Until the '60s, when they were abolished, much of Nissim's movement in Bombay, used to be by tram. When he was a boy of ten, Jewish passengers enjoyed special privileges on trams, and later on buses. They could buy their tickets for travelling on Saturdays and Jewish holidays in advance, and be assured of seats. Trams were an integral part of the scene in Bombay, and he was sorry when they were discontinued. 'Even in California and Germany, things are retained for historical reasons, unlike in India,' he laments. As a man who has always depended on public transport all his life, Nissim has well thought-out views on the subject. He feels that both buses and trams should have been allowed to coexist, buses contributing to, say, eighty per cent of the total transport, and trams to twenty per cent. This way the common man would have had an option, as he does in Calcutta, where tram fares are cheaper than bus fares.

Bombay is a modern Indian city. One thing that the term 'modern' here implies is that the quality of life in it will be preserved as best as possible. Nissim feels that in this respect, Bombay's administrators have failed us. Roads still exist in the same condition that they did many years ago; there is scant improvement. Public transport, especially trains and buses, doesn't come anywhere near the city's actual requirements. Above all, modernity, according to him, has not really touched the lives of the people. Nissim has been a strong critic of, for example, the way Indians indulge in loud talk in public places, or spit, pee, and blow their noses wherever they want. Some of these observations have gone into his poems:

> All Hindus are
> Like that, my father used to say,
> When someone talked too loudly, or
> Knocked at the door like the Devil.
> They hawked and spat. They sprawled around.

('Background, Casually')

'Can you call that modernity?' he asks.

And yet, in spite of all its faults, he gives Bombay a clean chit, and says there is something about the city—call it mystical or mysterious—that cannot easily be defined. He objects to the word 'hate' when I tell him that his relationship with Bombay is a love-hate relationship. 'It's only love,' he says. What he loves most about the city is that it gives him a 'sense of belonging', and this is not something he can say of any other city in the world. Joy, sadness, success, failure, all these are experienced by him in the context of belonging to Bombay. His best friends are in Bombay.

I ask Nissim whether he thinks such a sense of belonging to be absolutely essential for a writer. 'I don't know. I feel it,' he answers. Then he provides an illustration: 'If I'm invited to a party in Bombay by XYZ, I say to myself, there'll be different kinds of people here, but one thing I'm certain about is that I'll be at home at the party. How can I tell? I don't know, but it's happened again and again. Whereas in England and America, you end up talking to only a few people, who may be just being kind.' As our conversation progresses, he disagrees with me when I suggest that 'belonging' is contradictory to, or outside the purview of, the globalism of today. He says: 'The exposure in Bombay is insular only part of the time; otherwise it's representative.' What surprises him is that people who have lived in Bombay for the most part of their lives, say they will leave after their retirement, and settle down in quieter places like Bangalore or Pune. To this day, he cannot imagine leaving Bombay and settling down anywhere else, though he enjoys short spells outside. 'I would never leave Bombay–it's a series of commitments,'[11] he once said. He also said: 'It is only here in Bombay that I have sought jobs, not in Calcutta or Delhi or Madras. In New York, you may get ten times the salary, but I was not interested in that.'[12] In 1988, when I told him I was 'leaving' Bombay to take up a teaching assignment at the University of Pune, his first reaction was shock and disbelief. Yet, Nissim contradicts himself when he says, almost in the same breath, that he doesn't consider other parts of India to be very different from Bombay.

Having discussed the significance of Bombay in Nissim's life, I would like to examine how, in the twentieth century, the city came to mean 'home' to the Bene Israel as a whole. Beginning with that first synagogue that they built at 254 Samuel Street, Mandvi, in 1796, which is still in use today (this possibly explains why Mandvi is the most favoured residential locality among members of the community), the Bene Israel went on to build several other synagogues in the areas occupied by them. By the time we come to the twentieth century, we find that the synagogue becomes the focal point of community life among the Bene Israel. This was particularly facilitated by the fact that the people themselves conducted the affairs of their synagogues–they had no ordained or professional clergy to lead them.

The Ezekiels maintained a distance from many of these social transactions. They would go to the synagogue, but not fraternize too much. In this they were not exceptional; several well-educated people of the community kept away, at least partially, from these congregations. Two of the Ezekiels' favourite synagogues were, as we have seen already, the Magen Hassidim Synagogue at Agripada, and the Magen David Synagogue at Byculla. The latter was all the more convenient because it is at walking distance from both Readymoney Mansion and The Retreat. Then there was the forward-looking Rodef Shalom Synagogue. In the '70s and the '80s, with young Bene Israel couples leaving the city and moving to suburban areas like Kurla and Thane, the new synagogues constructed in the suburbs witnessed a greater number of visitors than the older ones.

The old ones in central Bombay remained half to three-fourths empty, and members were sometimes even 'bribed' by the authorities to attend prayers, for according to rules, one cannot pray in a synagogue unless there is a minimum of ten persons. Nissim himself was never very strict about his visits to the synagogue. He would go there whenever he felt like it, though it is true that in old age he became increasingly involved in the social and cultural affairs of the community.

In Bombay, class had almost completely replaced caste as a means of determining the status of the three Jewish communities. This has been attributed to 'the leavening influence of Indian Independence, and to the fact that all the three Jewish communities . . . were drastically shrinking in size as a result of emigration.'[13] The upshot is that the Bene Israel, who were earlier accorded the lowest status among Jews in India, were now able to identify with a white-collar middle class, a slot that had until then belonged to upper-caste Hindus. While caste is determined by birth, class is flexible. As a result, all the three Jewish communities could boast not just of a sizeable white-collar class, but also of achievers in different fields. Some of them even rose to become celebrities. If the Bene Israel had a celebrity poet in Nissim Ezekiel, the Baghdadis had their film stars; Nadira was a well-known actor in the Bombay film industry. Economic prosperity, however, did not significantly contribute toward a decline in conservative attitudes. Isenberg notes that most Bene Israel of Bombay have followed the traditional Indian pattern, conservatively keeping themselves socially separate from their communities.'[14] This, of course, does not apply to Nissim, who has always been more liberal than the average person in the community, and who has friends from virtually every community in the world. However, it may have applied to his parents in the pre-Independence years, and in the years that immediately followed. Nissim cannot remember too many friends of his father and mother, or too many visitors to their house, who were either Hindu or Muslim. But this may have had little to do with communal-mindedness; it may simply have been Moses' and Diana's way of life, and way of protecting their privacy. By this yardstick, their doors would not have always remained open to the people of their own community either. Nissim himself has always been particular about receiving all his visitors, including close friends, at his office; rarely at his home.

While the ordinary Bene Israel may be finicky about mingling with people of other religions, it is fascinating how their homes in Bombay have come to exactly resemble those of their Hindu and Muslim counterparts. They live in crowded rooms, usually rented rather than owned, with as many as ten people of a joint family sometimes sharing a room. To this, guests are always welcome; there is very little, if any, of a sense of privacy, which is said to be confined merely to bathing, dressing and sexual intercourse. Speaking of cramped living conditions among the Bene Israel, Isenberg informs us that as early as 1920, a certain judge named Ezra Reuben wrote a pamphlet called 'The Housing Problem and the Bene Israel', in which he recommended that the Bene Israel develop a cooperative housing project for themselves in Bombay, on the lines of similar projects undertaken by the Hindus and the Parsis.'[15]

Bene Israel homes in Bombay invariably have a mezuzah at the entrance, and a hanging oil lamp to be lit on the eve of the Sabbath, and on Jewish festivals, as they used to do in the villages. Then there is the Old Testament in Marathi. Other common things include prayer books, and framed portraits of family members, scenes from the Bible, and sometimes even Hindu gods! Like the people of other communities, they like to give feasts during happy occasions.

The Ezekiels, too, always had a mezuzah and prayer books at Readymoney Mansion and The Retreat. There were a few framed portraits of elderly relatives. But, as seen earlier, they had a very strong sense of privacy. They hardly ever gave parties, though on Friday nights, after the prayers were said, they had a sort of party among themselves, drinking wine. Even among the educated Bene Israel of Bombay, they were exceptional. Their unconventionality manifested itself in their secularism, which meant not flaunting their religion and culture, and making a public display of it, howsoever indirectly.

During the lifetime of Moses and Diana, The Retreat still resembled a 'regular' household, with everyone in the family living there harmoniously. After their death, the circumstances were such that one by one everybody began leaving the place. Today, Nissim lives alone at The Retreat, and hardly anyone knows how he lives. Even by the standards of the rich middle class, who can afford to set up separate households from their parents, he is unusual. At the time of writing, it just so happens that Nissim, Daisy and Elkana each live in three separate apartments in Bombay–Nissim at The Retreat, Daisy at Kala Niketan, and Elkana and his wife in company quarters at Prabhadevi. In a city where the housing problem is more acute than anywhere else in the world, this surely is luxury.

Bombay is Nissim's city, and he would always depend on it for image and metaphor. 'I feel I am a Bombay city poet . . . I am oppressed and sustained by Bombay,'[16] he has said. It is a metaphor that he has consistently used throughout his poetic career. As a consequence, it will again come up for analysis in the chapters that follow, as we discuss his individual volumes of poetry. Here, however, we must tackle certain fundamentals, such as the distinction between his Bombay poems, actually set in Bombay, and those that are merely urban in nature, without necessarily using Bombay as a locale. While almost all his poems would automatically fall into the latter category, only selected ones would qualify as Bombay poems on the basis of our definition. For example, the following poem from his 1976 collection Hymns in Darkness is a Bombay poem:

> He said:
> 'In a single day
> I'm forced to listen
> to a dozen film songs,
> to see
> a score of beggars,
> to touch
> uncounted strangers,
> to smell
> unsmellable smells,
> to taste
> my bitter native city.'
> ('Hymns in Darkness, XIV')

In many of his Bombay poems, Nissim puts forward the radical view that in India, rootedness need not be only to one's native village; one can discover one's roots in the city as well. This idea is unfamiliar to Bombayites, who often regard the city only as their place of work, while home is elsewhere, in Kerala or Uttar Pradesh, or even a hilly district of Maharashtra, to which one must travel in the holidays with one's children. The assumption underlying such a belief is, of course, that if one can relate only to Bombay, and to no other village or town of one's supposed origins, one is rootless. Nissim's position, on the other hand, is closer to that of second and third generation settlers in the city, who were born here, and who think of their roots as existing in Bombay, not in an India of abstractions situated in the faraway countryside. In short, one can live in Bombay all one's life and still regard oneself as a true Indian, with Indian values, although Bombay has many outward tokens of Westernization that may prove to be a 'corrupting' influence.

Two of Nissim's most well-known poems about Bombay, 'Urban' and 'A Morning Walk', occur in the book *The Unfinished Man,* published in 1960. Although he uses the third-person method of narration in both the poems, this is only a strategy, a mask, to distance the poet persona from the poet in either case. But the details are autobiographical, and Nissim relies here on personal experience. For example, in 'Urban' he writes:

> At dawn he never sees the skies
> Which, silently, are born again.
> Nor feels the shadows of the night
> Recline their fingers on his eyes.
> He welcomes neither sun nor rain.
> His landscape has no depth or height.

Both the first and the last lines of the above stanza reveal the setting to be a not-too-tall building, say Readymoney Mansion or Mazda Mansion, from where he could see neither the sky, nor experience a sense of depth or height. (One cannot imagine, say, Adil Jussawalla, another Bombay poet, writing these lines.)

Again, in 'A Morning Walk', when Nissim says, 'His native place he could not shun, / The marsh where things are what they seem,' we know he is prima facie talking about himself, whose native place is Bombay, allegedly a marsh. (There is an interesting discovery I made about the poem 'A Morning Walk', in which the oft-quoted phrase 'barbaric city' occurs. I found precisely the same expression used by Raja Rao in his novel *The Serpent and the Rope,* to describe Bombay, as he talks about his protagonist Ramaswamy's visit to the city, en route to Paris. Considering that both *The Unfinished Man* and *The Serpent and the Rope* appeared in exactly the same year, 1960, I can't say which of these two famous writers plagiarized the other's phrase; or whether their existence in the two books is purely coincidental.)

The Exact Name (1965), Nissim's fifth collection of poems that followed *The Unfinished Man,* also contains poems about Bombay. One of these is 'In India', in which India virtually becomes Bombay, and Bombay a microcosm of India. In the first section of the poem he writes:

> Always in the sun's eye,
> Here among the beggars,
> Hawkers, pavement sleepers,
> Hutment dwellers, slums,
> Dead souls of men and gods,
> Burnt-out mothers, frightened
> Virgins, wasted child
> And tortured animal,
> All in noisy silence
> Suffering the place and time
> I ride my elephant of thought,
> A Cezanne slung around my neck.

In the fourth section, his setting is '... the large apartment / With cold beer and Western music' in which there is 'Lucid talk of art and literature,/ And of all "the changes India needs." The poem being what it is, 'In Bombay' would have been a more accurate, and therefore better title, than 'In India'.

It is in his poem 'Island', included in *Hymns in Darkness* (1976), that Nissim firmly and finally expresses his commitment to Bombay:

> I cannot leave the island,
> I was born here and belong.

These lines also echo the famous concluding lines of 'Background, Casually', the previous poem in the book, autobiographical in nature:

> I have made my commitments now.
> This is one: to stay where I am,
> As others choose to give themselves
> In some remote and backward place.
> My backward place is where I am.

Another poem, 'Occasion' takes us to the unglamorous, relatively unaffluent suburb of Ghatkopar in north-east Bombay, to meet Ramanathan (or is it Krishnaswamy?), a south-Indian, middle-aged, balding typist 'without a face or figure.' This man works in a bank by day, and types in the evening, 'for another hundred rupees or so a month.' He has three children, a mother and an invalid wife to support, and travels to and from work every day by bus and train, spending half an hour in the bus queue, fifty minutes in the bus, and forty in the train. Besides, he has to take a long walk from Ghatkopar station to the slum in which he lives. His wretched life causes the poet's friend, a freelance journalist, to remark that 'He ought to be a smuggler . . . we should have left this country twenty years ago . . .There's no future for us.' And the poet-narrator seems, on the whole, to be in agreement.

Nissim's continuing interest in Bombay, and his poetic evocations of it in the manner of Yeats and Eliot, eventually gave rise to a school of poetry that is sometimes referred to as the Bombay school. It is made up of poets who, like him, were born or bred in the city and, regard it as home, and who, of course, write only or mainly in English. Some of the more well-known among them are Adil Jussawalla, Gieve Patel, Saleem Peeradina, Dom Moraes, Eunice de Souza, Santan Rodrigues, Menka Shivadasani and Ranjit Hoskote, but there are numerous others. All of them were born after Nissim and looked up to him for inspiration and guidance. And all of them, like him, have written at least some poems that are specifically about Bombay. It is this that led me, in 1987, to guest-edit, to the great delight of the editor, L. Adinarayana Rao, a special anthology number of the Hyderabad-based journal *The Literary Endeavour*[17] on Bombay poetry. But in July that year, when the issue was out, with seventy-three poems by forty-nine poets, no one's happiness surpassed Nissim's. Not only did he arrange a special reading at the PEN at Theosophy Hall, Churchgate, but he also went round talking excitedly about it to almost everyone he met, suggesting that ten years earlier such an issue would have been unthinkable.

The critic Bruce King was perhaps not being very original when he 'invented' the term 'Bombay school' in his book *Modern Indian Poetry in English* (1987). But no one else can take the credit for doing other things to the word, like 'Bombayizing' it.[18] In this, King was recognizing Bombay as an important locus of modernity in Indian English poetry, a modernity that could not have existed outside the cultural parameters laid down by the city.

And it was Nissim Ezekiel who first made all of us aware of it.

Freedom at Midnight

In the summer of 1939, Nissim was vacationing at his grandfather's house in Tal, waiting for school to reopen, so that he could enter his final year, and be done with school life once and for all. He picked up a copy of the Bhagavad Gita in an English translation, and went through all the eighteen chapters. He assiduously read both text, and translator's comments that followed each stanza of the holy book. He was shocked. His peace-loving sensibilities and his ethical sense were offended by the doubts Arjuna had expressed, and particularly by the advice Krishna gave him–to go to battle in the name of duty. He simply couldn't see sense in such reasoning, no matter how hard he reflected upon the matter. The shock of those boyhood days in relation to Hinduism's, and India's most sacred text, would stay with him for life. It is as if his Judeo-Christian foundations, with their notion of virtue and sin, were acting as a barrier here and interfering with his ability to grasp the logic of Krishna's teachings: all battle is evil and cannot be justified, even if the ends are noble; ends do not justify means. And to think that Nissim wouldn't have even bothered to read the Bhagavad Gita at that time, had the school fathers as orthodox Christians not run it down! It is incredible that a man who harboured such convictions should, less than a decade later, relinquish religion to become an atheist and a rationalist. Yet this is the course that Nissim's life takes, and it constitutes a major segment of the present chapter.

Upon successfully completing his matriculation in 1941, Nissim joined college. It was the Wilson College at Chowpatty where his father taught, founded by the Presbyterians, and he took admission to the four year BA course. On the whole, Nissim seems to have been a better student in college, than he was at school. In a first-person account to a Bombay magazine, he said '. . . it was not till I joined Wilson College that I applied my mind to studies seriously. I won a scholarship there throughout my four years and graduated in English literature with a first class. This inspired me somewhat for my Master's degree . . .'[1]

We may attribute his preference for college, as compared to school, to two essentials: one, life in college was less regimental than life in school, and more conducive, therefore, to creative freedom; two, there were far less subjects for which he did not have a taste (like Physics and Algebra) that he had to compulsorily study. Moreover, it was in college that he began taking his poetry seriously, and realized that, possibly, it would be his vocation in life. He says: 'I had already started writing poetry at age twelve and had become quite certain that poetry was going to play a very important part in my life. All through the years, no matter what the job– and I have had many-writing poetry is an activity that has never stopped.'[2]

The Wilson College magazine was one of the first magazines in which Nissim began publishing his poems during those years in the early '40s. The experience of seeing his handwritten poems transformed into print was hypnotic, even if it was only a college magazine. This emboldened him, and he ventured out in other directions, sending poems to various established journals and magazines, some of them with a large readership. One of these was *Thought*, edited in those days by K.M. Munshi. There were others, but not all of them accepted his work. Those that did sometimes paid him a fee for the poems they had used: Nissim's first earnings. None of this, though, made him over-confident about his abilities. The natural diffidence, the sense of failure, were always there, hanging over his head like the proverbial sword of Damocles. Partly, it was also the need he has always felt, to be modest. Thus, he says : 'I was certainly writing poetry during my college days, but hadn't begun to think of myself as a poet.'[3]

What's more, the lack of confidence had its positive side. It made him excessively critical of his own work. It helped him fashion an approach to poetry he would profitably pursue in later years, to evaluate both his own work, and that of others who came to him for literary advice. 'At the age of twenty I became the worst critic of my poems, looking at most of them as too trivial,' he said in a newspaper interview.[4]

Nissim passed his Inter Arts in 1943. It was time for him to decide the special subject he would graduate in, and he opted for English literature. It was as a BA student of English literature between the years 1943 and 1945 that he first seriously acquainted himself with all the great masters of the Western literary canon, from Chaucer to T. S. Eliot. He read avidly and did well in all his exams. His reading helped him shape his own ideas about literature in the modern period, and constituted the foundations on which the edifice of his own poetry would be built. He was especially influenced by the ideas of Eliot and Ezra Pound, and what has come to be known as the Pound-Eliot revolution, that brought modernism to English literature.

The decision to graduate in Eng. Lit, was entirely Nissim's own, his parents having no say in the matter. If Moses had had his way, he would have liked at least one of his children to follow in his footsteps, and become, like himself, a lecturer in Botany and Zoology. Nissim recalls that his father even kept books on these subjects in the house, hoping that his children would read and develop an interest in them. Finally, of course, the choice was theirs, for Moses did not believe in imposing his will on his children. As it turned out, none of them became professors of Botany and Zoology. But Moses' attempts to inculcate a love for the sciences in the minds of his children paid off. All of them developed a curiosity about the subject, and were fascinated no end by its marvels. They also developed a scientific attitude. Nissim says: 'Since my college years, I've read with great pleasure articles and books on the relation of science to society, to religion, and to everyday life. Well before I was twenty, I had become science-oriented, or so I thought, though my emotional life was largely in terms of poetry. Asked about my beliefs, by equally confused companions and acquaintances, I would say "I believe in the scientific attitude to life." Before I knew what was happening to me, I had started announcing my atheism and my faith in a future society dominated by scientific attitudes and values.'[5]

He also regards it as significant that though the 'ethos of science' had begun to change around the mid-'40s, when he was a college student, so that an overly scientific view of things quickly went out of fashion, he retained his 'fundamental loyalty' to science, drawing his inspiration from the mood that was prevalent in the nineteenth century, and in the early years of the twentieth.[6]

How did Nissim spend his time in college, apart from writing poetry, reading books? From his childhood, he had hobbies, and some of them like stamp-collecting, stayed with him through his years in college, though he was no philatelist. He enjoyed watching English films, mostly at the Alexandra arid Palace Cinemas, both close to his house. Then he had an interest in political thought, and became a member of M. N. Roy's, Radical Democratic Party. Later, in the '50s, he developed other interests, like bird-watching, in the company of his friend Zafar Futehally, the naturalist, and became a part of Futehally's Nalanda group. However, he apologized to Futehally and gave up bird-watching when he found he was no good at it. He also began seeing Hindi films, many of them starring his former classmate, Raj Kapoor. And, of course, he flirted with the girls of the college and the neighbourhood.

The headache that Nissim suffered from as a schoolboy, persisted in college, right until the time he graduated. Since reading and writing formed an important component of his daily activity, there was little chance of its receding or disappearing; on the contrary, it intensified, and sometimes even led to sleeplessness. But it did not worry him too much, and he cannot remember any particular course of medicines that he took. His parents too did not attach much importance to his headache; they told him it would go away on its own.

In 1945, Nissim passed his BA with a First Class. His performance in the examinations motivated him to register for his MA in English Literature at Wilson College. He had already won a scholarship throughout his four years as an undergraduate student. Now he became a Fellow of Wilson College for two years, from June 1945 to June 1947, with a monthly stipend of Rs 40. This meant that alongside his course work, he had also to take tutorial classes for the First Year and Inter Arts students of the college. At the same time, he began teaching at the Hansraj Morarji School at Vile Parle, which fetched him a small income. But he had to give up his job after a term's teaching in 1945, because the Wilson College authorities took objection to it: as Fellow of their college, he wasn't permitted to take up outside assignments. The Hansraj Morarji School understood; they only requested him to continue his classes until the end of that term, after which they relieved him.

Both his fellowship and his job at the school gave Nissim his first taste of teaching, and he loved it. He realized there was this wonderful thing about the profession, whereby even as one taught others, one learned things oneself. He was as diligent a student in MA, as he was during his BA. The very authors who fascinated him in his BA classes, Eliot and Pound and Joyce and Yeats, were now to be studied at a more advanced level. There was also a good deal of literary criticism on the syllabus. For the first time he was in his element in a classroom situation, taking an active part in discussions, doing exceedingly well in exams. The result was that in 1947, Nissim not only passed his MA with a high Second Class, but also topped the university, and won a coveted prize, the R. K. Lagu Prize.

Nissim's fellowship ended as soon as he completed his MA. He was twenty-three and needed to have an income of his own. As a young man with a postgraduate degree from the University of Bombay, he was eminently qualified to teach in a college, and that is where his sights were set. His first choice was his alma mater, Wilson College, but there was no vacancy for the post of lecturer in English. In response to newspaper advertisements, he sent out applications to various other colleges, and was called for an interview to the Khalsa College at King's Circle. Without any difficulty, Nissim got the job, even before his MA results were declared. In all, he spent twelve months at Khalsa College, June 1947 to June 1948, teaching undergraduate students. Then, by his own admission, he grew restless in his job and resigned from it, spending the rest of 1948 doing nothing in particular except 'wandering aimlessly'[7], writing poetry, freelancing for newspapers and magazines (he mentions *the Times of India, Free Press Journal* and *Bharatiya Vidya Bhavan Journal*), giving tuition, and of course, working for the Radical Democratic Party. This went on until November that year, when 'an unexpected thing happened'[8]– Ebrahim Alkazi took him away to England.

Nissim's youthful years in college and beyond, from 1941 until the time he left for England in early 1949, were also India's most politically important and politically sensitive years. These years, as everyone knows, not only witnessed the Quit India Movement in 1942 and Independence in 1947, but also culminated tragically with the assassination of Mahatma Gandhi on 30 January 1948. Nissim's reactions to these events must be seen from two perspectives: one, his, own, and the other, that of the Bene Israel community. Often the two overlap.

As a community, the Bene Israel were in those days, much less politically inclined than, say the Cochin Jews, who had a history of political dealings with the Hindus, as well as with the various Europeans that ruled India, like the Portugese, the Dutch and the British. Isenberg informs us that throughout India's freedom struggle only three Bene Israel were known to have been involved in active politics,[9] not surprising, perhaps, when we are told that according to the 1921 Government Census for the British Districts of Bombay Presidency, the Jews as a whole constituted only 00.06% of the total population, in stark contrast to the Hindus who comprised 76.78 %, and Muslims who comprised 19.57 %.

A popular reason that is put forward for poor Bene Israel participation in the freedom movement is that, in the twentieth century, the community was only just reinforcing itself economically, and members were too busy looking for opportunities to make a decent living, to have the time to take part in politics. This no doubt is true, but there is another factor that must not be overlooked. The struggle for freedom in India, in both the nineteenth and the twentieth centuries, has always been linked to Hinduism, the religion of the Indian majority. Nationalism, thus, was at best religious nationalism, a thesis that is corroborated by no less an authority than V. S. Naipaul in *India: A Wounded Civilization*. Microscopic minorities like the Bene Israel were bound to feel alienated from such a movement, and keep at a distance from it. One thing is certain: as a community, the Bene Israel did not know, even after Independence was won whether Gandhi's methods of satyagraha and non-violence, were ideal. This is directly reflected in Nissim's own doubts about the philosophy of Gandhi, and his preference instead for the beliefs of M. N. Roy.

Even so, several Bene Israel contributed to the freedom struggle in their individual capacities. Among these, mention may be made of Dr Joseph Benjamin, who was an active member of the Indian National Congress, and Dr Jacob E. Solomon, Secretary of the Ahmedabad Branch of the India Home Rule League. Again, Aaron Daniel Talkar lent his support to Lokamanya Tilak, while Dr Elijah Moses was one of the first Bene Israel to have contested and won a public election, becoming eventually the Mayor of Bombay.

One of the community's most 'political acts' was a letter dated 22 November 1917,[10] addressed to Edwin Samuel Montago, the then Secretary of State for India in the British Indian government. It was signed by as many as nine highly-educated and highly-respected members, including Dr Jacob E. Solomon. The other signatories to the letter were Shalom B. Israel, B. J. Samson, M. S. Ezekiel, Rahamim J. Ezekiel, Abraham S. Erulkar, Samuel S. Mazgamkar, Jacob B. Israel and I. J. Samson. Basically, the letter requested the Secretary of State to ensure that the Bene Israel not be represented communally in electorates in India, because 'we feel that smaller communities stand to lose by communal representation, in as much as they are marked out, and whatever special representation they may get, can never be very effective.' Besides, 'by giving a separate electorate to a community, the racial feeling is accentuated and the interest of the community is narrowed down to its own activities. Such communal elections do not foster the development of the Indian nation; they rather retard it.' However, 'if the principle of communal representation be extended to smaller communities, we beg to submit, that there should not be separate communal electorates. In place of communal electorates or Government nominations, we would recommend that communal representatives be co-opted by the representatives of the general electorate, which must then necessarily include all the persons with franchise irrespective of caste or community.'

The soundness of reasoning in the above letter must not give us the impression that it had the tacit approval of the entire community. There were many who disagreed with the point of view of the signatories, and argued that the latter could not be taken as spokesmen of the whole community. In other words, they were asking for communal representation in elections. When it came to matters political, the Bene Israel were themselves divided in their opinions.

Of course, the Hindu majority paid lip service to the issue of communal harmony from the very beginning. In 1921, Mahatma Gandhi's Bene Israel physician, Dr A. S. Erulkar, who supervised his health during his various fasts, and who later became a rationalist and an admirer of M. N. Roy, asked him what role Indian Jews could play in the freedom struggle. Gandhi, it seems, scribbled the following answer on the back of an envelope: 'If you could influence the Jews, or put me on to some, I would like it. They must feel absolutely secure from molestation by Hindus and Mussalmans [sic].' Furthermore, 'If the Bene Israelites have not been injured or affected, one need not worry. The English Jews I class among Englishmen, who don't need any special assurance.'[11] The reference to Englishmen in the latter part of Gandhi's statement is generally taken to mean that he was making a distinction between the Bene Israel and other Jews, regarding the former as Indian.

The following year, a day before Gandhi was arrested in March, he spoke about what he called 'the four pillars of swaraj', one of which was Hindu-Muslim-Sikh-Parsi-Christian-Jewish unity. The other 'pillars' were non- violence, the abolition of untouchability, and the manufacture of hand-spun and hand-woven khadi to prevent the use of foreign textiles.[12]

The letter of Dr Jacob E. Solomon and others to Edwin Samuel Montago in November 1917, and the statements of Gandhi notwithstanding, a Jewish (Indian) Nationalist Party was mooted, towards the end of the '20s, by none other than Gandhi's physician, Dr A. S. Erulkar, together with I. J. Samson. Its aims, obviously, were to emphasize that the Bene Israel stood for independence, but that they had to put up their fight separately. Support to the party wasn't, however, unanimous. The All India Israelite League and the Bene Israel Conference passed resolutions of loyalty to the British, which implied they were not really keen on independence. Many Bene Israel who owed allegiance to these groups identified themselves with communities like the Anglo-Indian community, who enjoyed a privileged status in British India, and who were given preferential treatment in the sphere of employment, along with higher salaries.

Be that as it may, the party named the Jewish Nationalist Party actually came into existence in 1930. A news item published in the Bombay Chronicle of 21 July 1930, announced its formation. About seventy-five members mostly of the Bene Israel community gathered to express sympathy with the national movement and to support it by taking up the Swadeshi and other boycott programs of the Congress.

No one in Nissim's family was directly connected with the politics of the freedom movement, although they stood for independence. Neither Moses, nor Joe, nor Hannan, were members of the Jewish (Indian) Nationalist Party, or of the All India Israelite League or the Bene Israel Conference. However, as pointed out earlier, Nissim was interested in political ideology as a college student, and became involved in it via another route: his fellow Bene-Israelite, Abraham Solomon, exactly ten years older than himself, whom he first met in 1941 during his very first year of college, ironically enough, at the Prayer Hall of the Jewish Religious Union. Solomon and Nissim became close friends, and Solomon introduced him to ideas on international atheism and rationalism. In those days, international rationalists were themselves divided into two groups, those who were both atheists and rationalists, and those who were only the latter. Solomon claimed to belong to the former set, and about the first thing Nissim recalls is that he started making very critical comments about religion in general, and Judaism in particular, stating categorically that he was a member of the Rationalist Movement, and did not believe in the existence of God. Yet he continued to attend the service at the synagogue only so as to not upset his mother, who was still alive. Though Nissim was not convinced by this argument, he did not fail to see the connection between rationalism and atheism. His father, who was a rationalist, also agreed that an atheist could not attend prayer services, and now Nissim, coming under the influence of Solomon, proclaimed he was both a rationalist and an atheist, and would henceforth stop attending the prayer services. The decision, of course, was not easy, and he went through weeks and weeks of soul-searching, becoming terribly upset in the process, before he made up his mind to renounce religion. But renounce it he did, and not even the fact that, like Solomon's mother, his mother too disapproved of his decision, made him change his mind.

The electric personality of Gandhi was not easy to resist in the '30s and '40s. Most writers of the period, including Rabindranath Tagore, Sarojini Naidu and Aurobindo Ghose, were taken up with his ideas, one way or another, although poets like Tagore also had their differences with him. Nissim, however, was never seriously drawn to Gandhism; he was always skeptical about it. Serious politics began for him in 1942, the year of the Quit India Movement. He would often go to the Chowpatty sands to listen to the speeches of Gandhi and Nehru,[13] finding himself in disagreement with them. Here he was relating to history strictly as a Jew, and a Royist, feeling it was disastrous to speak about non-cooperation when the War was on. As suggested earlier, the Bene Israel as a community were of the opinion that Gandhi's demands in 1942 were inappropriate, considering the political exigencies of the day. They were also wounded by the fact that anti-Semitic sentiment, which was responsible for wreaking havoc in the lives of Jews all over the world, meant little to the people of India. Nissim's friends in the First Year and Inter Arts classes at Wilson College were themselves divided on the issue of non-cooperation, and over the need to be anti-British in response to Mahatma Gandhi's call. Those who supported Gandhi's and the Congress' line of thinking were cheesed off with him for not being anti-British enough; but there were others who shared his views. These students had the stupendous task of explaining to the pro-Gandhi lobby that, as M.N. Roy said, World War II, was, after all, a war against fascism, and opposing the British at that stage would be tantamount to supporting the forces of fascism, against which the War was being fought.

It is remarkable that these views that Nissim held in the early '40s, have stayed consistently with him for over fifty years. In 1994, N.V.K. Murthy wrote an article on the popular Hindi film, "1942: A Love Story" in *New Quest* (formerly Quest), a journal that Nissim himself was associated with in the '50s. Murthy said in his article: 'Those of us who were fortunate to be young during 1942 had a similar feeling [as those, according to Wordsworth, who lived during the heady days of the French Revolution, captured in Wordsworth's lines "to be young was very heaven"]. People, especially the young, were swept off their feet by a typhoon of emotions. Young men and women who belonged to an apolitical middle class suddenly found themselves in the midst of an epic struggle. They discovered the rationale of the movement later, most of them in jail. But the first response was overwhelmingly emotional. There were many Hari Singhs, Nandus, Raos, Pathak Babus, Beg Sahebs, Subhankers and Major Bhists [presumably, characters in the film] in actual flesh and blood.'[14]

I asked Nissim how he reacted to this effusive piece, 'If I was left alone by other politics-M. N. Roy-I would have been like everyone else. It was the M. N. Roy speeches and articles I read that made me agree that there was a case against fighting for Independence when the war against the Nazis was still going on after World War II, which was more important. Roy said we shouldn't give up our struggle for freedom, but postpone it. I don't think the anti-Nazi sentiment appealed to me only because I was a Jew, but that must have been there too, though it was not the dominating factor.'

Around that time, Nissim even lectured on Gandhi at Rotary Club-type meetings in Bombay. One of the things that he invariably brought out in his lectures was that, what Gandhi had in mind in relation to a certain subject, was not necessarily what other people had in mind vis-à-vis it. In other words, it was easy to misunderstand Gandhi, because there was often a wide gulf between precept and practice. For example, Gandhi was very much in favour of Hindu-Muslim friendship, and yet, when one of his followers once hinted that he would invite some Muslims to a certain political dinner, he was aghast; for, what if they expressed an interest to marry your daughter! According to Nissim, there was a genuine dilemma here that Gandhi was facing; some may choose to call it hypocrisy.

The disenchantment with Gandhi was one of the factors that directly led Nissim into the heart of the Royist Movement. Manabendra Nath Roy, whose real name was Narendra Bhattacharya, was born in Urbalia village, Twenty-four Parganas, West Bengal, in 1889. He had a chequered political career as a nationalist and a communist, before he arrived at the philosophy of humanism in the last ten to fifteen years of his life. Roy was a member of the Communist Party, first in Mexico and then in Moscow, and led a successful movement in China, before he was expelled from the Party for refusing to follow their ultra-leftist insurrectionary methods. He had the sensibility of a poet, that perhaps made him incapable of adopting a very hard line. On being dismissed from the Communist Party International, he wrote, in a tone full of contempt: 'No evidence whatsoever was produced to show how a traditional "leftist" has become a right opportunist, how one suddenly becomes a "renegade" after more than twenty-five years active service to the revolution.[15] But his experiences with Gandhian nationalism were equally unpleasant. As a student, he ignored Gandhi's call for swadeshi, and opted for the path of militancy, joining Yugantar, a group with like-minded aims. As he grew older, he couldn't share Gandhi's out-and-out dislike for British imperialism, devoid of references to feudal exploitation within India, where, according to Roy, the real problem lay. Coupled with this was his inability, as a Marxist thinker, to accept Gandhi's philosophy of satyagraha. Things came to a head during World War II, when Roy, who had been a member of the Indian National Congress ever since he ceased to be a Communist, declared that he couldn't adopt Gandhi's anti-British, anti-war policies, because he saw the War as a war against fascism, and believed in it. It is this that provided Nissim the immediate impetus to join Roy, because, as pointed out earlier, to him too, World War II was an anti-fascist war that gave the Jews of the world an opportunity to avenge themselves.

Shortly after his release from jail, where he spent six years soon after his return to India in 1930, M. N. Roy was expelled from a political party for the second time. It was the Congress, this time, and he was asked to leave for refusing to toe their line. The year was 1940, when World War II was at its peak, and in December that year, Roy founded his own party, the Radical Democratic Party.

Actually, even before the Radical Democratic Party was started, those who were close to Roy suspected he was on his way to taking off on his own. This was because of his idealism, which always made him see flaws in the groups he was associated with. In 1937, V.B. Karnik, one of Roy's most ardent followers, said in an article that contrary to the hopes of the so-called left-wingers who wanted Roy to keep aloof from the actual work of mobilizing the radical forces, so that they may put him on a pedestal to be looked on as a hero and revolutionary, Roy went straight to the task of organizing the people in their revolutionary struggle. 'He did not' says Karnik, 'appreciate the role of a highly applauded, but an ineffective hero. . . He joined the ranks of the people, and moving in their midst, thinking their thoughts, and giving expression to their feelings and aspirations, undertook the ostentatious, but essential work of organizing them.'[16]

In the eight years of its existence, till it was dissolved in 1948, the Radical Democratic Party, under the leadership of Roy, exercised a great deal of influence on thinking Indians. It succeeded in splitting up the Trade Union Movement under the auspices of the All India Trade Union Congress, to form the rival Indian Federation of Labour, which actively supported World War II.

Roy was a charismatic leader, who from the '20s onwards, attracted young intellectuals by acquainting them with the ideas of Marx, both personally, and through his books like *India in Transition,* published in 1922. Nissim came under Roy's influence only during the last ten to twelve years of his (Roy's) life. He was a young man of less than twenty when he did. Apart from political reasons, there were psychological reasons that drew him to Roy. As G.D. Parikh says, 'Roy released the creativity of men; he made even the most mediocre of persons feel that life was beautiful, and that they were wanted.'[17] He saw failure as the inevitable consequence of intellectual and moral integrity, and this appealed to Nissim, who was himself afflicted with a sense of failure. Moreover, reason was Roy's sole guiding principle, and reason was always something that Nissim held in very high esteem.

In order to ensure that my perceptions were right, I asked Nissim how he saw his involvement in the Royist movement, after nearly half a century. This is what he said: 'Even before I read material by M.N. Roy given to me by Royists, one thing is certain–I was attracted by some of the concepts of socialism, and also nationalism, and desired to participate in the struggle for freedom. In class, when I was a student, almost everyone felt involved in the struggle for freedom, at least mentally, even if we did not actually do anything. If anyone said anything in praise of the British, we would be contemptuous of him. This was before I became a Royist in the first two years of college. It was at this stage in the Inter Arts class that I was first given Royist material to read, and then attended a lecture by him in Bombay. Things written by him–he brought out a journal called Independent India–were passed on to me, and I felt closer to his ideas than to Gandhi, Nehru and Congress nationalism. Roy also stood for Independence, but many nationalists who attacked him, accused him of not wanting India to get free. But I was convinced that he wanted Independence. Roy's personality, his question-answer sessions, his essays, editorial articles, statements about the nationalist situation, I sort of felt sold on all that. But at that age–I was eighteen to twenty–this sort of thing happens to most people. But I was also attracted to Roy's rationalism, his critical attitude to God and religion.'

Roy preached the message of revolt, and in the cultural sense, revolt was the catchword of the English modernists as well: it made Roy especially attractive to Nissim.

Another of M.N. Roy's experiments was the principle of cooperative social or community living, where one's rationality, which, to him, bore an inseparable connection to one's morality, could be put to test. Accordingly, in 1948, when Nissim was a lecturer at Khalsa College, he left his parents' home and started to live on his own, first in the political office of the Radical Democratic Party at Girgaum with other members like V.M. Tarkunde and V.B. Karnik, and then in a sort of slum with Royist political workers, at the office of the Municipal Workers' Union situated there.

He was even appointed Secretary of the Municipal Workers' Union and enjoyed his job, though he lost the municipal election that he stood for. His lectures at Khalsa College were mostly in the morning; so he had the rest of the day free to carry on with his political activities. Luckily for him, Moses and Diana did not construe this as his walking out on them; there was little unpleasantness at home. They knew of his involvement in the Royist movement. Though it occasionally led to arguments between Moses and Nissim, his parents, once again, respected his freedom of choice, even if it upset them in the bargain. As a matter of fact, Moses would visit him in the slum every morning, with tea in a flask and something to eat.

In about seven years from its inception, Roy outgrew the Radical Democratic Party. In its place, he developed his philosophy of New Humanism. India had become independent; perhaps he felt that a movement with a starkly revolutionary base was no longer the need of the hour. What was required was a softer movement, with a more positive, more futuristic vision. New Humanism has thus been called 'a mid-twentieth-century version of the Renaissance,'[18] and Roy became to his followers a philosopher of the modern Renaissance.

The genesis of the new movement, as explained by Karnik, took place at the famous summer camps which were held regularly every year at Dehra Dun or Mussoorie. Here issues would be discussed calmly and intelligently until they found general acceptance. They were then put in the form of Twenty-two Theses. They were discussed by a conference of the Radical Democratic Party held in Bombay in December 1946. It was the first time that 'a political party was called upon to discuss such a highly intellectual, philosophical statement on the origin and growth of man and society, on the development of ideas and on the social and political institutions that could serve the purpose of man in the twentieth century. . . Roy was asked to draft a statement based upon the social and political ideas contained in the Twenty-two Theses. It was to be the Humanist Manifesto. It was published later under the title New Humanism.'[19]

M. N. Roy himself described New Humanism as a cosmopolitan commonwealth of 'spiritually free men' motivated by the will to remake the world in order to restore the individual of his primacy and dignity and show the 'way out of the contemporary crisis of modern civilization.'[20]

New Humanism led to the disbanding of the Radical Democratic Party in December 1948, exactly eight years after it was founded. Roy seems to have felt that there was no room for a political party in the New Humanist's scheme of things, for a political party only prevented people from exercising their sovereignty, and was an obstacle to democracy. The majority of his followers were willy-nilly in agreement with him, even though it was not an easy decision to take. The party had grown during the eight years of its existence, it had its branches in most parts of the country, and had a large cadre of intelligent, devoted and selfless workers. They had sacrificed everything for their political and social work under the aegis of the Party. They had stood by it through thick and thin.'[21]

Nissim, however, was disappointed at the dissolution of the Radical Democratic Party. He couldn't see eye-to-eye with Roy on this business of the party being a hindrance to sovereignty and democracy, or of its having outlived its utility generally. Nor was he enthusiastic about New Humanism. The result is that he grew distanced from politics after 1948. Literature and the arts came to replace politics as his first love by the end of the '40s, and coincidentally, this is marked by his departure for England at the end of the decade. To the list of friends such as Abraham Solomon, were now added new names like George Coelho and Ebrahim Alkazi, both predominantly interested in the arts.

Nissim's disenchantment with Roy did not mean, of course, that New Humanism was dead. After 1948, Roy changed the name of his journal from Independent India to the Radical Humanist, and the journal continues to come out as a monthly journal to this day, under the editorship of V.M. Tarkunde. Public interest in Roy's ideas also continues, as is evidenced by two edit-page articles on him in The Times of India recently, the first by R.M. Pal on 'Roy's Humanism' (21 March 1996), and the second a letter in response to the above piece, by R. Meganathan (30 March 1996). Needless to say, both the articles were highly appreciative of Roy's contribution to the humanist movement.

My own analysis is that Nissim's relationship with M.N. Roy was parasitic. He had neither the dynamism of Roy–at one stage in the early twentieth century, Roy even became a sanyasi and toured parts of northern and eastern India on foot–nor his astute political sense. At the same time, he realized how important it was for young men with a university education to have a grasp of the goings-on in the country, in what was evidently India's most tortuous political phase. Royism provided the peg.

Had it not been for M. N. Roy, Nissim probably wouldn't have had strong convictions about issues like Partition, which he claims made him 'very upset and angry', for he had assumed there would be Independence without Partition. This, he says, made him bitter about Nehru, whom he and his friends felt was in a hurry to become Prime Minister. They were opposed (and to this day he continues to be opposed) to what he calls 'Nehru's compromises', and he is of the opinion that had Nehru listened to the advice of other nationalist leaders, India could have become independent without having had to go through the trauma of Partition. Likewise, he had by then come to disagree with most of what Gandhi was saying, although his assassination on 30 January 1948 made him unhappy. Yet Nissim admits that since he left India soon after these events took place, he was spared of the obligation 'to take all kinds of decisions about politics,' as for instance, the need to choose which political party to align himself with. In the final analysis, he knew that his real commitment was to poetry.

What is commendable about Nissim's approach to politics is his honesty. He realized that to be in politics also meant being an activist, and this he could never be. In this context, he said to me: 'One reason why I kept away from politics, even during my M. N. Roy years is because I could never accept in toto statements made by leaders, as a person with a lifetime of involvement in politics must do.'

Thus, compared to his other associates, there was very little actual political activity that he was involved in, even as a Royist.

When it comes to writing, Nissim has once again kept away from issues that are overly or overtly political. True, he did edit the journal *Freedom First* for a while and also wrote letters to newspapers, but then, as he puts it, 'Nine times out of ten, I'm not even in a group of writers who make public statements denouncing this or that.' At the time we were discussing this (1994), the Taslima Nasreen affair was being hotly debated in the national and international media, and Nissim confessed that he was apprehensive about having to sign a resolution condemning the harassment of Taslima Nasreen, 'because there may be some part of it with which I don't agree.' Here, of course, he was adopting the familiar stand that he had taken during the Salman Rushdie episode in 1989. He had shocked the literary world then by declaring that he supported the ban on *The Satanic Verses,* because, to him, upholding a writer's freedom of expression was not more important than safeguarding the religious sentiments of the people. At the root of the matter was, possibly, also this feeling that controversy was an all-too-easy shortcut to fame–fame of the kind that he had never tasted.

Perhaps the acid test, that proves he was a novice in politics, exists in the fact that in his entire corpus of poetry, there isn't a single poem on a nationalist theme, although he was actively writing poetry even during his Royist phase. Nissim cannot be called a poet of Indian democracy, as Walt Whitman was a poet of American democracy. He is aware of this, and when heckled about it, says in his defence that in his early years he would attempt to write poems on political subjects, but soon discovered that he couldn't. So he gave up, realizing that a political poem, in order to be successful, had to be a good poem first. He had read and admired some of the work of other nationally recognized poets of the period, Tagore, Aurobindo, Sarojini Naidu and Armando Menezes, all of whom had enough poems that could properly be called political. However, none of them acted as an influence. On the contrary, he was extremely critical of most of what he read, ranging from the puerile rhymes of Harindranath Chattopadhyaya, to spiritual extravagances of Aurobindo Ghose. On occasion, this got him into trouble, as when the PEN of which he was a member, received a letter addressed to Madame Sophiya Wadia, its chairperson, asking that he be expelled from the association for saying nasty things about Aurobindo Ghose.

I discovered, while working on this book, that I was not the only one who was surprised by the lack of a political dimension to Nissim's poetry. On 26 June 1994, Nissim was in Cochin, Kerala, where he gave an interview to the daily newspaper Indian Communicator. Interviewer V.C. Harris, begins his interview by saying:

'One of the first and most important questions that I resolve to put to him [Nissim] concerns his early involvement with M. N. Roy's Radical Democratic Movement. To me this is an extremely interesting bit of biographical/historical detail, for Ezekiel's poetry–and Indian poetry in English in general–is rarely read in terms of politics. The largely apolitical stance taken by a majority of these poets and the reluctance with which their works address issues concerning the political life of the nation are commonplaces of scholarship on Indian English poetry. But here is its leading exponent, Nissim Ezekiel, coming to the vocation of poetry via a startlingly political, Royist route.'[22]

However, Harris is soon disillusioned, as he realizes that 'Ezekiel is not the kind of person who would go beyond his immediate perceptions, his own appraisals of the situation, in addressing the wider political implications of his involvement with M. N. Roy.' The rest of his interview proceeds along largely apolitical lines.

There is one last point that I wish to make before I move away from the subject of Nissim's inconsistencies: like his politics, his atheism too may be attributed to the overpowering influence of M. N. Roy. In other words, there were no convictions here, and he tried to have his cake and eat it too. As an atheist, there were contradictions in his attitude, and eventually, in the late '60s, he gave up atheism altogether. Not that Nissim isn't aware of the contradictions. Speaking about those years, he says: 'Paradoxically, I was also a persistent student of religious doctrines and mystical texts. When questioned about this habit, I would agree that I responded to religion and mysticism only as poetry and not as belief. In fact, I needed them to compensate for the spiritual dimensions I had lost.'[23]

Between 1942 and 1955, Nissim and Abraham Solomon frequently exchanged letters, in which they discussed ideas of common interest, and advised each other on what course of action to take, when it came to issues concerning their respective futures. (There is more advice from Nissim than from Solomon). Seventy-eight of these letters exist today, throwing invaluable light on the mindset of Nissim in those years. They also form the basis of his poetry. In later life, he would lose interest in writing letters, except of the most routine kind, because, as he said to me, 'the same time could be spent in writing a poem and revising it, whereas a letter is just written and posted.' So, in a way, these letters are the only serious ones he wrote in his life. What is particularly striking about them is that although they were written by young men, one of whom was merely eighteen when they begin, the tone of the letters is mostly austere, there is plenty of idealism and scholarship, but they are astonishingly free of banter. This is strange, considering it was close friends who were writing. Most of Nissim's letters are handwritten–a practice he has retained throughout his life–with the characters slanted to the left. Several of them are on ruled sheets torn out of exercise books.

Others are on note paper, or foolscaped paper. After Independence, a few of them are on inland letter cards. The letters stop in 1955, a year after M.N. Roy's death.

In the summer of 1996, I tracked Mr Solomon down to his residence in Bombay's Prabhadevi, and interviewed him. He was all of eighty-two years, but extremely well-preserved for his age. He reiterated it was the Rationalist Movement he was interested in, rather than the Radical Democratic Party, having been raised by his uncle rationally (his father died when he was three years old). It was the well-known d'Avoine Blasphemy Case of 1933, known as the Reason Case, that brought him centre stage in Rationalist affairs. Eventually, he became the joint secretary of the Rationalist Association of India, and helped them to publish their journal, "The Reason". Later, he subscribed to (and occasionally wrote for) "The Secularist", a journal founded by A. B. Shah in 1969.

Solomon had a lonely childhood but cherished the company of the few friends he had. He regards Nissim as one of his dearest friends of those days, whose company he found stimulating. That Nissim was ten years younger than him did not act as a deterrent–he was no ageist. But Solomon was less bothered by political issues than Nissim, and he sets the record straight by informing me that while he got Nissim involved in the Ratonalist Movement, it was Nissim who got him interested in the Radical Democratic Party, although he had heard of M. N. Roy, and knew he was the only politician in India who frontally attacked superstitious beliefs. Solomon also did not possess Nissim's understanding of art and literature; the letters make it evident that sometimes this led to tensions between them, and threatened to destroy their friendship. He tells me that among the Ezekiel children, it was not just Nissim he was close to, but also his brothers Joe and Hannan, and especially his sister Sarah. It was a youth movement of the Bene Israel that drew them together, more specifically, an annual gathering held every year, when young people below thirty discussed subjects of general interest, while their parents sat in the back rows and listened. I asked Solomon whether their correspondence ending in 1955 had anything to do with M. N. Roy's death. He told me that while that was not a possibility he would rule out, it was also true that his job with the International Confederation of Free Trade Unions (ICFTU), that took him to Calcutta in 1952, Delhi in 1956, and finally to Brussels in 1963, kept him busy. But he got in touch with Nissim whenever he came to Bombay on vacations, once every two years. Nissim would give him a copy of his latest collection of verse.

Cut to. . .

31 October 1942

Writing from The Retreat, Nissim complains to Solomon of the heat that makes his 'poor brain' non-functional and prevents him from writing. Solomon is in Matheran, probably vacationing, Nissim refers to a dance at which he and 'our boys' expect him. Then he mentions Youthopia, a six-page newsletter that is in press. He wants to raise the number of pages to sixteen in four months' time. He confesses that he's never been to Matheran, complains that his handwriting is horrible (but he cannot help it), announces that college re-opens on Monday, and he's both longing for and dreading it. He's not doing any serious reading, but reading seriously (Nissim was always good at wordplay). He informs Solomon that reading *The Picture of Dorian Gray* by Oscar Wilde was an adventure, he found Wilde's views on art striking, and 'passed through a series of experiences' as he read it, and 'came out feeling rather cynical about this life of ours.'

3 November 1942

Nissim has received a letter from Solomon (irretrievable) in which he has quoted a few lines of verse that Nissim likes; he wants to know who the poet is.

There is a reference to 'our boys' of the previous letter. Nissim says: 'Of course our feminine friends are included in "boys". Did you doubt it?' (However, there are no references to any actual girl/woman). He calls Solomon's descriptions of Matheran graphic, but says, in turn, he doesn't suppose Solomon expects him to give him similar descriptions of Bombay. He disagrees with him about his 'inability to express' and his 'poverty of words' (Solomon's phrases). He quotes Oscar Wilde: 'Art can express everything. It is the spectator and not life, that Art really mirrors.' Solomon has had a horse ride in Matheran. Nissim envies him the horse ride, saying even if the horse had no horse power, he's sure it had horse sense (wordplay again), though if it had a combination of both, it wouldn't have agreed to carry Solomon! Although college reopened yesterday, Nissim didn't attend it, but 'remained at home–just a sort of finishing touch to the long holiday just completed.' He hopes to be at his desk by eleven in the morning, 'listening to the dull voice of the professor doling out ancient platitudes in a slightly modern garb and indulging now and then in hallowed autobiographical reminiscences.' Yet he thinks of college life as worthwhile for two reasons: one, the time he gets to spend in the library, and two, the free periods between lectures and between the departure of one professor and the arrival of the next. Then, naughtily, he says: 'For some of us who are aesthetically minded, there are other "things" that are attractive . . .

Importantly enough, this is followed by the sentence: 'I too have been indulging in dreams . . . seeing my name beneath the blazing title of a bestseller etc. etc. etc.,' indicating his desire to become a writer. But he laments that the atmosphere here (in Bombay) is not quite congenial to dreams, that it is difficult to live even a few minutes in complete solitude, although he is trying his best. He discloses that he has attempted to weave his literary theories before schoolchildren, from whom he knows he cannot get any intellectual response, 'with the hope of getting some unconsciously naive opinions on the subject.' And he wasn't disappointed: 'I behave as if the person I'm talking to is supremely superior to me . . . touch upon a few themes in a manner so full of trust (cleverly put on, of course) that the other party feels confident it knows all about the subject and blurts out statements that are thought-provoking even if they are childish.'

And in the next paragraph: 'I have my select victims . . . I only speak thus to people I'm very fond of [a quality that Nissim has retained]. That's a fault perhaps but I can't help it. It has become a little hobby of mine. I hope my victims don't see the twinkle in my eye, as some sweeping generalizations are made by them, with an innocent foolhardiness. I learn quite a lot from them and I'm grateful. Yesterday one little girl came to stay for a minute (her mummy wanted her soon) and remained for a couple of hours. How's that?'

12 December 1943

Nissim tells Solomon he has always wanted to write to him about so many things, and now that Solomon is on the threshold of a great adventure, he must begin. His intention is 'Not to advise you. Not to instruct.

Simply this, that in my life I have found certain values [not specified] worth preserving.' He himself is attempting to see these values in proper perspective. He doesn't want to be 'any the less crazy about them' but wants to be balanced, and depends on his friendship with Solomon for that balance. But he also thinks that Solomon too needs balance, and in turn can attain it by his contact with Nissim. He is aware that this may sound like conceit, but all the same risks saying:

'If I can at all diagnose your case and prescribe a cure I would say . . . more poetry, more richness, more sensuousness, more intoxication with beauty.' Then, in parentheses: 'All this because you have the foundations.' He quotes Andre Gide: 'All knowledge, that is not due to sensations is to me, useless.' Wordsworth, an extract from Aurobindo Ghose's essay 'National Value of Art', a few lines from Pater to Rossetti are quoted in the letter. Nissim declares that it is only by following the dictum of the greats that they stand a chance of developing the intellectual stature and penetrative vision required for *nation-building work* (my emphasis). He describes all these 'Great Personalities' as the bane of India, confusing issues and obstructing clear thought by their slogans. India, he says, needs genuine workers, modest and industrious, competent and powerful. He feels he and Solomon are at the foot of the ladder which they must one day climb.

Nissim next refers to the hint Solomon has dropped of his becoming associate editor (he does not state of what), and wonders whether he's serious. On his part, he says he is prepared to do quite a lot of work, 'with or without my name being given out.' However, he insists he must be 'quite definite' about what his work is to be.

A poem called 'Exhortation' accompanies this letter. It bears the date 13 December 1943, and Nissim's signature at the end. It has the familiar metrical and rhyme schemes of Nissim's early work:

> Fight and dare the darkness
> Though the soul be numb,
> And cold despair caress
> The solitude you plumb.
>
> Speak and scatter shadows
> Though your lips be bled,

By the urgency of blows
You dealt that Truth be fed.

Your lips were made to sing
But a hand is at your throat
Though warm white arms may cling
Fight, a madness is afloat.

23 April 1944

Nissim makes an offer of help to Solomon. He is willing to do all the clerical and outdoor work, excepting accounts, the buying of paper, and the making of declarations at the magistrate's office, relating to the publication of *Reason* under the editorship of R.D. Karve. He is keen that the journal should come out again, and soon, preferably from 1 June.

The next paragraph is interesting. It says: All this work to be done by me for you, Abraham Solomon, who must assume sole responsibility for the work and will be expected to guide and direct me. I am not to be on the committee or be directly related to it in any way. My name to be strictly kept out and no mention of my work [to] be made either in the *Reason* or elsewhere except in the committee. (This is asked for because I have unfortunately not been a member of the Association and do not want to be accused of opportunism).'

6 February 1945

Nissim tells Solomon he is going over to his place on Thursday, 8 February, at 7p.m., and wants to know if any of his friends is likely to give him a subscription for the 'Independent India' week. He informs Solomon that, as part of their campaign for popularizing the Draft Constitution of India, the Students' Union is holding a discussion on Saturday, 10 February, at 6.30 p.m. in the Dadar office of the Radical Democratic Party. He asks him to come along, together with other Renaissance Club Members. The subject for discussion is 'Problems of the Indian Constitution'.

Nissim tells Solomon that M. N. Roy is still in Bombay, not keeping well–one of the first references to Roy in the letters–and a few paragraphs later grumbles that the report of Roy's lecture in the *Vanguard* was as distorted as it was in the *Free Press Journal*. Then, significantly, 'I am at a dead end now between poetry and politics; it is a most unholy mess.'

A long exposition follows on the meaning of the words 'integrity' and 'wholeness'. They fascinated a friend of his (unnamed) for long, with all that the words came to represent to him. Nissim's own conclusion is that 'what is lacking in politics is integrity. Everywhere a dehumanizing process is going on, a distortion of human values, a death of all intellectual freshness and "free thinking". He adds, with mock-modesty: 'If I say such heretical things to anybody, I would be ridiculed as an "intellectual". Isn't it crazy?'

He claims that the emphasis has now changed for him—it is the quality of conviction held that matters a great deal. And he lapses into a sort of lecture: 'I was troubled by Athaide's speech. It was typically "superior", fascist unconsciously. We need not mere rationalists, we need men of vision. We need men who have realized that it is more difficult to be than to do. What is important is that the self should not be impoverished in a frantic effort at public service. That in a sense is the tragedy of communism. We need a book to be titled "Heresies of a Communist" in which the whole problem of ends and means is examined anew . . . some obsolete concepts given up and emphasis readjusted.'

Nissim promises to write to Solomon again, some day, with more on Communism and free thought. He ends on an interrogative note: 'Am I not right when I say that the essence of the free thought position is the right to think freely; and the ability?'

Six untitled lines accompany this letter. Once again, the finished poem seems to figure nowhere in Nissim's published collections of verse:

> Let me be filled,
> Let my movement be like stillness,
> My silence radiate
> Significance of speech,
> And speech signify
> The struggle with its own uselessness.

20 October 1945

Nissim writes on his father's letterhead, with the address of The Retreat on one side and that of Wilson College on the other. He begins thus: 'Just when I've got an opportunity to pour out my heart to somebody, somehow or the other I'm in no mood to do it.' As in his letter of 31 October 1942, he complains about the hot weather. (It is significant that in both these letters he complains about the heat in October, whereas his letters of April and May, when Bombay is appreciably warmer, contain no references to the weather).

There is party talk, with references to a set of folders, required in all likelihood for party work, and to Maniben, a co-worker in the party, with major administrative responsibilities who 'is managing things well.' Nissim says further: 'I shall not tell you any party news because you will be returning soon to create it.'

He discusses an article on economic planning that he has read in the Modern Review: he finds the author's objections to economic planning, on the ground that we cannot hope for the kind of democratic state visualized by the People's Planners, sensible. This leads him to the subject of Gandhism, the study of which he is continuing, reading currently the 'Economics of Khadi' and an anthology of Gandhi's selected writings. He says: 'If I could put in three years' regular work on Gandhism, I would begin writing on it. I would not like to produce much transient polemic writing. It is necessary to look to something stronger, more lasting and more noble.' Later in the letter, he also says: 'Gandhi is not so elusive in his methods as is generally made out. You know that "dilemma" stuff That's all nonsense. Already with the scrappy work I've put in I think I can discern a crooked thread running through his "actions".' He then informs Solomon that he has started reading a book called *The Interpretation of History* by Max Nordan, which 'is interesting, though the joint view borders on cynicism.'

Nissim reveals that he wants to do 'pampleteering' (sic) for the next six months, but finds there is no one to publish his pamphlets. And he cannot ask Solomon to invest his money on what would be unproductive publishing. Besides, his suggestion that the provincial office of the Party should take up the task of publishing pamphlets wasn't received well by Maniben, who wants things like that to be left to the central office. This is followed by the doubt: 'I am afraid I'm drifting into party small talk again. I suppose it cannot be helped.'

20 October 1945

Surprisingly, Nissim writes a second letter on the same day. This is because he thinks he has answered Solomon's last letter hastily, and has thus done both Solomon and himself an injustice.

In great earnestness, and with a terrible sense of diffidence, Nissim says there was a time when he felt himself a rich, inexhaustible source of ideas and emotions. At that time, he did not think that a day would come when in the middle of a letter, he would have nothing more to say. 'Today that fear has taken a very acute form; its cause is a certain dissipation of energy which has made me less sure of my creative powers. I intend to cure this malady by a fresh series of efforts. If some stabilization is not achieved at an early date, I shall be lost. Any further drifting aimlessly along will result in utter bankruptcy.'

He realizes, of course, that he is beginning his efforts on a note of compromise, by 'continuing on a plane of activity which is not mine [politics]. That I am doing because I find no difficulty in accepting the urgency of the call made upon me. If ever I feel that urgency to be exaggerated I must begin life all over again. Yet within the universe in which I find myself it is possible to be more purposive and rhythmic than I have been hitherto.'

And then, significantly, 'I must cling to Art. Of that I have not the slightest doubt. What I have to determine is whether the social responsibilities I have accepted are congenial to devotion–for devotion it must be–to Art.' He goes on to speak of the need to integrate his present experiences 'into the complex from which my art productions must spring.'

In the next paragraph, Nissim puts a series of questions to himself 'What are the duties of my station? Is it not to strive for the preservation of moral principles in a fundamentally immoral world? Is it not to strive for an adequate pattern of living in a world whose processes kill all such patterns?' He attempts to answer his questions: ' . . . by now it is quite obvious to me that my poetry must express a certain totality of human experience; it must move from the purely personal plane to a plane at once intensely individual and universal. This task, I realize at the very outset demands an honesty which I do not possess. To achieve that honesty then becomes the need of the hour. Everything else, I feel, will be added on to that.'

Nissim interprets his statement above as a search for elusive values, that, because they are elusive, are responsible for the poverty in his life. Worse, if he doesn't 'exterminate' this poverty, it shall exterminate him. And if all this seems vague, he says, the vagueness shouldn't be confused with profundity, but should be seen as a stage that leads up to it: 'Subtlety and profundity should be the characteristics of any philosophy of life worth the name.' Although he doesn't expect 'spectacular or external results' from these efforts for very long, he resolves to pursue the matter a little further.

He encloses four typed poems with his letter. Two of these, 'Townlore' and 'The Recluse' appear in the *Collected Poems*, in the section entitled 'Early Poems (1945-8)'. The other two, 'Sonnet to Miriam' and an untitled poem of twenty-five lines, seem to be unpublished.

> But your eternal silence does not fail,
> Companionable to this loneliness,
> Withered by the deathless magic of your eyes
> And laughter earnest as the Holy Grail
> Then Miriam help this soul to organize
> That every act with Time's ripeness may grow wise.

('Sonnet to Miriam')

12 February 1948
Solomon writes to Nissim. He wants to visit Nissim at his place, but thinks he may not be home, or may be busy with more 'aesthetic' friends. He also thinks that Nissim might visit him and carry out his threat of taking away his books on art! However, 'the personal perception of things beautiful is simpler and more pleasurable than the tedious task of interpreting the joy felt by others.'

Solomon claims that reading Nissim's letters has been a vital experience for him–all that they talked and did, thought and dreamt, felt and imagined during five years, which Nissim managed to 'concentrate' into a few minutes. He wonders whether Nissim remembers the many penetrating remarks he has made in his letters, which acquire a new significance for him today. He also adds that he values Nissim's prescription of 'more poetry, more richness, more sensuousness, more intoxication with beauty.'

23 March 1948
The address at the top of the letter is: The House of the Foolish Virgin, Neral Road, Matheran. Nissim has at last accepted Solomon's advice and gone on 'retreat' to Matheran, while Solomon himself seems to have stayed back in Bombay. The name of the house in Matheran may have something to do with their atheism.

The first half of the letter talks about affairs of the Radical Democratic Party and about the books that Solomon must send to one Mr P. R. Ramachandra Rao who is writing an article on M. N. Roy for an anthology. The rest of the letter deals mainly with the logistics of meeting and sorting out their businesses.

25 March 1948

This letter to Solomon contains one of the first references to Shibnarayan Ray who was an active member of the Radical Democratic Party and whom they affectionately call Shib. Solomon is expecting a manuscript by Shib and Nissim looks forward to it. Henceforth Shib is mentioned frequently in their letters.

On a more personal note, Nissim expresses the view that Solomon and he must continue to be friends, that there is work for them that they must do together. At the same time, he feels that both of them must make new friends, some of whom will be more intimate than others, and that their respective friends should know each other. 'Beyond that things are bound to be elastic but no situation will be willed by me. It will emerge out of my way of life and it will be dynamic.'

5 May 1948

Nissim is in Lucknow, at the Wayside Boarding House, Station Road. He has gone there on Party work. He thinks it may have been possible for Solomon to attend the Dehra Dun Camp (of the Party). He names one Radheylal, who has not yet made his appearance, but who acts as a kind of distributor for Renaissance Books in Lucknow. He refers to these books as 'our books' and says most of the bookstores in Lucknow stock them. He wants Solomon to write to Radheylal and seek his assistance for the distribution of Modern Age Books as well. In this context, he mentions Thinkers Library Books and Pioneer Press Publications, complaining that apart from the former, he cannot find any other rationalist publications in the city.

Once again, he inquires about progress on the 'Shastriji' book, and asks Solomon when he plans to bring out Shib's essays, for which he has not yet thought of a suitable title.

He grumbles about the complete lack of reading matter in a recent issue of the *Guide*. He also wants to know whether Solomon has done anything about getting his (Solomon's) article on 'Science, Rationalism and Philosophy' published.

It's at this point that he mentions his brother Hannan, wondering whether Solomon has met him recently, and told him of Nissim's reviews of the books *Materialism Restated* and *Grammar of Free Thought*. However he's offended that 'my reviews of the books you stock have not helped so far to increase the sales.' And adds: 'I think we should try to find journals with greater circulation to publish such reviews.'

Nissim sounds manipulative enough when he says to Solomon that, as an experiment, Hannan and he should select two or three popular but decent journals and then send him books to review for them, which if they *want* (my emphasis), he shall return after writing his review. 'It is doing very little actually for the cause but we are not in a position to do anything more.'

11 May 1948

Nissim hasn't left Lucknow yet, but has shifted to the residence of R.L. Nigam (probably a Party worker) at 36, Ruttledge Road.

Shib's essays are referred to in the previous letter as something that Solomon intends to bring out (possibly as a Modern Age Book). This letter makes it clear that it is Nissim who has been entrusted with the task of editing them, which he hasn't done (he wonders whether Hannan has informed Solomon about this). This is because he has come to the conclusion that they cannot be brought to the condition he wants them in, unless he has Shib with him for consultations. He has therefore opted for minimum changes in the manuscript, some of which 'even made me feel rather timid.'

Nissim hopes that Solomon has made him a subscriber of *the Marxian Way*. He also hopes he has no personal debts to pay, but if he does, 'Do let me know and I shall struggle as usual to pay them.'

6 June 1948

Lucknow still, back at the Wayside Boarding House, Station Road. Several new people figure in this letter: Dalvi, who was supposed to hand over a bound volume of *The Marxian Way* to Nissim, but did not; Sarah, Nissim's sister, whom he directs Solomon to pass on the volume to, once it has been traced; Mr Kirloskar, whom Sarah will in turn give the volume to, and for whom Nissim wanted it in the first place; and Hussein and Akbar, common friends with whom 'we have had some gay times together.'

Nissim's disillusionment with politics is apparent in this letter, and this is somehow linked up with the ever-widening gulf between himself and Solomon. He writes: 'My interests have not become narrower though my activities have, for the present. So it cannot be that you have nothing to write of interest to me. If you are feeling disinclined just now, for reasons which I can well imagine, I can wait. And I do hope you will write to me from time to time. My interest in friends does not easily diminish except apparently and one can never judge from appearances alone.'

19 July 1948

Although he has said he will return to Bombay in September, Nissim is back in Bombay already. He talks about his 'new plans which have just been provisionally completed.' Basically, these concern Ebrahim Alkazi with whom he's working on a production of *Hamlet*. He says, '. . . my hours of duty are so irregular that when I am free others are not.' Then he adds: 'Anyway, I hope you will accept this substitute [it's not clear what he means by this] in the spirit of our long and fruitful friendship, now and in the future.'

He announces that he is to leave for Paris on 20 September or thereabouts for a stay of approximately three years, where he says he will study the theory and history of art as well as French literature and thought. (Eventually, of course, he goes to London and not to Paris). He hastens to say, 'As you must have guessed this is entirely due to the Alkazis and I will make no secret of it. Elk and I are going together and Roshenara [Ebrahim's wife] will join us in April next.'

The rest of the letter is devoted to advising and helping Solomon to make a crucial decision of his life, viz., whether to stay in the Radical Democratic Party, or whether to resign from it and concentrate entirely on his rationalist and personal interests. To start with, Nissim expresses his own 'helplessness in the matter'. Even so, 'as a friend' he says two things to help Solomon decide: one, if Solomon feels that within ten, twenty or thirty years the Radical Democratic Party will become a force to contend with, then he should continue with it with 'renewed efforts', for the Party, for Modern Age Publications, and for himself. This way Solomon might find 'new ways of conquering old difficulties.' Furthermore: 'The struggle will be worthwhile for its own sake and there will be enough elation to make you carry on.'

On the other hand, if Solomon does not believe that any of the above gains shall accrue, then he will have to separate the radical Democratic Party from his rationalist interests and 'decide whether the latter struggle will be worth undertaking for a second time.' If the answer to the latter question is no, then Nissim's 'final and absolutely no-other-alternative decision' to Solomon is that he should chuck it all up and turn entirely to personal interests. Having done this earnestly, he 'is bound to be soon in a fair way' with his 'competence and conscientiousness' bringing him victories in no time. And finally: 'You will not be in the struggle any longer but there will be some balance and adjustment in your life and ultimately stoicism and contentment. There will still be friends and a home, reading and writing, and the thousand enjoyments which an intelligent man can wring out of routine existence, unheroic though it be, without selfishness.'

It is worth noting that, after this time, while Nissim himself lost interest in politics, in the Radical Democratic Party and even in rationalism, he advises Solomon to stick on with them if he thinks it proper. The last letter discussed above gives the impression that he is washing his hands off issues that have now become burdensome or bothersome. From Abraham Solomon's point of view, it even seems like betrayal, especially as Nissim has found a new friend, anchor, mentor, in Ebrahim Alkazi, and dumping everything he was closely associated with, would be taking off for another country before the year is out.

To Say Hello to the Queen

After Nissim disassociated himself from M. N. Roy, he was able to look at Roy objectively and weigh both his strengths and weaknesses. He realized that what he admired most about Roy was that he was a good man in his dealings with his followers, never said a word that upset them, and gave a reasonable reply to every question he was asked. In addition, 'he was a very hard-working man, steadily transforming into writing whatever ideas were in his mind. It's another thing that today nobody wants to read the immense body of writing he has left behind, except his followers.'

But it is not as if Roy was without his faults. Nissim feels that one of the greatest mistakes Roy ever made was to accept a gift of Rs 13,000 from the British Indian government for promoting the Trade Union Movement in the country. He didn't disclose this to his followers but kept the fact hidden from them. It was only later that an Indian journalist discovered and wrote about it, putting Roy and his supporters to considerable embarrassment. What is worse, the news undermined Roy's laudable approach to World War II, and led to widespread suspicion that he was a British agent.

As far as Nissim was concerned, these revelations about Roy helped demystify the man for him, and enabled him to move on without a sense of guilt.

It is at this point that another father-figure, Ebrahim Alkazi, enters his life and steers it in an altogether different direction. His first meeting with Alkazi could not have been at a more inconsequential place–a platform at V.T. Station, late in 1947 or early in 1948, when Nissim was still a lecturer at Khalsa College. Both Nissim and Alkazi had gone to the railway station to see off George Coelho, a mutual friend. Coelho himself was a sort of litterateur whose family knew Nissim well, and who became a central factor in his intellectual life, partly because he lived not far from Wilson College. It was Coelho who introduced him to the poetry of Rilke.

When the train left, Alkazi invited Nissim over to lunch, regardless of the fact that he was meeting him for the first time. They got on instantly; Nissim says he was very close to Alkazi from that time onwards, until many years later, when the friendship ended.

It is obvious that Nissim found Alkazi's company much more stimulating than that of friends like Abraham Solomon and members of M.N. Roy's entourage. This was because Alkazi was a man of the arts, with a strong interest in painting and theatre. He did some painting in those days, but eventually gave up aspirations to become a painter and concentrated on theatre. He owed his success in theatre to his wife Roshenara's elder brother Sultan (Bobby) Padamsee, who produced a couple of plays with Alkazi in the lead. He learnt all the basics of acting from his brother-in-law.

Alkazi managed to transmit both his interests to Nissim. By then, theatre in Bombay was synonymous with Alkazi; but he also fuelled Nissim's interest in the visual arts through persuasion and jokes, teasing him about the fact that although he was a Master of Arts, he knew nothing about art! As for theatre, he made him realize for the first time, the importance of acting, direction, costume, music and sets in a play.

One day in 1948, Alkazi told Nissim that he had plans to join the Royal Academy of Dramatic Arts in London. As the year advanced, he became more and more serious about joining it, until, towards the end of the year, he announced that he was going to London for an on-the-spot interview at the Academy.

The turning point in Nissim's life came when–unbelievably enough–Alkazi asked him to accompany him to London, as if going to London was like going to Lonavla. At first, Nissim thought Alkazi was joking, or worse, he had gone mad! But he realized soon enough that Alkazi was serious. Still, it was hard for him to digest the news. He has expressed his reactions at that moment in various interviews. 'It's all very well for you, Elk, but what about me, where do I get the fare from?'[1] he asked Alkazi. '. . . I said you can go because you have the money. I can't. Where will the money come from?'[2] And, 'You can afford to do that, you are a millionaire, but I'm the son of a poor teacher.'[3] Indeed, time-wise Nissim was free, having resigned from his job at Khalsa College, and biding his time giving tuition. Yet financially, neither he nor his parents were in a position to pay for his travel abroad. Alkazi himself was much more comfortably off than the

Ezekiels, with rich family connections in the Arab world. He offered to pay for Nissim's journey to London, and in order not to make it seem like charity, said he could take it as remuneration for all the theatre work he had done for him in Bombay.

For Nissim, it was more than a dream come true. One of the things that he resolved to do was to join an arts school in London and learn something about painting. His parents were happy, although they were also full of parental anxiety, for their son was going abroad for the first time, without adequate resources to back him up, and without any definite plans as to how he would spend his time.

Alkazi meant business. Before Nissim could recover from the shock of his offer, he landed up at The Retreat with a steamer ticket, which cost Rs 620. He also took him to a secondhand-clothes shop in Bhendi Bazaar and bought him warm wear. He sailed a month before Nissim, so Nissim had to undertake the voyage by himself. He remembers his parents, brothers and sisters coming to see him off at the pier and waving him goodbye as the Jal Azad left. He had to face the prospect of a twenty-six-day voyage at sea, via the Suez Canal, with barely ten pounds in his pocket. But as meals were included in the ticket, he had virtually no expenses on board. The voyage passed off uneventfully, with Nissim spending the bulk of his time reading. Unlike Dom Moraes, who in his autobiography *My Son's Father* demonstrates that his maiden voyage to England was full of romantic adventure, Nissim cannot recount any tales of fun and mischief.

On arriving in London, Nissim took a taxi and proceeded to the place where Alkazi was staying, but found it locked. He then directed the taxi driver to the address of Baloo, another Indian friend who studied at the London School of Economics. This guy was out too, but the landlady opened up his room and allowed Nissim to deposit his luggage. Eventually Alkazi came and picked him up.

Initially, Nissim stayed with Alkazi. He did not experience much of a culture shock, as he had read enough about England throughout his six years in college. Certainly, however, there was a 'climate shock', more so because it was November by the time he arrived, and winter was setting in, with its icy cold winds.

The big question that faced him now was how to spend his time. He discovered that London was a cultural oasis, full of museums, art galleries and theatres; Alkazi and he regularly visited all these 'hideouts', especially on weekends, and had a rollicking time. Nissim was possessed by this feeling, fairly common among Indians who go to England for the first time, that it was only now that he was becoming educated in the real sense–all his years at college in Bombay were merely like preparatory school.

Alkazi himself had secured admission to the prestigious Royal Academy of Dramatic Arts. His course work entailed the directing of student plays. Sometimes he took Nissim along. The late '40s and early '50s were turning out to be what was then regarded as the golden age of English theatre, and Nissim was having a terrific time seeing plays that featured Sir Lawrence Olivier, Richardson, Gielgud, Scofield, Redgrave, Fonteyn, Helpmann and Peggy Ashcroft.

In the mornings, he would read at the India House Library. It was here that he first heard rumours that Krishna Menon, the Indian High Commissioner and a friend of Nehru, a man who had done a lot of propaganda for the Indian freedom struggle in England, was giving jobs to needy Indians. All it took Nissim was a meeting with Menon, and an interview, and he was in possession of an appointment letter to a clerical post in the Internal Affairs Department of the High Commission. His office was at Aldwych, where he would commute by bus, as he did back in Bombay. One of the things that he was expected to do–although his job was clerical–was to bring out a weekly newsletter which was sold for four pounds. Menon, realizing that Nissim's special gifts as a writer could be put to effective use, asked him to edit the newsletter. This, he said, would make his job less monotonous, more challenging.

Exploring the area around which he worked, Nissim discovered that at barely five to seven minutes walking distance from India House, was the City Literary Institute that offered academic courses of interest. He at once enrolled for evening classes in Chinese and Western Philosophy, Art Appreciation and a couple of other subjects. The fees, in his words were 'rock-bottom' because the Institute was partially funded by the government of the UK. As a result, he paid merely seven to ten shillings for each three-month course.

At the same time, he registered for a BA in Philosophy at Birbeck College, affiliated to the University of London. Here he was taught by the legendary philosopher, C.E.M. Joad, from whom he learned much, particularly about Plato, Aristotle and the Existentialists. Then he tried to learn Italian through a correspondence course–and failed. The courses at the City Literary Institute and Birbeck College proved to be beneficial to Nissim, though he did not complete his BA. They cleansed his mind of ideas on rationalism, and he was able to see life anew. He told me, 'I discovered there [in London] while studying philosophy, that the rationalist thing was too simple, almost as dogmatic as any religion. Just as religious people say there's God, the rationalists say there's no God. None of the professors of philosophy in London were basically championing faith. Rather, they lived in a complex world of ideas, trying to come to grips with the problems of philosophy, and I found that stimulating. In any case, it transformed my state of mind and prevented me from falling into a simplistic pattern of either/or.' So much so, that when he received a letter in London asking him to promote Royist ideas there, he felt compelled to write back to say that since he didn't feel good about Royist ideas any more, to do so would be incorrect.

The courses in London were so intellectually enriching that not once did he feel he was wasting his time, as he sometimes did in Bombay while doing his BA and MA. However, as he attended classes in the evenings, after a hard day's work at the India House, he began to feel the pressure. Besides, he found that the job was eating into the time he wanted to spend on his poetry. So a little over a year after he got the India House job, he chucked it. This is one of the famous episodes of his life, heroic and all, and he has often talked about it to journalists. For example, he said to V.C. Harris: '. . . my experience in England, studying, working, shutting myself up in an underground room for hours together and thinking and writing poems . . . Yes, that's when I take a drastic decision: I resign the job [at India House] and take to full-time writing, earning a pound here and a pound there.'[4] In the *Bombay* magazine interview, he claims he grew tired of the 'soullessness' of the job at India House.[5] And to *Mid-Day* correspondent Neema Kamdar, he suggests he was making a sacrifice by quitting his job.[6]

How did Nissim earn a pound here and there after resigning from his post? Well, not only by sending poems and reviews to the editors of British journals like the *Strand Magazine,* and Indian magazines like *The Illustrated Weekly of India,* for which he got a small fee, but also by 'delivering Christmas mail, selling masalas in basements, and grabbing at any means of livelihood' (as he says in *Bombay*). Even so, according to Behram Contractor, his 'life was tough, he sat in a cellar, starved and wrote, living on whatever little money he could garner from reviews and articles.'[7]

It is also true that to help Nissim tide over his financial difficulties during these 'toughest' years of his life, his brother Joe started sending him some money, about ten pounds per month, from Bombay. (Many years later, it was left to his wife Daisy to return this money to Joe's wife Khorshed, and this embittered her.) He had by then moved out of Alkazi's flat and found accommodation in a basement room in the same building. It was the cheapest he could find in London. In a way, it was like betrayal on Alkazi's part, for having got him there, Alkazi now asked him to make way for his wife Roshenara who joined him. Also, on completing his course at the Royal Academy, Alkazi and Roshenara went back to Bombay without offering to take Nissim along with them. But these hardships were offset by the happiness he felt at being able to spend his time the way he wanted. He said to Tara Patel: 'The greater part of the day was spent in reading poetry, or writing it, or listening to it [at poetry readings], or listening to lectures on it, or visiting local libraries. . .'[8]

Nissim reached the highest levels of self-discipline as he forcibly shut himself in his room to read and write–a self-imposed exile. When he went out, he especially sought out poetry readings and attended them, not only because he had a soft corner for poetry as compared to the other arts, but also because entrance to poetry readings, unlike plays, was free.

His life in the basement room has a special aura of romance about it, for which Nissim alone is responsible in no small measure. He immortalizes it in his autobiographical poem 'Background, Casually', where he speaks of Philosophy, Poverty and Poetry as the three companions that shared his basement room. There were other companions, more human ones, like the Spanish woman and her daughter (her husband was killed in the Spanish War), who cooked in their own room and left the kitchen entirely at Nissim's disposal; and still others, who, though they did not live in the infamous basement, were nevertheless 'of my impecunious tribe, and we usually scraped together the few shillings we could to go to as many plays, films, art galleries, museums and libraries as we could.'[9] Some of these events were far away from the city centre, so they travelled there by the London tube.

Companionship though these people of his 'tribe' provided, they were not friends on whom Nissim could depend. For that, he had to turn to his native India and prevail upon an old acquaintance, Krishna Paigankar to whom he sometimes wrote, to come to England. Paigankar did, following virtually in Nissim's footsteps, and obtained a job at the India House, with which he supported both himself and Nissim. Paigankar was the 'husband' who went out to work and did the shopping, but could be 'assured of a meal whenever he returned home from 'wifey' Nissim, who stayed in and did the cooking, whenever he was not writing poetry. They also enjoyed watching TV–Alkazi had lent them a set–especially the plays.

It is necessary to put the kind of poems that Nissim was writing in those years to scrutiny. Most of these found their way into his first book *A Time to Change,* for which he found a publisher in England, and which came out in 1952 before he returned to India. He regards it as significant that he was writing these poems away from home, from happenings in India, experiencing a new kind of reality in which he was trying to find his own personal voice: they were personal rather than political poems. This is what he said to me: 'When I made the decision in England to write poems all my life, I read lots of books on poetry and articles on it, along with poems themselves. I was not satisfied with reading poems alone. When you sit down to write a poem, you realize it's not a simple process. I had a scrap book with me, but I did not preserve it. Some poems would take ten times longer to write than others. I wouldn't regard that as a waste of time. Revising a poem after one has written it can be very slow, but one has to accept it. I still feel strongly that even if you have completed a poem, it doesn't mean that you shouldn't look at it again, even to change a line or an image.'

While Nissim was working on his poetic drafts and discovering his voice, help came from an unexpected quarter–from the editors of the various journals to whom he sent his poems. Even if the poems were not good enough, the editors often gave him their time to explain why they had rejected them. This advice he found immensely useful. It enabled him to go back to their offices with greater confidence and a better set of poems. So much was Nissim moved by the attention he got from British poets and editors, that when he returned to India, he decided to follow their example. The famous generosity with his time, that has become his trademark in Bombay literary circles, has its roots in those early years in England, when poets and editors in positions of power took him under their wing, when easily they could have spurned him.

Nissim's reading in London was vast. Apart from subjects like literature and philosophy, which directly concerned him, he found the time to read other things, like psychology. The habit to read books on subjects unrelated to his curriculum was an old one. At home, as a boy, he would read his father's books on science. In Wilson College, as a student of English literature, he attended classes on philosophy a certain professor would take every afternoon, from 3.30 to 5 p.m. Now, in London, he started borrowing books on psychology from libraries. In one such book, in a chapter on headaches, he came across a statement that provided a 'miraculous' cure to the headaches he had been suffering since childhood. The writer of the article claimed that people suffered from headaches because they blamed others for their troubles. If they learned to blame themselves, instead of others, the headaches would automatically disappear. This was because taking the responsibility for one's actions released the anger and tension in one's system and prevented a headache from setting in. Nissim says the statement had a tremendous impact on him: he resolved that from then onwards he would only blame himself for his woes. Call it his suggestibility, but to this day he has never again had a headache. So impressed is he with the wisdom of the article, that he describes the episode as 'one of the major events in my life'.

Similarly, he was influenced by something he read in another book in London, which advised people not to start wearing their warm clothes all at once, but gradually, as the winter set in, so that their bodies got acclimatized. Nissim tried this out and found it to be true. Of course, he also had to constantly put up with the question 'Aren't you feeling cold?' To which he learned to answer, 'I'm warm-hearted.'

To the question, 'Did you get involved in the literary scene in London?' posed by *Celebrity* magazine, he replied: 'Not actively, no, but as a visitor, as a member of the audience. The British literary scene was on a small scale, remember this was after World War II and I had nothing to compare it with, anyway.'[10]

The 'audience' metaphor in his reply is significant: in the ultimate analysis, Nissim was a spectator in London, not a player. He must have got a taste of this time and again, as when, for all the friendly advice of editors, only seven of the twenty-five poems he sent for publication found their way into print. This was discouraging all right, and was responsible for the attitude that he developed, of not seeing his poems in terms of books or collections, but simply completing a poem and moving on to the next one, being as self-critical about it as he could.

And yet, the desire to publish a book was there, as natural in his case, as in any other poet's. It was compelling enough to lead him to knock at the doors of Fortune Press, London, at best a vanity press, though he was sincerely advised (by all the English poets he had spoken to) not to publish with vanity presses. But it struck him as the only way out. Apparently, when Fortune Press asked him for ten pounds as their publishing fee, Nissim willingly paid the amount, although he was opposed to it in principle. The next day, a representative of the Press came to his basement room and picked up the manuscript of his first book, *A Time to Change.*

Despite all the artistic and intellectual gains that life in London provided, Nissim was fast reaching the end of his tether. The most pressing problems were financial: he realized he hadn't paid his rent for seven weeks, and had to depend almost everyday on friends for lunch and dinner. The money Joe sent from Bombay, and his earnings from the newspapers and magazines he freelanced for, were far from sufficient. So what if he had all the time in the world to attend to poetic drafts and poetic craft? The decision to quit his job at India House was a rash one.

There was no other alternative, but to think of returning to India. 'I could no longer remain a wanderer. I decided to return to Bombay–to my roots,' he wrote.[11] But once again, this was easier said than done. Ebrahim Alkazi was nowhere on the scene now, in 1952, as he was in 1948: how was Nissim going to find the money for his passage? At the same time, Krishna Paigankar began to get letters from home saying his mother was seriously ill, and that he should come back to India. He too was penniless. Yet, being more practical than Nissim, he hit upon a solution. Indian students in England who were hard-pressed for money, had in the past, earned their passage home by working on the ships in which they travelled. Paigankar followed leads, made inquiries, and learned that a certain warship, carrying ammunition to Indo-China, was desperately looking for staff to join them on the voyage, as their own sailors were on strike.[12] The work that these people were required to do was by no means flattering: it included the 'lowest of low' jobs, like washing decks, stoking coal and wiping furniture. Faced with no other option, Paigankar and Nissim approached them, and were at once appointed.

It didn't take them long to wind up the affairs of their meagre existence in London, and travel to Dover from where they were to board their ship. It was already March (1952) by the time the voyage began, and as they were to soon discover, it would take much longer than the stipulated twenty-six days. Not only had the ship to frequently berth at various ports of call en route; but it also happened that the Suez Canal was by then closed to traffic, and ships had to take a circuitous route round the Cape of Good Hope. The most important of these mid-voyage halts was at the French port of Marseilles, from where the ammunition had to be picked up. Nissim recalls that they stayed there for nearly a week.

The work was hard and laborious and went on for eight hours a day. But he lived up to it. Not once did he think it was work too degrading for a man of his education and talents, nor did he ever feel he did not have the energy. His ancestors had led rugged working-class lives back in the village, and there was something of their stamina and their sense of dignity in his bones, that gave him the determination to keep going. It was likewise with Paigankar.

There were compensations, of course. The greatest of these was that they were getting to travel absolutely free, without having to pay even for their food. But a much more exciting thing happened, when, to his surprise, Nissim received copies of *A Time to Change* at Marseilles, while the ship had docked. The Fortune Press people with whom he had left his itinerary, were kind enough to send him the books by parcel post, possibly to make up for the goodwill they had lost by not bringing it out on time.

Everybody on board the ship was pleasantly astonished to learn that one of their compatriots was a poet. The attitude of the ship-owners changed somewhat after that–they were extra kind to Nissim and Paigankar. Even the sailors were delighted, although few of them were equipped to understand the niceties of poetry. One of them knew a couple of journalists, who were invited on board to interview Nissim. The interview, along with his photograph, appeared on the front page of the local tabloid newspaper. All of them marvelled at the fact that here was a poet, toiling away, scrubbing decks like any humble person.

The voyage continued as if it were endless. After they pulled out of the Mediterranean Sea, Nissim remembers stopping at an East African port where Spanish was the language spoken. This was another long halt, like the one at Marseilles, so the crew was allowed to have a quick tour of the city. At such times, he always took advantage of the opportunity to stroll about, and add another place to the list of places he had already visited.

The vessel on which they travelled was not scheduled to go all the way up to India. But it was expected to touch the port of Colombo in Ceylon, and Nissim and Paigankar were promised train fare from Colombo to Bombay. With all the stoppages, and with the additional nautical miles they had to traverse around the Cape of Good Hope, the voyage lasted all of forty-eight days. Both Nissim and Paigankar were thoroughly exhausted when they reached Colombo. But once again there were compensations. In Nissim's case, it was the certificate of 'Able Seaman' that he was awarded for honest and impressive work on board. It was an 'honour' that he cherished as much as all the literary awards he would win during his lifetime.

The journey from Colombo to Bombay was partly by boat (probably up to Dhanushkodi in Tamil Nadu) and then onwards by train. But the travelling companions did not set out for Bombay immediately. There was a woman in Colombo Nissim knew (!) with whom he corresponded, either from London, or while he was on board the ship. On landing in Colombo, he and Paigankar spent some time with her, before they caught their boat again.

Another two or three days, and they were in Bombay, their native city, with family and friends welcoming them. Nissim emerged a changed man. Talking about his state of mind on returning to India after a lapse of over three years, he said to me: 'When I returned from England, I became philosophical. That meant being very critical of all ideologies, including one's own. I was prepared to make allowances for all kinds of faults from the highest levels to the lowest, facing the reality, as it were.' What he specifically had in mind here, was his complete loss of faith in movements like Royism, which he had outgrown: and it was England that was responsible.

The memory of their unusual voyage, too, was deeply ingrained in his mind. Fifteen to twenty years after returning to India, Nissim wrote in 'Background, Casually':

> So, in an English cargo-ship
> Taking French guns and mortar shells
> To Indo-China, scrubbed the decks,
> And learned to laugh again at home.

The journey remains one of the most theatrical things in his life.
Cut to...

1 December 1948
Nissim writes his first letter to Solomon from London. The address he is staying at is at 38 Lansdowne Crescent, London W11. He greets Solomon on his birthday and says: 'How I long at the moment for sunny

Bombay! A heavy fog is over London ever since I arrived, the heaviest for years according to the press here!' He goes on to explain how, when he went out a couple of hours ago, to buy the airmail on which he is writing, the visibility was so poor that he could scarcely see twenty yards ahead of him. He walked through the streets in a state of 'mingled anxiety and bravado,' but was lost still, and learnt a bit about his neighbourhood, in the bargain. Over and above that, he had 'the strange experience of being asked the way by pedestrians. His reaction: 'Do I look like a policeman?'

There is a reference to Baloo, who stays close by. He feels it was a mistake to come to London in winter, when the cold and the fog make it difficult for him to familiarize himself with the roads, the bus routes and the tube.

He describes his visit to a Hyde Park orators' meeting with Elk (Alkazi), Baloo and Dinoo, 'a common friend'. He was greatly impressed by what he saw at Hyde Park. 'From the serious, scholarly speaker of the London Forum to the madman speaking without an audience, it is democracy with its pants down, so to speak.' Then he provides an actual account of what went on while he was there, in the form of a dialogue, ending with the word 'Curtain'.

Solomon has asked Nissim to do some work in London (concerning his Rationalist journal). He regrets he hasn't, because Elk is busy and Baloo has an examination on 6 December. Nevertheless, he promises to do Solomon's work, also Hussein's, plus wander a little in London, when his friends are free to take him round, so that he feels less 'helpless'. They even plan to visit France, though he dismisses thoughts of living in Paris on a long-term basis, 'as there seem to be some prospects for me here.'

17 December 1948

Solomon receives Nissim's letter and replies to it in pencil, thanking him for the birthday greetings, which came only a day late. His letter is, as usual, sentimental. He says: 'I hope it was not the fog that reminded you–of the foggy friend you left behind in Bombay.' In turn, he too wishes Nissim for his birthday (which was yesterday), and hopes that his first birthday in London 'will mark the beginning of whatever you desire most in your life.'

20 January 1949

Solomon writes his second letter to Nissim after his departure for

London. He has good news: he has been appointed managing editor of *Motion Picture* magazine. He finds it hard to believe that he has landed such a plum job. He promises to send Nissim a copy of the journal by book post, and is so excited about the assignment that he even thinks he might be able to go to London to see Nissim. He wants Nissim to send him 'ideas for the magazine', also contributions by way of 'light humorous stuff' for which he guarantees payment.

24 January 1949
Nissim is glad that Solomon has got a nice job but he cautions him not to hitch his wagon to the [film] stars, even if he flirts with them, for 'most of them are smokescreen on the silver screen but off it they are after your gold. Silver no longer satisfies them.'

In response to Solomon's request for light humorous stuff for his magazine, Nissim wonders whether such stuff 'is in my line'. Instead, he offers to send Solomon articles of serious film appreciation if that's okay by him, for which 'payment should be made by postal orders, which are available from the General Post Office.'

It is interesting how, having landed in London himself, quite by accident, Nissim is hell-bent on making all his friends in Bombay, or their relatives, walk in his shadow. Here he wants Solomon to ask Hussein to write a detailed letter to Dr Kosla, Education Officer at India House (and he underlines the word 'detailed' for emphasis) asking for information. One of Hussein's cousins wants admission to a British university, which Nissim warns is not easy. Dr Kosla has told him that 'oral inquiries or anything that does not pass through the files is not respected.'

So he goes a step further and actually drafts the opening paragraph of the letter, which reveals his skill in business correspondence. It reads as follows:

'I am taking the liberty of writing to you as my friend in London, Nissim Ezekiel, wrote to me very highly of you. I hope you will let me have the desired information as soon as possible.'

He goes on to advise Hussein to enclose International Reply Coupons worth two shillings in his letter, for airmail replies. He also advises him to ask Dr Kosla for a room for his cousin in the Indian Students' Hostel 'for at least a month in the first instance.'

Then there's more advice of the practical sort: 'One needs about Rs 350/- per month to live reasonably. It is possible to economize by doing one's own cooking as I do. So do Elk and Roshen. So does Baloo. Food is cheap. I get a meal for less than twelve annas. In a cafe it is Rs 2/-. One picks up the technique quickly. . .' Nissim offers to 'initiate' Hussein's cousin into the art of daily living in London.

Having said this, he is suddenly overcome by doubt, as he writes: 'If Hussein doesn't mind my being frank, I hope the boy is intelligent and hardworking well above the average and has a good academic record. I know Bombay MA's returning to Bombay after five attempts to pass the Inter Arts of the London School of Economics. This is God's own truth. Papers are judged for originality and definite talent, not for textbook information. Therefore our Indian students are putting up a poor show here. Government scholars fail elementary tests.'

We learn from this letter that, while he was in England, Nissim tried very hard to secure admission to a Ph.D. programme, but failed because the universities wanted him to learn Latin and take a preliminary examination, which he wasn't prepared to do.

29 January 1949

Nissim writes to Solomon on a picture postcard of Paul Gauguin's 'Two Tahitian Women with Mangoes' from the Coll. William C. Osbern collection. He says: 'Selected this excellent reproduction especially for you. Hope you will like it. We should see more colour in the world, in all senses. The eyes are most difficult to train of all, I think. We rarely gaze steadily, we just glance. Here is voluptuousness indeed.'

20 June 1949

Nissim seems to be in a reflective mood throughout this letter. He writes: 'Corresponding with friends can be an intoxication; it reached the limit when I was in Lucknow. But one must really learn to rely less and less on things outside us. It is a temptation to want to write a letter and a fine discipline to postpone writing it. I now enjoy most a desultory correspondence, slow and leisurely and serene like the course of nature.'

Commenting on the pessimism with which Solomon concludes his last letter regarding the uninspiring political and social atmosphere back home, Nissim asks: 'Why sum up the Indian situation as "far from inspiring"? Why not curse and stamp and hit out right and left and feel free? Must you repress your feelings all the time? . . . Just say Damn, Damn, Damn, Damn, Damn, instead of counting sheep jumping over a fence and I bet you will feel better and sleep sounder.' To this, he adds a footnote: 'This is not advice by the way but a reaction to your recent letters.'

Having denied that this statement amounts to advice, he continues in the same vein: 'The individual must make his own adjustments. That is why advice is so futile. On the other hand I have never yet found advice useless even when I was unable to take it. . . Ripeness may be all but in the meanwhile growth is something.'

And he gets progressively abstruse, as he writes: 'The idea of Compensation and the Idea of Reconciliation (as distinct from Compromise) are advancing to embrace me. Rhetoric? No, just the progressive vividness of abstractions as one tries to live them.'

Nissim's letters, especially when he is writing to less artistically inclined people than himself, can sometimes be arrogant: consider his claim here, for instance, that 'May be in such matters I am WISER than you are because more ERRING. My life is more of a mess than yours; there has been so much waste and I have been so slow to learn that my main ambition in life at present is to be less of a fool every year for the next ten years or so. The time limit is necessary because my patience is not inexhaustible.'

Finally, he reveals that he is slowly studying and beginning to understand India and the East.

He recommends Iqbal Singh's *Gautam Buddha* to his friend very strongly, because 'it is as fascinating as a good novel.'

11 October 1949

Nissim sends Solomon a picture postcard from Maldon, Essex, where he has had 'a very restful holiday with an English family.' The picture postcard depicts an eleventh-century abbey in Maldon.

8 November 1949

Krishna Paigankar has arrived in London, and Nissim writes to Solomon to say so. He comments on the issues of the *Motion Picture* magazine which Paigankar has brought along, with Solomon's articles in some of them. He is particularly impressed by an editorial that speaks of the need to show continental films in India. He says: 'It struck a chord in me somewhere. I wonder whether any definite attempts are being made in this direction or is it just "pleas" and "exhortations"?'

He says he is becoming quite a film fan, and is certain he is at least as serious about film as about literature. But he regrets that he didn't quite succeed in being 'spiritually involved' on the stage, 'although the idea of writing verse plays appeals to me.' However, 'at the moment it is definitely the film and not the stage which has caught my fancy. London is among the best places in the world, incidentally, for studying the film [sic]. Two-thirds of this airmail is on the subject of film. In the same paragraph, Nissim claims he has seen 'some of the greatest films in film history,' many of which he didn't like, but which have nevertheless been influential. Then he lists some of these films: *Intolerance, The Battleship Potemkin, Ivan the Terrible, The Cabinet of De Caligari.*

He talks of celebrating his completion of a year in London by going to Cambridge on a visit, where he knows an Italian professor who lectures in his language, and who has promised to look after him. He has just returned from a holiday in Oxford–his second visit there–which 'I liked very much.' In the spring, he plans to go to Paris. 'My zest for life is undiminished,' he says. 'I should say rather that it is increasingly taking its true form and helping me to cast away the burden of my anxiety and depression.'

At this point, Nissim seems to suddenly realize that 'I have written all about myself.' So he adds hastily: 'I shall expect you to do likewise. Are their new turns of fortune's wheel?' This is followed by his next question, which he regards as much more important: 'Are you better adjusted to life now and are you as open to influences, impressions and persons as you have always been?' His concluding comment is: 'You can easily judge the train of my thought from the words and phrases I have used: reconciliation, adjustment, open to influences.' There is a cryptic remark directly below this: 'I have learnt a little of husbandry.'

1 December 1949

Nissim writes from Oxford (where he has unexpectedly gone for the third time) on a 'souvenir letter card', comprising five picture postcards depicting Oxford's various colleges. He writes on only one of the postcards and leaves the other four blank, saying 'I wish I had the time to fill this inviting space with words of cheer, goodwill and fond remembrances. But there isn't really.' Also, he is writing the letter from a post office with a 'public pen'. This prompts him to ask: 'Am I not above all, personal?'

11 December 1949

Solomon thanks Nissim for the souvenir letter card, greets him for his birthday. He often writes whole sentences, paragraphs even, and scratches them out. He tells Nissim that 'in your previous two letters you make a few remarks about yourself which gives me some inkling [sic] to your trend of thought but not quite enough.' Then, like Nissim, he lapses into philosophy. He scribbles out a couple of paragraphs on the nature of adjustment and reconciliation, relating them to this own intellectual, restless and 'emotionally disturbed' state of mind (for not having found yet 'a central source of security, material and spiritual'). In Nissim's company, Solomon has grown habituated to the use of metaphors. Here he says: 'For years as you know I was like a restless ship tied to the docks unable to sail into the open sea and discover new lands. I broke myself loose but unfortunately at a time when there was a storm brewing. Now that storm has come, and threatens to develop into a blizzard. A severe economic blizzard from which I am trying my best to find shelter.' He concludes his letter by stating that if he's lucky, he'll find the means to go to London to see Nissim for a few months (something he eventually never did). However, 'for the present I do not know what tomorrow will have.'

1 January 1950

Nissim writes on a picture postcard of Paris, showing the Paris Et Ses Merveilles (1806-1826). He says his new year wish for Solomon is that he may always be renewed.

5 January 1950

This letter makes it clear why Nissim sent Solomon a picture postcard of Paris: he had been there in December, having had only a week at his disposal. 'The prospect was brilliant and seemingly inexhaustible,' he claims. Sometimes, Nissim's letters sound nostalgic. Take the paragraph where he says, 'On my return I found a large number of letters awaiting me and the sense of belonging to intimate groups of friends grew in me. I wanted to indulge in an orgy of letter-writing. But there was one factor for which I had made no allowance. The holiday hangover. It was really distressing. . . There were two days of the most utter depression I have known for a long time.'

We also have evidence of his impetuousness here. He says his stay in England is to end soon, for 'I am likely to shift to Paris and remain there for a year or more.' He goes on to say that he hopes to return to Bombay in December 1951, so will move to Paris by April or May 1950. Whether Nissim was serious about this, or it was merely another aspect of his holiday hangover we shall never know. What we do know is that these plans were never carried out; he continued to stay in London until his return to Bombay in 1952.

What redeems him somewhat from the charge of impetuousness is, of course, the paragraph that follows, where he honestly admits that 'the apparent confidence of such statements is . . . problematical as I have little to build on except my new states of mind . . .'

But in the next paragraph, Nissim says something that gives us a sharp insight into his own nature as he perceives it: 'Your difficulties are so practical, so concrete, that an ounce of direct assistance would be worth tons of advice. So I am obliged to keep silent, being unable to offer direct assistance.' The implication: Nissim is only good at giving tons of advice. And the advice he does give, before he signs off is: 'Keep up your reading. Make new friends.'

3 February 1950

Nissim tells Solomon he wrote to Professor Dalvi, 'a moment ago' and was reminded of a certain editing project that he and Solomon had jointly planned, 'a selection of some sort or another.' He thinks highly of editing work, and describes it as 'second best to original creative work and honourable, useful, necessary.' Then he discloses: 'I am still experimenting with modes of living and very stimulating it is.' There is an element of ambiguity here which doesn't quite make it clear what he means by 'modes of living'. Furthermore, as far as he is concerned, there is no 'fullness of life' without activity ('Fullness' is a word Nissim often uses in these letters). At the same time he is overcome by uncertainty. 'Sometimes I think much could be gained by decisively sacrificing one aspect or more of my life, to strengthen the others.' He rounds this off with: 'Fortunately I no longer have any romantic ideas on this subject and that gives me poise and serenity.' Jean-Paul Sartre is quoted to substantiate: 'Reality alone is reliable.'

While he complains that Solomon is reserved and reticent, that he wishes he would let himself go so the air is cleared between them, and they can get down to communicating, he also sermonizes: 'Don't be overscrupolous. Sometimes, scruples, which are admirable in themselves, act as inhibitory factors. We must talk and write a lot of nonsense.'

Returning to metaphor, Nissim says speaking nonsense is preferable to being 'bottled up . . . we must wring the neck of the bottle and let the drink spill all over and laugh aloud over the mess.' And the next sentence is: 'Now throw this letter into the waste-paper basket.'

In the last paragraph, Nissim describes in detail the seasonal changes in the weather that are taking place in England. Coming from India, this apparently is of great significance to him because 'I have been occupied a great deal with the weather which rings the changes on one's moods with quite remarkable mastery.'

5 March 1950

While two months ago, Nissim had a large number of letters awaiting him on his return from Paris, he now laments there is 'no news from anywhere for ages. All my dearest correspondents have kept silent for many weeks.' The air between Nissim and Solomon doesn't still seem to have cleared, for he says he's writing this letter 'rather haltingly'. And if he writes about himself, 'that might be tedious'. Taking into account the date of this letter, Nissim discloses, importantly, that 'I have been writing poetry, which you will see sooner or later. It comes to me now with renewed force and nothing will make one desert it.' (It was less than two years after this that *A Time to Change* was out.) But this letter is revealing in more ways than one. It gives us a clue about the kind of relationship Nissim now had with his family back in Bombay. He tells Solomon: 'If you meet Hannan or any of my people will you please say I am thirsting for news from home?' It is significant that Nissim doesn't want to write to his family directly, but makes Solomon an intermediary. Solomon, of course, was very close to Nissim's family, particularly Joe and Sarah, and there is even a hint of a romantic involvement between himself and Sarah.

Yet another thing that this letter lets us know, almost for the first time, is that Nissim was facing a dilemma as to how to divide his time between life and art. He confesses: 'At the moment I am feeling unduly isolated and even a bit lonely. The result is I go in for a lot of company here which I should spare myself. My special problem now is to strike a balance between Art and Life. I never could believe that there was any antagonism between them but now I see the point. Taking large doses of life makes me happy . . . and disorganized. I need a large canvass [sic] (which means a large purse).'

20 June 1950

As if acting on Nissim's advice, Solomon tells Nissim that he now has much time for deep thinking. This is because his assignment with *Motion Picture* magazine has come to an end. He describes it as 'a big blunder,' and adds: 'The legacy of that blunder . . . remains to add to my usual worries.' But he doesn't provide the details, and only says 'It is a long story . . . but I shall not bother you with it.'

More importantly, Solomon strongly expresses his disillusionment with the political scene in India: '. . . our worst fears are coming true . . . the whole mass of people seem to be going on and on from misery to misery and even the proverbial last straw cannot break their back because they have no backbone, no desire for a fuller life, no urge for freedom. Simple honesty is forgotten, as for friendship it is the illusion of fools like us, and love . . . well, that is a little interesting. It is the overwhelming theme of all the idiotic Indian films. But since we value "spiritual" things so much, we are naturally interested in the exchange value even of love.'

1 August 1950

Nissim seems to have lost some of his earlier enthusiasm about life in England. At least that is the impression his opening remarks give us: 'I don't want any longer to expound plans or elaborate ideas of doing something either alone or in collaboration . . . If there is something for us to do it will have to wait till I return.'

He informs Solomon that he has returned to live with Alkazi in the basement flat, which he calls 'cheap but comfortable.' Furthermore, '. . . almost for the first time since I left Bombay I feel I have a home.' Surprisingly, he finds it more necessary to speak about himself than about his writing. When it comes to the latter, all he says is: 'Have done a bit of writing, some of which you have probably read. No need to give an account of it.' It is unclear whether he says this because he finds Solomon incapable of responding to literature, but it's likely. For in the next sentence, he declares: 'Intend to stick, on the whole, to the written word.'

A few paragraphs later, he asks, rhetorically, 'What shall I say about myself?' And answers: 'I try to put it into my writing and after that I live a little and for great stretches of time I contemplate and always I sleep and everything considered life is good and I relish it more and more.' His outlook here seems, on the whole, to be much more optimistic than it was a few months ago, when man and writer were in conflict. He almost seems to have sorted it out for himself, because having commented on his role as a writer, he now comments on life itself. 'I know very well what is happening to the world and why. It is difficult to cut myself completely from it and also it is wrong. But it is necessary because life is good only when it is quiet and lose [sic] to the fundamental realities, eating, drinking, sleeping, breathing, being friends, making love, working and resting and talking a great deal and finding solitude and silence and seeing and touching and feeling.' Later he calls these things 'primal . . . essential . . . without them we are lost.' And he doesn't end his letter before rubbing in the point: 'I am trying to know these things and when I think I know a little I try to make literature out of it because for me that completes the knowing on one level. And then I want to live again and write a little in the intervals of living. The world is in a sad state, but may be learning how to live will make me lessen that sadness a little.'

Sometimes Nissim can say things that verge on self-pity. Take this, for instance: 'I was knocked about a great deal after I left my job, particularly during the last three months.'

16 August 1950

Solomon writes one of his longest-ever letters to Nissim, on note paper as usual, but four pages of it, as against his normal one or two. He begins by saying that he met Sarah for the first time after Nissim left for London, and was surprised to hear from her that Nissim had referred to him in his letters home. This quite irritates him, as the tone reveals; it may have something to do with his romantic interest in Sarah around this time. He refers to one of Nissim's letters, (probably not posted), in which he has spoken of 'fanciful flights', and says he wished Nissim had sent him that letter because he is 'still interested in "fanciful flights" in spite of a drab existence here or perhaps because of it.' He informs Nissim that the rationalists in Madras have formed an Indian Rationalists' Association. Then he asks him his most hard-hitting question: 'Why are you coming back to this wretched country anyway?' And goes on: 'This so-called spiritual country where human beings have less value than cows. Where the sights one sees and the things one hears are enough to rape the aesthetic and moral sense of the . . . sensitive.'

His advice is: 'Why don't you try and go to Sweden? From what little I have heard of its people and institutions I am inclined to think of it as the most civilized . . . place in the world.'

Solomon continues to complain about the lack of money in his life, and the lack of a regular job, that he is accustomed to describe as 'entanglements'. He simplistically dismisses people with money as being devoid of qualities of soul. It is evident from Nissim's letters that he doesn't entirely agree with his friend here.

23 August 1950

Nissim explains to Solomon that what he meant by 'fanciful' in his unposted letter, was that they should collaborate in preparing anthologies of interest to India. As an example of what he has in mind, he mentions–of all things–the writings of G. K. Gokhale. He harps on the 'Indian' thing at length, as if, now that he's in England, he's seized by a sudden bout of patriotism and love for his motherland: 'This idea is part of a larger attitude, without which, I feel our generation in India is lost. We must find something to do in India. We must relate ourselves to things Indian. India is home for us. It is wrong to think we shall be at home in Sweden . . . or Switzerland. In English society we shall never be accepted and in any case you will not like it in many respects.' Later in the letter he also says that if Solomon finds life in India wretched, then 'Damn it, lets do something about it. I am far from resigned to the present state of things.' His advice in turn is: 'Keep up your interest in life and all will be well . . . One must be in the stream of life, always.' Something as platitudinous as that!

He uses another clichéd expression–'experience of a lifetime'– when speaking of a certain cultural festival in London for which he wants to be present. The optimistic tone of his letter is in direct contrast to Solomon's pessimism. He speaks of wanting to travel, and of being 'full of confidence'. This, in spite of what he discloses about himself a few lines later: 'We must make full use of our experiences, which, in my case, have been painful. My sufferings are almost entirely due to memories of the past, the errors, the illusions, the irresponsible behaviour, the unreliability, the moodiness and the meanness.'

Nissim equates 'inner emptiness' with death. And follows this up, for a change, with some practical information about himself. 'Perhaps you don't know that I intend to return to the academic profession. It suits me in every way and enables me to keep in touch with my subject. Also, I enjoy lecturing and it provides me with that niche in society without which I find, I am not strong enough to do.' But again: 'All this must be in a context. That is India. We cannot live in a void. One must be in touch with the environment, even if it is rotten. That, at any rate, is a necessity for me.'

1 December 1950

Nissim writes: 'I am anxious to get out of the habits I have slowly formed here and restore to my attitude some of the freshness and adventurousness of the first few weeks in London. I want to live as though I have only just arrived.'

Once again, the tension between himself and his family in Bombay is apparent in the remark: 'Do you meet Hannan often? What is he about?' Then he swings back into the idealistic mode again: 'I feel there is a great deal to be done in India, if only we can get out of ourselves and link up with something bigger. I've been nursing this idea ever since I left the party. I realize the value and significance of political activity, which must be rediscovered in some other form of activity.'

The rest of the letter is philosophical: Nissim reflects on the nature of time, energy and equilibrium. In his words, '. . . I feel it becomes easier if we are strongly related to something outside ourselves . . . This gets the pettiness out of our lives. During the last ten months or so, occupied with poetry and "inner" problems, I experienced very forcefully the sheer artificiality of these "inner" problems. I feel now that the inner must communicate with the outer at every stage and that leads to the fulfillment of our nature.'

Before he ends his letter, Nissim informs Solomon that he is due for a BA in philosophy from London University one-and-a-half years from now. This, of course, is a degree he eventually never managed to obtain.

8 January 1951

After several letters heavy with ideas and advice, Nissim, for a change, writes one that is mostly full of urgent business to be attended to. This includes finding accommodation for one Mr Norman A. Merchant who is expected to arrive in London soon. An interesting thing he says in this context is: '. . . he may bring as much tea, sugar and Indian condiments as he is permitted to, but I wouldn't advise him to bring anything else (200 cigarettes, perhaps, from the ship, whether he smokes or not).' For a man who has spent his entire life running domesticity down, this almost seems out of character! The other businesses that take up his time and attention here, are the impending visit of his friend Hussein's brother, who hasn't turned up in London yet; and copies of a critique that Solomon had sent to him, which met with 'negative responses' that discouraged him.

Nissim requests Solomon to attend the plays staged in Bombay by the Theatre Group and the Experimental Group Theatre, and let him know what he thinks of the performances. He sends him the address of the secretary, which is 7 Walton Road, Fort, Bombay-1. He reiterates he is looking forward to returning home, but calls the next year and a half 'intense' because his philosophy course is proving to be 'arduous' and he cannot give up his reading in literature. His recent philosophical reading, he points out, was a little collection of essays called *My Philosophy* by Croce, and Schweitzer's 'petite' *Philosophy and Civilization* in two volumes. Over and above all this, he has to write, 'no matter how little.'

Moving finally to the subject of friends, he asks Solomon whether he keeps in touch with the 'old set' at all, and adds: 'My need for human contact is still great.'

13 March 1951

Solomon regrets his 'last letter was full of things I want you to do for me which is not what a letter should be.' How much progress Nissim was making in the writing and publishing of his poems is evident from Solomon's remark that 'I have not read your poems and articles for a long time as it is difficult [for me] to keep track of the various papers in which they appear.' He also informs Nissim that he met Sarah recently, and admonishes him for having not written to her for nearly a year: 'Now will you please immediately sit down and write to her?' Once again, this makes it clear that Nissim often got information about his family from Solomon. In a previous letter, it was Nissim who complained to Solomon that Sarah did not write to him; here the implication is the other way round. However, Solomon cautions Nissim that when he does write, it should be 'just a casual letter about nothing in particular.' Furthermore, 'don't say I told you to write.' These phrases are underlined for emphasis. Occasionally, a refreshing light-hearted touch creeps into the letters, as for instance, when Solomon writes: 'Say what about sending me a snap of yours lest I fail to recognize you when you come back. Besides looks speak more than words

. . . I might be able to know things you have not been telling me. Perhaps you don't want me to know.' Such remarks serve to remind us that it is close friends who are writing to each other–something we are easily apt to forget in their case!

26 April 1951

Both Nissim and Solomon need each other's letters badly–Solomon rebukes Nissim for not writing to him 'at shorter intervals.' He comments: 'It is difficult to be insensitive to our daily problems without preventing oneself from becoming insensitive to the finer things of life as well.' Nissim's influence on Solomon is apparent in his remark, 'I have not read anything in philosophy and literature for a long time and feel like kicking myself for it.' However, what is more revealing about the youthful times they spent together in Bombay, is his next sentence, underlined, once again, for emphasis: 'Many times I also feel like spending an unplanned aimless day as we used to before you left. But it does not happen and I cannot find appropriate company.' He adds that he finds his attitude to life changing slowly (though not fundamentally) but doesn't attribute it to age; and that he wants to 'think and think' about problems and people and himself. The concluding sentence is: 'I do not know what you will make of these incoherent thoughts, whether you will understand my moods or detect any meaning in them.'

13 May 1951

Nissim states the reasons for his 'painful and shameful' delay in replying to Solomon's letters: he has become 'something of a prisoner of poetry,' and finds it difficult to attend to anything else. Therefore, 'I am putting poetry aside for the next month or so to do the various things waiting to be done . . .' He returns to the topic of Sarah and gives his version of the story: 'Sarah does not write to me, you see. I write home frequently. However, I shall write to her separately'. This is followed by a cryptic remark, that may be a sly reference to Solomon's romance with Sarah: 'It is nice to find that you are still chivalrous and romantic and young.'[13] The next few paragraphs or so of his letter are–as usual–devoted to advice: 'Don't meditate any longer on the characteristics of old age . . . When you don't feel like reading, don't read.' Lest Solomon feels Nissim is too condescending, he adds: 'Actually, I am advising myself when I advise others so I hope you will take all this in the right spirit.' But the advice continues: 'I think everything can be made use of including disappointment, suffering, restlessness, uncertainty, fatigue etc... If we can be human that is enough. For the rest, damn.' And so on.

The advice given, Nissim turns to things practical. He tells Solomon that the simplest way of getting hold of his poems is by paying a visit to Joe and spending an evening glancing over the stuff. He would welcome Solomon's reactions to the poems. Responding to Solomon's request for a photograph, he also says: 'I will send you the next snap of me I can spare. Joe has heaps, however.'

Nissim's final comment is of importance, for it throws light on the pangs a struggling poet goes through: 'I feel very much rooted in poetry at present and it is difficult to write of anything else. It disturbs me because I want to be free even in poetry.'

17 May 1951

Letters in the '50s took less time to travel from England to India, it seems, than they do today! Solomon's letter is written only four days after Nissim's. There is a sense of joy at having at last received a letter from his friend, and Solomon says in an emotional voice: 'I am really angry with you.' One of the things Solomon laments here–and he's done this before– is his incapability to make 'literary use' of his pain, disappointment and restlessness. As explained earlier, Solomon was simply not artistic in the sense Nissim was, and this is one of the reasons why they eventually grew apart. Before long, he shifts to the topic of Sarah: 'I know Sarah does not write to you. But have you cared to find out why? When I told you to write to her I expected you to understand that there must be a definite reason for it, and would do it immediately unless you had reasons for not doing so.'

Curiously, Solomon rejects Nissim's advice to go over and spend an evening at Joe's place, if he wants to see his poems and photographs. 'It isn't so simple', he says, curiously. Instead, he suggests he will borrow them from Sarah when Joe, in turn, lends them to her, though he doesn't think he would be meeting Sarah, too, that often.

Then he comes to the part where Nissim, in his letter, has said he wants to be free, even in poetry, and asks: 'What are you trying to be free from, Nissim? Yourself? Why? Let us discipline our emotions and then let our intellect be their slave. We might then find harmony and perhaps a little happiness.' His parting advice is: 'Do read *Man by Himself* by Erich Fromm.

1 June 1951

Sarah seems to constantly refigure in their letters. Now Nissim lets Solomon know that he 'wrote to Sarah, a gay, whimsical letter with a whole poem in it.' However, 'I have not yet heard from her.' This is followed by a whole, emotionally charged, paragraph: 'Naturally, I do not know why Sarah does not write to me. How can I, unless I'm told? I remember when I first came here I was anxious to keep in touch with the family individually but that proved impossible. They were absorbed in their own activities. My world is obviously a very special one and I had no right to expect their perennial interest in my poetry.' Furthermore, 'Persistent questioning would only embarrass people at home. I have done so on several counts during the last two years and rarely succeeded. I don't know very much of what is happening at home and among my friends. They know equally little about me. I think this is natural.'

Yet, he also says: 'When I write to Sarah next I shall ask her to send you some of my poems.'

He moves on to the business of freedom in poetry, that has been occupying them for the last couple of weeks: '. . . I don't know what you meant by asking whether I am trying to be free from myself. Certainly not. It is the sense of freedom I am interested in and, intellectually, freedom as a social and ethical idea.' Moreover, 'I experience a sense of freedom mainly in my creative work but I believe it is possible to make it last longer than the time required to write a poem. That implies a way of life.' He elaborates on this, somewhat arrogantly: 'If you read my recent poetry you will see at once how, through poetry, a certain way of life is sought, found and recommended.'

While Solomon recommended a book by Erich Fromm to Nissim, he in turn recommends Henry Miller's *The Wisdom of the Heart,* claiming it 'has been a major influence on me during the last year or so.'

15 August 1951

The Sarah saga continues. Solomon writes to Nissim: 'I read your letter to Sarah. I believe she has not replied to you yet. I really cannot understand why she is acting in this way. She very much wants to receive letters from you but still does not write to you. Would it be too much to ask you to write again? And pull her up a bit. I have not seen her for some time now'.

Did Nissim ever feel bossed-over at the Weekly? He admits that the chief sub-editor had the right to summon any one of his subs at any time of day and assign editorial tasks to him. Nissim was mentally prepared. When the work was light, he formed the habit of doing his own reading at his desk, even working on his poems; but he did not resent it when, at such times, he was interrupted by the chief sub-editor. He was a dedicated employee who attended to all editorial work as soon as it was handed down to him. If this amounted to being treated as a junior, it was made up for by the freedom he was given to start new features like book reviews, not just in the *Weekly* but also in the Bennett and Coleman company's prized publication, *The Times of India.* Moreover, he was pragmatic enough to realize that hierarchies existed in every organization; one had to get used to receiving orders. Also, this wasn't his first job.

Nissim seems to have taken up the *Weekly* job with an open mind, and with virtually no expectations, except his monthly salary. The fact that nine-tenths of the material they received for publication was rubbish, and had to be rejected, did not disillusion him. It was easy to reject a bad article, he felt: at any rate, that was the assistant editor's business, not his. His job was only to sub the copy that was passed on to him after it was accepted for publication. Although even the accepted stories often left much to be desired, he learned with experience not to be too contemptuous of what he was reading.

The year 1952 was important for Nissim in several ways. Not only did he return to India after three years in England, and begin his association with *The Illustrated Weekly,* but by November that year, he was married. It is with great reluctance that he reveals anything about his marriage, which remains for him a highly personal affair. He describes it as a 'compromising' marriage and a 'semi-love marriage', and says that soon after he got back from England, someone from the community met his mother and took her permission to introduce him to his daughter. Nissim met her, the wedding was fixed. The girl's name was Daisy Jacob Dandekar. She was the daughter of Isaac and Lily, who had nine children–four sons and five daughters. Daisy's brothers were Benjamin, Shalom, Joseph and Aaron, while her sisters were Sarah, Ruby, Mozel and Ivy. There wasn't much courtship–'the courtship wasn't very short or very long'–to quote him. What was important was that he gave his word and stuck to it. 'My parents wanted me to take a decision one way or the other, so that it didn't create an awkward situation for the girl,' he says. The marriage happened just like that, with a proposal from a matchmaking third party, as is often the case with the Bene Israel. He was pleased that he was marrying within the community. Although he's fond of projecting himself as a liberal Jew–and liberal he is in many respects–in his heart of hearts, he has always believed that the Bene Israel should form marital alliances strictly with people of their own community. This, of course, is his personal belief that did not come in the way of his consenting to the marriages of his two sisters, and later of all his children, to outsiders. Within his immediate family, it's only his two brothers and himself who married Bene Israel women. Like his marriage, their marriages too were 'arranged behind the scenes'. But it is something he has held close to his heart, and it has to do with ideas of purity: one of the reasons why the Bene Israel are looked down upon by Arab Jews, is because they frequently marry Hindu women.[1]

Nissim and Daisy were married on 23 November 1952 at the Magen David Synagogue, facing the J. J. Hospital. It is difficult to say whether their respective families settled for this date because it was auspicious. Perhaps it was. There are many marriage-customs among the Bene Israel, most of these inspired by local Hindu rituals. Isenberg, citing other scholarly sources, lists practices such as calling out the names of five unwidowed or unmarried women; waving a copper or silver coin before the couple as a sort of "arti;" throwing rice on their bodies as a sign of fertility; making them pull out leaves from each other's mouths; and so on.[2] Once again, it is likely that some of these customs, like the applying of mehendi on the hands and feet, or the fastening of the hems of handkerchiefs, were adhered to, while the more obscure ones were disregarded. Both Nissim and Daisy came from educated families that did not place too much emphasis on ritual. The poem 'Jewish Wedding in Bombay', which he did not include in any of his individual collections until *Latter-Day Psalms* in 1982, gives us the most complete account there is about his marriage. One of the rituals he mentions in the poem is Daisy's brothers hiding his shoes and making him pay to get them back. He also talks about Daisy's father asking him how much jewellery he expected as dowry (though he doesn't use the word).

As pointed out earlier, the Ezekiels lived in The Retreat at the time of Nissim's marriage. After their marriage, Nissim and Daisy continued to live there for a while, before they moved out. Their home in The Retreat came closest, at this time, to resembling a traditional Indian home. Of the five children, only Joe was out. The parents were both alive, and a couple of aunts and uncles had also moved in with them. Now there was Daisy. With so many people living under one roof, and that in a neighbourhood which is known for its din, The Retreat was no longer the quiet retreat where Nissim could be inspired to write. It is at this time that he developed the habit of leaving home early, in order to escape the 'tyranny' of domestic life. Writing was something that had to be done outside the house–in the library or even at the office, but never at home. Nissim's famous contempt for domesticity has its origins in life at The Retreat around this time. It repeatedly finds expression in his poems and private conversations, in which he, for example, refers to the way servants are shouted at, and pities a man for being 'damned in the domestic game.'

Thus the year 1952 was crucial for Nissim. He was twenty-eight, employed and married. His wild brahmachari days had come to an end, so to speak, as he now settled down to the life of a householder. Except, of course, that he hated it.

Poetry afforded a break. *A Time to Change* was already published, and during the two years that he was with the *Weekly,* Nissim managed to bring out his second collection of poems, *Sixty Poems,* which appeared in 1953. Then there was theatre. Even if a little unpleasantness had developed between himself and Alkazi, he decided to let bygones be bygones, now that both of them had returned to Bombay. So after work, he would go straight to Alkazi's place in Colaba 'to resume my theatre relationship with him.' It is here that the idea of writing plays germinated in his mind, and Alkazi encouraged him. But a rift soon took place among the members of the Theatre Group. This was because Alkazi wanted the group to be involved in the production of only serious plays, Shakespeare, Ibsen, Beckett, while the others wanted popular plays as well. It was a policy decision on which there had to be a consensus of opinion, if the group was to stay together. Unfortunately, Alkazi and the others could not see eye to eye. Nissim was entirely on the side of Alkazi. He says that Alkazi came one morning to The Retreat and stated categorically that he couldn't continue with the Theatre Group. He decided to resign, and Nissim too would resign with him. The committee was shocked by their decision, but they were determined to abide by it. They then thought of forming their own theatre company. Alyque Padamsee, who was also on the committee of Theatre Group, joined them, and Theatre Unit was born. It fell upon

Nissim to frame the constitution of Theatre Unit, with Alkazi attending to the more real tasks. A schedule of plays that they would produce was prepared, and rehearsals were started. Nissim somehow felt very involved in this activity. He began to attend all rehearsals, which were usually held after office hours when everybody was free, and often he stayed on till late evening. The result was that he got home very late, ignoring the fact that he was now a married man with husbandly responsibilities. The first seeds of discord between himself and Daisy were sown at this point.

In spite of the efforts of Alkazi, Nissim and Alyque Padamsee, Theatre Unit did not pick up. Alkazi felt that the people he was hiring were not committed to theatre: they would attend a few rehearsals, and then disappear. Nissim, however, has a different story to tell. He says many of Alkazi's actors would meet him (Nissim) privately and complain that, while they admired Alkazi's talent and his dedication to theatre, they did not like his method of refusing to explain why he wanted them to, say, act out a scene or deliver their lines in a certain way. Nissim found himself sympathetic to their point of view. He tried to reason it out with Alkazi, but it wasn't something Alkazi was willing to discuss. He was therefore left with no option but to bring up the matter in a committee meeting, where Alkazi, in retaliation, asserted that it was he who would call the shots. Nissim walked out of the meeting. He was very unhappy, and so was his family, for he had every reason to be grateful to Alkazi. Yet he 'couldn't swallow Alkazi's dictatorship.'

Meanwhile, Alkazi obtained a job at the National School of Drama and moved to Delhi. With his exit, Theatre Unit collapsed. Nissim's relations with Alkazi continue to be strained to this day, though whenever they have met, neither has once referred to the events of that year, that thrust a wedge between the friends. While the existence of Theatre Unit abruptly came to an end (though Alyque Padamsee would later revive it), it left Nissim with some of his most trustworthy friends, such as Minakshi Raja and Toni Patel who first met him at a meeting of Theatre Unit.

The job at the *Weekly* was proving to get monotonous, and Nissim felt it was time to look for another job. He had stayed with the *Weekly* for two years, which, by his standards was a long time. It's not as if he had another job waiting for him, but he started to look around and respond to newspaper advertisements. One such advertisement simply said: 'Wanted: Young man capable of writing in English.' It did not mention the name of any organization but gave only a post-box number. It didn't even specify what the exact nature of the work was. Nissim applied for it, and soon realized that the ad was issued by an advertising agency known as Shilpi, run by the Sarabhais, based in Ahmedabad (though the post was for Bombay). Gira Sarabhai who was in charge of Shilpi told Nissim at the interview that she had heard of him through a friend. She offered him the job, which turned out to be a copywriting job, and he accepted it, although he didn't know a thing about advertising. One of the incentives that led him to take it up, was that the salary was more than what he earned at the Weekly: it was around Rs 600 per month. Nissim says that some of his friends, like the Futehallys, felt it was 'disgraceful' that a poet should go into advertising. Such friends he would pacify by stating that he'd stay in the agency for at the most a year a two, after which he would quit.

Once he started work at Shilpi, as the only copywriter in the company, it was okay: he had no reason to complain. However, within a year, it became clear to him that he would eventually have to move on to something else. For the present, though, he stuck it out at Shilpi, and made frequent trips to their head office at Ahmedabad, where he had the privilege of meeting Vikram Sarabhai, the scientist. If this was a job he was doing only in order to earn a living, there were other things that he did for his personal satisfaction: he began editing the magazine *Quest*, and apart from poetry, also began writing art and literary criticism with great seriousness, having learnt a thing or two from Ebrahim Alkazi.

In 1956, when he had completed nearly two years at Shilpi, Nissim reviewed the situation once again, and explored the possibility of resigning his job. But as luck would have it, the Sarabhais unexpectedly offered him the top administrative post in the agency, that of manager, after the earlier incumbent had left over a disagreement.

He was flattered at the honour and accepted his new assignment, although he knew he was once again getting into something about which he virtually had no knowledge. What the Sarabhais liked about him was his intelligence and his sincerity, and a work ethic that made him do well whatever he was doing. Management was no doubt something that he didn't have a clue about, but he was good at human relations and had abundant common sense; it is solely on the basis of these attributes that he pulled through the first couple of months. Luck was still on Nissim's side. The Sarabhais made him another surprising offer: they would send him to New York for six months to learn more about advertising's hard-sell techniques. Although he was no opportunist, he was attracted by the offer and was not going to refuse it, even if he didn't see himself running an ad agency for the rest of his life.

Unlike London, to which he travelled by steamer, Nissim went to New York by plane, making his first-ever air journey, to commence what he describes as his 'American experience'. Some Indians like to think of Bombay as New York's sister-city (step-sister, perhaps, is more accurate). In the '50s, Bombay did not, of course, have its high-rise buildings yet, but it is true that some streets in downtown New York look like some streets in downtown Bombay, though there the resemblance ends. The point is: Nissim lived in a somewhat familiar environment in New York, and spent his time calling on various advertising agencies in the city, as the Sarabhais had instructed him to. His training in New York was rigorous. He was put through all the different departments of advertising, where he met a number of professionals, some of whom invited him to their homes. Their professionalism was impressive, quite unlike anything he was used to at Shilpi. But there was time for social and cultural activities as well. He was put up at a hotel in Manhattan, from where all the art galleries, playhouses and movie theatres are within easy reach, New York being the great walking city it is. So he enjoyed life, and made contacts with a few American poets and artists. Since it was the Sarabhais who were paying for his entire trip, he was never out of funds.

There was more to come. Nissim was offered a grant by the Americans to travel to other cities and learn something about American culture. It must have been the poets he was meeting in New York who worked this out for him. But he had to write to the Sarabhais in India first and take their permission before he could accept his grant. He asked the Sarabhais if it was okay that, of the six months he was in New,York, he spent about six weeks travelling. The permission was granted. One of the first places that he headed off for was California, the cities of San Francisco and Los Angeles, where he attended poetry readings and familiarized himself with other cultural happenings. 'Nothing to shout about', he told me, reminiscing about those days, but he was happy.

This is the official account of how Nissim spent his time in America. The unofficial account is much more salacious. Rumour has it that he accepted the American assignment given to him by the Sarabhais principally to be with Linda Hess, with whom he had one of his most flamboyant love affairs. Linda Hess came to Bombay in the '60s, and I shall save up the story of what Nissim and she did together–and why–for a subsequent chapter. Here I shall only quote from what my 'secret source' said to me: 'He [Nissim] went to America ostensibly with the Shilpi job, but actually to be with her [Linda Hess] for one-and-a-half years [sic]. He would have even managed to convince the Sarabhais–he's always oscillated between the bohemian and the conservative, and this would be considered a good example of his bohemianism.'

At the end of six months, Nissim returned to Bombay. As he wrote in *Bombay* magazine, he had learnt more about art and other related things in America, than he did about advertising.[3] The year (1956) was nearly over, and he would soon begin his third calendar year with Shilpi. As with his job in the *Weekly*, he grew tired of this job also. Resignation, of course, was at this stage out of the question, especially as he was committed to the Sarabhais by a sort of bond, having enjoyed their hospitality in America. They themselves were willing to give him a long rope by which to hang. Rather than discontinue him, they spoke of involving him in their unique textile museum in Ahmedabad, though this didn't materialize. But Nissim says he knew by then that sooner or later he'd have to give up advertising, which was simply not his scene. The moment when he would make a break with the profession kept getting postponed, however, and he continued with Shilpi for another five years or so, beyond the turn of the decade, before quitting.

His disassociation from Shilpi was not free of unpleasantness. Some advertising professionals whom Nissim had met in New York now visited India, and their reports to the Sarabhais about his performance were not very favourable. Thus, while he was on the verge of resigning from the company, having reached 'the end of the road', he himself got a letter of termination from them, giving him three months' notice. Although Nissim was unruffled by the letter, it was a blot on his otherwise impeccable record. As far as he was concerned, he had regained his freedom, the freedom to do other things, explore new avenues. But he was a married man with a wife whom he had left in Bombay, while he had had a good time in New York. The family couldn't have taken it very kindly, therefore, when he now came home and announced that he had resigned from his job.

Apart from work, how did Nissim otherwise spend his time in the '50s? One of the things that kept him occupied was the poetry of aspiring poets, who frequently sent him their poems for comment. This of course was something he had voluntarily opted to do. Thus, when he was faced with the alternative of (i) doing his own thing and not wasting time on others, and (ii) corresponding with others, offering opinions and conducting workshops, he settled for the latter course. It's not as if he did not anticipate the dangers of this policy–endless numbers of people would come to him and make demands on his time. But he resolved that he would ration his time, and spend at least a little of it on each poet who came to see him. Among the first poets whom Nissim thus began to 'educate' was Dom Moraes, whose father Frank took him to meet Nissim and show him his poems. In course of time, there would be innumerable poets (and pseudo-poets) whom Nissim would become acquainted with; some of them, like Gieve Patel, R. Parthasarathy, Adil Jussawalla, Kamala Das, Enuice de Souza, Saleem Peeradina, Santan Rodrigues, Menka Shivdasani, Tara Patel, Charmayne D'Souza and Ranjit Hoskote would go on to become established poets in their own right. Nissim became a sort of expert in understanding the mindset of these people: if they did not come back a second time, it meant it was not criticism they were looking for; it meant that the only thing they wanted was help in getting their poems published, no matter how bad they were. This 'investment' of his time paid off; it gave him some of his most dependable friends.

In the '50s, Nissim also began another life-long association: that with the PEN (Poets, Essayists, Novelists). This, as everyone knows, is an international organization with branches in many countries. In the late '40s and early '50s, PEN in India was headed by Madame Sophiya Wadia, who had founded it and edited its newsletter, the *Indian PEN*. Its office, in those days, was situated in Madame Sophiya Wadia's house at Harkness Road. It was a large mansion, with a front garden and a dozen or so bedrooms on the first floor. Nissim entered the scene around the year 1952, when he began assisting Madame Sophiya Wadia in editing PEN in Indian and the *Aryan Path*. Eventually, the newsletter would, under his stewardship, change its character to become a full-fledged literary magazine that ran poems, short stories, book reviews, and articles of a literary nature, besides the usual reports on cultural events. Madame Sophiya Wadia had faith in Nissim's abilities. She gave him the freedom to develop the journal as he thought best. Other people on the editorial board, mostly writers, academics and litterateurs, also welcomed the changes he was bringing about. Of course, the changes didn't take place overnight. Nissim says he had a long series of discussions with Madame Sophiya Wadia and members of the editorial board, in order to convince them about what he was doing.

I glanced through several old issues of the *Indian PEN* at Nissim's office at the PEN All India Centre, Theosophy Hall. The 1948 issues are larger in size than the later ones. In 1948, Madame Sophiya Wadia's name figures as editor in the masthead, and in 1972, she is still mentioned as editor, with the names of Urmila Rao and Nissim figuring as joint executive editors. It was not until Madame Sophiya Wadia's death in April1986 that Nissim took over as the editor of the journal. While Nissim worked closely with Madame Sophiya Wadia, he did not share her interest in Theosophy and made this fact known to her. His association with her would be strictly confined to matters literary. Commenting on the stand he took, he says: 'Otherwise, I do not think I would have survived. I have nothing against Theosophy, but you know how one feels about being compelled to do something. I did listen to her Theosophy lectures. The first time I went, the entire hall was full and people were standing on the staircase. She was a good speaker, had a good personality.'[4]

At the PEN All India Centre in 1952, Nissim met Rameschandra Sirkar who was one of its early members, and they have remained close ever since. I had a chat with Sirkar at his flat on the fifth floor of the Theosophy Hall building one Saturday afternoon. I allowed him to reminisce about those early days. He told me that as far as he could remember, he first met Nissim at an annual general meeting of the PEN (held in those days in Madame Sophiya Wadia's Harkness Road house, and followed usually by a literary do). This particular meeting, though, was probably at the residence of the then Governor of Bombay, Hare Krishna Mehtab, who was also a member of the PEN. Nissim was introduced to Sirkar by Mumtaz Motiwalla (later Mumtaz Karim), one of the first assistant editors of the *Indian PEN*. Sirkar cannot precisely recollect the year when this happened, but feels it must have been sometime between 1954 and 1958. It was in 1958 that the office of the PEN was shifted from Harkness Road to the Theosophy Hall at Churchgate, where it continues to be. Although Nissim is seven years older than him, Sirkar considers them to be of the same generation. He says his immediate impression about Nissim was that he was extremely alert-looking. He was friendly to younger people like Mumtaz, but never made small talk with them, confining his conversation only to issues relating to the job. He never showed an interest in one's personal life or background: spoke to them only about work.

In fact, one of the things that strongly came across in my interview with Sirkar was Nissim's professionalism and gentlemanliness. Talking of the time when Nissim was elected secretary-treasurer of the PEN for a three-year term in the late '50s, and had to work with Sabar Balsara, the secretary, and Iqbal Bakhtiar, the assistant editor of the *Indian PEN,* Sirkar says that these two young women spoke very highly of his keen involvement in the work he was doing. They were especially impressed by the fact that he visited the office regularly, unlike previous secretaries (he mentions Anand Kanitkar, Gulabdas Broker and M. M. Jhaveri). Nissim was accessible; the people with whom he worked liked his liveliness, liked having him around.

But it was not just on account of his friendly nature that Sirkar was drawn to Nissim. He was closely associated with him in various editorial capacities, even as he edited the *Indian PEN* and several conference volumes that the centre published. He found that Nissim's editing had a particular slant to it–he allowed a writer enough latitude (too much latitude to Sirkar's way of thinking), and as far as possible retained his/her original turn of phrase. Here was a human being who felt compassion for other, less-gifted persons than himself, though he did not have a proof-reader's eye and often overlooked many obvious errors. As the years went by, Nissim would become involved with more editorial projects, journals like *Freedom First* and *Quest,* where he would display the same qualities. In this respect, Sirkar compares him to what he calls the intelligent, cultured and humane people of the world, people like Stephen Spender, Arthur Koestler and G. D. Parikh.

The centerpiece in *A Time to Change,*[5] dedicated to Elk and Roshen (The Alkazis), is *'On an African Mask'.* The poem figures in Nissim's conversation with V. C. Harris as recently as June 1994.[6] Speaking about the poems in the collection, as a whole, he says he sees them as written 'away from home, away from everything happening in India at the time, [bringing him] face to face with a new kind of reality, a new kind of experience, trying to find my own personal voice . . . The poems reflect this experience, personal experience . . . and they are not political pieces.' Harris then zeroes in on 'On an African'd and quotes phrases from the poem, like 'equilibrium of art' and dialectic oppositions' He wants to know whether the poem can be considered a valid statement on Nissim's kind of art in general. But Nissim cannot answer the question. All he says is: 'Yes, something in that direction.' For Bruce King, 'the poem moves from an appearance of disequilibrium to a final order.'[7] However, I cannot agree with his view that 'there is a bit too much of William Blake's *Tiger* in the background of the poem waiting to spring out at us as model or influence on the ideas and phrasing of some lines.'[8] If King makes this remark in order to prove that Nissim is unoriginal here, he is being unfair to him, because no matter what was present at the back of his mind when he wrote the poem, the poem itself is ultimately his.

The other poems in *A Time to Change* are on diverse themes. The theme of sin and redemption comes up in the opening poem '*A Time to Change*', which gives the book its title. It is also present in '*The Double Horror*', where he says, 'Corrupted by the world I must infect the world /With my corruption,' and in 'Something to Pursue'. Women become the topic of several poems like 'An Affair', 'The Old Woman', and 'To a Certain Lady'. In 'Birth', Nissim describes a newly-born child and its mother, and speaks of the woman rising to his kisses as she bears him the child. The poem makes us wonder whether there actually was such a woman and child when Nissim was in England. In some poems, his attitudes come across as anti-intellectual, the way he runs the business of learning down. This is especially true of 'On Meeting a Pedant', 'Commitment' and 'Reading'. Of these three poems, it is 'Commitment' that puts its finger on the problem: 'There is a world of old simplicities /To which my calling calls me.' On the other hand, there are poems in which he reveals his contempt for things domestic. 'To a Certain Lady' in four sections is particularly demonstrative of this, because he suggests that while the man-woman relationship is appealing, marriage that transforms men and women into husbands and wives is boring. A few poems in the first collection anticipate other, more well-known poems he would later write on the same theme. Thus 'On Meeting a Pedant' anticipates 'Philosophy'; the wordplay in 'And God Revealed' prepares us for 'A Conjugation'; 'Planning' anticipates 'Enterprise'; and 'Declaration', 'Poet Lover, Birdwatcher'. There are also other miscellaneous poems here, on the difference between emotion and intellect, with emotion put on a pedestal ('In Emptiness'); on racism in England ('Preferences'); and on greatness ('The Great'). This last poem offers a definition of greatness to which Nissim himself would one day measure up:

> The great are egoistic, sensual,
> Self-sacrificing, self-controlled, unique
> And universal, lovable and damnable,
> Selfish and sympathetic, married happily

And sex-frustrated, listen to the voice
Of God who favours them, and play the host
To all the devil's favourite sons and daughters,
Daring in the vigour of their cowardice
And in their shameful failures dignified.
The great provide a pattern for our lives,
Illustrate the paradoxes of the real
To which we are exposed, alone.

There is a view, made famous by the Canadian critic Christopher Wiseman, that all Nissim's early poetry is formal, written strictly in rhyme and metre.[9] This, Wiseman argues, destroys the spontaneity of some of the poems. Nissim is very touchy about this view because he thinks it is incorrect. He points out that in all his collections published in the '50s and '60s, there are poems which may not be 'radically free' in terms of style, but are not formal either. What he is primarily concerned with is 'variety'. 'If I were a painter, I wouldn't think of doing all my paintings in only the abstract mode,' he claims. In 1994, when Nissim was in Kerala, he said: 'I dislike to be described either as old-fashioned or modern. But if you like, call me traditional–in the sense I do like poetry to have some kind of form and system like metre and rhyme. One who writes good poetry within the confines of metre and rhyme will write as well in free verse too.'[10]

Nissim is right. In *A time to Change*, the title poem as well as poems like 'On an African Mask', 'The Worm', 'Words in a Gentle Wind', 'Preferences', 'The Prophet' and 'Encounter' are more 'open' than 'closed' in form.

Bruce King has also popularized the idea that Nissim Ezekiel writes poetry, not poems.[11] But it is Nissim himself who first makes us aware of the distinction, in a poem called 'Poetry':

A poem is an episode, completed
In an hour or two, but poetry
Is something more.

Similarly, when King compares Nissim to W.B. Yeats for writing poetry to heighten self-awareness, he gets evidence from Nissim himself, whose poem 'Something to Pursue' (especially Section IV) makes it clear that he uses poetry as a means of self-realization, spiritual evolution. (For this reason, 'Something to Pursue' brings to mind both Tagore and Prince Gautama.)

A living, educated poet has often to guide his critics and put them on the right track, so that they do not go berserk in their interpretations of his work. Nissim is no exception. It is he who has had to point out, for example, that there were two role-models available to him when he decided to become a poet, and that he had to choose between them, sometimes settling for a combination of both. The two were, of course, W.H. Auden and Rilke. Nissim explains their method of writing to Behram Contractor: 'There are two ways [of writing poetry]. There is W. H. Auden's way. He advises, not to worry about subject, form or metre. Isolate yourself, sit at a table, pick up a pen and write the word "the". Then continue writing about the tree outside the window, last night's dream, anything. When you have written seventy to hundred lines, you have possibilities of a poem. Work on that, cut, revise, change, use the thesaurus, look up the dictionary. The other is Rilke's way. He was a German poet. He advises, wait for a poem, wait for a day, weeks, months, it will come, and when it comes, you will finish it in ten to fifteen minutes. Revise, but do not rewrite.' And then Nissim discloses the method he follows: 'I believe in revising, rewriting, I look up the thesaurus which provides fifteen to fifty alternate [sic] words for each used. I strive for the exact word. I work on my poems.'[12]

A Time to Change did not get many reviews in London, though it was published there. This causes Nissim to remark, somewhat bitterly, 'I think it fell flat, it won no prizes. '[13] But there were several reviews in India, both in the popular and the literary press. Reviewing the book in the 28 June 1952 issue of *Thought,* poet and scholar P. Lal wrote:

'Mr Nissim Ezekiel is, I think, one of our better poets because he is the most consistent in maintaining a happy balance between experiment in technique and the introspective urge. Now and then the balance is replaced by a fusion, and the result is a memorable poem.'[14]

Commenting on the title, Lal felt however, that 'There could be no more misleading title as an introduction to his poetry. There is really no notion of change in the sense of the poet moving from one stage into another, or of development of one idea into another. There is movement, but not change; growth, but not paradoxically, development'.

Lal opened his review by condemning 'romantic' poets like Leo Fredericks and R. L. Bartholomew for their 'bright, glittering vowels, consonants and rhyme-schemes' and their 'tortuous psychological probes.' He suggested it was Nissim Ezekiel who was the messiah with a fresh, original voice and a streamlined style.

Professor Inder Nath Kher of the University of Calgary (Canada) published a scholarly article on *A Time to Change*.'[15] He introduced his article by asserting that the volume 'focuses upon modern man's search for meaning and identity in the here and now of existence, while at the same time it highlights the human conditions which frustrate such an attempt.' In the conclusion, Kher wrote:

'. . . on the whole, *A Time to Change* is a remarkable achievement for a young poet in his twenties. Ezekiel makes several experiments with prose rhythms and shows the ability to handle metrical verse. The longer poems in the volume reveal his sure sense of structure and the complex nature of his perceptions. The shorter poems show his lyrical, contemplative, and ironic insight into human masks and realities. The influence of T.S. Eliot's poetry is clearly felt in this collection, particularly on the few longer poems, but the sources of poetic inspiration and the voice of affirmation are entirely Ezekiel's own.'

A year after the publication of *A Time to Change,* Nissim privately brought out a second collection of verse, which he called *Sixty Poems*.'[16] He dedicated the book to Elizabeth, one of his basement-room girlfriends in London. The year of publication of the book was 1953; but it contained not only new poems written after *A Time to Change,* but also old ones written in 1950-51, and between 1945 and 1948. The total number of poems is thus sixty-five. Nissim's thematic concerns in *Sixty Poems* often overlap with those in the first collection. There is a whole group of metaphysical / moral /philosophical /religious poems, beginning with the very first poem, 'A Poem of Dedication':

> I do not want the yogi's concentration,
> I do not want the perfect charity
> Of saints nor the tyrant's endless power.
> I want a human balance humanly
> Acquired, fruitful in the common hour.

This is followed, elsewhere in the book, by seven consecutively-arranged poems (beginning with 'Nothingness') in which he comes up with lines such as: if I could pray; the gist of my /Demanding would be simply this: /Quietude. The ordered mind' ('Prayer I'); 'Let me not be isolated' ('Prayer II') 'Do not, in vanity, the tenuous thread /Of difference flaunt, but be /Asserted in the common dance'; 'Holiness reveals itself in everything ('Transmutation'). Nissim's Judeo-Christian religiosity in these and other poems like 'Psalm 151', 'Nocturne', 'Cain' and 'Creation' seems inconsistent with the atheism of his M. N. Roy days. The inconsistency is somewhat offset by the ironic or near-ironic tone of some of these poems, but in the end the poems are faith-affirming. In 'Prayer I', there is even an idea that is borrowed from the Buddha Dhammapada, as a footnote to the poem informs us. And 'Creation' ends with the following stanza:

Child of flesh and fancy,
Be equable, as the sages recommend,
And God-like make a universe
From chaos,
Of fire and air and earth and water.

As in *A Time to Change,* there are several poems in this book that make women their titillating subject. These are, specifically 'Situation', 'The Old Abyss', 'For Her', and 'The Female Image'. The last poem, for example, begins like this:

She lies, the female image
On the lonely pillow, in the single room,
Incessantly reborn, rolling the senses
Down through several circles to the solid ice;

Related to these poems is the famous hatred for domesticity and for day-to-day living, expressed earlier in poems like 'To a Certain Lady'; it reappears here in 'Portrait', where he speaks disparagingly of

Jazzy picnics,
Cooking on a smoky stove,
Shooing beggars from the back-door wall,
Bargaining in cheap bazaars
And other tame or wild vulgarities.

A couple of poems have an autobiographical element. 'A Short Story' reveals what Nissim's own nature is like, and the experiences it could lead him to. 'First Theme and Variations', like 'Background, Casually' later, uses the third-person mask, and alludes to the basement room, where he lived when he was in London. (In another poem, 'A Visitor', he refers again to 'my basement room'.) If 'First Theme and Variations' anticipates 'Background, Casually', 'The Crows', a comment on Rimbaud's *Les Corbeaux,* anticipates 'The Visitor' (not to be confused with 'A Visitor', included here). There are miscellaneous poems, like the pompous 'Stuffed Owl', which we are told was written after reading much bad poetry (it could equally be used to critique some of Nissim's own work); and 'The Problem', that advocates the resistance which differentiates Nissim from his pre-Independence predecessors. Poems like 'After Rain' and 'The Fisherman' seem pointless, and remind us of 'And God Revealed', an equally meaningless poem in *A Time to Change.*

There is nothing much to be said about form in *Sixty Poems.* As in the previous collection, the poems are composed in a mixture of styles, ranging from formal to free verse. In 'Sotto Voce', there is a song-like repetition of the lines with which he experiments. 'Prayer II' has an abab rhyme scheme and, like most of his poems, initial capitals for every new line. 'Tribute' is a perfect poem in iambic tetrameter, where Nissim works wonders with the four-foot line:

> Let's go to see the lights, she said,
> And so we went. She knows the things
> To see, the shortest way to reach
> The place, the joy an outing brings.

'My Cat', on the other hand, skillfully uses pentameter, and makes for an interesting 'anthology poem', though, to the best of my knowledge, it has never been anthologized.

Professor Inder Nath Kher also published an article on *Sixty Poems*[17] He wrote, somewhat rhetorically:

'The volume does not represent any major thematic development; the themes that continue to occupy Ezekiel's mind are love and sex, poetry and existence, body and mind, flesh and spirit, private meditation and participation in the world, self-identity and concern for the other. However we witness here (in all the sections) a greater involvement in the theme of human passion and sexuality, and a suggestion concerning the possible relationship between the female form and poetic creation. The volume also does not show any advancement in Ezekiel's craftsmanship; compared with the overall brilliance of *A Time to Change,* this collection is somewhat disappointing. Many poems here . . . suffer from looseness of structure, confused imagery and discursive rhetoric.'

Cut to...

28 October 1952

Nissim writes to Abraham Solomon (who is in Calcutta) from The Retreat, announcing his marriage on 23 November. No details about the wedding are provided; the matter is dealt with in a single sentence, which is also a paragraph by itself. Before informing him of his marriage, he talks about having posted a copy of *A Time to Change* to Shibnarayan Ray, and says: 'As I told you, this is only a gift to him but should he write something about it somewhere I will not be displeased.' He then reminds Solomon about the advertisement of the book he promised to carry in the *Radical Humanist.*

Nissim flaunts his youthfulness in the letter. He wants to know all about Solomon's 'activities' in Calcutta. He tells him: 'If you feel like writing don't shirk repeating the news (with variations) or invent something new. And don't leave anything to my imagination which is sluggish at the moment. Put in all the details of amatory and other adventures.'

He wants Solomon to send him all the leaflets and booklets published by his 'alphabetical organization, I.C.F.L.P.Q etc. provided it is free.' This is because 'I like to know what is important to other people.'

In the concluding paragraph, he lets Solomon know that Sri Lankan poet Tambimuttu spoke at the Silverfish Club on the Young Modern Poets. His impression: 'It was trash but there didn't seem to be anybody capable of detecting it.' Perhaps that is why he refused to preside over, or make the introductory speech, or give the vote of thanks at the meeting. In the last sentence, he says: 'Tambimuttu is a pleasant person, though.'

2 December 1952

The opening sentences in this letter are: 'Thank you for your telegram. The wedding exploded well and landed us in Panchgani. I've just returned with my wife, bewildered, calm, happy, tormented and restless as usual.'

Mungat is mentioned in the letter, especially since his wife came over to see Nissim and Daisy with a little gift and good wishes for their wedding. The last paragraph betrays Nissim's anxiety about his work, natural in any poet. It says: 'Any news about Shib's reaction to my book?'

31 January 1953

Nissim sounds unhappy that six weeks have passed since he last heard from Solomon. He's also unhappy with the descriptions Solomon gave him of his life in Calcutta, 'five-mile journeys to office in antedeluvian buses, early morning rush–rattling home at a set time for dinner–Sunday spent in darning, polishing, dhobi etc.' And he is particularly put off by Solomon's statement that 'I do not find time to go anywhere.' His own view is: 'I know how the days pass that way and then one feels one hasn't lived at all!' What we get here, yet again, is his distaste for the ordinariness of day-to-day living. Hence he spends the next few minutes lecturing his friend: 'You must try to live somewhere near your place of work and the hub of things–good, bad and indifferent. You must go places in the evenings even when you're dead beat. You'll find you're not so dead after all. It can be done but not if all your spare time is spent in a bus. Somehow, desperately, you must break from that.' Then there are his poetic fears and anxieties: 'I saw the advertisement of my book in the *Radical Humanist* but there was no response. I've been waiting eagerly for Shib's note on my stuff but there's no sign of it yet. Is it coming, do you know, or has he dropped the idea?'

Nissim encloses five poems with his letter. Of these, four are later included in *Sixty Poems*. They are: 'Nothingness', 'Marriage Poem', 'A Visitor' and 'Sotto Voce'. The fifth poem, which is untitled, doesn't seem to have found its way into any of his individual collections; probably because he didn't think much of it:

> To give and not to demand
> Even in the lunar-dream of love,
> Abandoning the sacred to an accident
> Upon an alien stair,
> As in my native city more-than-dead,
> Pleases me, beyond the things I cared
> To win in the boom-time youth of yesterday
> That brought me virgins, fame and bread.
> This crime against the me and mine creates identities
> As various as the masks discarded
> For which there is no need to moan.
> But still there is a need to drink–
> Sad reason, angry at the source

Between the thighs, or in the concert-room
The cafe and the naked street.

5 April 1953
Solomon writes to Nissim. To the poems that Nissim enclosed in his letter, his reaction is: 'The poems . . . were indeed a pleasant surprise. I liked them, particularly "Nothingness" and "Marriage Poem".' He refers to something known as the MRA plays, asks Nissim if he's seen them, wants to know what he thinks of them. His own opinion is: 'I wish this movement had a sounder philosophical foundation.'

7 April 1953
It's obvious from the dates on the letters that this one by Nissim crossed the above one by Solomon in the post. Hence Nissim sounds angry and hurt when he asks Solomon in his very first sentence: 'Why have you not written all these months?' He is concerned that Solomon should have prolonged his stay in Calcutta, and in this context asks him: 'By the way, is there anything I can do for your mother?'

There is a reference to the 'legendary' Shanbagh of Strand Bookstall on P. M. Road, Bombay. This in connection with Nissim's complaint that 'I've been buying quite a lot of books lately but still feel quite unprovided with the stuff I need.' He adds, however, 'Shanbagh is a great blessing. I get most of my books from him.'

The letter ends with a plea in which Nissim sounds completely out of character, because for the first time he expresses the feeling that he is sick and tired of his native city, Bombay, and would like to consider moving out of it, to say, Calcutta. His exact words are: 'Do you think I could get a job in Calcutta? Want to move out from here definitely.'

However, it is clear that this was an impulsive remark, based on the mood of the moment. In reality, Nissim never ever left Bombay.

18 October 1953
Solomon expresses his shock at Nissim's claim that he wants to leave Bombay and consider living in Calcutta. He says, matter-of-factly: 'Why? You will not be able to do anywhere else all that you are doing in Bombay. Not in Calcutta at least. I still do not like Calcutta, though I appreciate some aspects of it, e.g. life is more leisurely here.'

26 October 1953

Nissim gives up the idea of leaving Bombay. He writes: 'I don't wish any longer to leave Bombay though I still occasionally like leaving the earth.'

Solomon is expected to come to Bombay, and Nissim seems pretty excited about his visit. In a reference to Alkazi after a very long time, he informs Solomon that, 'There will probably be a Theatre Group production in town during your presence here, but it will not be one of Elk's productions.' The word 'Elk's' has been underlined.

Paradoxical statements, which often come up in the poems, sometimes find their way into Nissim's letters as well. Here he says, for example: 'It is really astonishing how busy I am and how little I do all the same.'

But it is the last paragraph of this letter that is most interesting. Here Nissim talks of his married life. He says: 'You'll like my little creation–a daughter . . .' To deflect this, he continues the sentence with '. . . even if you don't [like] my second book of verse which should be out by the middle of next month.'

10 November 1953

Responding to Nissim's letter, Solomon writes: 'I am delighted to hear about your two creations and anxious to see them.' He refers to the two creations as 'two projects', and thereby adds his own share of colour. He says he's excited about the impending visit to Bombay, but doesn't know the exact date of his journey yet. Then he reacts to Nissim's statement about leaving the earth: 'I also . . . often feel like leaving the earth but that guy Newton seems to have made this impossible by discovering the law of gravitation.' The remark proves how infectious Nissim's sense of humour was, how it begot humour in others. Solomon's letter ends with philosophy: 'One has to keep alive so that at least one can move about or else be swallowed up and be confined to nine square feet of "good" earth.'

12 November 1953

Once again their letters cross in the post. Nissim writes this one with the express purpose of reminding Solomon to bring from Calcutta the names and addresses of as many theatre groups and cultural organizations as he can. He particularly mentions groups such as Bohurupee, Little Theatre and Uttar Sarathi (that perform in Bengali); and Dramatic Club, Light Opera Group and Theatre Group (that perform in English). He recommends James Jones' novel *From Here to Eternity*, calling it 'a good modern novel'. He also lets Solomon know it is available 'in a cheap glossy paper edition.'

Calcutta doesn't seem to have got out of Nissim's system yet. Once again he flirts with the idea of going there, at least on a visit: 'Are there any little magazines in Calcutta? What's the intellectual life like, and life generally? I feel I would enjoy a visit to Calcutta, for a fortnight or so. I should certainly prefer that to a sedate holiday for "rest and recuperation".'

This is followed by a wise, concluding remark: 'If one is not rested while working then it's a failure.'

13 February 1954

M. N. Roy's death is mentioned in this letter, though it is dealt with in just half a paragraph. Nissim writes: 'Roy's death is a tragic end to a tragic career. In spite of my persistent gnawing doubts about him, I feel now rather melancholy to think he is no more.'

The fact that Nissim invokes both his 'father-figures' in this letter– Roy and Alkazi–makes it especially poignant. About Alkazi, he says: 'He is the only person today about whom I have almost no doubts, though I am an intensely sceptical person.'

The letter contains important revelations about the business of writing: 'Sometimes I feel it would be wisest for me to work in one medium only, that of the written word. *Unfortunately I am not strong enough to bear the isolation and the solitude*' (emphasis mine).

22 February 1954

Quite a serious letter in which Solomon responds to the statements Nissim makes about art and writing, M. N. Roy, and so on. He begins by thanking Nissim for a bulletin that he has sent him, in which his notes on art were thought-provoking. He wants to know from Nissim how 'an ordinary mortal like me' may know the difference between good art and bad art–'the modern kind, I mean.' This is followed by: 'Or am I asking an absurd question.'

Reacting to Nissim's decision to stick to one form of artistic expression, Solomon asks a series of rhetorical questions: 'Why must you confine yourself to one medium? Is the modern tradition of one man one medium so unbearable? Is not all art fundamentally the same? Why should not one individual use two different instruments for the expression of his artistic urge? Why the arbitrary limitation?' Then he pronounces his own, somewhat incomprehensible view: 'It is my belief that in the process of artistic expression there is no isolation in solitude but only in the absence of it, of whatever quality that expression may be.'

As for M. N. Roy, Solomon agrees that his death is tragic, but feels 'More tragic is the long time he took to shift the emphasis of his efforts from politics to philosophy.' Furthermore, 'About his philosophy, I had few doubts and none at all after his formulation of *Radical Humanism.* My interest in his politics was secondary.'

Solomon dwells on the subject of Roy's death more than Nissim. In the next paragraph, he responds to Nissim's claims about his 'gnawing doubts' about the man: 'I do not know what kind of doubts you had about Roy as you never spoke to me about them nor do I know the reasons for your *sudden withdrawal* (emphasis mine). But that is all over now.'

Then, in a final stroke: 'Roy himself killed Royism–and that's no small thing.'

Solomon was disappointed with his holiday in Bombay, and with the party at Roshen Alkazi's place. He says: '. . . individual meetings with friends reminded me that each of us have our own problems to face which we try to cover with a mask called "Everything is fine".'

28 March 1954

Nissim tells Solomon that for a long time he was planning a letter of some length on 'one or two intriguing statements made by you.' However, 'such plans seldom seem to come off these days as *more and more I hesitate to express myself* (emphasis mine). He challenges all of Solomon's beliefs: 'On the one hand you say "Must we live simply because we are born?" On the other: "About his [M. N. Roy's] philosophy I had few doubts and none at all after his formulation of Radical Humanism." Do you not see the contradiction? The philosophy you have accepted does not, apparently, give you the answer you want to the first question.'

Yet, strangely, he says: 'I am not going to discuss this now. It seems to me obvious that there is no point in assenting to certain ideas if those ideas do not fill your being and provide you with the incentive to live on from day to day and find fulfilment or endure its absence.'

Coming to the subject of art, he makes a small speech, indicating he feels strongly about it: 'About the difference between good art and bad art, in particular the modern kind, you have to ultimately rely on your own judgement, while taking into consideration the judgement of others. For instance, if you take *The Impressionists and Their World* which contains fifty pictures in colour and costs only Rs 12/8, you are not bound to consider them all good, even though the compiler thinks so. Besides, even a good painting may have weak points. You should read *Understanding Art* by Ana M. Berry.'

The speech sort of continues in the next paragraph: 'You ask why I confine myself to one medium. Actually, I don't, but perhaps it would be better if I did. People who are interested in "everything" generally know less than those who have a thorough grasp of one subject. That mastery gives them an awareness of what it means to know a subject.' It is in the last paragraph that Nissim informs Solomon that he will be leaving the *Illustrated Weekly of India* soon to join Shilpi, 'a firm which does the publicity and public relations of the Sarabhai concerns.' He says he joins Shilpi as publications editor. 'The set-up looks good from outside but one doesn't know anything from outside.' Then: 'At any rate it does mean an immediate improvement materially, though I'm planning to make it mean more than just a change of job–so help me God!'

8 and 9 April 1954

Two short, almost identical letters about one Mr Carmes Saleh who, presumably, was with the (*Times of India*) *Filmfare* magazine. Apparently, there was a legal notice served on him by the *Times* (which was later withdrawn); but the letter doesn't go into the reasons for the notice. No context to the letters is provided either. In the first letter, Nissim says Saleh 'comes here sometimes to clear up arrears of work and settle other matters.' In the second, he writes: 'He is in his room at present and I am told he is to continue on *Filmfare*.' These remarks show he knew Carmes Saleh well and was in touch with him.

20 June 1954

The letters of Nissim and Solomon are always serious, sometimes excessively so. This one by Solomon, for example, opens in the usual friendly manner, with him thanking Nissim for his book of poems (presumably *Sixty Poems*) and acknowledging that 'It was a timely reminder that . . . I put some poetry into my reading.' It ends with Solomon jocularly asking Nissim: 'Have you joined Shilpi's? What about taking me as your assistant?' The body of the letter, however, is riddled with abstruse philosophical statements like 'I am my own purpose' and '. . . there is no purpose in life outside oneself. There is no destiny besides oneself.' In fact, three large paragraphs are devoted only to Solomon's philosophy of life, which he needs to clarify, since Nissim had detected a contradiction in some of his arguments. This makes their correspondence tedious.

30 July 1954

Nissim needs to discuss a 'big question' with Solomon, and asks if he's going to be in Bombay soon. The question concerns the new quarterly, *Quest*, which he is to edit for the Indian Committee for Cultural Freedom: he wants to know if he can count on Solomon's help and 'cooperation' in bringing out the journal. The first issue has to be brought out in the first week of January (1955). Nissim is anxious that the journal 'should have an all-India character from the start.' The other useful information that this letter contains is the exact date on which he joined Shilpi: 1 May 1954.

About the job, he says, 'It is good here and in many ways I am pleased with myself.' He also asks Solomon to come to Shilpi if he's serious.

The rest of the letter becomes contagiously philosophical, making us wonder whether the vision expressed is that of a poet or a thinker, or both:

'I agree with all you say about human limitations and the individual's problems. My only point is that in experience ideas are tested, not by our intellectual assent only or by logic. Therefore, when we complain about "life", we are, in a sense, complaining that our ideas about it don't work. This is at least a possibility and one should consider it. The ideas should not remain sacrosanct while we go on making diverse experience whose creakings and groanings we usually ignore.

'I don't see why we should justify our existence to ourselves-constantly, as you say. It is better to think in terms of quest which is never ending but also blessed with frequent discoveries. To give those discoveries meaning one must live them until fresh discoveries or insights are demanded of us. Without this perpetual freshness there is no wisdom, only obstinacy in holding ideas which may be quite correct in themselves. I would go so far as to say it is not only the ideas that matter but the personality through which they express their force and weaknesses. The blend of strong ideas, personality and character–to put it another way–primal *energies* [emphasis original] of life + moral energy (will to *do* good), this blend does not have to justify itself constantly. It is so fulfilling, so right, so inevitable, it has no time or need to look for excuses.'

The last paragraph contains his conclusions: 'I have no illusions on one score, however: what is says [sic] in this manner is theory. It must be vindicated in action.'

10 August 1954

Solomon admires the name *Quest* that has been chosen for the magazine Nissim will edit. He thinks no other word could be more appropriate: 'You have a couple of editorials locked up in that one word already.'

He pledges his support to the journal, though he is not quite sure in what way he can cooperate in bringing it out, especially as he is unlikely to go to Bombay before December. As if answering his own question, he informs Nissim that during the last two weeks he learnt much about printing and printing machinery.

Solomon dwells on the subject of Nissim's job at Shilpi once again, and about his own job, says: 'It is difficult for me to explain in a letter why the thought of leaving my present job enters my mind.' Yet the reason is provided a few sentences later–'Mungat is a very difficult person to work with.' Furthermore, he emphasizes: 'I do not like Calcutta but coming here has eased a number of my difficulties though also created one or two others.'

The rest of the letter is ponderous: 'All those who try to comprehend existence by means of thought are knowingly or unknowingly trying to justify their existence.'

4 October 1954

Nissim complains that the arrangements for publishing *Quest* are not yet finalized. What is certain is that the journal will be a bi-monthly instead of a quarterly. 'This means so much more work, but the budget looks more reasonable and the writing will probably be more effective and topical.'

The letter makes it clear that he is enthusiastic about the editorship of *Quest.* He tells Solomon: 'I wish I could meet that typographical expert of yours. One can't learn everything from books. I have brought Oliver Simon's Pelican on typography but I'm afraid we do not get "Indian Print and Paper" at the Shilpi's.'

What makes this letter invaluable is the news that Theatre Group has split up: 'Alkazi and I with a host of others have got out and formed Theatre Unit.' The reasons for the rift are also provided: 'It was not possible to carry the Group with us in accepting *training* as the main activity . . .' (emphasis original).

The next issue of Theatre Group's bulletin is to carry the story of the rift, and news about the formation of Theatre Unit. The plan is to open a drama school by June 1955. More ambitiously and incredibly: 'Within two months a 60,000-rupees structure is going up at 89, Bhulabhai Desaj Road to house the Unit and the school. We have already collected a part of this money.'

Nissim confesses that 'I am less happy now at Shilpi than I used to be. Several times I nearly resigned.' However, 'what restrains me is my attachment to Gira Sarabhai, and the feeling that the structure of Shilpi may change in the near future. There are plenty of things to do—and I am happy doing them—so I should wait, really.'

5 January 1955

Solomon made it to Bombay, finally, but irony of ironies, Nissim wasn't around to receive him at the railway station! This is because he was called away to Ahmedabad that night, and 'It was absolutely necessary for me to visit the Theatre Unit headquarters before I left, and make a few arrangements.'

There is a new task that he entrusts Solomon with, apart from looking for likely subscribers to *Quest* ('please be as active as possible, I am almost alone') and the Theatre Unit bulletin: he wants to be introduced to people interested in textile history. This is because Gira Sarabhai and John Irwin (of London's Victoria and Albert Museum, India Section) are commissioned to jointly edit an annual entitled *Journal of Indian Textile History* and Nissim has been given the responsibility of providing the contacts.

27 February 1955

The opening paragraph of this letter sounds pretty alarming. Nissim writes: 'I feel I have become quite grotesquely functional, and must really make some room in my life for pure, friendly exchanges, with no extraneous compulsions. There is little prospect of this for several months to come . . . I am even losing my touch in poetry, which has a devastating effect on my morale.'

The first issue of *Quest* is to be out in May. He says they have secured an excellent, though expensive, room in the old Army and Navy Building, which is to be used as an office. (He actually started working here–going in the mornings, giving instructions to the full-time person in the office, and then returning to his regular job at Shilpi.) He wonders whether Solomon is seriously considering spending the rest of his life in Calcutta, a prospect that seems strange to Nissim.

This is surely the age of his involvement in movements, of one kind or the other. Speaking about the Cultural Freedom Movement in which he is also active, he says: 'Straight literary work is essential if the Cultural Freedom Movement is to make headway in India. Shib is the only man who could really do anything solid but I am not sure how free he is for new commitments.'

9 March 1955

Solomon has married Hussein's sister Ruby, Hussein passes on the information to Nissim, Nissim calls it 'good news' and congratulates Solomon. 'May it prove a turning point in your life!' he says. 'Please give her (Ruby) my regards and good wishes for a long and happy married life.' Then, in a manner slightly less banal, 'Don't let any of your external problems touch the domestic refuge. I am sure you will feel a changed man.'

It's ironic that Nissim should here be talking so tenderly about the 'domestic refuge'. After all, his own married life turned out eventually to be not the happiest thing in the world. Charity, of course, never begins at home.

It is also interesting how he likes to pose as the absolute big boss of *Quest*: 'While I am eager to see you settled in Bombay again, I must tell you frankly it is not possible through *Quest*. For all practical purposes, the appointment you have in mind has already been made. I am not happy about it, but there were no outstanding applications.'

The last sentence in the letter reads: 'With regards to both of you (nice to be able to say that).'

19 May 1955

One of the first letters in which Nissim scribbles Solomon's address at the top: Abraham Solomon Esq, Eden Court, 64, Theatre Road, Calcutta-17. The letter is on the Quest letterhead; printed below the word *'Quest'* (which is in red) are the words 'a bi-monthly of arts and ideas'. Then, in bold: EDITOR NISSIM EZEKIEL.

The letter is mainly about overdue subscriptions from Solomon, Mungat and other common friends.

These letters certify one thing: Nissim always worked at his jobs with dedication, no matter how interesting or dull he found them.

1 June 1955

Another letter on a *Quest* letterhead, smaller in size than the last one. The opening lines are: 'Don't be alarmed. I'm a patient man, and there's a great deal of faith in me.' This almost seems contradictory to statements made in previous letters, where he called himself 'cynical'. However, there is a touch of honesty in this letter: as his poems show, he is, deep down, a man of faith.

19 September 1955

Nissim and Daisy have finally moved out of The Retreat, and gone to stay at their new apartment at Breach Candy. This is the first letter that bears his new address. The address is: Mazda Mansion, Ground Floor, 67 Breach Candy, Bombay-26. About his present location, and life, he says: 'I am now near the Theatre Unit, which is a great blessing. We have a small flat, with a lawn in front. To see the baby playing in it makes me feel at peace with the world and myself. Somehow we sit out late evenings and the open sky is an endless revelation of one's neglected moods and conflicts. So little is resolved, so much postponed and lost on the way.'

There are other facets of Nissim that the letter makes known, like his preferences in colour and design. Speaking about the cover of the next issue of *Quest* he tells Solomon: 'The cover this time is blue but the geometrical get-up remains and is even reinforced inside. It suits my taste. Any sort of illustrative, pictorial or decorative designing would have been quite unacceptable to me.'

Nissim refers to the 'crisis at your end' which, as usual, has to do with Solomon's jobs. He grumbles about *Quest's* commercial lack of success, though editorially the magazine has been successful: *'Quest* evoked strong and articulate responses everywhere, which is a measure of its "success". The only trouble is that appreciation in this country is not necessarily followed by support. The trickle of subscribers, which became a slightly wider stream for a bit, has now definitely dried up.'

? October 1955

Nissim claims this letter was written several days ago–as Solomon can judge from the date–but not posted in time. However, no date is actually given anywhere in the letter, which is on notepaper. (The only date mentioned is 11 October 1955, the date on which Solomon received the letter.) 'I don't know what destiny prevented me from posting it,' says Nissim. There is a reference to Solomon's proposal to move from Calcutta to Delhi. Nissim gets back to the avuncular mode: 'You can't remain perpetually unhappy at your place of work. I think you should at least make the effort to get out and fix yourself up at Delhi or Bombay . . . You must try, try, try.'

13 October 1955

One of the few letters in the entire bunch of correspondence between Nissim and himself, that Solomon has bothered to type. He praises Nissim for his editorial in *Quest:* 'Whenever I read things written by you I almost know what you are going to say next, but if I were to try and write it myself I wouldn't be able to write the next word in donkey's years.'

Of his own job prospects, Solomon laments that he has no qualifications, that he would give anything to be back in Bombay, and that he recently put an advertisement in the *Statesman*, but did not get a single reply; only wasted a lot of money. He has come to believe that 'one cannot get a suitable job these days unless one knows very influential persons.'

24 October 1955

Professor A. B. Shah of Poona figures in the opening paragraph of this letter. He has written an article for the third issue of *Quest,* which Nissim calls a 'strong rationalistic article' because it 'attacks the view that religion or religious inspired movements [sic] should be regarded as helpful to the democratic cause.' So impressed is he with the article that he has decided to print it as the lead story.

The last page of this three-page letter betrays some of Nissim's own idealism. He tells Solomon : 'There is one sentence in your letter which I did not like–that one cannot get a job these days without knowing influential persons. Knowing the right people certainly counts today as it has always counted, perhaps throughout the history of the world, but surely people get jobs on the strength of experience, personality, qualifications and ability.'

He advises Solomon, therefore, to maintain his faith and self-confidence without being blind to his limitations and weaknesses, for so long as one is growing and learning, there is room for both sets of things. Then he suddenly turns apologetic: 'Sorry I had to moralize on that one.'

3 November 1955

Another typed letter from Solomon. Most of it concerns the editorials in *Quest* and other scholarly journals, and the news that M/s Makhuram & Co. to whom he has spoken, are not interested in stocking *Quest*, because they feel it has no demand.

It's amazing how Solomon and Nissim sometimes continue to debate an issue over several letters, without letting go. Here Solomon has the last word on the business of obtaining a job through influence:

'As regards my remark about the difficulty of getting a job, I was not thinking of people who had qualifications and ability. Even if I assert that I have experience and ability who is going to believe it except those who know me, and it is not necessary to tell them in any case.' Furthermore, 'This things called self-confidence is a very curious thing, it is difficult to have it when you need it most. It is usually there when everything is fine.'

10 November 1955

A note from Nissim on the *Quest* letterhead. He informs Solomon that he leaves for Delhi that night (by train?) and will be there till the 14th. His address in Delhi is: C/o Thought, 35, Faiz Bazar [sic], Delhi. If Solomon would like Nissim to do something for him in Delhi, he should write to him at this address. All within a span of four days, minus the time spent in travelling!

15 November 1955

Mainly an 'official' letter. Solomon lets Nissim know that he has persuaded Oxford Book & Stationery Co., Park Street, to display *Quest*.

Also that an agency known as *Journal's Corner* at Chowringhee has taken over the distribution of *Quest* in Calcutta.

Solomon, on his part, wants to know what Nissim thinks of the idea of the Congress for Cultural Freedom (or its Indian Committee) opening a small office in Calcutta, with someone appointed to run it on a full-time basis. It's obvious that he has himself in mind. At the same time he realizes that '. . . naturally, a Bengalee [sic] who should also be well known here would be more suitable.'

30 November 1955

Solomon has finally lost his job in Calcutta, and Nissim is sorry. However, he's careful not to show too much regret. 'This is quite the worst thing that can happen to a person these days but in your case I feel it might turn out to be a good escape out of a hopeless position. You could hardly have hoped to work for a lifetime with one you could not stand. Sooner or later the break had to come, so perhaps the sooner the better. I don't know if you're looking at it that way.'

As to Solomon's desire for a Calcutta office of the Congress for Cultural Freedom, Nissim is dismissive. He tells him: 'You should have only one simple objective at present: to get a stable tolerable job in a commercial organization in Bombay.'

26 December 1955

There is anger in Nissim's tone when he speaks of the way *Quest* is faring: 'There is much dissatisfaction about *Quest,* mainly from vain mediocrities who do not like my right to reject articles. Fancy that!' More positively, he discusses a publishing project he has in mind: 'Yesterday a new idea came to me on which I shall start working immediately–to edit an anthology entitled "India Speaks To America". There would be six to eight contributors and an American publisher. More about this later.' One wonders why this idea came to Nissim at this point. The visit to America on behalf of the Sarabhais, had not yet materialized–it was to happen the following year (1956). Eventually, the proposed volume did not come out.

Everyman in His Humour

Around the mid-'50s, when Nissim was just over thirty, his attitude to life changed. His years at school and college were characterized by a seriousness that persisted during his working phase as a lecturer at Khalsa College. It was Alkazi and his penchant for humour that influenced Nissim. In any case, life in London had become stressful for him towards the end of his stay there, and it is with the aid of a sense of humour alone that he was able to cope. By the time he returned to India, he was a changed man. Humour became a part of his make-up, though he feels that this happened only gradually.

In course of time, humour permeated his poems as well; it gave rise in the '60s and '70s to a set of poems he would come to call 'Very Indian Poems in Indian English', which would serve as a counterpoint to the seriousness of his other work. Nissim ceased to believe, as he had done earlier, that humour and seriousness did not go hand in hand. This belief is central to his own growth as a poet and a human being; it is something that has enabled him, over the years, to live up to his commitment to India in spite of its 'backwardness'. And it has manifested itself, not just in the serious business of writing poetry, but also in mundane business of everyday living. Nissim excels in wit and repartee; a general sense of mirth informs his being.

Another way of looking at it is that Nissim used humour as a defense mechanism to help him deal with his anxieties. Perhaps it is this that has enabled him to come to terms with his own clumsiness and fear of technology. The fear is real, has been one of his lifelong companions. Take his attempt at learning how to drive. He seriously gave it a try when he was at Shilpi, enrolling himself in a driving school. But he was awkward behind the steering wheel, possessed by the thought that he would run over somebody. In the end, he failed his driving test and, in spite of taking several lessons, did not obtain a license. Daisy shared his phobias here, for she too attempted to learn driving and gave up. The result: Nissim has been dependent on public transport all his life; it is just as well that he lives in Bombay, where the transport scene is much better than it is in other cities. It is a different matter, of course, that with present-day traffic conditions and the rising costs of fuel, socially-conscious people would prefer using public transport, rather than owning their own car. Also, the concept of private ownership has always been alien to Nissim–in his lifetime, he wouldn't even come to own his apartment. In that sense, he has remained a socialist, though he prefers to explain it in terms of his inability to handle buying and selling, which to his mind are (for some reason) associated with litigation and lawyers' fees.

Driving thus, may be an art with its own ramifications. But what excuse can Nissim have for not learning how to type? As a writer, this is one of the first things he should have attended to. The idea of taking lessons of any kind, whether in driving or in typing, does not seem to have appealed to him, he who was a teacher and was responsible for instructing others. So all that he managed to do was to practise on a typewriter by himself; several years later he was able to type with one, or at the most two, fingers. This would have its effects in later life, when he would submit poems and articles laboriously written out in longhand, with a request that the editors have them typed on his behalf! Because of his incompetence at typing, there was no question also of his switching over to a computer later, as writers all over the world were doing.

What Nissim may or may not have realized at the time, was that he was living up to the 'stereotype' of the artist as impractical, useless at things worldly. He may have even justified it to himself in terms of his asceticism (and Marxism): many creative people all over the world especially in the nineteenth and early twentieth centuries, were like that. But the notion is a romantic one, and it proves that while he is usually credited with ushering in cultural modernity, in the material sense he was–to use a strong word–anti-modern.

In all likelihood, there were many other activities involving the use of skill that he ignored. Viewing him as stereotypical here is one way of approaching the problem. But to be fair to him, there is also the other side, which is that he was not flattered by his limitations, and, as we have seen earlier, often thought of himself as a failure.

Yet it cannot be denied that in Nissim's mind, there was a sort of a priori relationship between the 'idea' of the artist and the artist in person;

the idea came first. I have already noted how in matters of dress, there could be something very cultivated about the untidiness with which he liked to carry himself about. Here, I should like to discuss the subject of smoking. Nissim smoked a lot during his middle years, as he said to Bharathi P.G. in his *Health and Nutrition* interview;[1] this was between the ages of, say, thirty and fifty. But he makes it a point to say that he never smoked cigarettes to relax, or for enjoyment, but 'only to stay awake, to meet deadlines, to complete theatre reviews, and so on.' I find this a little far-fetched. I am not opposed to the pomposity of the statement here–as a poet he has a right to his indulgences. But I can recall any number of occasions when I have seen him smoke for enjoyment and *relaxation*. A smoker is a smoker is a smoker; if one is habituated to cigarettes, one cannot restrict them only to the times one is writing a review! Things get worse when he states in the interview: 'After some years, I stopped smoking cigarettes and took up beedis instead, because a beedi would get over in a few minutes. Of course this meant that I smoked about three beedies to get a review done, but after that was done I didn't smoke.' Yeah? What about the fact that it was fashionable to smoke beedies in the '60s and '70s, when there were more beedies smoked in the campuses of St Xavier's and Elphinstone, than in the labour areas of Parel and Lalbaug?

On a more sincere note, the time that Nissim spent giving advice to aspiring poets and writers that visited him increased. I decided to cross-examine him on this subject, and discovered that his poetic social work originated in the belief that no human being can be a hermit; those who 'reject' people are never entirely isolated; they have to pay the price in terms of loneliness and suffering. Nissim likes to rationalize on what has now become a famous aspect of his personality–the time he gives to young poets. He refers, in this context, to poets like Robert Frost and Rilke, and the American novelist William Faulkner, all of whom he used as role models. He points out that Frost, who loved giving himself away to students and audiences, was the opposite of Faulkner who never replied to any letter he got from his readers, never agreed to speak at lectures and seminars. But Frost never felt that the time he spent on people ate into his own time. On the other hand, Nissim feels that Faulkner's must have been a 'tough life'. Even Rilke's advocacy of solitude, which he believed in, was limited, as far as he was concerned, to the act of writing a poem. It didn't extend to life in general, and once the poem was written, he would feel the need to meet people, talk to them. Clearly all this has to do with individual temperament, some people being the 'outgoing' type, others withdrawn. Nissim has no hesitation in describing himself as an extrovert who likes to be surrounded by people. That is why Yeats' method of writing poems–writing a line, destroying it, meeting people and coming back to the line later–appeals to him so much. Throughout his career, he has often written his poems just like that.

After he chucked his job at Shilpi, Nissim remained unemployed for just a short time. Within days of his resignation, as he was brooding over what to do next, he was approached by Kekoo Gandhy, who dropped in at his house and made him an offer. It was for the job of manager in Gandhy's frame-manufacturing factory, Chemould. At Shilpi, he had already done some work for Chemould as part of his duties there; Gandhy was impressed by his work. Besides, he knew Nissim personally, as he frequently visited Gandhy's picture-frame shop at Fort. Nissim accepted Gandhy's offer, and was appointed on a monthly salary of Rs 1200, which was high. One of the reasons why he took up the job was because the product was picture-frames; he felt he would be able to relate his work in the factory to his own growing interest in painting and art criticism.

The factory was situated at Andheri, while Gandhy himself lived at Bandra. His suggestion was that Nissim should go to Bandra, and travel to the factory with him in his car.

Nissim liked the nature of his job at Chemould, although it was mainly routine administrative work that he did. He says he was happier here than at Shilpi, even though his fellow-employees were not particularly friendly. Somewhere along the way, he even seems to have got a promotion–to the post of factory manager. He could now discuss with Gandhy (on more equal terms) the various practical problems the factory was beset by. One much appreciated suggestion that he came up with was that Gandhy should start an art gallery that would complement the activities of the factory (which existed, after all, to manufacture frames). Gandhy liked the suggestion, took it seriously, and eventually started the Chemould Gallery that still exists above the Jehangir Art Gallery. Both his wife and his daughter assisted him here.

Nissim couldn't have stayed at Chemould for more than a couple of years: as always, his restlessness got the better of him. One day in 1960 or 1961, as Kekoo Gandhy and he were driving to the factory, Nissim told him that he was tired of the job, didn't want to be factory manager all his life, and felt it was time for him to do something else. Gandhy couldn't force him to work against his will, even if he was unhappy to lose him.

Immediately after leaving Chemould, Nissim applied for a job with *Design* magazine, edited and published by Patwant Singh, who later made Delhi his base. He was appointed as manager once again, even though he sometimes assisted Patwant Singh with editorial tasks. It was a small set-up, consisting of six to seven persons, with an office in downtown Fort. But Nissim didn't continue for long. He says that soon after he joined the magazine, one member of the staff after another, began to complain to him that much as they enjoyed working there, they were not paid their salaries on time; sometimes they didn't receive their salaries for months. The contributors to the magazine, too, grumbled that their payments were always delayed. As manager, Nissim looked into the matter and came up with incriminating evidence. His conscience told him it was incorrect to work in such a set-up. He had been with the magazine for barely three months, when he decided to leave. Significantly, his own dues were never withheld by Patwant Singh; even after he decided to quit, he was promptly paid whatever they owed him. He feels this may have been done as sort of an incentive, to retain his services. But he couldn't go against his conscience and work in a place where all was not well. Nissim did not see Patwant Singh at the time of handing in his resignation; he simply left him a letter.

While the jobs he took up in order to earn a living did not give him a sense of satisfaction, satisfaction came from another source, from the art and literary criticism he had started to write; and from the middles he published in the *Times of India*. The middles date back to the time when he worked for the *Weekly*, from 1952 to 1954. But even after he left the *Weekly* he continued to write them, and by the late '50s, close to ten of them successively appeared, making him feel proud; they also supplemented his income.

As for art and literary criticism, two prominent reviews that he wrote around this time were (i) a review of a brochure on Indian painter Francis Newton Souza, issued by Gallery One of London; and (ii) a review of dancer Ram Gopal's autobiography, *Rhythm in the Heavens,* published by Secker and Warburg of London. Both the reviews appeared in *Thought* in the year 1958. One striking feature of the reviews is that they do not hanker after balance; Nissim takes care not to bestow too much praise on the work (and the people he is reviewing); but he doesn't mind being excessively critical. In fact, many of his reviews of the '50s, '60s and '70s were marked by a harshness of tone that (he believed) originated in the very strict standards he was setting; it could also be on account of professional jealousy, and a misuse of the power he had as a critic. In the Souza review, for example, Nissim called his piece 'Souza: Crude Power'.[2] (The editorial staff of the magazine changed the title to 'Souza: The Painter', much to his annoyance. So upset was he with their interference, that he actually scratched out the words 'The Painter' and laboriously replaced them with his own words, 'Crude Power', in every copy he could lay his hands on.) The oxymoron of the title more or less sets the tone of the entire review. Beginning with a small introduction of Souza, for those readers who do not know anything about him, Nissim goes on to demolish him in as civilized a manner as he can. The review is replete with sentences such as: (i) 'I complain against the misuse of distortion as a technique to create something formally monstrous, unrelated to any element corresponding to it in the artist's vision'; (ii) 'These paintings are closer to whodunit horrors than to the tragic view'; (iii) 'What they [the paintings] lack in feeling, form and meaning they attempt to make up in intimidating technique'; and (iv) 'Whatever modern art has done, Souza seems to say, I can do too.' On the other hand, where Nissim thinks praise is due, he is sparing in his enthusiasm: 'A word about the two landscapes. I find them impressive if not engaging. There is obviously a certain authentic simplification of form here, a definite atmosphere of the stark, almost the barren. The inspiration, nevertheless, is more from modern art than from nature. A feeling of having seen much that is similar cannot be avoided.' Yet, the last paragraph, with its standard phraseology, is inconsistent with the general tone that he adopts in the rest of the review; it makes one suspect that either he was being tactful and making a last-ditch effort to avoid bad blood, or simply that the editorial policy of *Thought* did not give him the freedom to be rampantly opinionated.

The last paragraph says: 'Despite these comments, I do not question Souza's talent and achievement as a painter. The talent is outstanding and the achievement is considerable. His [Souza's] place among Indian painters is with the few who are in the highest class. There is little of the fumbling amateur in him. Most of his work is on a scale, which makes it unchallengeably professional. He handles his tools with tremendous confidence, and his prolific output gives a cumulative impression of vitality which it is impossible not to admire.

'His task, in my opinion, is to liberate his talent from the paraphernalia of his egoistic theories and ideas and to let it find its own honest level.'

The aesthetic principles that Nissim adopts in this early review, remained more or less constant in the large numbers of art reviews he would write in the years to come. Some of these principles, he claims, he learnt from his 'guru' Alkazi, who taught him how to write art criticism, though he never wrote it himself.

With book reviews, on the other hand, he appears to have evolved a method of his own. As a poet, he was more qualified to deal with the interpretation of texts than with paintings; there is a greater degree of conviction in the statements that he makes here. His review of *Rhythm in the Heavens*[3] is full of choice quotes that sound familiar to those of us who have got to know Nissim over the years. In the opening paragraph, he refers to claims about the book made in the blurb, and spends much of his time, in the paragraphs that follow, pooh-poohing these claims, and showing how the book is, in fact, not one bit what it is made out to be: 'Blurbs provide book reviewers with their most convenient props. The publishers of Ram Gopal's autobiography have been liberal in supplying them. By contrasting the claims made with choice passages from the relevant chapters it is easy to arrive at a fair estimate of the book. Too easy, perhaps . . .'

In the next paragraph, he goes on to dismantle the 'brilliantly described opening scene' (in the language of the blurb), where the writer, as a child, runs out of his house during a monsoon thunderstorm to dance naked in the rain. This innocent act is invested with great symbolic meaning in the book, and is interpreted as the child's desire 'to become one with the storm.' Nissim feels, rightly, that this is a 'romantically banal situation' which has been blown out of proportion by the writer and his publishers and editors. He says: 'While I am writing this review, my four-year-old daughter is dancing naked under the tap in her bath. She may well grow up to describe it in her autobiography as her impulse to become one with the terrific tap water.' (The reference to his four-year-old daughter, incidentally, is one of the few references Nissim has ever made of his children in his poems and articles.)

The next claim in the blurb that comes in for scrutiny is that *Rhythm in the Heavens* is an admixture of 'Western self-analysis and Oriental mysticism.' Nissim's response to this is direct: 'Of course, there is no self-analysis in the autobiography, but I take it the publishers are referring to the critical outlook, which is part of the Western tradition. It is this, presumably, to which Oriental mysticism is contrasted.'

The last two paragraphs of the review are worth quoting in full: 'There are a number of photographs in the book, and if none is outstanding there is at least one which is remarkable. It is of the author's living room. A door, a cupboard full of books, some outsize framed pictures and a generously carpeted floor can be clearly seen. It is all very touching.

'Indian dancing is a great art but how watery the tradition is in those who have made it known abroad may be learned from this book.'

In his lifetime, Nissim would come to write hundreds of book reviews; once again this early review displays all the characteristics that would distinguish him from other book reviewers: irreverence, sarcasm, the deliberate lack of generosity, often in the name of high standards.

The experience that Nissim gained from writing reviews stood him in good stead when he finally took up the editorship of *Quest,* between 1955 and 1957. Unlike the *Illustrated Weekly of India*, where he had previously worked, *Quest* was a scholarly journal founded by A.B. Shah, with different editorial policies from those of a popular magazine thriving on advertisements. But he adapted himself to the situation quickly and easily, his own training coming in handy. In future, all the journals he would become associated with, such as *Poetry India* and the *Indian PEN* would be little magazines like *Quest;* literary, scholarly, catering to only small numbers of conscientious readers. Of course, there was *Imprint,* which like the *Weekly* was a popular magazine, but Nissim was strictly in charge of only the literary section, for which he had to select poems and short stories, and assign books for review.

In 1958, Nissim published his third collection of poems.[4] For some reason, he did not give this book a regular title either, but like *Sixty Poems,* simply called it *The Third*. One explanation for titles like *Sixty Poems* and *The Third* is that he was sensitive to the dangers of choosing titles that were pompous or pretentious, where the poems in the volume did not measure up to the grandeur of the title. Here, on the other hand, he was on safe ground, for there is something very tentative about titles like *Sixty Poems* and *The Third*. His third collection too was privately published, but, like *Sixty Poems,* distributed by the Strand Bookshop of Bombay owned by his friend Shanbhag; it was 1959 by the time the book was out in the bookshops. Strand Bookshop was not a regular publisher of poetry, but they seem to have agreed to distribute Nissim's books as a personal favour. In the '50s, Strand, situated at a crossroad of the Pherozeshah Mehta Road, was possibly the only 'respectable' bookstore in Bombay which book-lovers could frequent; a fair amount of goodwill was established between Nissim and Shanbhag. Perhaps it is they who offered to market the books, for he had by then earned a considerable reputation as a poet. This is especially borne out by Nissim's claim (discussed earlier) that he himself never thought of his poetry in terms of books at this stage, but was only concerned with completing a poem and moving on to the next one.

The Third, dedicated to Krishnanath whose identity remains a mystery, is made up of poems that were written between 1954 and 1958. There are thirty-six poems in the book, and they often cover the same bases as poems in *A Time to Change* and *Sixty Poems.* The cycle of philosophical-moral-reflective-self-analytical poems is repeated, as is that of poems that concern themselves with sex and romance; in fact, the bulk of the volume is made up of these two kinds of poems, leaving very little room for the odd travel or animal poem that also makes its appearance for the first time. In several poems, Nissim wears a third-person mask to disguise himself, and deflect suspicion that the poems may be about the conflicts he was going through as a real person. This strategy also adds a degree of complexity to the poems, causing Bruce King to remark that 'Part of the achievement of the volume results from the creation of a persona of someone watching himself as if he were a case study in bad faith, as if all the philosophizing of the early poems were self-deception.'[5]

Among the philosophical poems, the terms of reference are set by the second poem, 'Division':

> For nothing can be hidden long
> From heart or intellect,
>
> . . .
>
> But welded they could seem and be
> A single architect.

The division of 'heart' and 'intellect' into a set of binaries, each heading its own paradigm, is, with some variation, the theme of many of the poems in the book: broadly, all that is dull and uninspiring is attributed to the intellect, all that is warm and passionate, to the heart. By the time he put his third collection together, Nissim realized it was not enough to make bland, abstract statements that expounded his theories. Some poems, therefore, resort to devices such as situational comedy, and draw their conclusions from this. In 'Waking', for example, he writes:

When the politician boasted
How he had made two hundred speeches,
'No, Tom,' his wife declared,
'You made the same speech two hundred times.'
So are we all
Making the same speech over and over again.
And now I hear the first birds
Spasmodic and repetitive–
I know I shall repeat myself.

Nevertheless, how moral (or moralistic or moralizing) Nissim can get, is borne out by the next two poems, 'Admission' and 'Memo for a Venture', which, between themselves, use the phrase 'do not' at least thrice. 'Admission' opens with 'Do not admit the monstrous truth, the touch / Of cold and cowardice in stubborn dreams', and ends with:

Do not reveal the face behind the mask,
Which almost any eye unguided sees,
Unblessed but bending blindly to the task,
Eclipse of the old passionate mysteries.

Likewise, 'Memo for a Venture' opens with the following lines:

You do not know
the outcome
nor should try to guess,
the secret
is the preparation of a role;

A noteworthy feature of some poems in *The Third* is that they keep the familiar use of irony down to the minimum, so that the poems mean what they say. 'Advice' is one such poem; the title of the poem leads to expectations of irony which remain largely unfulfilled, because the poem actually gives advice, again of a moral kind. The only redeeming factor is the last line, which says, 'I prefer the company of spiders' (and prepares us, thereby, for the few, refreshingly different animal poems in the book). 'Tonight' continues in the same platitudinous vein: 'The world is for the living, is there more?' Nissim asks, and in the next stanza, only slightly offsets the banality of the question with: 'The world is for the dying, is there more?' The message contained in 'Two Adolescents' is that '. . . clumsy to the normal sight/Are gropings of the inner light.' However, this poem is redeemed by its contrast of two young people, one articulate, the other awkward, with the poet siding with the latter. Several poems in *The Third* use words and phrases (or even entire lines) to weave disparate elements together, and give the poem organic form. In 'Episode', such a phrase is 'romantic restfulness'. There are lines in this poem that stand out, as for example the penultimate line, 'God sent three beggars', reminiscent at once of Gautama Buddha's spiritual quest. However, much more interesting, from my point of view, is the line 'She lied to be with me.' This very line is to be found in 'Situation', another poem in *The Third*; it suggests there is something autobiographical that is responsible, ultimately, for the break up of Nissim's marriage, though I am fully aware of the dangers of using a poet's work to draw conclusions about his life. We shall return to this issue shortly, when we come to a discussion of the 'love' poems in *The Third*.

'Episode' is followed by 'Wisdom', a title that has more ironic resonance than 'Advice', since it seeks to establish that '. . . the old are weak and on the shelf', and '. . . the old are stale in the morning light', subverting, in the process, the traditional Indian idea of the old as wise, the young as naive; in fact, the poem attempts to define, at some length, what wisdom is and why the old cannot be wise. 'Prayer', on the other hand, like 'Advice', gets rid of irony once again, and goes on and on, in praise of prayer, asceticism, austerity etc.

> Now again I must declare
> My faith in things unseen, unheard,
> The inner music, undertone,
> The silence of a daily friend,
> The dignity of trust, the fervour
> Of an erring choice, the hidden
> Sacrifice, the wordless song.

'Insight' too is exactly like 'Prayer' and 'Advice', serious and straightforward in tone. Much more surprising is 'Insectlore', the first few lines of which easily make it an 'animal' poem, but which later lapses into the philosophical mode and reminds all 'lower' forms of life 'That you exist and are gone, /Claimed by mortality /Even more than we, / Within some dim intent /Which comprehends /Moon and Man.' 'Song of Desolation' anticipates the much-anthologized poem 'Enterprise', that Nissim would write many years later. The line 'You lifeless moralists prescribe your laws', almost tempts one to steal it from the poem and use it to describe the overall quality of Nissim's work in this collection. Finally, there's 'What Frightens Me', a poem of self-analysis where the title and the first line, 'Myself examined frightens me' nicely complement and balance each other; and 'December'58', in which he says:

> I must define myself, the place
> And time, the starting line or tape,
> To mirror for the seeking face
> What love of self distorts its shape.

The 'love' poems begin with the eighteen-line, two-stanza poem 'For Her', which, in a way, proposes Nissim's 'theory' of love: '. . . We cannot love /Without the idea of love . . .'; all the other poems in this category are about the practice of love. In 'Paean', an attempt is made to sing praises of the body minus all the trappings of the soul, but the language remains decorous and therefore tedious. Nissim does not succeed in bringing the body to life, complete with all its odours and secretions, as, say, Kamala Das does in some of her poems. There is an image of 'shaken breasts', another of 'arm and armpit', the best that Nissim could do to destroy the psychological block that prevented him, throughout his poetic career, from using imagery that was explicit, especially in its capacity to revolt.

A point that seriously needs to be made about Nissim's poems on women, both in *The Third* and in volumes that preceded and succeeded it, is that he invariably constructed the woman as other and 'gazed' at her with chauvinistic male eyes. In 'Declaration' he writes, without the slightest remorse:

> . . . certain vases
> And women are too expensive, or else

Fragile, exacting, best enjoyed
From a distance, with delicate affection.

Such instances abound in poem after poem after poem, in a long innings spanning nearly five decades. When, many years later, Nissim would be questioned about this by younger writers and critics with a poststructuralist or feminist orientation, he would lamely defend himself by arguing that, as a poet, his duty was only to record the attitudes of people at a given time; that at the time these poems were written, men habitually looked at women as sexual objects; that there was no notion of personal politics or political correctness then. The truth of the matter, however, is that this is how women appeared to him. Had this oppressive view been confined to his poems, he would have been a happier man than he was. But he extended it to life itself, with the result that he led a somewhat promiscuous and debauched life that alienated him from his family. Bruce King, trying to be as circumspect and restrained as possible, puts it in these words: 'In *The Third* . . . many of the poems concern love, marriage, the discontent of marriage, affairs pursued or failed to be pursued outside marriage, memories and fantasies of other loves. While it would be foolish to translate the poems into real life–after all these years Ezekiel remains married–and to forget that poets create personae who live their imaginings and conflicts, Ezekiel's poetry from *The Third* onwards will often be concerned with the conflicts of marriage, new romances and the delight of new loves.'[6]

It isn't time yet, to name some of the women with whom Nissim had extra-marital affairs. Nor is it time to ask why these women, several of whom were accomplished individuals in their own right, gave in to his desires. We're still analysing the 'love' poems in *The Third,* where 'A Conclusion' declares blatantly and uninhibitedly:

> . . . women, trees, tables, waves and birds,
> Buildings, stones, steamrollers,
> Cats and clocks
> Are here to be enjoyed.

Similarly, in 'At the Party', women, addressed directly, are told:

Ethereal beauties, may you always be
Dedicated to love and reckless shopping,
Your midriffs and your thighs unruly,
Breasts beneath the fabric slyly plopping.

Nissim, as I have already hinted, developed a great fondness for parties, and this stayed with him until old age. 'At the Party' may provide a clue as to why he liked to attend parties so much; the third 'me of the poem tells us that at parties, he often 'scrutinized the women for the kill.' In this context, 'Gallantry' needs to be quoted in full because it spells it out clearly:

This is a face
A man may look upon;
Do I stare too long?
Well, then, I shall
Lower
The gaze-
Your bosom likes me well.
Or let me be humble,
Taking in the thighs,
Forgive me madam.
Now I bend my eyes lower still
To fall upon your knees.
How low shall I fall?
Down to your ankles then
But now
It's time to rise
And look again upon your face
Do I stare too long?
Well, then, I shall
Lower
The gaze . . .

And 'At the Hotel' tries to be equally explicit:
Our motives were concealed but clear,
not coffee but the Cuban dancer took us there,
the naked Cuban dancer.

On the dot she came and shook her breasts
all over us and dropped
the thin transparent skirt she wore.

Unlike earlier poems in *The Third,* where it is Man who makes the first erotic moves, the later poems, including 'At the Hotel', present Woman as seducer. In 'For Love's Record', for example, the line 'Who gathered men as shells and put them by' (referring, needless to say, to the pastime' of a certain woman), is repeated thrice in three separate stanzas as a sort of refrain. Once he arrives at this view of the 'fairer sex', nothing stops Nissim from being as nasty towards women as he can. The opening stanza of 'The Language of Lovers' has this to say about a certain woman:

Poetry, some foolish critic said,
Is the natural language of lovers-
Looking at her destroyed even my prose.

That last line is a punch line, for sure, and at whose expense!

There are other poems in *The Third* that can be classified as 'love' poems, especially 'Encounter' and 'Night and Day'. But before we bid farewell to the volume, it is worth examining some of the stray poems on miscellaneous subjects, and commenting on Nissim's use of form. Of these poems, the ones that are about insects, birds and animals are easily the most interesting. I have already referred to the last line of 'Advice' ('I prefer the company of spiders'), that, to me, lifts the poem from the morass of abstraction into which it sinks. The word 'spiders' may be the last word in the poem, but it also allows spiders to have the last word, although it does no more than mention them. It also proves, importantly, that Nissim was observant. 'Insectlore' has opening lines that do more for the poem than 'spiders' do for 'Advice':

Worm, moth, serpent, toad,
Gleaming in the sun
Or slimy in mud,
Helpless round a flame
Or as the joys of love

Fragile in evening air
Tame the wanton tongue
With flash of wonderment,
That you exist and are gone.

The sense of observation is much more evident here, and in the latter half of the poem, the observations are used to make conclusions about life itself (as discussed earlier). 'The Cur' and 'Sparrows' are strictly about the creatures they refer to in their titles, but like 'Insectlore', they go beyond description and reflect on the human condition. The first stanza of 'The Cur' is moving in its compassion:

It came upon me with a vicious crawl,
Gangrenous in a vital limb
And drawn by some disorder of the brain
To foul decaying stuff. I stared as one
Who sees at dawn the face of God.
For here, locked into life and helplessness,
Is what one cannot hope to understand,
Hounded by the worldly view
And free from dreams and dogs.

In the third stanza, Nissim interprets the hapless look of the animal thus:

'I too am life',
The image seems to say,

'Sparrows' follows the same strategy as 'The Cur'–it starts out by describing the ways of sparrows, and then becomes meditative. The opening lines are:

You may not doubt their single aim,
Which is to fly and then to mate,
Aroused to build with twig and leaf,
A nest sufficient for the need–
Open, warm, and planned to give
A truly bird's-eye view of things.

Nissim's 'animal' poems, as far as their descriptiveness is concerned, are nowhere near the animal poems of, say, Ted Hughes, or even a younger contemporary like Manohar Shetty. They do not quite manage to 'describe' the animals, birds and insects they purport to speak about, and are anthropocentric in their tendency to attribute human qualities to animals, and to see them in human terms. But they still have their place in his oeuvre. Unfortunately, they are rarely included in anthologies and college-level texts (with the obvious exception of 'Night of the Scorpion'). Hence they are not widely known.

'Letter from Rangoon' is the only travel poem in *The Third*, and possibly in Nissim's entire body of work. During my conversations with him, he told me several times that he envied writers (Tara Patel, for instance) who wrote poems–or at least travelogues–on the places they went to. Whenever he tried to work his peregrinations into poems, his attempts always ended in failure. Given this 'handicap', a poem like 'Letter from Rangoon' must be celebrated. What strikes me about the poem is that, unlike his 'animal' poems, it does not turn metaphysical at the end. However, some readers are apt to see the last stanza as partially metaphysical. Nissim probably went to Rangoon when he was a Royist. The poem is based on his impressions of Burma's capital city, possibly recorded in his journal.

> Pagodas illuminated
> Women tightly wrapped
> Slanting eyes
> Prices all inflated
> City still unmapped
> Food, exposed to flies.
>
> Saffron monks with heads clean shaved
> Trishaws (cycle rickshaws)
> Taxis are jeeps
> Whole market for gewgaws
> Pavements unpaved
> And refuse in heaps.
>
> Pornographic books (in Burmese)
> Chinese taking bets

Indian waiters coolies lawyers
Pawnbrokers soothsayers
Palms requiring grease
Love under mosquito nets.

Like home in many ways
We belong to the East
This Buddhist city smells
Of God and the Beast
Here the gong marks the days
There the temple bells.

Another poem that is a throwback to his Royist days is 'Road Repairs'. Once again, this is among his few poems on the working class, and reminds me of the work of W. H. Auden. The first stanza of this two-stanza poem may seem somewhat condescending; yet it reveals Nissim to be a part of the real world of blood and sweat, toil and tears. This is in marked contrast to all the other poems in *The Third,* which make him out to be something of an armchair philosopher, comfortable only in the realm of ideas. The first stanza is as follows:

At six the staggering drone begins,
The lorry brings 'the working class' in loads
Who start at once the ritual of their fate,
Digging as for gold or golden speech.
They leave no stone unturned but bend, unbend,
And sweat like horses on the broken road.

Like A *Time to Change* and *Sixty Poems, The Third* has a mix of formal and informal poems, still others being semi-formal. I should like to discuss the formal ones here. The rhyme-scheme that is almost uniformly employed is abab. 'Portrait', the first poem, uses such a rhyme scheme, together with the four-foot line; three lines in the poem have an additional ninth syllable. 'December '58' also uses the four-foot line, but iambic tetrameter is used consistently here, without any variation. By contrast, 'Sonnet' deliberately avoids the use of rhyme, even though the poem is in iambic pentameter, with an octave-sestet kind of stanza division. The last six lines of the poem are as follows:

> The truth is in the face when morning breaks
> I love the perfect modulated voice
> But let it be ambiguous, not assured.
> Reality is not concealed by what
> The wards display. In bitter secrecy,
> A central image grows or shrinks away.

Nissim carries out various experiments in his poems. In 'Situation', which is a four-stanza poem, he manages to end the four lines of each stanza with the word despair/eyes/hair/lies. From the point of view of form, the poems I particularly like are ones which have a unity of time or place, becoming invested, in the bargain, with a dramatic compactness. In 'In the Queue', for example, the entire action takes place in a bus queue, where the poet-narrator is (as usual) engaged in games of sexual harassment:

> Now savage red, now mildly pink,
> Are thoughts I cannot help but think:
> Exposed to mountain air or sea,
> Her unashamed anatomy;

Likewise, in 'At the Party', the poem happens at a party, in 'Encounter', at a date. 'Encounter', incidentally, is one of the few poems where the generally indifferent Nissim displays a sense of dress: 'I wore my tie of brown and green, /She came in white'. 'Mid-Monsoon Madness', which uses rain as a central metaphor, has an immediacy about it that prevents the poem from being all over the place.

Having analysed and evaluated the poems in *The Third,* it is perhaps necessary to pass judgement on Nissim's overall achievement. To me, the poems in this book do not seem to reflect a major development in his talent. As I have tried to demonstrate, they proceed on more or less the same lines as the earlier poems: his best is yet to come. I therefore find Bruce King's claims somewhat exaggerated, when he says: 'In 1958 Ezekiel was a better, more skilled poet than a short time before.'[7] Or, 'Suddenly Ezekiel had become a real poet rather than a promising one; partly this results from a colder, more distant and ironic tone towards himself and his emotions.'[8]

'I'm a Poet and I Know It'

The end of the '50s marked, in several ways, the end of a period of uncertainty in Nissim's life. This is especially true in relation to two important things: his job and his career as a poet. As regards the former, he found his vocation, at last, in teaching; as for the latter, he consolidated his position with the publication of *The Unfinished Man* (1960) and *The Exact Name* (1965). Let us chart the course of events that filled his chequered days, as the '50s gave way to the '60s.

Nissim's stint at Bombay's Mithibai College, located strategically where the erstwhile Ghodbunder Road (now Swami Vivekananda Road) intersects a road coming from Juhu beach, is no doubt a turning point in his life. No longer was he at a loss as to what to profitably do for a living. Having 'experimented' with college teaching for a year or so in the'40s, he now stuck it out at this other suburban college for as many as eleven years, till the assignment paved the way for a more prestigious one at the English Department of Bombay University.

The events that led to the Mithibai College appointment seem quite ordinary. Professor G.D. Parikh who was an M.N. Roy supporter, and whom Nissim knew well, had by then become the Rector of Bombay University. It was a post created especially for him. One day, early in 1961, he called Nissim over to his office in the university campus at Fort, and told him that a new college was opening in the Vile Parle area; it would be known as Mithibai College. The management and the principal of the college were known to Professor Parikh—he emphasized the point that all of them were Gujaratis. Professor Parikh had enough clout with the authorities to assure Nissim of a lecturer's job in the Department of English. Nissim, sceptic that he is, was himself doubtful whether the thing would work out; but Professor Parikh was confident that it would. On Parikh's advice, therefore, he travelled to Vile Parle to have an interview with the principal, A. B. Yajnik. At the end of the interview, which couldn't have lasted very long, Nissim was offered the job, as well as the headship of the English Department. Without second thoughts, he accepted the offer.

The interview took place several weeks ahead of the opening day of term, in June. This gave him enough time to familiarize himself with the neighbourhood in which he would be working. He says he made frequent trips to Vile Parle, simply to get his bearings, so that once the college began, he did not have to waste time finding his way. I asked Nissim what he thought was the main reason he had been selected for the job. He said the G.D. Parikh factor of course mattered, for Parikh and Yajnik who had worked together at Ruia College were close friends. However, the principal was also impressed by the fact that he was a known name, who frequently wrote for the *Times of India.* This, at any rate, was what Professor Parikh himself reported to Nissim later, and it doesn't surprise me that the principal was unable to differentiate between the journalistic writing that Nissim did for the *Times of India,* and academic writing that genuinely distinguishes a scholar from others; it was a confusion that Nissim would cash in on throughout his teaching career.

When Nissim joined Mithibai College in 1961, there were only a handful of teachers in the English Department besides himself, Pramod Kale and Victor Gaikwad being two of them. Although he was offered the department's headship, he was initially given only junior classes to teach–First Year Arts and Inter Arts; it was only the following year that he began teaching Junior and Senior BA. Nissim recalls that as the years passed, the college expanded, so that in course of time the strength of the English Department swelled to as many as seven or eight lecturers, who also taught Science classes, in addition to Arts classes. (English was a compulsory subject for Science students in those days. By the mid-'60s, the lecturers who joined them were the poet R. Parthasarathy, G. D. Antarkar, M. K. Kutty and Srinivas Rao). Nissim's period of probation may have lasted for a year, after which he was confirmed.

Vile Parle is a long way off from Warden Road, where Nissim lived. In order to reach the college, he first travelled by a B.E.S.T bus from Warden Road to Bombay Central station, and then took a Western Railway suburban train to Vile Parle. From Vile Parle station, tired of smelly buses and trains, he walked to the college, ten minutes away, in the refreshing morning air. However, I'm probably viewing the entire situation from the point of view of today's conditions. Back in the '60s, Nissim says the buses and trains that he travelled by were not terribly crowded, and he did not have much difficulty boarding either the bus at Warden Road, or the train at Bombay Central. Moreover, the journey from Bombay Central to Vile Parle would have been against the 'tide', so that it was possible for him to comfortably step into a train and find a seat–even a window seat–although he had a third-class season ticket. Still, the entire operation would have lasted at least an hour, which is more than the time it took him to reach the *Times of India* at Bori Bunder during his stint there. Considering that lectures at Mithibai College commenced at 10.30 a.m., Nissim must have left home around 9 a.m. everyday, after being served breakfast by Daisy.

Like any other faculty member, he had three to four lectures per day, on an average. His classes finished by 3 p.m., which was, at any rate, the time all of them were supposed to be in the college till, though the principal was not bossy. (Nissim was always opposed to teachers who left the college as soon as they finished their lectures.) Sometimes he finished his classes by lunch. This was particularly so during the early years of the college, when it was 'still getting off the ground'. As the '60s advanced, he started teaching postgraduate classes in the evenings, at downtown venues such as the university campus, or St Xavier's or Wilson College. This meant that his evenings were also occupied–another factor that could have contributed to the rift that was slowly developing between himself and his wife.

Compared to any other job that he did, Nissim enjoyed his work at Mithibai College. It made him realize that teaching was indeed in his blood, and that there is something to be said for hereditary occupations, as the ancient Hindus believed! Besides, unlike his assignments at the *Times* and Shilpi, the work he did here as a lecturer was an extension of the poetry he wrote, so that the two nicely complemented and balanced each other. Since college jobs necessarily entail vacations at least twice a year, it gave him the much-needed breathing space that a poet benefits by. It was because he was functioning in an atmosphere that he found congenial, suited to his temperament, that Nissim did well and managed to rise in his chosen profession. He was already head of the English Department. This led, eventually, to his being appointed vice-principal of the Arts Section, a post that is admittedly superfluous in an academic set-up, but not without its glamour, all the same. Especially in Nissim's case, being vice-principal did not mean very much more than enhancing the college's reputation, as it enabled the college to state in its prospectus that a well-known poet was on its faculty. Most of the routine administrative work (Nissim says ninety per cent of it) was done, in any case, by the principal and the clerks, though the principal did make it a point to consult him on certain matters.

Nissim expected little from his jobs. Call it complacence or cynicism, he seems to have walked into every job with the feeling that it was just a source of livelihood; he could function with a minimum of job-satisfaction. This I would attribute to his stoicism and asceticism.

The standard of English at Mithibai College was, to put it bluntly, low. This was natural, since the majority of students were Gujaratis who had done their schooling in the Gujarati medium. In his estimate, out of a hundred students in class, sixty to seventy had problems with English; eight to ten were above average; and five or six lived on a different ('superior') intellectual level. However, where any other lecturer of Nissim's calibre may have been put off, he turned it to advantage by engaging special classes of a remedial kind, Monday to Friday, much to the delight of the principal. (Nissim did not teach on Saturdays–he reserved it for writing poetry.) He realized that if one wanted to be critical, the criticism had to be directed against the educational system, what with everything being geared only towards examinations. As far as the students were concerned, his relationship with them was a question of attitudes. He believed it was his duty to help them solve their problems, without sitting too much on judgement. Condemning them for their ineptitude did not help. And then there was the brighter side. If the students in junior classes were weak in English, those at the BA level had enough of a mastery over it to make his lectures with them enjoyable. The texts were challenging, the classes, in their own way, cosmopolitan in their make-up. This was more true of the MA classes he engaged in the evenings, where new subjects like American Literature were gradually being introduced into the curriculum. His postgraduate classes also enabled Nissim to view his undergraduate teaching in a different light, when he discovered, to his astonishment, that even M. Phil students wanted notes to be dictated to them, and in the exams and class tests, reproduced what he had said on Pablo Neruda or Octavio Paz verbatim.

Nissim's dedication to teaching did not go unnoticed. It won him praise from the principal of the college who was proud that they had a world-famous' teacher on their staff who brought out books of poetry, and–in 1964–was invited to lecture at the University of Leeds.

Though this may sound like dark comedy, it's true that yet another way in which he converted his working conditions at Mithibai College to his advantage, was by observing closely the speech habits of the students (and professors), and taking notes. A few years later, he would return to these notes to compose his very first poem in Indian English, which, in course of time, would lead to more such poems. Speaking of composing poems, Nissim found that he had enough time at the college to write during 'free' lectures. In his own words: 'It wasn't like doing a nine-to-five job. Even if teaching does make heavy demands [on one] in the Indian context, it still meant that a greater part of the day was yours.' As he talked about his days at Mithibai College, I could perceive an excitement in Nissim's eyes. One of the things he said to me was: 'When I went back to college teaching, I felt this was an important change in my life [for the better]. I made up my mind never to go back to any other kind of job, even if it meant more money. Teaching came to me much more simply and naturally. I enjoyed it immensely.'

As I was conducting my research, I discovered that two of Nissim's colleagues at Mithibai College, Pramod Kale and Victor Gaikwad, had both settled down in Pune. I interviewed Gaikwad to find out what kind of man Nissim was in those days, how did his colleagues see him. 'Nissim was full of life, and very encouraging,' Gaikwad began. 'I thought of him as a father-figure. He got on famously with everyone in the staff common room. He was a cut above the principal and everyone else in the college. Yet he didn't demean anyone–he didn't need to put people down because he had no inferiority complex. This was his plus point.' I asked Gaikwad to tell me something about his own interaction with Nissim. 'Like me, he was interested in sports in those days. A couple of times we played table tennis together in the college. I was on the Sports Committee. We once organized a hundred-metre racing event for teachers, and Nissim participated. As far as teaching was concerned, he was very accommodating. Both *Romeo and Juliet* and *The History of Mr Polly* were on the syllabus. At first, Nissim taught *The History of Mr Polly* and I *Romeo and Juliet*. After a few years, Nissim suggested that we should exchange texts, so that the students would have the benefit of both the teachers. Nissim encouraged me to write poetry and even published one of my poems in the *Illustrated Weekly of India.*'

Later, Gaikwad provided me with an anecdote. It seems Mithibai College once invited Harindranath Chattopadhyaya to address the students and faculty. This was shortly after Nissim had reviewed and panned a book of his in the newspapers. But the college didn't know of the review, and asked Nissim to introduce Chattopadhyaya to the audience. Nissim began his introduction by saying: 'Mr Chattopadhyaya is one of the wittiest persons in India. I hope he doesn't make fun of me,' Few people in the auditorium, of course, caught the joke.

Finally, Gaikwad told me something that quite surprised me. He said, back in the '60s, Nissim had plans to start an 'autonomous institute' that would give its own degrees and pay teachers handsomely. But it fell through. G. D. Parikh, in particular, who was an office-bearer of the university, wasn't too happy with Nissim's utopian ideas.

Kale did not want to be interviewed. However, from time to time he telephoned me and offered snippets of information. He said Nissim hated Vile Parle as a neighbourhood and playfully called it 'vile' Parle. There was open hostility between him and the popular Marathi poet Mangesh Padgaonkar who taught in the Marathi department of the college. As Nissim arrived in the staff room, Padgaonkar would remark, 'Here comes the blue aristocrat.' (The 'blue aristocrat' is a phrase Padgaonkar borrowed from one of Nissim's own poems.) What was going on here was the familiar nativist-versus-Indian writing in English battle.

In the '60s, exercise took up a significant chunk of Nissim's time in the mornings. He was an early riser then, as he continues to be even today. He usually woke up at 6 or 6.30 a.m. Occasionally he got up at 7, which by his standards, was late. His day began with deep breathing exercises, limb movement exercises, dumbbell exercises, standing-on-the head exercises, exercising on a stationary bicycle and jogging. It is not as if he did all this everyday, but it formed the entire range. Some of these things he picked up from books and articles that he regularly read, though he emphasizes that 'what suited me are the comparatively simple exercises.' He also devised his own exercises and was not disheartened if he couldn't do things exactly as they were supposed to be done. Nissim even tried visiting a gym in his neighbourhood, and enrolling at a local yoga class, but he says he never succeeded either in mastering yoga, or learning to use the various sophisticated gadgets available at the gym. 'After all, my exercises were for health, not for athletics,' he said to me, as he talked about those years. After finishing his exercises he would make himself a cup of tea. (Daisy woke up after him, so he made his tea on his own.) Even as the tea was getting ready, he would walk up and down the corridor. No single day in Nissim's life passed without exercise. If on occasion, he was unwell, or simply did not feel up to it, he would at least do a certain amount of walking within or outside the house, for 'I knew that exercises had to be done everyday, as a daily habit.' The exercises and tea were followed by other things in quick succession–bathing, reading up for his lectures and eating breakfast, before he took off for college at 9 a.m.

One reason why Nissim relied so much on exercise at this time, was because, health-wise he perceived himself as belonging to the high-risk bracket. There were several factors responsible for this. First, he was, by nature a man who worried a lot. 'I've done a lot of worrying in the past,' he told me, 'about food, health, relationships with friends, relatives and family, harbouring sometimes the feeling that so-and-so was unfair to me.' He tried to overcome the habit of worrying by reading books on health and psychology, but realized that reading alone wasn't enough. Worries can lead to stress and hypertension, which in turn can lead to blood pressure and heart disease; regular daily exercise was one of the simple preventive measures that Nissim took to keep such ailments at bay. In fact, it surprises him that although it virtually costs nothing, few people he knows believe in exercise.

Then, there were other 'unhealthy' habits that he picked up, like smoking. When he was at Mithabai College, there was a short spell when he smoked six to eight cigarettes a day and this soon increased to a whole pack of ten cigarettes. Sometimes he substituted beedies for cigarettes, depending on how broke or 'rich' he was at a given time. Cigarettes may have helped Nissim to compose a poem or write a review with a degree of ease, but he was aware that they also damaged his body. Exercise was a way of making up for some of this harm he was causing himself.

Life, however, went on, Nissim's job as a professor of English helping him in no insubstantial way to come to terms with it. Even in those days, he did not take English literature to mean merely the literature of England, but regarded translations from Russian, Japanese, German, French and Indian languages as a part and parcel of it. His own reading was wide enough to incorporate this diversity, and he advocated it to his students as well. I asked Nissim how he managed, way back in the '60s, to introduce such maverick ideas in a college set-up, which, by very definition, is orthodox, and whose orthodoxy influences the thinking of teachers and students. He replied that when he lectured in class, he never imagined that he was simply addressing a narrow audience of exam-oriented students. Within a short time, he felt it necessary to draw the attention of students to literature's variety, and to provide, in the broadest terms, the historical and cultural context of a poem he might be teaching. This, he felt, was quite different from how an Englishman would approach a work of English literature–he would relate it to the English literary context alone. On the other hand, Nissim, as an Indian, tried to relate texts to India. The attempts paid off, for he was able to arouse the interest of students. Other teachers in the English Department, of course, could not always appreciate his point of view. They felt comfortable and secure following the Englishman's way of looking at a text. Some of them, according to Nissim, may even have felt that the Indian cultural context was not worth relating a work of English literature to, for this would destroy the sanctity of English literature. If he did not have a confrontation with them, it was partly because, in the '60s, these issues were not discussed as widely and universally as they are today. Occasionally, however, such matters did come up, as the teachers had their tea or relaxed in the staff common room, and Nissim always found himself in disagreement with the typical English teacher.

Here was a man, then, who had strong convictions and lived by them. His life in those days existed almost entirely in the realm of ideas and opinions; there were always others to look after the nitty-gritty, like money matters that were handled by Daisy. It was she who did the budgeting, shopping, saving, and buying of stocks and shares. Nissim's duty, as the breadwinner of the family, was only to hand her his monthly salary. Having done that, he was free to direct all his energies towards work. The result was that he became something of a workaholic who couldn't envisage spending his time in any other way, than at his desk. Speaking of that time, Ramesh Sirkar told me: 'When I married and came here in 1961, Nissim certainly gave me the impression of being driven. He would refuse invitations to parties, exhibitions etc., saying if he attended them, when would he do his own work?' And yet if he wanted it, he could always find the time to socialize. Adil Jussawalla recalls an evening that he, Kersy Katrak and P. Lal (who had come down from Calcutta), spent at Nissim's apartment at Mazda Mansion. It wasn't a party, according to Jussawalla, for Nissim never threw parties, but it was a 'meeting' at which Nissim's two little daughters, Kalpana and Kavita, were also present, along with their mother. It seems to have been especially arranged so that Jussawalla could be introduced to Katrak and Lal. This was sometime in 1961 or 1962. Jussawalla, in fact, was a frequent visitor to the Ezekiel household in the early '60s. This was partially facilitated by the close proximity of his parents' house, at 47-B Warden Road, to Nissim's, which, if not exactly a stone's throw away, was at least within walking distance. He liked to go there because although it was a small apartment, it was lined with books. Jussawalla thus got to know Nissim's family–the man himself, his wife and children. But he had no way of telling how strained Nissim's relations with Daisy had grown by then—outwardly at least they gave the impression of conviviality. As an emerging poet, himself it was natural that what attracted Jussawalla to Nissim was, first and foremost, his poetry. He says: 'I'd met poets in London, when I first went there in 1957, but in Bombay Nissim Ezekiel was about the only one, and I certainly felt he was a kindred spirit.' (Dom Moraes, it will be recalled, says identical things in *My Son's Father.*) What poets like Jussawalla and Moraes cherished about Nissim was that he was the only one who could help them network with other like-minded souls. For example, Jussawalla says that apart from Lal and Katrak, it was Nissim who told him about R. Parthasarathy. From a stranger, who first read Nissim's poem 'Mid-Monsoon Madness' in the *Illustrated Weekly of India* in the '50s and liked it, and who occasionally saw him from a distance at shows, Adil Jussawalla went on therefore, to become a close friend and confidant of Nissim, and the association continues in all its glory to this day. It really seems to have developed in the early '60s, when Jussawalla returned briefly from England, and Nissim told him to send the manuscript of his first book of poems, *Land's End,* to P. Lal, to publish under the Writers Workshop imprint.

Upon close examination of Nissim's friendships, it becomes evident that this business of first meeting or getting to know of him in the '50s, and then picking up the threads ten or twenty years later, is a pattern that applies to more than one individual who found a place in his heart. Like Adil Jussawalla and Toni Patel, Minakshi Raja too first met Nissim in the early '50s, when she joined Theatre Unit. However, she does not remember him as a 'clear person' in the '50s. For that, we have to wait for another ten or so years, when she returns to Bombay from Columbia University (in much the same way that Jussawalla returned from Oxford). Her 'reunion' with him is dramatic enough. In her own words, 'I came back from Columbia University in 1961 and was walking down Breach Candy one day with Shakoor [another member of Theatre Unit, whom Raja became friendly with], when we saw Nissim coming in the opposite direction. He greeted me very warmly, but I mistook him for his brother Hannan whom I'd met at Washington, and I said, "Hello, Hannan, when did you get back?" and he said he wasn't Hannan, he was Nissim.'

Raja saw Nissim fairly regularly after that, more so as she needed his help to find a job; as usual, he was generous with his time, especially because the person in question was a lady as elegant as Raja. As he himself wrote for *Imprint* then, he put her in touch with Gloria and Authur Hales, the publishers of the magazine, who gave her an editorial job on the basis of the qualifications she had acquired at Columbia University. Nissim's letter of recommendation, of course, made a difference. Soon after Raja received the *Imprint* offer, she was given a job in the *Times of India,* which obviously was a better place to be at. What prevented her from accepting it at once was the feeling that she would embarrass Nissim by ditching the Hales, to whom he had, after all, introduced her. But when she met Nissim and told him of her dilemma, it wasn't his embarrassment that he thought of, but her welfare; he advised her to take up the *Times* job without hesitation. Raja interprets this as his concern about her future. It endeared him to her, and from then on Nissim and she remained 'very good friends' for a while.

The Hales, of course, weren't upset with either Raja or Nissim, for no one is indispensable; moreover, Raja was only at the beginning of her career, setting out to make a name for herself in journalism.

Nissim's own association with *Imprint* was complicated. He was on their staff on a regular basis for a while (in the late '50s), but after he joined Mithibai College, he couldn't continue with the magazine. He continued, however, to work for them in an advisory capacity, advising them especially about the poems and short stories to be published, and about reviewers to whom books could be sent for review. He himself reviewed books frequently for which he was even paid a kind of regular salary, although he was only a 'freelance' reviewer on paper. The job at Mithibai College gave him enough time to review books, with the result that at times he published four book reviews in a month (in *Imprint* as well as in other newspapers and magazines). This is what took his review tally so high–in the future, one of Nissim's 'selling points' in his curriculum vitae would be that he reviewed over five hundred books in his life! As for *Imprint,* he kept writing for them, and served as their literary editor for at least six to seven years.

Another friend that Nissim made in the early '60s was Gauri Deshpande, who later became a well-known Marathi poet and writer, and an honorary spokesperson for women's issues. Exactly thirty years after

Deshpande met Nissim, I met her at the University of Pune, where we were colleagues in the Department of English. Deshpande was as young and effervescent in the '90s as she must have been in the '60s. She spoke to me at length about the days when she first met Nissim and got to know him. But it's best that I allow her to speak for herself: 'I think it was way back in 1962 or 1963 that I met Nissim first. I just had been published by my favourite editor in my favourite weekly, Mr Gorawala's *Opinion*. Even then Nissim was the big cheese. I was thrilled to meet him and even more thrilled to find that he was a nice man and that he was not at all prone to "talk poetry". That was the time in my life I met the whole lot of them: Kamala Das, Kersy Katrak, Keki Daruwalla, Gieve Patel, Adil Jussawalla, Eunice de Souza . . . And they were all great guys and never "talked poetry". Well, perhaps Kamala was a bit peculiar, but that was the persona she had chosen for herself and we went along. Essentially, they all did their own thing and left me to do my own. It was an exhilarating time for me. I loved and admired them all and was no end thrilled to be considered "one of them". And all of us thought of Nissim (or at any rate we all said to one another that we thought of Nissim) as the guy who had made it, or was sure to make it.'

Deshpande hastened to add that she was not being condescending when she applied phrases like 'make it' or 'made it' to Nissim. What she meant was that while no one in those days, except idealists like Mr Gorawala, wanted to publish Indian writers who wrote in English (poems by Indian English poets were sometimes used as fillers in newspapers!) there was Nissim, whose poems were being published in respectable journals abroad. 'Without going into the colonialism-post-colonialism of it, I think we felt that to be heard in the world, you had to be published "over there" . . . And this Nissim who had "made it" thus, was friendly, approachable, generous with his time and made constructive and useful suggestions about your poetry, but only if you asked for them. A boon.'

Whatever advice Nissim gave her, Deshpande found to be truly beneficial; it helped her do some literary soul-searching and determine the direction in which she would proceed: 'I did not rate myself very high as a poet–a correct estimate, considering the valuation of posterity–and when eventually I found my metier, I gave up writing poems in English–at least for a good thirty years. For this I have Nissim to thank. He asked me once–it must have been in the late '60s or early '70s–what it was that I wanted to say in my poems. That was about as "critical" as he ever was.

But it gave me pause. Having been brought up on "spontaneous overflow of powerful feelings", I had never stopped to think if there really was anything I wanted to say, other than myself. I considered Nissim's point and had to admit, reluctantly enough, that I had nothing to say; and then came his more devastating question: even if I had anything to say, did I have to say it in a poem? That was it. I had to stop and ask: what is a poet? I knew: Nissim is a poet, Keki is a poet and Gieve is a poet; but am I a poet? It was hard, but necessary to say I was not, not then; and now only occasionally. But it went even deeper: I had to ask myself am I an English-writing Indian poet? The answer was a resounding NO. Oh, I could and still can turn out Indian English poems by the bushel; but I began to see, thanks to Nissim, that what I have is a knack, a talent, not a calling. My calling is narrative fiction, mostly in Marathi, and thanks to Nissim, I discovered it. If he hadn't asked that question, and mildly as is his way, I may have gone on producing perfectly respectable poetry; that is, poetry that did not fall below a certain standard, and yet never saying anything–linguistically or poetically–until I discovered the futility of it all for myself. I would have; but I would have wasted a lot of time that I could ill spare. And that is the sort of friend Nissim has been, a friend who can make you think about yourself with just a mild question. Valuable'

Deshpande does not use the word 'friend' casually. She means it when she calls Nissim a friend. She pointed out to me that back in the '60s, his friendship was especially important to her because she thought of herself as 'the odd-woman out among them all, a small fish thrown into a big pond and asked to sink or swim' She wasn't 'plagued by paranoia and anxiety complexes,' but neither was she overly self-confident. The fact that she had never known 'any one like any of them before' often caused her to misread persons and situations and land herself into trouble. And she's certain that it was the fortitude and generosity of these beautiful people– especially Nissim Ezekiel–that saw her through those difficult years.

Nissim had already been abroad twice–once to England, and again to America. Both these trips happened just like that, with him having had to shell out virtually nothing from his own pocket. The trip to England was courtesy Alkazi, that to America courtesy Shilpi and the Sarabhais. These two early foreign trips had set the ground rules for all his numerous travels abroad in the decades that followed: whosoever invited him, would have to cover all his expenses from–to use his favourite phrase–A to Z. They did. To that extent, Nissim has been exceptionally lucky in his foreign travels, though I do not mean to suggest that he did not deserve what he got. Yet it's true that he was cashing in on his popularity as post-Independence India's first major poet in English; it was taking him literally around large parts of the world. Over the years, there are few places on earth that he hasn't at some time or the other visited, to give lectures or readings from his poetry, with the exception of the two poles! But rarely, if ever, has he had to pay for his fares. If his hosts couldn't afford to sponsor him, there were always grant-disbursing agencies (such as the Tatas or the Indian Council for Cultural Relations) that came to his aid. The international Jewish community has also been an important source of support. Often the airfare came from their coffers; after all, they were using the money to promote a fellow-Jew from a poor third world country!

It is in this spirit that, in 1964, Nissim went abroad for the third time, to England once again. The visit was at the behest of Professor Norman Jeffares of the University of Leeds. The British Council in India gave him a travel grant. The sequence of events that led to the prestigious lecturing assignment at the University of Leeds is as follows. Professor K. R. Srinivasa Iyengar, a previous incumbent at Leeds, had upon returning from the UK, published his well-known book, *Indian Writing in English*.[1] Some of his lectures at Leeds were incorporated in the book, which came to Nissim for review. Nissim ripped the book apart. Someone who was strong on worldly wisdom–he does not know who–sent a clipping of the review to Professor Jeffares. It worked. Professor Jeffares invited Nissim to be the next visiting Professor at the University of Leeds. The British Council stepped in and awarded him a grant.

The offer was attractive. Since it was Indian Writing in English that he had to lecture on (a subject that he knew well), he didn't have to spend much time in the library. The only hitch was, would the Mithibai College grant him leave? Nissim convinced them. He wrote to professor Jeffares to say that instead of lecturing from October to March (October is the month when term commences in British universities), he would arrive in Leeds in January and lecture until June, so that he could make use of his vacation. This was acceptable to both the Mithibai College management and the University of Leeds.

Unlike his trip to the United States where he went alone, Nissim took Daisy along with him to England. But neither the University of Leeds nor the British Council paid for her passage; Nissim used the airfare that he received to travel by sea, so that both their expenses could be covered. Daisy was travelling with him to a foreign country for the first time in her life, much to her delight. As far as Nissim was concerned, he was perhaps allowing her to accompany him, so that his own wayward ways in strange lands–as evidenced by some of the things he did on previous trips-were kept in check.

They left Bombay by steamer sometime in the first half of December 1963. The ship travelled via the Mediterranean and the Suez Canal, taking about eighteen to twenty-two days to reach England. Nissim recalls that the fare was about Rs 800 per head, which was slightly more than what it had been when he returned from England by sea over ten years ago, washing decks as the ship sailed. As is his wont, he pointed out to me, however, that the fares included 'everything from morning tea to dinner.' When they reached England towards the end of December, celebrating Christmas on board, and docking at either Plymouth or Dover, they were immediately met by representatives of the University of Leeds who made arrangements to take them to Leeds, situated in magnificent Yorkshire. As he remembers it, 'When my wife Daisy and I reached there, our host instantly assessed our needs, and to our astonishment, and eternal gratitude, advanced a lump sum to us.'[2]

Within a few days of their arrival, Nissim began teaching, and found that compared to conditions in India, the workload was not at all heavy. In all, he is supposed to have delivered fourteen lectures on Indian Writing in English, though according to his own calculations, he lectured for about two-and-a-half months at the rate of two lectures per week. If this were true, the total number of lectures that he delivered would have been well above fourteen! In fact, he says that the above break-up applied to regular faculty at Leeds; in his case, as he was a visiting lecturer from abroad, he agreed to engage more classes than the rest, so that he could cover as much ground as possible. He recalls, for instance, that he often took an extra class on Saturdays, for students of courses other than Indian Writing in English (or Commonwealth Literature as it was then called). The turn-out of students was good–there were more than just the mandatory eleven or twelve that he was accustomed to seeing at the Special English classes at Mithibhai. He cannot recollect the exact authors/ topics on which he lectured, but it isn't difficult to imagine what they must have been–all the hot favourites of the time, such as Mulk Raj Anand, R. K. Narayan and Raja Rao. As far as poetry was concerned, there was probably no way in which he could completely avoid reference to himself, though self-effacement, which has been a significant attribute of his personality, would have naturally made him shy away from focusing too much on himself.

Being the big city person that he is, Nissim appears to have found life in Leeds too peaceful for his taste. Yorkshire may be one of the most beautiful parts of Britain, next only perhaps to the Lake District and the Scottish Highlands, but there was only so much of it that he could take. He began to explore the possibility of travelling to London and spending as much time as he could there. There were several reasons why he was eager to shift base to London. For one thing, he was familiar with London, having lived there a good three to four years. Nostalgia tempts a human being to visit the sites and the spots where he has spent an earlier–and in this case freer–part of his life. Secondly, as Daisy was visiting Britain for the first time, London was definitely on their itinerary; as spring approached and the weather warmed up slightly, Nissim wanted to show her London without further waste of time. Thirdly, someone he knew in Bombay and liked–Toni Diniz–was at that time in London. It made sense to call on her. Toni was working then for a magazine called *China Quarterly*. After getting in touch with her, Nissim started to enjoy her company so much, that he became a regular commuter from Leeds to London. In Bombay, Toni and he were as yet only on 'hi-bye' terms. Now, isolated in a foreign country, and a cold one at that, the two like-minded people sought the warmth of each other's company. According to Toni, it was in London at this time that she and Nissim really struck up a friendship, got to know each other, as it were. She said further: 'This was before my wedding or before I got to know Gieve [Patel, whom she eventually married]. We met quite often in London. Nissim then returned to India, and I followed a year or so later.'

Where did Daisy figure in all this? She did not accompany her husband on all his journeys to London. They had been given comfortable family accommodation in Leeds; she stayed at home while he went to London under one pretext or other, say, to look up publishers or check out an art exhibition. Moreover, Daisy was pregnant during that time, and her mobility was restricted. It's worth noting here that Nissim did not let her stay in England for all the six months that he was there. Somewhere in between, giving her the excuse of her pregnancy, he packed her off to Bombay, introducing her to some Indians on the ship who looked after her. He was especially concerned about her pregnancy this time, as if he knew intuitively that after two daughters, it was their turn now to have a son, the son whom he would fondly name Elkana, in memory of his friend Elk (Alkazi). After Daisy's departure, his trips to London–and elsewhere–became more frequent.

What about his teaching assignment at the University of Leeds? Nissim completed his term successfully, but towards the end, spent virtually no time at the university, going back only once in a while to examine answer scripts. All said and done, then, his visit to England in 1964 was only marginally different from that to the United States in 1956, as far as his recklessness and restlessness were concerned. In both cases, he made sure that he did exactly as he pleased, and that, above all, he entertained himself while the trip lasted. This attitude puts Nissim in the rather unfortunate shoes of the stereotypical Indian, who views the West as a hedonists' paradise, especially as it is miles away from home, where parents, family, job and all the emblems of authority are located.

In June 1964, Nissim returned to Bombay and resumed his duties at Mithibai College. One of the gifts that he brought along with him was a book on how to grow tall, which his wife's niece Jessica had especially asked him to bring. A year later, when Toni Diniz arrived in Bombay, one of the first people she thought of calling on was Nissim. This was, of course, to collect the threads of a valuable friendship that had begun in Britain; but it was also because, like everyone else, Toni needed his help to embark on a career in the arts. She managed to find a job with the Committee for Cultural Freedom, where one of the things she was expected to do was organize art exhibitions. But it wasn't smooth sailing. Wherever she went, she met with resistance, as people continually downplayed the significance of the arts and overrated politics. (This was at a time when, although postmodernism was making its presence felt in the West, India was still in the throes of modernism and formalism. The artificial division that people created between art and politics was only an outcome of this.) Fed up with the hostility that she encountered, Toni left the Committee for Cultural Freedom and joined a publishing firm. Here too, her desire to publish the work of Indian writers in English was treated dismissively. She was frustrated. It is here that Nissim stepped in and gave her a shoulder to cry on, so to speak. She says: 'Nissim helped me a lot in those early years by encouraging me. He was very sympathetic to what I wanted to do. He was among the only people I knew who understood what I meant when I said I didn't want a wretched commercial job.' As it turned out, it was more than just a comforting shoulder that Nissim gave Toni. Together, they were able to persuade India Book House to publish the work of some Indian writers.

But it is unfair to portray Toni as an opportunist who got close to Nissim only because of his contacts. There was a personal factor at work here, as Toni grew fond of Nissim, Nissim of Gieve, and Gieve of Toni. Toni was also very fond of Gieve–she married him in 1969, and 'this cemented the bond between the three of us.' This mutual fondness has lasted over three decades: the Patels today are among Nissim's only friends, when so many others have deserted him.

Toni is also one of the few people who, back in the '60s, dropped in at the Ezekiels' flat at Mazda Mansion for chats. Although this didn't happen too often, she distinctly remembers going there at least a couple of times. She's reluctant, however, to divulge what went on inside the house. It's the occupational hazard of being a biographer–people are immediately on their guard while talking to you. But it means that from her point of view, all was not exactly as it should be.

While Toni first met Nissim at the Theatre Group, and then again in the UK, Gieve was introduced to him under altogether different circumstances. He was an aspiring poet then, who like other young hopefuls of the day turned to Nissim for encouragement and guidance. He says he 'sought' Nissim out, primarily with the intention of showing him his poems, 'and got very lukewarm responses.' This was in 1958 or 1959. Gieve had just begun writing then, and the idea of showing his poems to Nissim actually came from Kersy Katrak; it was because Katrak saw the talent in Gieve's work that he took him to meet Nissim. The meeting did not serve its purpose, for Gieve left Nissim's house with his confidence shattered. 'He didn't give me very many suggestions for improvement,' Gieve told me. 'I remember him saying rather half-heartedly that there are so many things around us which we don't respond to, thereby making a negative comment on the poems. The only positive thing he said was–"let me see the next batch".'

Nissim's hostility did not discourage Gieve. He continued to write, and a year or so later showed him his new work as Nissim had suggested. This time he reacted much more positively. After that, things quickly went to the other extreme; it was Nissim who published Gieve's first collection of poems.[3]

Gieve recounted how it all happened. He was then a medical student at Bombay's J. J. Hospital. He kept showing his poems to Nissim as he wrote them, till one day in 1965, Nissim unexpectedly suggested that they could be brought out as a book. Gieve was shocked; he hadn't thought in terms of a book of poems yet; wasn't sure, in fact, if he wanted to bring one out at this stage. The thought made Gieve uneasy. He went back to Nissim, to say that his exams were approaching and he couldn't afford to have his concentration ruined. Nissim laughed at this, and told him examinations were forever, but that couldn't prevent a book from coming out when it had to! The rest, as they say, is history–or almost–for the book actually came out in 1966; it launched Gieve's illustrious career as a poet.

Nissim published Gieve's book under his own name. It was supposed to be the first of a series of books in a larger publishing programme funded by a Vadilal Dagli, a Bombay industrialist. The project, however, failed to take off. Gieve's book remained the only book that was published, together with six issues of *Poetry India,* which Nissim edited.

I was curious to hear from Gieve what kind of editor and publisher Nissim was. He said: 'There was no major difference of opinion [between Gieve and Nissim] as we were putting the book together. May be there were a few minor things, like deciding the order of the poems. I may have listened to a few of his suggestions of this kind, but most often he was willing to concede to my view. As a publisher he was professional enough, though distribution [of the book] was as usual a problem. The book was widely reviewed, all due to his efforts.'

If Gieve tried to paint a picture of Nissim as he looked at the time, what would it be like? He remarks spontaneously that in his late thirties, Nissim displayed none of the sloppiness that was to become his trademark in later years. He was better-dressed then, though he was never a dandy. His features, however, have remained more or less the same.

I asked Gieve whether Nissim, who lost his own father in 1960, ever felt like a father to him. His answer was precise: 'In my case, in the early years he definitely did feel like a father-figure, but soon he became a friend-figure.' Gieve pondered over the question, and a short while afterwards, came out with a slightly more detailed reply: 'It would be inaccurate to say he ever was a father-figure for me–he was more of a supportive-figure who thought well of my work, for which I was grateful. And very soon this developed into a fine and abiding friendship.' About Nissim's reputation for being a father-figure generally–I remember journalist Nikhil Lakshman once referring to him as the 'Big Daddy of Indian English Poetry' in a private conversation–Gieve is uncertain. He told me two seemingly contradictory things. He first said that, in his view, Nissim was definitely a father-figure who was 'constitutionally helpful', by which he meant that he enjoyed helping younger writers with their drafts. But in Gieve's opinion, Nissim also went out of his way to discourage paternalism by his constant self-irony and self-deprecation, and his ironic statements about the world. If, in spite of this, he continued to be the great patriarch that he was, it meant that the need for this kind of thing is very great, with people clinging to whatever they can.

While on the subject of filial relationships, it is worth noting that like Jussawalla and a few others, Gieve graduated to the level of a personal friend who could visit Nissim at his house, and be introduced to his parents. Nissim's father had passed away by the time Gieve and Nissim had become close, but he has clear memories of his mother, whom he met on a couple of occasions at Mazda Mansion and at The Retreat. She was, like all mothers, kind and affectionate, and welcomed her children's friends who visited them, even though the children were now married and were parents themselves.

According to Gieve, there are two major events in Nissim's life that are responsible for changes in his personality. One is his relationship with Linda Hess. The other is LSD. As both these issues are discussed in the next chapter, I shall not say much about them here. However, I should like to record Gieve's impressions, as a sort of prelude to what follows in the next chapter. His views are remarkably non-judgmental, considering the subjects they deal with: narcotics and extra-martial affairs. On the contrary, Gieve feels that the two events contribute towards improving Nissim's outlook on life: that is why he refers to them as dense.

To deal with the second issue first, Gieve calculates the benefits Nissim derived from LSD by comparing his poetry readings before and after. Before LSD, Nissim's readings at public places were 'cool, distant and they seemed to say "take what you can and forget the rest".' On the other hand, in the late '60s, when he was in the middle of his LSD trip, he 'reached out to the audience to a much greater extent.' Hence, 'one should not underestimate the importance of his LSD experience,' says Gieve.

As for the Linda Hess affair, Gieve points out that it was Hess and Toni, in fact, who were responsible for cementing the friendship between Nissim and himself. He calls Nissim's involvement with Hess 'an important turning point in his life.' It made him realize, once again, that he was not reaching out to people. It was only after he got to know Hess that he began to 'open out towards other people.' Furthermore, 'The affair also brought out other qualities, like his insistence on clarity–at a time when there was so much woolliness around you in thinking, talking, writing–for which I especially admired him.' This 'woolliness' Gieve thinks of as a 'national disease', and says that Nissim responded to his admiration and appreciation, because he knew precisely what he admired and appreciated– and why. And it was Linda Hess who was directly responsible for bringing out qualities in him which might have remained dormant, had he carried on with his humdrum existence.

As I have noted earlier, Nissim knew Hess long before she actually visited India in 1966. Daisy was aware that there was an American woman known as Linda Hess in her husband's life, and from time to time there were the usual outbursts that often take place in such situations. Minakshi Raja narrates an incident that proves how volatile the atmosphere at Mazda Mansion was:

'I used to drop in [at Mazda Mansion] on Sundays to borrow books from Nissim. Daisy would be working in the kitchen, doing domestic chores. I enjoyed visiting them. One day my friend Bilkees Alladin who lives in Hyderabad wrote a play and wanted Nissim to read it, so I took her there along with me. I went in, while Bilkees sat in the car, but Nissim wasn't home. Daisy was walking in the garden with the baby [Elkana] in her arms. I asked her if I could leave a message for Nissim. She said: "Don't you know? He's left me for this American woman!" Then she said: "Please tell him to come back to me. I need him." She said this a couple of times. I was startled. I rushed back to the car. I avoided Nissim for a long time after this. I reported the incident to Nira Benegal.[4] She just heard me out.'

Before I'm accused of getting gossipy, I must bring my narration back to a 'respectable' level, where I speak of my subject's work, rather than his private life.

In the '70s and '80s, Nissim would create a genre of verse in quintessential Indian English, abounding in, among other things, the use of the present continuous. He would call these poems 'Very Indian Poems in Indian English', and they would acquire the status of Kishore Kumar-type film songs in a farmaishi-geet programme. Requests to read these poems would pour in constantly, especially at academic seminars, where a large number of English teachers from the rural areas had gathered. The poems would generate endless debate about Nissim's snobbery and his sense of humour, and lead people to ask whether he had the moral justification to make fun of those who obviously came from less privileged backgrounds than himself. Everyone wanted to know, in other words, if the poems were politically correct. I shall discuss these controversial poems and the issues that, to my mind, they bring to the forefront later. But I wish to remind readers here that the origins of the 'Indian English' poems lie in Nissim's experiences at Mithibai College. It all began with a chance remark that someone in the college once made, about his inability to speak English the way most people in India spoke it. After that, 'I thought it would be a good idea to observe how Indians spoke English,' he said to me. 'I started listening to people's English on my train journeys from Bombay Central to Vile Parle and back. I took down lots of notes. I found that the Indian English of Bombay was different from that of, say, Calcutta.' One of Nissim's famous (infamous? notorious?) Indian English poems is called 'Goodbye Party for Miss Pushpa T.S.'. Few people know that the words were actually used, more or less as they occur in the title of the poem, by none other than the principal of the college, A.B. Yajnik, to whom Nissim is naturally indebted (and whom he has no qualms about thus exposing). But it was not during train journeys alone that he got all the inspired phrases that went into his Indian English poems; there were enough of them that, besides the principal, he obtained from the professors and students. So what he was really inventing was Indian English as people from Gujarati homes spoke it, prompting some people to remark that the poems were really in Gujarati English rather than Indian English.

India went to war with China in 1962, and Pakistan in 1965. One would have thought that Nissim, with his political affinities of the '40s and '50s, had a definite position on the war, which would find expression in his poetry and prose. But these upheavals in India's recent history simply passed him by, without his taking particular note. The reason for this, according to Nissim, is that 'Everytime I tried to write a poem about these events, it would be bad . . . as bad as my trying to write, say, a travel poem.' To be sure, he did write a few poems on the wars, but was dissatisfied with them because he thought of them as journalistic poems, and is relieved they were never published. Nor did he care to preserve them–I couldn't trace any of them among his papers, scattered all over his PEN office. Nevertheless, Nissim cannot explain why the poems could not be brought up to a certain standard, no matter how hard he tried. My own answer is that it has to do with aesthetics; he is suspicious of anything that is perceived as topical. This, to my mind, is a limitation because it is perfectly possible to tackle topical subjects in a poem, without letting the poem degenerate into propaganda. The history of literature is full of examples of writers who have been able to negotiate the seemingly contentious issues of art and politics, and arrive at a via media. The most positive (and reassuring) remark that comes from Nissim, in this context, is that he hasn't given up yet!

Most of the poems that Nissim wrote when he was at Mithibai College, were included in *Hymns in Darkness* (1976). 'Goodbye Party for Miss Pushpa T. S' appears in this book. The poem that follows 'Goodbye Party' is 'Guru', and Ranjit Hoskote tells of how he once overheard Nissim saying to someone that the poem is actually based on a real-life godman he happened to visit with (as usual) a colleague from the college. I did not know this when I discussed the poem in my article 'How Secular is Modern Indian Poetry in English?' (1992).[5] What I said about the poem, quoting its last two lines ('If saints are like this /what hope is there then for us?'), was that although these lines (together with the rest of the poem) give readers the impression that he was being ironic about godmen, he was actually sympathetic towards them; the irony, then, was only an eyewash. Since this poem appeared in *Hymns in Darkness,* I assumed it was a post-LSD poem: after LSD, he completely gave up whatever atheism was left in him, and went the other way, proclaiming he had seen God under the influence of the drug. I thought, therefore, that on the face of it, the poem was inaccurate, hypocritical even, not realizing it was possibly written before his 'addiction'. I still have not been able to establish the exact time at which it was composed. It seems unlikely it was written in the early '60s, for if that were true, it would have been included in *The Exact Name,* which appeared in 1965. It's most likely that it was written between 1965 and 1970, just as Nissim was embarking on his narcotic adventures, and, following the example of the Beat poets, experimenting with pop spirituality. The information I obtained from Hoskote's eavesdropping also testifies to this, for by 1965, Nissim was well entrenched in Mithibai College, and familiar enough with his colleagues to accompany them here and there. The comment I made in my article therefore stands.

The Unfinished Man,[6] dedicated to Laeeq and Zafar (Futehally), was published by the Calcutta-based Writers Workshop in 1960. The Workshop itself was founded only a couple of years earlier by P. Lal, a poet and scholar. Although Nissim and Lal eventually fell out, (Nissim earned a reputation for quality and Lal–so to speak–for quantity), it remains to Lal's credit that the Writers Workshop brought out two of Nissim's most widely-appreciated collections, *The Unfinished Man* and *The Exact Name.* In the '70s the high-profile Oxford University Press would take him under its wing; but the two books it would bring out, *Hymns in Darkness* and *Latter-Day Psalms* would not meet with the same applause as the earlier collections. Perhaps the highest of praise comes from Jussawalla, who told me that some of the poems in *The Unfinished Man* made him wish that he had written them! N.P. Acharya, a former colleague of mine, says in one of his articles: 'The five years from 1959 to 1964 . . . proved to be the most productive years in the poetic career of Ezekiel. Almost all his finest poems were written during this period. *The Unfinished Man,* a thin volume containing just ten poems, all written in 1959, appeared in 1960. The Writers Workshop, Calcutta, which published this book, also brought out Mr Ezekiel's next volume of verse *The Exact Name,* in 1964 [sic], containing twenty poems. I believe Ezekiel's reputation as a poet rests solely on these thirty poems.'[7]

The epigraph of *The Unfinished Man* is from a poem by W.B. Yeats; Yeats, together with W.H. Auden, T.S. Eliot and Ezra Pound, influenced Nissim deeply. In the lines that Nissim chooses for the epigraph, Yeats speaks of the ignominy and distress of boyhood, as it changes into manhood, and of the pain and clumsiness of the man who is at best unfinished, and knows it. The persona that he creates in his poems is exactly like that; human, imperfect, subject to failings; not much can be expected out of him.

If the ten poems in the book have to be classified, only a few of them that are in the moral-philosophical-spiritual mode will be found to go over ground covered in previous volumes. The rest chart unexplored territory. Special mention must be made here of the two Bombay city poems, 'Urban' and 'A Morning Walk', and of a biographical poem on the painter Jamini Roy, which, coming at the end of the book, serves as a counterpoint. There are autobiographical poems and love poems, which are of great interest to me as a biographer; they show that, as he matured, Nissim became less inhibited about writing in the 'confessional' mode. All the ten poems in *The Unfinished Man* are formal, making judicious use of rhyme, stanza and metre, over which Nissim by this time had attained mastery.

To begin with the Bombay poems, both 'Urban' and 'Morning Walk', as I point out in an article,[8] are concerned with the clash between a bucolic dream world and a rotten actual one, on which one cannot turn one's back. In the article, I reject the view of Chetan Karnani, who sees these poems as the lamentations 'of a man who wants to run away from the city's turmoil, but does not know where he should go.' I use Nissim's own statement, made in his interview with John B. Beston, to refute this; in the interview, he says categorically: 'I would never leave Bombay–it's a series of commitments.' I consider Nissim's use of prosody and rhyme; I agree with Acharya who says that the metre and rhyme actually bring out the claustrophobia of the poet persona . . . Finally, I argue that although the images in the two poems seem allegorical, the poems are specifically about Bombay if we take into account the manner in which Nissim stands in relation to the images, weaving into them autobiographical facts from his life. To support my contention I refer to his use of the term 'barbaric' to describe Bombay (which, of course, coincides with novelist Raja Rao's description of the city in *The Serpent and the Rope,* published the same year as *The Unfinished Man*).

Nissim's Bombay poems inspired a whole lot of younger post-Independence poets to write poems on the city. As pointed out in Chapter Two, by the '80s, there were so many of them that I was able to compile an anthology of poems on Bombay city for a special number of the *Literary Endeavour*.

Like all his previous volumes, *The Unfinished Man* has some poems with a moral. 'Enterprise' is the most well-known of these; it has been included by R. Parthasarathy in *Ten Twentieth Century Indian Poets.*[9] There are poems in the earlier books that anticipate 'Enterprise', though none of them quite comes to the conclusion that 'home is where we have to gather grace.' (When Nissim published his *Collected Poems* in 1988, he, for some reason, replaced 'gather grace' with 'earn our grace' in the last line of the poem. To this day, no one really knows why he did so; most critics and reviewers regard it as a change not for the better. I remember asking Nissim about it after I had read a review of *Collected Poems* by Elizabeth Reuben. But his answer was vague. It is possible that the revision was made at the insistence of one of his editors at Oxford University Press.) The other moral poems in *The Unfinished Man* are engrossing, not for the morals they expound, but because they shed useful light on Nissim's married life in the late '50s. 'Commitment,' which makes use of English proverbs such as 'look before you leap', 'slow and steady wins the race' and 'a bird in hand is worth two in the bush', ends with the following stanza:

> The fog is thick, and men are lost
> Who wanted only quiet lives
> And failed to count the growing cost
> Of cushy jobs or unloved wives.

In a general way, I would like to interpret these lines in terms of Nissim's familiar contempt for domestic things. Specifically, however, they indicate that by the end of the '50s, six to seven years after he had got married, he began to think of his marriage as a mistake and regretted it. The lines project Daisy as a demanding wife who did not let her husband be; she was like any other woman who wanted material comforts, forgetting that her husband was a poet. Similarly, 'Morning Prayer', which opens with the words 'God grant me privacy', is important, not for what it says to God (by way of prayer or otherwise), but for the revelation that (i) Nissim had no privacy at home–or thought he had no privacy–after marriage; and (ii) he felt marriage to be at cross-purposes with a higher kind of contemplative life. These conclusions emerge, even if we take into account that it is poems we are reading, where the persona in the poem need not represent the poet himself; and that the poet may be being ironic.

There are two love poems in *The Unfinished Man*, but once again in at least one of them, the distinction between fact and fiction is blurred. 'Event' is about the boredom the man-woman relationship is capable of generating. While Bruce King wonders whether the woman being talked about is 'another woman'[10] with whom Nissim was having an affair, it's equally possible that she is Daisy, especially as sexual intercourse is depicted in the poem as monotonous. On the other hand, 'Love Sonnet', which is more about the mechanics of lovemaking and less about a relationship, may be based on an extra-marital affair; in the eleventh line, Nissim says: 'We lose ourselves in mingling with the crowd' (this also makes it a Bombay poem). However, it is the last line, 'A certain happiness would be–to die', that establishes it as a love poem. Vilas Sarang criticizes the line for taking a particularly unoriginal view of love. He says: 'Ezekiel's numerous poems about love are, as might be expected, chiefly analytical. When he tries to express the emotion of love, the result is poor. "Love Sonnet" offers Romantic cliches, undistinguished detail, and ends with that most cliched of Romantic ideas: "A certain happiness would be–to die!" '[11]

Finally, however, Nissim comes to the point directly. 'Marriage' and 'Case Study' are by no means veiled autobiographical poems–they are forthright. In the first poem, the marriage is Nissim's own. The last three stanzas of this poem are as follows:

> I went through this, believing all,
> Our love denied the Primal Fall.
> Wordless, we walked among the trees,
> And felt immortal as the breeze.
>
> However many times we came
> Apart, we came together. The same.
> Thing over and over again.
> Then suddenly the mark of Cain
>
> Began to show on her and me.
> Why should I ruin the mystery
> By harping on the suffering rest,
> Myself a frequent wedding guest.

'Case Study' anticipates 'Background, Casually', and like that poem, may be described as Nissim's autobiography in verse. It contains all the details of his life, such as his involvement with the Royists, his switching of jobs, and his marriage, 'the worst mistake of all'. He wears a third-person mask in the poem, as if he were having a dialogue with someone who is really himself. In the last stanza, he says:

> He came to me and this what I said:
> 'The pattern will remain, unless you break
> It with a sudden jerk; but use your head . . .
> Not all returned as heroes who had fled
> In wanting both to have and eat the cake.
> Not all who fail are counted with the fake.'

In advocating caution and moderation, rather than brashness and violence, Nissim was settling for the familiar 'middle path', which to some of his friends (Toni Patel, for instance) feel is responsible for the lifelong suffering he brought on himself. These friends feel that if he was dissatisfied with his marriage, he should have divorced Daisy and set both of them free.

Although King feels that Nissim's autobiographical poems are guarded, as compared to, say, American confessional poetry,[12] they reveal enough about his personal life, despite the various strategies that he adopts (such as the use of a third-person mask).

The last poem in *Unfinished Man*, 'Jamini Roy', stands in contrapuntal relation to the other poems in the book. This is because 'Jamini Roy' is a biographical poem about a painter from Bengal who '. . . started with a different style /He travelled, so he found his roots /His rage became a quiet smile /Prolific in its proper fruits.' The lesson Nissim learns from him is that if one changes to a style that is harmonious with the aspirations of the people, one automatically finds one's roots. To me, however, this is merely gibberish that betrays his desire to be assimilated into the mainstream; throughout his life, Nissim would self-consciously attempt to be a little more Indian than he actually was.

The meta-text of 'Jamini Roy' is religious: being one with one's surroundings, the way the Bengali painter was, also implies that one settles for a Hindu way of life. This, at last, serves as an eye-opener to King; while he earlier insisted that all Nissim's poetry is secular, he now qualifies his stand to say: '. . . in Ezekiel's initially agnostic vision the experience of the secular world is seen as in itself having a kind of religious nature, although it is difficult to define the precise nature of this experience beyond it being moral and life being holy.'[13]

This is especially important to me, because it endorses my belief that Nissim is a religious poet. And 'Jamini Roy' provides the first clues.

Flower Power

A man is married to a woman, howsoever unhappily. Suddenly there's a 'foreign body' released into the bloodstream of this bond that threatens to destroy it. Eventually the bond is not destroyed, but it is considerably weakened. I'm talking of Linda Hess and her passion for Nissim. I'm talking of Nissim's affair with Hess, which until now was carried on in safe and distant lands, far from the suspecting eyes of Daisy. But Hess's visit to Bombay in 1966 brought the issue centre stage: the action, as it were, was taking place on home turf. What Daisy may have known of earlier, but only in the form of rumours and hearsay, was now confirmed: her husband was in love with another woman.

Who exactly was Linda Hess? She was an American of German-Jewish descent. She was a Kabir expert who produced some of the finest translations of Bijak. She was educated, intelligent and articulate, attributes that Nissim found lacking in his wife. Ranjit Hoskote feels 'Linda Hess must have represented to Nissim everything that his own conservative wife was not: beauty, brains and liberation. She enabled him to live the way men in the '60s wanted to–with a dutiful wife at home and a liberated girlfriend outside. Nissim has always oscillated between the conservative and the bohemian, and the presence of Linda Hess in his life would be considered a good example of his bohemianism. Besides, both of them would have seemed exotic to each other.'

Nissim, by temperament, is secretive (especially about his love affairs), so his biographer comes up against a wall when he tries to ferret out information from him. Linda Hess, on the other hand, is today based in California, where she teaches in the Department of Eastern Religions at the University of Berkley. Because her specialization is Medieval Hindi, she is a colleague and friend of Philip Lugtendorf who teaches Hindi at the University of Iowa. I met Lugtendorf when I was at the University of Iowa in the latter half of 1996, for the International Writing Program. I tried to contact Hess with Lugtendorf's help to get her version of the story. But I was unsuccessful in my attempts. Even the fact that I was headed for California in November to do readings from my work did not make my access to her any the more easy. I came away from the US without meeting Linda Hess.

Jussawalla remembers meeting Hess when he returned from England in 1966–the very year she came to Bombay. He says: 'It's possible the affair with Nissim was already on when I met her.' Then he adds: 'Those were the days of Allen Ginsberg and the Beats.' Connecting a poet's infidelity to a popular cultural movement (as both Hoskote and Jussawalla do) is another way of looking at his bohemianism. Later in this chapter, I interpret Nissim's 'experiments' with drugs in the same way: by taking drugs he was only responding to the social and cultural trends of the age.

My 'secret source' revealed some highly classified information. He said: 'One day Nissim decided to walk out of the family. Daisy took her two daughters, Kalpana and Kavita, who were not in their teens yet, and went crying to Adil's [Jussawalla'sJ mother. She at once asked Daisy to "leave him".'

Jussawalla himself is uncertain of this. He says: 'I don't know when– and why–my mother told Daisy to leave Nissim. Maybe she was upset when she said so. Neither my mother nor Daisy are the easiest of women.' Jussawalla took the trouble of contacting his mother on my behalf, to see if she still remembered what exactly had happened. This is what she told him: 'Kavita and Kalpana came to my house, along with Daisy, and said that Nissim was leaving them. Kavita said, they would like to live here, at my place. After that, Daisy would keep phoning me. So I said to her one day, if you're so unhappy with Nissim, why don't you divorce him? Daisy was shocked. There was an Indian lady [sic] who was supportive of Daisy. She used to take her out in her car. Daisy said to me: "You're no longer my friend; this lady is." But she still continued to visit me, and talk to me on the phone.'

There are other dimensions to the story. One of these is that the rift between Nissim and Daisy, for which the immediate impetus was Linda Hess, was further aggravated when Daisy wanted to settle down in America and Nissim refused. This was around the year 1967, when Nissim was invited to the University of Chicago to deliver lectures on Indian Writing in English.

He had several reasons for doing so. For one thing, he had a confirmed job in Bombay. For another, Nissim has always been opposed to emigrating to the West for good, though he enjoyed short visits to foreign countries. However, on a more gossipy note, I am tempted to suggest that as Linda Hess lived in America, Nissim would have never really wanted to take Daisy there. He had made that mistake once, when he went to Leeds, but he certainly wouldn't want to make the same mistake again. It's also likely that, at that point, Hess herself was unsure of where she wanted to live– Bombay, LA, London–and Nissim's decisions would be tied up with hers.

What was the upshot of the Linda Hess affair? Nissim could have divorced Daisy and gone away with Linda Hess. But that is not what he chose to do. Like some of his close friends, I had a serious chat with him on the subject, and asked him why he did not set both himself and Daisy free, if misery was all there was left to their marriage. I discovered it was the moralist in him that opted against such a course of action.

The Jews in India are in a unique situation. They do not have a personal Jewish law (as the Muslims do). They are also not governed by the 1955 Hindu Marriage Act, which forbids polygamy.[1] As far as the synagogue is concerned, a husband and wife who want to mutually part, have only to inform it of their decision; they do not have to state their reasons. The synagogue itself doesn't grant the divorce, but it gives advice. This being the case, Nissim would have had much more leeway than the average Indian. If he was serious about Hess (who is also Jewish) and wanted to have her as a second wife without divorcing Daisy, he would, in all probability, have been able to bring it off, without too many legal hassles.

Like many creative and thinking people, however, Nissim is law unto himself (or even above the law, like Plato's philosopher-king) when it comes to taking decisions that affect his personal life. This is how he rationalized it for me.

He began by distinguishing divorce from separation, and argued that while most people would prefer the former, with him it was the other way round. This is because, to him, separation, unlike divorce, did not imply a complete severance of ties. Nissim sees marriage as sacred. He still regards women as helpless without men, dependent on them for economic and emotional sustenance (though he agrees that this may change in the next century). A separation then–as opposed to a divorce–allows a man to have the best of both worlds. He lives away from his wife, and is free to do as he pleases, but he also continues to provide for her, visit her periodically, and give her the feeling, above all, that she hasn't been abandoned. In short, Nissim sees divorce as sinful. These are some of his statements: 'Marriage can be a failure in so many different ways, but if it comes to the point of enmity between partners; then to preach to either one of them would be folly.' (I see this remark as an honest attempt on his part to take the blame for the failure of his marriage). He says further: 'In marriage, the rules of the game are known to both parties,' and he defines these rules as 'having children, bringing them up, and becoming grandparents in spite of all the quarrels.' About the question of fidelity, Nissim believes that 'within marriage, fidelity is assumed, unless both partners have an understanding that they can each do what they like.' I probe a little on the business of fidelity, and he says it would all depend on the individual, though it's true that a lot of people have relationships outside marriage and yet continue to stay together.

These views are directly linked to Nissim's ideas about the family. It just so happened that 1994, the year in which we were discussing the role of the family, was declared by the UN as the Year of the Family. I let Nissim speak in a somewhat rambling manner, and this is what he spontaneously said:

'Traditionally and historically, the family has always been an important part of every society. In every family there are specific problems that may come up, as the family grows and develops—quarrels between brothers and sisters, for example. Sometimes these problems may be marginal and may be dropped. But I can't see any alternative to family life. If you have a family, when you die there are at least people to come to your funeral.

'The Indian traditional attitude, where a family holds together [despite all the odds] is sounder than the Western approach to family, although even in the West, they are going back today to the concept of the family. It's true that sometimes the family may seem like a superficial phenomenon, but I wouldn't endorse Western individualism of the extreme kind either. I know it for a fact that in the US, attitudes towards the family are rapidly changing.' When I suggest, after he has finished talking, that the family is also conducive to the undesirable notion of patriarchy, Nissim simply answers that he would take it all as a part of the reality.

As stated above, Nissim's ideas on sensitive issues such as marriage and family, no matter how objective they appear, are, in the last analysis, a throwback to his own personal life, and the way he has organized it. In a way, he is only justifying the fact that he did not divorce Daisy, although he was involved with another woman. He is prioritizing sin, separation to him being a lesser evil than divorce. But Jussawalla seems to say it on behalf of us all, when he refutes Nissim's claim that he did not divorce his wife because it's sinful; he goes to the extent of alleging that his Judaism itself is suspect, because it did not prevent him from adultery, which is also sinful.

Toni Patel is less scathing. She admits that she was his confidante, with whom he would discuss personal problems; but she claims he had a way of talking about these things generally, without being specific. She also believes that if Nissim was circumspect and secretive about his private life, to the point of imposing a sort of censorship on himself, it was because he could empathize and sympathize with the opposite party. This did not necessarily mean, of course, that he was taking the blame for his actions. At the same time, it proved he still had a conscience.

The five years between 1965 and 1970 saw the friendship of Nissim and the Patels flower. The reason for this, according to Toni, is that 'we had many things in common, he was the art critic of the *Times,* and I was doing exhibitions of the work of Indian painters. He would give me advice as to what to read and so on, which I found valuable, though I did not necessarily follow it.' Together, Toni, Geive and Nissim formed a fine threesome, with Toni and Nissim helping to set Gieve up in his artistic pursuits, and he in turn becoming their medical consultant. While Nissim published Gieve's first book of poems in 1966, Toni helped him to hold his first art exhibition the following year.

It became crystal clear to Toni, that of the two men she was close to, both of them remarkable and unusual human beings, it was Gieve she was interested in romantically. About Nissim, her feelings were much more ambivalent. This is how she analysed their relationship:

'I've never intruded on Nissim's personal boundaries or territories. I've never talked to him about his affairs with women–I may have heard about them, but I never knew anything at first-hand. I was simply not interested. I was much more interested in the creative aspect of the man. He's a very, very complex and mysterious person. For example, he doesn't value anything brilliant he's written more than he values anything mediocre. He's grossly undervalued in some of his work–like the plays. I do not have a large number of gut-level friendships, but with Nissim it is one such, for such a friendship also has to be with someone with whom I have an equal relationship. So it is with him as well.'

Toni went on to discuss Nissim's attitude to women, and sounded almost like his defense counsel, defending him against the charge of being a chauvinist and a womanizer. Nissim himself has always felt that he was unlike a whole lot of men who had hang-ups about women. Toni is in agreement with him here. She has no doubts that, for him, men and women have always been equal. Yet, from time to time, he has innocently betrayed this sense of equality. One such time was after her marriage to Gieve, when he started to introduce her at parties as 'the wife of a well-known painter'. When Toni objected to this, Nissim did not quite understand her. On the contrary, he was surprised, for he felt most women would have loved to let the world know that their husbands were famous. Toni says: 'I had to educate him on this chauvinistic aspect.'

Similarly, she had a grouse against him (she calls it his weakness) for spending his valuable time on people, trying to help them to become writers, even if he knew they did not possess the talent. Toni herself was a recipient of this largesse, but then no one can say that she isn't talented. Toni's real interest was in theatre direction, but she also knew she had it in her to be a critic. It is here that Nissim came to her aid. 'He encouraged me to write a great deal–art and theatre criticism, things literary. He never criticized it, but then he did not praise it either, except occasionally. He once said to me when I reviewed a novel: "That was a good review. I almost wish I'd written it myself." Occasionally, though, he could be very generous in his praise. For example, when I wrote a review of Alyque Padamsee's "Jesus Christ Superstar", which the *Times of India* refused to publish, Nissim published it in the *Indian PEN* and gave me several offprints. However, I never consciously expected him to give me a critical appraisal of anything I did. It would be too much, coming from a man of his stature.'

After their marriage, Toni and Gieve formed the habit of travelling to Sanjan on the Gujarat coast, just beyond the Maharashtra-Gujarat border, where Gieve was doctor-in-charge at the primary health centre. Nissim would board a train from Bombay Central station on weekends, and go all the way to Sanjan, a two- to three-hour ride from the city, to be with them. He enjoyed their company that much. They also provided him with an alternative to family life, which, for him, was by now over. It is for this reason that he also made regular visits to their flat in Bombay, situated in Malabar Apartments on Napean Sea Road, almost at walking distance from Mazda Mansion. Recalling those days, Toni says: 'Avan, my daughter, was a baby then. She would sit under an umbrella and listen to our conversations on Soviet Russia or whatever. She's very fond of Nissim and she loved listening to us.'

Around this time, the Mazda Mansion on Warden Road was pulled down by its owner, to make way for a new apartment block that was to come up in its place. As compensation, Nissim and Daisy were offered a two-bedroom flat in a nearby building, Kala Niketan, for which they did not have to pay anything extra. Minakshi Raja rightly describes this as 'a stroke of luck', for the price of the flat today would be over a crore of rupees. The irony, of course, is that Nissim wouldn't be spending the rest of his life at Kala Niketan. It would be Daisy's home, where she would bring up the children, who were well on their way to becoming adults, while Nissim himself would retreat to The Retreat, from where, in a sense, he started out. The Retreat, an old building, cannot stand comparison to Mazda Mansion or Kala Niketan, just as Bombay Central, as a neighbourhood, is no match for Warden Road. Raja, probably one of the few people who has been to all Nissim's dwelling places, recalls a time she visited him at The Retreat with Shakoor, who passed away in 1972. She describes it as 'bare, there was nothing attractive about the flat, it didn't even have a fridge.' Raja herself is known for her tasteful interior decoration; when she says 'Nissim loves my bedroom because it's nicely done. . . it was his dream bedroom,' one knows exactly what she is talking about. She reveals that Nissim even invited her to The Retreat to give him a couple of suggestions as to how to improve the place. But when she did so, he was not really interested. She attributes this partly to the fact that he has never had enough money, for most of the family stocks and shares are in Daisy's name.

Nissim's friendships with the opposite sex were of two kinds. There were those women with whom he was sexually involved. Then there were women like Toni Patel, Minakshi Raja and Gauri Deshpande, who were friends of the 'platonic' variety. These were, no doubt, women he could confide in; however, as is proved by some of Toni's remarks, certain social barriers continued to exist. In other words, all these women respected his privacy and did not possess a voyeuristic curiosity about his sexual life. Gauri Deshpande speaks of the time Nissim went to spend a few days with her at her flat in Pune:

I think [it was] '66 or '67. . . when he was undergoing some sort of a personal crisis, and so was I. But the nature of our friendship was not the sort that invited such revelations. And I think both of us welcomed this formality-cum-friendship which allowed us to talk of matters that were important to us, but not family-related-personal. He talked of his experiences in California, LSD, religion, God; things that were turning his life around; and I talked about the trials and frustrations of teaching English at the undergraduate level which were soon to turn my life around.'

Deshpande's reference to LSD sets the stage for a discussion of this very important phase in Nissim's life, which, as far as his poetry is concerned, serves as the boundary line that separates the early from the later Ezekiel. What exactly did he do? Between 1967–the year he went to Chicago–and 1969, he took LSD twenty-four times, to find out what the drug would do to him as a human being and a poet. In his interview to *Health and Nutrition*, he speaks of the genesis and the outcome of the experiment:

> I heard a lot about LSD and had attended several meetings [in America] where people (mostly writers and artists) took LSD, but I had never tried it myself. Then somebody suggested why don't I take it. I said, 'No, I don't want to. I've heard that people lose control after taking the drug.' The person said, that happens only when it is taken in large doses, in limited quantities there is no risk. And then I realized that everything that people said about LSD is true: there is a mind expansion, you do have visions and you do hear voices, which perhaps is your subconscious talking. It was these voices that told me to become a vegetarian. I was a non-vegetarian at the time but had been wavering for a long time. This experience kind of decided things for me.
>
> I took LSD several times after that, but stopped about fifteen years ago, when the drug was banned abroad and the doses that were sent to me were of dubious quality and quantity. In any case, taking the drug made no difference to the quality of my poems. In that sense, LSD was a disappointment.[2]

A more elaborate, first-person account is to be found in an unpublished essay he wrote during the time he was taking the drug. He called the essay, 'DRUGS: A Personal Footnote.' I reproduce it for the benefit of readers. The emphases in the essay are original.

I am interested in the disciplined use of drugs for expanding the consciousness, and for the variety of emotional and intellectual experiences which they offer. Drug addiction is another matter. The abuse of drugs is another matter. To know how to use drugs, in what way they are dangerous, their specific qualities and dosages, the expertise that is available for exploring their potential, these are among my areas of interest and concern.

It was not always so. I first made an LSD 'trip' in April 1967, when I was forty-two years old. My age was a great help, and so was my motive which was to know what happens . . . The subsequent trips were carefully organized to go deeper into the experience and to obtain the maximum benefit from it. I learnt how to avoid the dangers, a kind of knowledge which assumes a measure of self-knowledge. There is [sic] a number of do's and don'ts which must be scrupulously obeyed. Indulgence leads to disaster but caution and a sound healthy approach brings revelations, even illuminations.

In a more limited way, I've found marijuana also immensely useful. My appreciation of music and art was broadened and intensified. I increased my capacity for concentration, my love of silence. I had glimpses of my true self which I had never dreamt existed in such depth and complexity. My understanding of philosophical, metaphysical and religious questions became keener and acquired greater immediacy. I also saw the limits of my abilities more clearly and developed a sense of destiny. I owe more to LSD and marijuana than to my reading, though perhaps without it I may have benefited less from them.

I am not dependent on drugs. Their value depends on what one does when not on drugs. An insight that is not applied, a revelation that is not tested in practice, an illumination that is not made to guide daily conduct, however imperfectly, loses its power very rapidly. All it leaves behind is vanity, spiritual pride, the delusion of wisdom. As it has been often said in different ways, it makes all the difference in the world whether you use drugs or are used by them.

I do not claim to have succeeded in using my drug experience fully or properly. To know the extent to which one has succeeded or failed is essential if the decision is to continue using them. It can be a source of strength or of weakness. Drug-taking cannot be a substitute for effort in advancing self-expression and self-projection but it can, definitely, aid that effort. As a servant, it is marvelous, as a master tyrannical. I never long for a drug or allow myself to feel that I must have it, I never take it when my morale is low, when I am discouraged or when I feel uncreative, emotionally and intellectually arid. I fight all those undesirable states of mind in other ways, practical and ideational. The time for taking a mind-affecting drug for me, is when my mind is on the top of the world.

Most of my LSD trips were taken in the company of a 'guide' whom I had instructed on how to guide. Today, I take my trips alone and work as my own guide. Marijuana I have taken in the company of friends, but I learn most from it when I have a single, sympathetic listener. If both of us take marijuana, I need to be prepared to be the listener. A full-scale dialogue or argument does not work. If there are distractions, nothing very valuable can be understood: the commonplaces are encountered. (Even this is not a waste of time, since we all tend to forget the commonplaces of life in the pursuit of sublimities. In reality, the commonplaces are sublime.)

When abandoned to laughter in a drug-session, there is a sense of liberation. Similarly, abandonment to weeping has a cathartic effect. Neither should be controlled but eventually it is necessary to examine the causes of the laughter and the tears. Without that examination, only the experience is made but its meaning is missed. That is why thorough preparation is needed for a drug experience. If you set out on a journey without adequate equipment, you may lose your way. The drug is only a ticket for the journey.

I have not explained anything but I hope I have hinted at possibilities. That is all I want to do in this note. I cannot expect to instruct but I wish to make it clear that for those really interested, instruction is easily available. Drugs for kicks provide only kicks, and some hard ones at that. The price is too high. The unbalancing, unhinging effects, particularly on the young, take years to overcome. And the return is only to 'normality' with nothing gained in the interim period.[3]

At the end of the essay, Nissim supplies a reading list, emphasizing thereby that for him drug-taking is serious, scholarly business. He mentions two well-known books by Aldous Huxley, *The Doors of Perception* (1954) and *Heaven and Hell* (1956), and one by S. Cohen, entitled *The Beyond Within: The LSD Story* (Atheneum Press; 1964). The two Huxley volumes are about this twentieth-century British author's obsessive interest in mysticism and parapsychology, that led to experiments with mescaline and LSD. He was undoubtedly a role model for Nissim here.

The above essay was written in the '70s, while Nissim was still on the drug. However, the glamour associated with drug addiction outlived his actual consumption of LSD. It went on to become one of the milestones of his life, about which he was interrogated by journalists, like his sea-voyage to India in 1952, when he scrubbed decks. His statements, when examined closely, often enable us to see how Nissim developed a perspective on his own activities. For example, he writes in *Science Age* of March 1984: 'My rationalism and anti-religious credo could not, however, stand up to my LSD experiences, which began in early 1967. From that phase in my life to my present one, I've found it more and more easy to reconcile all values based on science with the reality of the mystical and the mysterious.'[4] Ten years later, when V.C. Harris comments that '. . . Ezekiel is not the kind of person one would associate with something like LSD–he looks too sober and genteel for that,' and proceeds to ask Nissim how he feels about LSD, 'looking back on the whole trajectory now in the light of his present-day concerns,' his answer is:

'I don't regret LSD. I did learn a little bit from that experience, but I never wanted to continue with it. You do such things–like travelling to China or Japan, to see things, to get to know life all around, but not to settle down there. You always come back.'[5]

By the time I started working on this book in 1994, Nissim, presumably, had nothing left to say about LSD: he had said it all. Yet the topic frequently came up in our conversation. During one such chat, what he said to me was a slightly more elaborate version of the statement he made in *Health and Nutrition* (quoted above):

'When I read Aldous Huxley, he claimed that LSD actually led to mind expansion and expansion of consciousness. Till the end of the drug trip, you heard things and so on, and after that you went back to normal. Apart from Huxley, I read everything else about LSD I could lay my hands on. Then one day someone [Nissim doesn't say who] came to my room in the US, may be after a lecture, and asked me pointedly whether I had actually taken LSD. When I said no, he asked, why not? My answer was that I had read so many stories about young people who had suffered after taking the drug, and becoming addicted–jumping from rooftops and so on. His reply was that if I took it under his supervision, the effect of the drug wouldn't last beyond an hour; whereas I had thought it would last over a day. So I agreed. This man was someone who was a part of this whole experiment [with drugs] that was taking place in New York. He was quite young, and there was a whole generation of young people, like himself, into it, and there were even seminars on it.

'When I took LSD, there was a companion of mine who didn't take it who was by my side. For the first twenty minutes or so nothing happened, but then suddenly this thing about mind expansion described by Huxley and others started to happen to me. When the man who supplied the drug to me turned up the following Sunday, I told him what had happened. He said he'd give me a larger dose, the effect of which would last the whole day. He did, and that's when all those things [described by Huxley] happened to me.

'I had one more dose in New York, before returning to Bombay. My supplier gave me the stuff to take to Bombay–large doses that would have a day-long effect. I took it once every three months at The Retreat. However, by this time, drugs were banned in the US, so my supplier-friend wrote to me saying he couldn't guarantee me my normal dosage. Besides, drugs also went out of fashion because of the havoc they created in the lives of young people, who thought themselves gods. So I stopped taking drugs completely.'

LSD had a certain long-term effects on Nissim. One of these was that it made him give up his atheism, attributable to his M. N. Roy days. But he dislikes the suggestion that, together with atheism, he also forsook some of his rationalism, and became prone to mystical states of mind. He said to me: 'In the post-LSD phase, I dropped my atheism, not my rationalism. However, I didn't then use the term "rationalist" as one who didn't have any connection with mysticism at all. The Rationalist movement both in the UK and USA definitely involved things like Russian mysticism. Besides, the courses in psychology that I had taken in London taught me that I could call myself a rationalist and yet behave as irrationally as I wanted.'

Nissim believes that LSD did not change his poetry for the better or worse. I expanded the scope of the question to ask him whether he had acquired control over his mind. His answer: 'I cannot claim to have hundred precent control over my mind. It could be anything from fifty to sixty-five per cent, which is manifested, say, when I write a poem or make serious decisions. I'm not completely reconciled to this fact, though. I would have liked perfect control. I'm not the type of artist who feels that control thwarts creativity. That is why, I can't drink in order to write. It was the same with LSD.'

The most visible effect of LSD was that it made him take to vegetarianism in a big way. He enjoys explaining how it came about: 'My vegetarianism was definitely a part of the LSD experience. I heard voices. One of the voices I heard told me you will never climb to the top of the spiritual mountain so stay where you are and be as good as you can be.'

Nissim took the dictates of the voice seriously. Giving up the eating of meat was one of the ways in which he tried to 'be as good as you can be'. If this seems irrational, so be it.

'Once I became a vegetarian, I decided I would never cook or eat meat-dishes at home. However, in order not to seem too fussy in others' homes, I would give in sometimes and have a piece or two of meat, along with the gravy. But then when I found that this was happening a bit too frequently, I decided to take a stronger line and make it clear to all my hosts (even in America) that I was a vegetarian.'

Nissim rejects the suggestion that his vegetarianism may have had something to do with his concern about health: 'No, I did not exactly become a vegetarian on health grounds. I'm not an expert in that aspect so I can't really tell. There are too many special concepts that come into the picture.'

On the other hand, he agrees that he is concerned about animal welfare and–in today's terminology–animal rights; and that his decision to become a vegetarian is a direct outcome of this:

'In the US those who advocate vegetarianism constantly emphasize on what it means to slaughter thousands of animals, particularly lambs, per day to feed a human population. Since the meat of baby lambs is more tasty, these lambs were sometimes killed within twenty hours of their birth.'

How do Nissim's friends, well-wishers and admirers react to his LSD trips? The harshest response comes from Ranjit Hoskote, young enough to be his grandson. 'The ontology of the LSD experience, on which Nissim's religious poems are based, is idiotic,' Hoskote thinks. He goes on to reveal that 'at an unguarded moment he even told me he saw Krishna with his peacock feathers in one of his visions (I think he's written about it somewhere), but I think there's something absurd about this non sequitur.'

Rameshchandra Sirkar is rather forthright in his disapproval:

'At one time Madame Wadia and I were concerned about the way he connected literature with LSD and drugs, influenced with books like Huxley's *Doors of Perception.* It seemed to us he was taking a favourable idea to experimenting with LSD. Madame Wadia was thirty years my senior, but we both agreed on this. Philosophically, both of us questioned the value of any experience obtained in that way, although Nissim was discussing it, and not taking a dogmatic stand.'

Toni Patel, on the other hand, is non-judgmental. She merely describes, as objectively as she can, what Nissim's state of mind was during and after the time he was on LSD:

'He was more open with me about his personal problems, than before, but that was also because I grew tough with him, I often quarrelled with him when he masked things, till he gave in.

'On occasion he would talk about his inner self, his feelings and fears, but this was rare. What he told us of his researches into psychic experiences seemed very authentic. He told me what he experienced at one of the seances he went to. But three days later, if I asked him to continue the story, he would go blank and express surprise that he had told me these things in the first place.

'I remember that one time, when Gieve was in Baroda, I met Nissim in the late evening and he suddenly began talking about his fear of death. I remember the evening and the event very clearly. I gathered that the fear of death to him was subtler than just an ordinary fear, it was a sort of long dialogue he had had with himself, taking into account the fact of death.'

Tara Patel's remarks were puzzling: 'Nissim certainly had a reputation with women after LSD,' she said to me, leaving me in a state of intrigue to put all the bits and pieces together.

How do I personally react to Nissim's use of LSD? My own feeling is that since he took LSD at the height of the Flower Power movement, he was, at one level, only responding to the cultural trends of the age. If he then called his craving for drugs an 'experiment', it was because his classical bent of mind made him frown upon anything that was too plebian; it was also a way of validating some of the guilt that drug consumption brings in its wake. Nissim saw himself as an emulator of literary greats like Huxley; he was no roadside hookie. Moreover, the champions of Flower Power themselves saw their concerns as revolutionary–after all, they were making a statement against culture.

The late '60s, when Nissim started taking drugs, was a time when sense-gratification was a mantra among young people, particularly in the West. It was a time, as the British Marxist historian Eric Hobsbawm explains in a recent book, when both sex and drugs were the most obvious ways of breaking and defying not only parental authority, but also that of the establishment–society, state law and convention. Both were seen as ways of attaining personal as well as social liberation. Drugs, Hobsbawm goes on to say, 'spread not only as a gesture of rebellion, for the sensations they made possible could be sufficient attraction. Nevertheless, drug use was by legal definition an outlaw activity, and the very fact that the drug most popular among the Western young, marijuana, was probably more harmless than alcohol or tobacco, made smoking it (typically, a social activity) not merely an act of defiance but of superiority over those who banned it.'[6]

In 1966, when he was still at Mithibai College, Nissim landed a prestigious assignment that came his way almost suddenly. This was the editing and publishing of *Poetry India* devoted as its name suggests (unlike the *Indian PEN* with which he was also associated), entirely to poetry. To start with, *Poetry India* was owned and financed by the Bombay-based Parichay Trust. The first issue (Vol. No. 1) which bears the date January-March 1966, describes the journal as 'A Parichay Trust Publication'. Inside, on the third page or so, there is a more detailed description of the activities of Parichay Trust, which is stated to be 'a non-profit trust founded in 1959 with the object of disseminating knowledge in its widest sense.' The name of Pandit Shri Sukhlaji appears as the Chairman of the Board of Trustees, while Shri Vadilal Dagli is the managing trustee. In addition, there are six other members on the Board of Trustees.

With the second issue of *Poetry India* (April-June 1966), the name of Parichay Trust is struck off from the journal. A note on the first page, entitled 'Transfer of Ownership and Management of *Poetry India*', dated 31 July 1966, and signed by Vadilal Dagli, declares the following:

We hereby inform the subscribers of Poetry India that the ownership and management of *Poetry India* has been transferred to Mr Nissim Ezekiel who has given an undertaking to the Parichay Trust that he will publish *Poetry India* hereafter . . .

The editorial address of the journal from the second issue onwards is Nissim's: The Retreat, Bellasis Road, Bombay-8. I asked Nissim why the Parichay Trust backed out from the venture all at once, and left the publication of the journal entirely to him. He said that although the idea of bringing out such a journal was initially theirs, he found, after the publication of the first issue, that the man who started the trust (probably Pandit Shri Sukhlaji) wanted to use the journal to publish the poems of his friends, regardless of their quality. Naturally, Nissim was annoyed. Also, it seems that the members of the Board of Trustees were unhappy with the kind of financial burden that the publication of this English language journal involved. For these reasons, they pulled out of the venture.

Yet, having successfully edited the first issue, with translations from Sanskrit, Marathi, Tamil and Punjabi, plus original poems in English by R. Parthasarathy and Gieve Patel, Nissim was unwilling to see the journal fold up so abruptly. That is why he agreed to have the ownership and management of it transferred to his name. Of course, this also necessitated the generation of alternative sources of funding, at which he was no good. The result: from the second issue onwards, he put his own money into the journal. This was courting disaster, because, as he soon realized, he simply couldn't cope with his financial troubles.

'When I put my own money into the journal, I took it for granted that I would recover it, when I sold copies,' Nissim said. But although the number of subscribers actually increased, it didn't simultaneously prevent the rise of debts. Even the few advertisements that he managed to obtain 'didn't add up to much'.

After taking over the ownership of *Poetry India,* Nissim managed to bring out a total of five issues. The third issue is dated July-September 1966; the fourth October-December 1966; the fifth January-March 1967; and the sixth (and last), April-June 1967. After that, *Poetry India* ceased publication.

The underlying 'philosophy' of *Poetry India,* its editorial policy, as it were, makes it a journal well ahead of its times. The six issues included poems (and articles on poetry) translated from Sanskrit, Marathi, Tamil, Punjabi, Kashmiri, Gujarati, Konkani, Urdu, Maithili, Hindi, Bengali, Malayalam and Oriya, in addition to original writing in English. That English should be seen as another Indian language, complementing rather than being in conflict with these languages, points to the kind of liberal humanist position that Nissim held: there was one literary tradition in post-Independence India, and all Indian languages, English included, were a part of that tradition. This was contrary to the view of the 'nativists' who automatically (and somewhat simplistically) assumed that as English was the language of our colonial 'masters', Indians who used it for creative expression only betrayed their alienation and marginalization from the mainstream. But the nativists had a strong and active lobby in the '60s and '70s, and journals like *Poetry India* amounted to an act of resistance (to nativism) on the part of people like Nissim. It is for this reason that he is to be commended for single-handedly bringing out the journal.

Like other journals with which he would become associated in the future, *Poetry India* did not carry a signed editorial by Nissim. He was no good at writing editorials. Each issue, on an average, contained sixty-seventy pages, though some were considerably thinner in size, owing to a lack of funds. The price per issue was Rs 1.50; it remained consistent from the first issue to the last. All the issues carried advertisements, which were of a varied nature. While there were advertisements of publishing companies like Writers Workshop, and bookstores like Strand Bookstall, there were also the other more commercial ads of Bata shoes and Charminar cigarettes. Actually, the first issue, brought out by Parichay Trust, contains more advertisements than the other five, published by Nissim. This was a direct outcome, both of Nissim's distaste for advertisements in a literary journal, as well of as his inability to procure them.

The literary world in India–and especially Bombay–lamented the closure of *Poetry India*. Adil Jussawalla told me what he particularly cherished about the journal:

'On the whole Nissim has never tried to be a highbrow poet, hence his exasperation with me, Dom, Arvind [Mehrotra] etc. If he can't get the meanings out of poetry that he's looking for, he's lost. But in his *Imprint* and *Poetry India* days, he went against his own judgement, and as an editor he succeeded.'

Around the time he was editing *Poetry India,* Nissim wrote his first play, 'Nalini'. Poets have often doubled as playwrights and novelists, and in his case too it was the urge to try his hand at different things that first led him to the writing of plays. He said to me: 'From time to time people want to do different things, [hence I took to the writing of plays]. But writing plays was not as casual an activity for me as, say, writing book reviews. May be I was possessed by the feeling of wanting to do many things at the same time.' In this context, Nissim disclosed that he has, on occasion, even embarked on a novel, only to give it up later. He has similarly attempted to write short stories, but in the end he 'destroyed them' because he was unhappy with the way they shaped up. Yet he reiterates that it was always poetry that was 'at the centre of my mind.'

As Nissim confesses, his first urge to write plays was because of the influence of Alkazi. In England, in the late '40s, he developed a fondness for seeing and reading plays under Alkazi's expert guidance. The irony is that by the time he started to write and publish his own plays, (like 'Nalini') Alkazi was no longer the central presence in his life. That is why he couldn't think of having his plays staged.

One criticism that came his way when he showed friends his plays, was that all his characters–without exception–tended to speak exactly like him, their creator. This upset him; he went out of his way, then, to make his characters sound different from each other, and different from him. This, of course, is easier said than done. What would have come in the way of noble intentions such as these, was that Nissim mostly associated with people of his own social and cultural class, whose speech habits were no different from his own. Also, when it came to plays, he tended to rely much more on direct observation than on imagination–this is evidenced by the way, say, he got the title of one of his later plays, *Don't Call it a Suicide*. Professor Sudhakar Pandey, the then head of Pune University's English Department, was telling him about the suicide of his son, when his wife interrupted the conversation, saying (in Hindi) 'Don't call it a suicide.'[7]

'Nalini' is the story of two men; Raj and Bharat; and a woman, Nalini, who happens to be a painter. Nalini wants to hold an exhibition of her paintings and Raj, who knows her, approaches his friend Bharat, an ad man, to organize the publicity for the show. Both men–and especially Bharat–have a set image of Nalini as they do of all women; one of the themes of the play is the dispelling of stereotypes by presenting the real Nalini as a woman of greater intelligence and substance than Raj or Bharat. But there is only so much that Nissim can do to 'liberate' Nalini from the male gaze. The play is no feminist statement; in the end, even the real Nalini (as opposed to the imaginary one of Bharat's fantasies) cannot completely be disassociated from her sexuality. The play is in three acts: in the first act we see only Raj and Bharat; in the second, we see Bharat with the two Nalinis, imaginary and real; in the third, we're back with Raj and Bharat in the aftermath of Bharat's encounter with Nalini.

Personally, my objections to 'Nalini' are not so much on account of its minimal build-up of action and sparse dramatic development; or because its intellectual content surpasses its dramatic value, as I suggest in an early article.[8] Considering my present concerns, I wouldn't criticize the play on any of the above grounds. I would even defend it by arguing that Nissim skillfully deals with his inability to handle conversation by consistently opting for short rather than long speeches. Yet, in the last analysis, in spite of Nissim's attempts to make the real Nalini a woman with a mind of her own, the play comes across as written to justify his own weakness for women, and for sex. There are several objectionable, chauvinistic lines put into the mouths of Bharat and Raj throughout the play, but especially in the first act. Consider, for example, the following speech:

Bharat: . . . The female writers are the most insufferable of all. Most of them write only middles of the *Times of India* and articles about their foreign junkets and intimate revelations about their quarrels with their husbands and difficulties with their children, all in a coy, giggly manner as if saying all the time, Look I can write too, I'm sensitive, I have feelings. It's awful.

> Or this:
> Bharat: The less women talk, the less nonsense they talk.
> Or even this:

Bharat: Besides, what do you mean by freedom and adventure and experience? For most of us abroad it only means encounters with women.

'Nalini' was published as a book by P. Lal's Writers Workshop in 1969. The book was called *Three Plays*.[9] Toni Patel, who produced and directed the play, has definite ideas about 'Nalini', about Nissim's other plays and about his capabilities as a playwright. She calls his dramatic achievement 'uneven,' and thinks 'Nalini' remains his best play. I asked her what she especially liked about the play. I also asked her to recount her experiences as she produced and directed it.

'On all counts, 'Nalini' is different from the other plays,' Toni began. 'It's good, it's much sharper.' She went on in a free-wheeling manner: 'I think Nissim's plays do present a problem of doing–if you do them as they're written, they came across as only a slice of life. But if you introduce a dream-like quality, then they improve. However, few directors can manage this. I think the director's vision is very important in these matters.'

Toni pointed out to me that much before she took it up, 'Nalini' was attempted by other directors, 'but all these productions were bad, they came to nothing.' This was partly because apart from a few noteworthy names, 'there were not many people doing English theatre in India at the time.' She then spoke of Nissim as a playwright: 'Nissim himself doesn't know which of his plays are good, and which aren't. He hasn't been able to assess them, he thinks they're all equally good. Luckily for me, he left me alone as I was directing 'Nalini'. He didn't come to a single rehearsal although I invited him, and he refused to talk to me about it. When the play opened, it was very successful. We did ten to fifteen shows at the Cymroza. But Nissim, as usual, was measuring its success in terms of audience reaction. Since the audience liked it, it meant the production was good. He never once told me what he thought about it. I don't think he realized that this play, in particular, handled by someone who didn't understand it, could have ruined his reputation.'

I asked Toni point blank whether she thought 'Nalini' lacked dramatic value. She said, emphatically, that she did not think so. 'It's one of the best plays I've done.' The rest of the conversation progressed on somewhat more general lines, with Toni touching on such aspects as Nissim's taste in drama, and on other productions of his plays.

'Nissim's taste in literature differs from mine,' she said. 'He loves Shaw, whereas I think Shaw is too garrulous, and lacks the fine delicate wit of Oscar Wilde. Although Nissim himself displays a tremendously sharp wit in some of his plays, he never once talked to me about Oscar Wilde, it was always about Shaw.' Toni feels that Nissim naively assumed that any theatre director could do any play if it was good and if he/she liked it. She reports how he once asked Alkazi to do a particular play by Bernard Shaw, which he refused. Nissim couldn't understand why. It was left to Toni to explain to him that it wasn't enough for a director that a play was merely good–the director had to have his heart and soul in the play before he took it up. It is in this context that she criticizes him for not being choosy about his own directors, acting on the principle that 'anyone willing to do his plays was fine.' Toni would have preferred that he gave only those directors the permission to do his plays, who understood them at gut level.

One production that Toni is full of praise for, however, is Patrick Beck's production of 'Marriage Poem' at the Alliance Francaise in the early '80s. Toni herself did not feel inclined to do the play, although she considered it, because 'my problem with it is that it's written in a realistic vein–it's a slice of life.' But what Toni especially liked about Beck's production–who is reported to have described the play as 'a director's play all the way'[10]–was that he managed to distance himself from it, and in the bargain, managed to 'get it on another plane.' Yet the play was not a big success with theatre audiences. 'It was not generally liked, and after two shows, Beck couldn't continue,' she informed me. According to Toni, Beck's not being able to continue with the play also had do with Nissim's response. 'Initially, Nissim got very upset with the production, he felt it was not his play that Beck had done. I think it was the ambivalent audience reaction that affected him negatively. However, when I told him not to be a bloody ass, that the production was very good, I think he changed his mind. But by then it was too late for Beck to revive the play.' I asked Toni whether she actually used the words 'bloody ass' while talking to Nissim. She said she did, and that this was not the only time: 'I'm harsh with him. Long ago, he showed me a bunch of poems and I told him to rework them. He lost his temper and said everyone liked them, I was the only one who was asking him to rework them. But later he did rework them. My hunch was proved correct when A.K. Ramanujan also asked him to rework those very poems.'

After my interview with Toni, the director was over, I turned to Gieve, the playwright. Luckily, one could find them under the same roof. I asked him the same question that I asked Toni: did he feel Nissim's plays lacked action. Gieve's answer: 'Earlier, I also tended to see the plays as less successful than the poetry. But that was only till I saw Toni's production of 'Nalini'. That suddenly made me sit up and I came to realize that you need a sensitive director's eye to tell you what such plays require for their staging. I think they require a very special understanding. For me, 'Nalini 'suddenly become incandescent.' Gieve added, after a pause: 'I would love to see similar productions of his other plays, where the director has been able to grip the pulse of the play accurately. Until that happens, we will not be able to fully assess them. So I think the real problem is that there haven't been enough good productions of Nissim's work.'

My third respondent was a critic, Vrinda Nabar, who has written papers on Nissim's plays. Nabar was a lecturer in Bombay University's English Department at the Fort campus in the '70s, when Nissim joined the Department as a Reader in American Literature. A close association developed between them, especially as she did a Ph.D. on Indian English Poetry under Nissim's supervision, and was keenly interested in Indian Writing in English as an emerging area of study. Nabar's opinions were forthright: 'I still feel Nissim is primarily a poet,' she said to me. 'I told him, as a colleague, that he should write more poetry than other things. I find women come off rather poorly in his plays, and sometimes I get the feeling that some of his characters, projected in part the kind of public image . . . whereby a public face of supreme confidence, of wanting to be the life and soul of a party, only masked a more private, diffident side of the man, which not too many people saw. Basically, I didn't respond to the drama very well.'

In one of her articles, Nabar discusses 'Nalini' in relation to 'Marriage Poem', only to conclude that for her, the latter is the better of the two plays because it's less pretentious: 'To me . . . the play 'Nalini' has always seemed limited by the very limited world it portrays. It is interesting as a glimpse of a slice of life, perhaps, but would have been more so if Ezekiel's dramatic output had been more prolific so that what was witnessed here was part of a wider spectrum. If the function of drama is chiefly to represent, then 'Nalini' performs its limited function adequately. But it is too isolated a reality, one that holds only a marginal interest.'[11]

'Marriage Poem', she says, 'is more representational and therefore more satisfying as theatre . . . It is not an ambitious play. Its theme and treatment are in the mode of conventional theatre. These are defining statements, not negative comments. What I mean is that the theme of the play–a marriage that is clearly disharmonious–is presented in a fairly straightforward manner. There are no elaborate attempts to superimpose formally, any philosophies of drama or theatre, merely because they are fashionable abroad. There is no deliberate avant-gardeism, just as there is no fake existentialism, sense of alienation etc. Nor is there any strenuous attempt to "modernize" the technique, which remains that of conventional theatre for the most part.'[12]

Together with poetry and plays, Nissim continued to write reviews–art reviews, book reviews, theatre reviews. Between 1964 and 1967 he actually functioned as the art critic of the *Times of India,* without being a full-time staffer on the newspaper. Perhaps, at some level academics and journalism, two professions that are perpetually at loggerheads with each other, overlap. This is borne out by the large number of conference volumes and student editions of popular literary texts that Nissim has edited throughout his long career as a professor of English. Between 1962 and 1969 alone, he edited five such volumes. They are: *Indian Writers in Conference* (1962); *Writing in India* (1964); the Indian section of *Young Commonwealth Poets* (1965); *An Emerson Reader* (1967); and *A Martin Luther King Reader* (1969).

Vrinda Nabar, another writer for whom academics has crossed boundaries and made friendly overtures to journalism, says that it was this quality that Nissim and she shared in common, that got her to know him, well before she joined Bombay University in 1973. Of course, there were also the Bombay English Association meetings which both of them attended regularly.

In those days, Nabar taught English at Elphinstone College. Reviewing his entire body of journalistic writing, she especially singles out the book reviews he did for *Imprint* in the '50s and '60s, which she greatly admired, although she was then only a schoolgirl. Unlike some of his later reviews, Nabar is certain that his reviews in *Imprint* were not facile. It is on the basis of these reviews alone that she feels Nissim should have aimed at being more productive as a critic, 'because he had such a lot to give.'

On 13 July 1966, Nissim wrote a review article based on Nirad C. Chaudhuri's *The Continent of Circe,* published that year by Chatto and Windus. It is worth analysing how he went about his task, by attempting a sort of close-reading of the review. Beginning by describing Chaudhuri as 'India's most formidable and thoroughgoing dissenter,' he goes on to explain that 'the main thesis [of the book] takes the form of a diabolic vision: Indians are "swine".' His response to a particular passage he quotes, in which Chaudhuri complains that Indians 'honk, neigh, bellow, bleat or grunt, and scamper away to their scrub, stable, byre, pen and sty' is strong. He writes: 'This is insulting rhetoric of righteous indignation. It seeks no cautious qualifications and reservations.' Nissim asserts that at the level of academic scholarship he does not wish to take issue with Chaudhuri on the various claims made in his book (one of them being that Hindus are really Europeans corrupted by the tropical environment). Instead, 'I propose to argue with him on the level that counts, the level of experience, observation and opinion.' And this is what he does. The review is an exercise in refutation; without exception, Nissim rejects every one of Chaudhuri's claims about life in India, the underlying desire being to prove that he understands the country better. For example, he disagrees with Chaudhuri that India is filthy, and that 'a man who cannot endure dirt, dust, stench, noise, ugliness, disorder, heat and cold has no right to live in India.' Similarly, he has problems with Chaudhuri's view that 'The Hindu spirituality of which the West spoke was the creation of a Western spiritual necessity, and was not to be found in India, either in books or among men.' He finds the Bengali author's attitude to Indology 'cavalier', and to Hindu thought and Hindu forms of artistic expression 'too negative to be convincing.' Chaudhuri's extreme opinions are spoken of dismissively by Nissim as his 'subjective dogmas'.

The implication of Nissim's statements, of course, is that his own experience has taught him otherwise. But there are two things in particular that I should like to comment on. One is Nissim's assimilationism: it doesn't matter to him that he is a Jew, to whom India traditionally has not been as accessible as it has been to Chaudhuri, an upper-caste Hindu. He assumes, like any theorist, that one's origins, one's antecedents do not matter; all phenomena are equally available for observation and comment to anyone who is willing to observe and study them. To me, this is a characteristically intellectual–but politically naïve–method of reasoning. Unfortunately, this has generally been Nissim's method. The other is a point I have already made: that, as a critic, he subscribed to a peculiar brand of aesthetics that required him to play the devil's advocate, and tear to pieces the work he was reviewing. I am especially tempted to repeat this now, when discussing his review of *The Continent of Circe*, because Nissim himself has any number of poems where he is critical about life in India. Yet he cannot stand an identical attitude in a fellow writer, and assumes a wholly contradictory and unpredictable method of reasoning when reviewing his book. To that extent, his review of *The Continent of Circe* is hypocritical.

Nissim's fifth volume of verse, *The Exact Name*,[13] published in 1965, contains twenty poems. Like *The Unfinished* Man before it, it was brought out by P. Lal's Writers Workshop. The book is dedicated to Partha and Adil (R. Parthasarathy and Adil Jussawalla). Some poems in the book were written when Nissim was a visiting professor at the University of Leeds. 'Night of the Scorpion', in particular, is supposed to have been written at the request of students and faculty at Leeds, who wanted him to capture the essence of India for them in a poem.

The phrase 'the exact name' occurs in the epigraph, in which lines from a poem by the Spanish poet Juan Ramon Jimenez are quoted:

Intelligence, give me
The exact name of things!

. . .

The exact name, and yours,
And his, and mine, of things!

Many of the poems have to do with binaries: the intellect versus the
senses; science versus superstition; heaven versus hell; Bombay versus
India. As in every other volume by Nissim, there are several love poems, a
couple of poems on ecology, and a final, somewhat pretentious poem ('A
Conjugation') whose first stanza reads like a grammar exercise:

Pretence, to pretend, I pretend,
You pretend, we pretend,
They pretend.

In the first set of poems, Nissim plays the senses up and the intellect
down. This, in the opening poem 'Philosophy', is illustrated by the lines 'I,
too, reject that clarity of sight /What cannot be explained, do not explain';
and 'The mundane language of the senses sings /Its own interpretations.
. .'

'In Retrospect' says, as it takes leave of the reader:

there is a point
in being obscure
about the luminous,
the pure musical
phases of living
which ought to be
delicately improvised
and left alone.

While the idea is also expressed in 'Platonic', in the lines 'But still,
defying time and place, / Perennial dawn is on your face', 'Art Lecture'
written for Ebrahim Alkazi has the following opening and concluding
stanzas:

He starts with dates and ends with praise,
Relates a subtle episode,

Points a moral or turns a phrase
On some historic formal code.
. . .
The final image, well explained,
Is whisked away. We clap and leave.
The habits of the eye, untrained,
Are granted here a small reprieve.

'Night of the Scorpion' contrasts the superstitiousness of the Indian masses with the rationality of Nissim's father. As pointed out earlier the poem is based on an incident that actually took place in Nissim's grandfather's house in the village of Tal. The nice thing about the poem is the neutrality of the poet-narrator, partly made possible because he is narrating an incident that occurred when he was a child, and was in no position then to come to any conclusions about its relevance. This makes 'Night of the Scorpion' one of the few poems where Nissim is content with 'showing', as opposed to 'telling', and where there is no moral or moralizing statement appended at the end. The narrator is neither on the side of the villagers, nor on the side of the father–he merely reports what he remembers to have seen, with a kind of photographic accuracy; this is what gives the poem its depth. The other positive thing about the poem is its manner: it is told in the first person, without poetic devices such as a third-person mask, and is informal in style, breaking free from the constraints of stanza, rhyme and metre. The lack of these 'regular' poetic attributes is atoned for by the sense of rhythm that permeates the entire poem. This varies from the conversational quality of the opening lines ('I remember the night my mother/was stung by a scorpion. . .') to the incantation 'May he sit still . . . /May the sins of your previous birth /be burned away tonight . . . /May your suffering decrease /the misfortunes of your next birth . . .' The one unfortunate thing about the poem is the stereotypical depiction of the mother as a passive, sacrificing goddess, who must be worshipped for allowing things to happen to her, instead of taking the reins of her life into her own hands:

My mother only said:
Thank god the scorpion picked on me
and spared my children.

But then we must remember that 'Night of the Scorpion' is a made-to-order poem, written for English academics and students, whom Nissim did not want to disappoint by giving them a portrait of India that didn't correspond to their own preconceived notions. In that sense, he was pandering to their needs, playing to the gallery.

'The Visitor' also juxtaposes superstition with reason, but in a less ambitious manner than 'Night of the Scorpion'. The superstition on which the poem is based is a popular one in India–a cawing crow indicates the arrival of a visitor. The crow caws, the poet-narrator waits expectantly, and to give both the crow and the narrator their due, a visitor does arrive after all; to that extent, the superstition is not debunked. Where reality confronts the superstition head on, and causes the narrator to reaffirm his faith in 'the ordinariness of most events' is when the visitor in question turns out to be a man (he expected a woman; needless to say, a young woman). Furthermore, 'His hands were empty, his need: /Only to kill a little time.' To me, what makes the point of view superficial is its heterosexism: what if either the narrator or the visitor or both of them were gay or bisexual? Unlike 'Night of the Scorpion', 'The Visitor' has a more formal style, with stanzas of equal length, though it tries to do away with metre and rhyme.

Three poems in *The Exact Name,* 'Perspective', 'Poetry Reading' and 'Fruit' are what I like to call 'heaven versus hell' poems. But it isn't as if Nissim is consistent in his rejection of one and acceptance of the other. In 'Perspective', the point of view seems to be that 'the prince of Hell /Can speak of love, although his heart is cold.' On the other hand, in 'Poetry Reading', the poet, whose reading is attended by his friends, is criticized for asking the question, 'Against those demons who can win?' The last two stanzas of the poem make us aware of the narrator's scorn in no uncertain terms:

> He drank, drugged himself, he went
> With wives and whores galore. In sin
> And song he spelt out what they meant.
>
> He stands before us now, remote
> From all that news of hell explored,
> And reads it with a steady throat
> As though unmoved or even bored.

But again, in 'Fruit', the narrator oscillates back to the position he took in 'Perspective'. Good and evil are both a part of our make-up, he attempts to remind us, and it's best that we come to terms with this soon. The poem is remarkable for its four-foot line, which is handled with dexterity:

> The sour grapes were just as firm
> And round as those I loved, smooth skin
> Reflecting light, flesh soft within.
> But victims of the silent germ
> They told the truth to heart and tongue.
> I paused, astonished. There they stood
> Delicate, downy, fair and young,
> Cool vessels of deceptive good.
> I took them as I took the good.

Images like 'promised land', 'angelic wings' and 'parables of hell' are also to be found in the poems 'Two Images' and 'Platonic'. It is a conglomeration of images such as these that compels Vilas Sarang to comment on Nissim's 'strong concern with moral corruption [and] sin,' and come to the conclusion that 'the concern is typically Judeo-Christian.'[14]

The paradox in 'In India' is that while the title of poem leads us to expect a pen-portrait of the country as a whole, what we end up getting is a picture of metropolitan Bombay. Whether it is the 'beggars, /Hawkers, pavement sleepers, /Hutment dwellers, slums,' of the first section; or 'The Roman Catholic Goan Boys /The white-washed Anglo-Indian boys /The muscle-bound Islamic boys' of the second, who 'bragged about their love affairs' and 'Drank whisky in some Jewish den' (pointing thereby to a cosmopolitanism and a permissiveness); or the women of semi-bare bosom in section three; or the dinner with the English boss in a 'large apartment /With cold beer and western music, /Lucid talk of art and literature, /And of "all the changes India needs"' (section four); the images are distinctly big city images. It awakens us to a fact we already knew, but which we are apt to sometimes forget: that Nissim's understanding of India did not extend beyond the cultural boundaries of Bombay city. But this was not a limitation he was ashamed of; on the contrary, it constituted a significant aspect of his psycho-cultural make-up.

There are six love poems in *The Exact Name*. They are, as I perceive them, 'Beachscene', 'Virginal', 'A Woman Observed', 'Progress', 'A Warning' and 'Love Poem'. These poems form the core of my ideological objections to *The Exact Name,* principally on account of the manner in which they revel in the 'male gaze'. For many years, I offered an M. Phil course on Modern Indian Poetry in English at the University of Pune. *The Exact Name* was one of the prescribed texts in my course, and I was often struck by the sophisticated readings of the text by my students. My own remarks, though pertinent, remained uncollected on loose sheets of paper that made up my lecture notes. But some of my more enterprising and resourceful students went back home and reworked the gems I had carelessly strewn into well-structured term papers for a class presentation. Br. Hector Andrade, a student of the 1997-98 batch, was one such disciplined student, who on my recommendation, ventured to submit his paper to the editor of a volume of critical essays at BHU, Varanasi. This editor, a senior professor of English, had actually invited me to contribute a paper, but because of a complete lack of time, I assigned the task to Br. Andrade. When he gave me a computer print-out of his paper, I was astonished by the razor-blade sharpness of his arguments, that were, in a sense, based on all the brain-storming sessions we had had in class. It is through Br. Andrade's paper that I should therefore like to present my views on the love poems in *The Exact Name.* In a section entitled 'Ezekiel's Women', he says:

'This is an inventory of the names and images that Ezekiel uses for women. . . burnt-out mothers, frightened virgins, sacrificing mothers, women of semi-bare bosom; wives of India who do not talk, drink, kiss and sit apart, wooden wives, sitting in disarray; women as objects of study; timid, surrendering; nagging women, temptation in unlikely shape, not meant to live like this, reconciled in sadness;

lonely wives and whores, demons, temptresses, prodigious human flesh to feed the eye and mind, naked blazing animals, unhinging speech and bone; pregnant women, sensual movement, women alone–who can be pushed into the sea with a touch, willing but unlovable with mocking sexual eyes, beasts of sex; women locked in a cage . . . women as erotic art objects at the art gallery.' The comment on these portrayals of women follows a few paragraphs later: 'So there is clearly an "othering" of women that is taking place. Women are represented as the exotic or immoral other . . . The same model of Western hegemony in which the colonizers is seen as a primary, active "gaze" subjugating the native as a passive "object", is operative. The gaze is in the possession of the male poet, thus depriving women of power and of significant subjectivity. Women are to be looked at . . . and it is only as objects that they can acquire legitimacy as a subject of literary discourse.' Br. Andrade ends the section by remarking that 'He [Ezekiel] is evasively and crucially silent on matters concerned with gender discrimination.' He also backs up this statement with a fine-tuned observation: that women are not represented in the poems 'Philosophy', 'Perspective', 'Poetry Reading', 'Paradise Flycatcher', 'Art Lecture' and 'Conjugation', all of which deal with 'intellectual' subjects; thereby 'going on to show that the world of reason is denied to women.'

How does Nissim himself react to criticism of this kind? He assumes a defensive posture and argues–as pointed out in previous chapters–that he was merely depicting things as they actually are; that women, particularly in the '60s and '70s did indeed have an 'inferior status' to men, and were, in the main, perceived as objects of sexual desire. And so on. But Nissim's poetry has rarely been a poetry of showing–it has usually been a poetry of telling. So it wasn't as if he was merely being a neutral spectator, who like the *sutradhar* of an Indian play, was disinterestedly but faithfully reporting on what went on around him. No, he was equally the participant, particularly in the love poems that were, one way or other, based on one or more of his own escapades–if that is not too strong a word; and through them he was telling us how (and what) he thought of the opposite sex. It is this characteristic that makes them objectionable.

I like to classify 'Poet, Lover, Birdwatcher' and 'Paradise Flycatcher' as ecology poems. Both poems invoke birds in their natural habitat, and the latter poem, which is dedicated to Zafar Futehally, actually has a note at the beginning of the poem which says: 'An entry in a bird-watcher's diary relates how, while dozing in his garden, he noticed the long, white streamers of a Paradise Flycatcher moving against the green of a casuarina tree. He is delighted for a moment, then remembers sadly how the previous bird he had seen of the same species had been shot down while he was admiring it.'

Futehally, the naturalist and ornithologist, was, as we have already noted, a close friend of Nissim, and if he managed to instill in him an awareness of 'animal rights', we must be grateful to him for it. Yet the thought of comparing women in 'Poet, Lover, Birdwatcher' to birds and poems, and suggesting that like them, women were under the control of men, provokes our wrath and indignation. To me personally, it detracts from all the other merits of the poem that numerous commentators keep talking of–its skilfulness, wit, etc.

How would I evaluate *The Exact Name* all in all? In my interview with Adil Jussawalla, he referred to the 'cloudiness of thinking' in the collection, and I tend to agree with him. And Br. Andrade writes: 'Although the poet desires to find the exact name, his pleas to "intelligence" remain unanswered, as he merely succeeds in reinforcing existing stereotypes.'

Both Jussawalla's and Br. Andrade's remarks imply that throughout the volume, the naming exercise is a failure, for the names end up being inexact rather then exact. This is the paradox of the book and it extends occasionally to the sphere of language, as words, phrases and images are used somewhat imprecisely and inaccurately. It is a serious lapse, this business of setting out to find the exact name of things, and not succeeding, or perhaps only partially succeeding.

Hymns and Fancies

The adventures with LSD changed Nissim for life. He came to be convinced that 'mystical' things happen to human beings, and he, for all his rationalism, was no exception. In order to explain what exactly he meant by 'mystical', he gave an example, based, he said on personal experience. 'Put the case that someone called X or Y says/does certain things to me, behaves in a certain way, and I am convinced that I should disassociate myself from him. What I've experienced over and over again, and I can't explain why, is that there is a sudden turn, very powerful, in this series of rational statements within one's own mind, and I find myself being urged to do exactly the opposite–pity him, help him, give advice, but don't turn your back on him; and I find myself behaving in that way.' Nissim then emphasized that neither those who believe in God, nor those who don't, can explain the reasons for this sudden change of attitude. When I asked him whether he was sure this was a mystical experience, he retorted, somewhat polemically, 'not "mystical" in the higher sense of the word, as applies to mystics, but "mystical" as opposed to "mysticism".' When I suggested that the reasoning seemed specious, if not simplistic, he was not ruffled. He merely said: 'However simple the approach may seem, acting according to those principles is not simple.'

The '70s saw Nissim switch jobs yet another time. But this time he was switching only jobs, not professions. The past ten years had made it clear to him that he was best suited for teaching, nothing more, nothing less. Now he was about to make a qualitative shift, as a university professor. American literature was slowly being introduced in the syllabus of English Departments all over India. Whereas in the past, universities invited American professors from abroad to come and conduct these courses, they now felt the need to appoint people from within the country, with special qualifications in American literature. That really was–or should have been– the bone of contention when Nissim responded to an advertisement for the post of Reader at the University of Bombay; for he did not possess a scholarly knowledge of American literature. But once again, a combination of good luck and personal charisma ensured that he was appointed to the post. The year was 1972, the vice-chancellor Professor Ram Joshi, and all that Nissim had to assure the Selection Committee was that he had taken some lectures on the subject while he was in America. In his own words, he 'walked into the job'.

The Head of Bombay University's English Department was, at the time, the legendary Kamal Wood. Another faculty member was the towering G. C. Banerjee. Although Nissim was younger than they were, he did not feel intimidated by their presence. If anything, considering the name he had made for himself as a poet and a critic, it was they who felt threatened when he joined them as a colleague. The Mithibai College people released him without any hassles; they realized he was leaving on a promotion, or as we frequently say in India, 'for better prospects'.

The English Department in those days was situated at the Fort campus in south Bombay, on the first floor of the East Wing (there was no campus at Kalina yet, though land for the purpose had been acquired). One thing that immediately struck Nissim about the job was that as a university teacher he was given a room to himself where he could read, write and meditate, unlike his previous job where teachers were huddled into a staff common room utterly devoid of privacy.

From its inception in the '50s, the English Department has followed the convention of conducting its courses in two batches-an afternoon batch for day scholars, and an evening batch for employed students. At the time Nissim joined the Department, the evening classes were usually held at the University Club House on C-Road, Churchgate. It was all very conveniently worked out for him. In the morning, he travelled by bus to the Department, taking in events in downtown Bombay before his classes began, such as an exhibition at the Jehangir Art Gallery across the road. Sometimes he went to the *Times of India* at V. T. to submit a review or an article. Then there was his work at the PEN All India Centre. In the evening, after his classes at the Department were over, he walked to the Club House, cutting through the Oval Maidan. Finally, he took a suburban train to Bombay Central and walked to The Retreat, five or ten minutes away.

What did Nissim think of his students at the university, as compared to those at Mithibai College? What kind of equation did he have with them?

As a university teacher, these questions are of special interest to me. He answered by pointing out, first of all, that unlike when he was at Mithibai, he himself was older, more mature and more experienced now. So this was reflected in his dealings with students. Of course, there was no denying that as graduate students, they too were more critical and more responsive. (In Maharashtra, university departments have traditionally concerned themselves with only graduate education, unlike some other states such as Gujarat and Orissa where both graduate and undergraduate programmes are conducted by university departments.) But even if some of them were mediocre, or not serious enough, Nissim never allowed himself to become cynical. He never felt bored. In any case, the work-load at the university was lighter than it was in Mithibai. At the Department, he taught for no more than six to eight hours a week. This was supplemented by some administrative work, coupled with his own writing and research, as well as the supervision of Ph.D. students assigned to him. The students still referred to him as 'sir', but he was liberated enough by now to encourage some of them to address him by name, as they did in American universities. He welcomed interruptions in class, provided the issues raised pertained to the text he was teaching.

Nissim rapidly rose in the academic hierarchy of the Department. Although he joined as a Reader, it wasn't very long before he became a full Professor. One of the controversies that surrounded his appointment, first as a Reader and then as a Professor, was that he did not possess a doctor's degree. Considering his eminence as a writer and critic, the selection committees always made an exception in his case. Nissim feels this is justified, as apart from poetry and reviews, he was also publishing academic books such as *A Martin Luther King Reader,* which he edited. Not only did they appoint him to senior faculty positions without a Ph.D., but they also did not insist that he should acquire a Ph.D. after he was selected for the job. Nissim did not have the patience to even consider doing a Ph.D. He saw it as time-consuming and tedious, while the other writing that he did brought quick dividends in the form of publicity and cheques. But this also led to a view in some circles, that he simply did not have it in him to be a scholar–the discipline and rigour that true scholarship demanded, were simply beyond his capacity.

There was a growing demand among students for new courses in American literature. Nissim realized that as he was appointed a Reader in American literature, he would have to spend much time reading up and preparing for his classes. This he conscientiously did. He approached his task with the same dedication that he did at Mithibai College. He prided himself upon the fact that, unlike some teachers, he did not merely dictate notes in class. He enjoyed all the preparation he had to do in the early years of his appointment. This thoroughness paid off as the years advanced, he became so well-versed in American literature, that he was able to tackle the entire history of American literature in his lectures. He came to be known as the resident American literature specialist. Yet it's not as if the job took up all his time; he still found the time to attend to poetry, journalism and editing. As far as editing was concerned, he was mainly occupied with the *Indian PEN,* which was still officially edited by Madame Sophiya Wadia, but over which he gained much editorial control.

As a poet of stature, how did Nissim feel spending his time interpreting the work of other poets and writers? He told me that although he was aware few students knew his work (most of them knew he was a poet), it did not upset him. Nevertheless, his soul was that of a writer; he saw himself as a poet who was also a teacher, not the other way round. He therefore never felt inclined to introduce new courses. However, whenever such a move was made by others, he invariably found himself supporting them. 'I felt that as a poet, I couldn't at the same time be a sort of educational activist,' he told me. He was also different from other teachers in another significant way. As someone who supplemented his income with the cheques that he got from writing, he was comfortably off, and did not have to look towards perks such as private tuition. The only tuition that Nissim remembers giving, is to the children of friends, whom he did not charge. He also remembers refusing lucrative offers to teach English at coaching classes. 'The money I made from my book reviews in *Imprint* magazine itself amounted to three-fourths of the salary I made as a lecturer, so where was the need to teach at coaching classes,' he reasoned.

In any case, Nissim's desire to see himself as an atypical teacher grew after he joined Bombay University. One of the 'atypical' things that he had to do at the Department was to discourage an Anglocentric worldview, prevalent especially among some students who came from affluent homes. This was often reflected in the attitudes that they had towards the courses that were taught. In the early '70s, it was only English and American Literature, but afterwards new courses like Indian Writing in English emerged on the academic horizon. Nissim was in a peculiar position vis-a-vis Indian Writing in English. On the one hand, he was a professor of American literature, on the other, he was an Indian poet in English. Students formed their own ideas of value; they placed English literature at the top of the scale, Indian Writing in English at the bottom. Ultimately, of course, it was from their teachers at school and college that they inherited these attitudes. To that extent, the question was political. 'Politics cannot be excluded,' Nissim concurs, and comments that 'Large numbers of MA students who studied English literature and went on to become teachers, thought themselves immensely superior to those who taught other languages.' This superiority arose, in all likelihood, from a desire to ape the West. While dealing with it in the classroom, therefore, Nissim had to spend a lot of time discussing the demerits of Anglocentricism.

He does not take the credit, however, for introducing Indian Writing in English in the syllabus. The efforts were those of others, but, as usual, he was strongly supportive. He came to believe that Indian Writing in English should remain a part of the English teaching scene in the whole of the country. Luckily for him, English departments in Indian universities were becoming independent, and the subject was to be introduced at many places. Eventually he had to confront his own poems in the course. This was both flattering and awkward. No, he did not lecture on his own poetry ('it would have been too embarrassing'); but sometimes he travelled to other universities at their request to comment on his poems.

At the same time, Nissim has refused to go to the other extreme. He does not support the move, initiated by some radical educationists in the '80s and '90s, to give English literature the backseat and foreground postcolonial literature. 'That would be stupid,' he says, 'because if you are studying the language, you have to study everything worthwhile written in that language, and English literature cannot be excluded.' When I suggest that we are talking here about the question of control, his answer is: 'It all depends on how you handle it. The question of [political] power can be given a perspective, not by dispensing with English literature altogether, but by forming our own relevant attitude to it.'

As a teacher, Nissim's methods grew increasingly sophisticated after he joined the university.

'Teaching can be complex when you practise it complexly, rather than simply prepare your classroom lectures, deliver them and come out.' His own approach he was certain, was complex enough. The simple approach often meant preaching without practising, talking about the appreciation of a poem, say, and failing to relate it to life. Nissim, on the other hand, learned to see the end of his classroom lectures as the beginning of something else, that would go on for ever. This is how he connected teaching to life. Lectures could sometimes be so illuminating, that he regrets he did not keep a journal to record discoveries made during classes. Had he done so, he would have been able to show the world how teaching and learning are two sides of the same coin.

It is worth keeping in mind that Nissim retained his enthusiasm for teaching till the end of his career. In 1983, only a year before his retirement, he said:

'In 1972, a vacancy arose in the postgraduate department of English of Bombay University, and I was invited to become a Reader in American literature. I was only too happy to accept, and that is what I teach now. It gives me several opportunities to travel; for instance, I conduct an advanced course for teachers at Hyderabad every year, and go to Goa annually as a visiting professor.'[1]

Rameshchandra Sirkar, who closely observed Nissim at the time, was struck by the fact that, inspired by their teacher, a number of Nissim's students wanted to themselves try their hand at writing. These students kept going to him for advice, and he always found the time for them. A joke began doing the rounds of the PEN: if Nissim wasn't in the office, he was probably at Sanman Restaurant across the road, entertaining visitors, many of whom were students, young hopefuls who came to show him their poems.

Vrinda Nabar provides one of the most vivid accounts of the kind of man he was in those days. As stated earlier, Nabar joined the English Department of Bombay University as a lecturer in July 1973, soon after Nissim. It was her first university appointment–her previous job was at Elphinstone College, where she worked for a year, taking at the most a few MA classes. 'Nissim was the only one who gave me a sense of being in the Department' Nabar said to me. 'He made me feel comfortable in the remote atmosphere of the university.' What contributed to this remoteness, as far as she was concerned, was that unlike at Elphinstone (or any other college), the teachers here were ensconced in their rooms. Nabar also refers to Nissim's more dedicated students, the ones, probably, Rameshchandra Sirkar found him having coffee with at Sanman. In particular, she mentions Santan Rodrigues, Shama Futehally and Charu Bhagwat (the first two of whom went on to become established writers). 'We used to have poetry readings on the lawns of Bombay University. What stood out then–and does still–is the amount of time he has for individuals, the amount he's willing to give as a writer to other writers.' This, Nabar believes, comes from a 'fundamental generosity' in the man, and is 'not a very common quality.'

The Indian university system as it then existed was somewhat alien to Nabar, even though her father was a professor at the University Department of Chemical Technology (U.D.C.T.), Matunga, and she grew up in an academic atmosphere. But she took off for Oxford soon after her schooling, and returned to India only in 1971, after completing her BA. When Nabar joined the Department, Kamal Wood was still the Head. After her death in 1976, it was R. B. Patankar who took over. In the bureaucratic melee in which she found herself, Nissim's seemed to be the only human voice. 'The unsparing honesty of the man was admirable,' Nabar says. This was manifested at two levels–intellectual and administrative. Intellectually, it was his essay on Naipaul's *An Area of Darkness*. Administratively, it was his 'willingness to stand up for injustices, even in an institutional set-up, full of bureaucratic rigidities.' Nabar gives several examples to back up her statements. 'We would frequently come up with the scenario of a student bringing an application form a day late, and being reduced to tears by the head clerk who did not accept it–Nissim would scream till the head clerk bent his rules.' Another time, a Readership was advertised by the university, and then set aside 'as it was tailor-made for a certain outsider.' The excuse given by the university for setting it aside was that, as Nissim himself was to be promoted to the post of Professor, there was no need for a Reader. Nissim, however, was unconvinced by this explanation, and did not accept it at face value. He said he could not stand by, and see injustice being done to someone else, just for the sake of his own promotion. His intervention partially remedied the situation–the advertised post was held back, but another Readership was advertised. 'Within a university set-up, this is saying a great deal,' Nabar believes.

I asked Nabar what she felt about Nissim as a teacher. 'He was on the whole a popular teacher,' she replied. 'He was innovative, especially in his class on Practical Criticism, in which he tried to make [the] students open up.' I then sought her opinion on a controversial matter–Nissim's appointment as a Professor without a Ph.D. 'He had publications,' she pointed out; 'even if they were not in academic journals, so the professor's job was not undeserved. It's true he wasn't like some others, who make all this–the producing of M. Phil's and Ph.D.'s, the publishing of papers etc–a small-scale industry. He should have been more productive academically, because he had such a lot to give.'

Many of Nissim's publications were art or book reviews in newspapers and popular magazines. Unlike other hardcore academics, for Nabar, this in itself wasn't cause enough to dismiss him as 'unacademic'. Each article or review would have to be assessed on its own merits. Having said this, she concludes that his reviews were not facile. As evidence, she once again cites the example of the book reviews that he did for *Imprint* in the '50s and early '60s, which even as a schoolgirl with a voracious reading appetite, she enjoyed reading.

I steer my interview in a different direction. I bring up the problematic issue of Nissim's 'cold war' with R. B. Patankar, when they were colleagues at the Department. Both Nabar and I were witness, in a sense, to the 'politics' that existed between these two stalwarts, one a poet, the other a philosopher; she as a staff member of the English faculty, I as a postgraduate student. 'I don't know whether there ever was a feud between them,' she began, 'though everyone seems to feel there was a feud. Nissim was mistaken to be the Head of the Department by the public at large, obviously because of his greater visibility, and this was one of the reasons for the tussle. But this sort of thing happens in all university departments. [Much later, a similar tussle developed between Vrinda Nabar and Vilas Sarang. Although Sarang was the official Head of the Department, the general public often mistook Nabar to be the Head]. There were insecurities in Patankar, but I don't know how they were projected. He was very upset when his attempts to induct Yasmin [Professor Yasmin Lukmani, the Head of the English Department at the time of writing] as Reader failed, and it went to very childish levels, when he wouldn't be on speaking terms with us. But it was blown out of proportion because someone like Nissim was involved, and Patankar had this new-found status in the Marathi literary world. So the issue became polarized in terms of English versus Marathi. Outsiders saw this as two ideological camps, but there was nothing like a confrontation.' This was Nabar's point of view, and it was only after I interviewed her that certain things about the Department became clear to me. It was a time when my own honeymoon with Nissim was just beginning, so to speak, with my enrolment in the Department as a postgraduate student. Knowing my passion for writing, my father got me interested in the man by informing me of his TV appearances and newspaper articles, whenever he came across them. My father was a medical doctor with the

Central Government. He often reported to me that as he was driving back home from his office in Colaba to New Marine Lines, where we lived, he saw Nissim crossing the road outside the university, heading towards the Oval. When I joined the university in 1978, my father's accounts were corroborated by what I witnessed personally. I frequently saw Nissim at exactly the same spot that my father did. Unlike my father, I wasn't in a car concentrating on the traffic, so I was able to observe him closely. He usually wore a guru kurta over formal trousers, and on several occasions I remember him buying a packet of groundnuts from the 'singwalla' who squatted just outside the ornate iron gates of the university. Yet I maintained a respectful distance from him, for he, after all, was my teacher–a teacher like none other that had ever taught me at school or college.

I was one more of Nissim's students, then, who went on to become a published writer. As the years rolled by, the number of such young men and women increased, with very illustrious people like Arvind Krishna Mehrotra heading the list.

When he was at the university in the '70s, Nissim was at the peak of his glory. Undoubtedly, the '70s were his decade. It was a time he became university Professor, and his books first came to be accepted for publication by Oxford University Press. His newspaper, magazine and TV appearances went up. In short, he was by this time, a celebrity. His celebrity status, coupled with the power he wielded in academic, literary and cultural circles, reinforced by his natural good looks, made him very attractive, if not irresistible, to heterosexual women. And Nissim was not the man to look a gift horse in the mouth. He made the most of all the opportunities that came his way.

When I asked Tara Patel about Nissim's reputation as a womanizer, she hesitated, and refused to divulge any information. She did not answer my question when I bluntly asked her whether he had ever made a pass at her. Instead, she told me that all the stories she had heard about him didn't scare her off one bit, for 'I was innocent.' She qualified this with: 'He's a charmer, intellectually; most women were attracted to him for very different reasons.'

I then asked Tara another personal question: what was the nature of her own attraction to Nissim–was it all sexual? She denied it was sexual. 'He doesn't fit my bill of a macho, good-looking man. I found him a fatherly figure, although for a while I was confused about my feelings.' Here Tara paused for a while, and then continued: 'I was so innocent [she was using this word for the second time in ten minutes] that when it came to physical things, he was a big shock to me. I never went beyond a certain preliminary point. I never had a relationship with him.' She ended this part of the interview by reiterating that Nissim fulfilled her need for a substitute father, her own father in Malaysia being insensitive and unsympathetic, forcing her thereby to migrate to Bombay.

No account of Nissim's fondness for women can be complete without recording Vrinda Nabar's views. At the time I studied at the Department, rumour had it that they were having a full-fledged affair. All the conditions were right: he was famous and good looking; she was young, intelligent and ambitious, and to all intents and purposes, stunningly beautiful. This combination of beauty and brains was somehow rare among Indian academics in the '70s. I left the Department two years later (1979) without being able to figure out whether they actually did have an affair. In any case, I wasn't interested. Affairs between men and women tired me. It was only when I found myself interviewing Nabar for this book–a situation I never dreamed of in the '70s–that I summoned up the courage to broach the subject. I detected a guardedness on her part as she spoke.

'He was susceptible to women but I didn't think he was a womanizer in the sense of the unpleasant connotations. He wouldn't make a nuisance of himself and I say this not just in relation to myself. He wouldn't chase a skirt.'

Nabar went on to remind me that, as a workplace, a university department is unlike a corporate office with bosses and secretaries, and differing power relations. She said this in order to underscore her point that Nissim was in an environment where sexual harassment and sexual exploitation were not possible. What she did not see–or choose to see– was that the secretaries of big corporations are easily replaced by junior colleagues and lady students in an educational institution.

Nabar described Nissim as 'subjective' but said it was a subjectivity that had nothing to do with gender. 'Several of us [she did not specify who] have teased him about not being able to assess who were trying to exploit him, men included.' She concluded by giving Nissim a sort of clean chit: 'As a male, Nissim was no more chauvinistic than most males in Indian society. Terms like "chauvinism" have to be seen in relation to their times. There are several things about his attitude that one would find questionable, but then that's how most men are, some obnoxiously so. Nissim is certainly not obnoxious.'

Tara Patel endorses Nabar's assessment of Nissim's character. Her statement about his 'reputation' with women notwithstanding, she stresses the point that as far as she was concerned, he performed the role of both substitute father and trusted friend. What especially endeared him to her was that when, after reading his poems in magazines like the *Illustrated Weekly of India,* she ventured to send him some of her own poems (she wrote under the name of Pankaj Patel then), he responded positively. She sent him the poems by post and he corresponded with her regularly. This did not mean that he always praised what she wrote–he often 'tore my poems apart.' But he encouraged her to continue writing and show him her work. This meant much to Tara who describes herself as 'shy and fanciful'. Before she met Nissim, Tara thought of him as 'too grand a personality' in whose presence she would feel 'intimidated'. And it's not as if this impression vanished the moment she set her eyes on him. On the contrary, his criticism of her work sometimes made her very angry. Recalling some of that anger, she said to me: 'Yet I realized on going back and rewriting the poem that it had genuinely improved. I decided to take all his advice about writing poetry seriously.' This process continued, until Nissim began to publish some of Tara's poems in the *Indian PEN,* and recommended them to the editors of magazines.

Thus it was poetry that helped their friendship to blossom. But Tara soon realized that, like her, there were several others–of both sexes, but mostly women–who came to Nissim 'to hear words of comfort and wisdom from him.' In Tara's case, these soothing words were required because she faced problems of different kinds: problems with her job in various companies, where for five years, she worked as a steno-cum-secretary; and problems at home. The latter were emotional in nature, and mostly had to do with the hostility she experienced from her parents; in the circumstances, 'Nissim was someone I could talk to.'

I gathered from Tara's statements that in some intuitive way, she also came to associate Nissim with Bombay. Both were things she turned to for refuge. 'Slowly I began to like Bombay,' she said. 'I wrote poems about the gulmohars of Bombay and showed them to him.' As the years went by, Nissim took on the role of confidant and counselor. It was no longer just poetry about which he advised her, but 'life in general'. Tara reminisces: 'I found that I could talk to him whenever I was low or depressed. He gave me advice, and even if I didn't take it, I was comfortable.'

Tara goes to the extent of giving Nissim the credit for offering her 'a perspective on life'; which she says she did not possess as a teenager. His office at the Fort campus of the university turned out to be a convenient meeting place, where she often met him. There were times, she claims, when she saw him every other day. These were interspersed with long stretches during which she did not go to him at all. 'There's lots I like about him and little I don't like,' she finally said, in an attempt to stress the point that, feminist though she may be, she does not view males like Nissim with suspicion. 'Nissim is one of the few persons who has contributed to me being me.'

The character appraisals of Vrinda Nabar and Tara Patel, based on the personal equation they had with Nissim, must not be taken to mean that he was a saint. There are several people who would be willing to come forward and swear that he wasn't exactly one. Ranjit Hoskote's father, Nissim's junior at Wilson College, swears that he (Nissim) was one of the 'most-chased men' at the college. Besides, if Nissim really had affairs, it is silly to expect any of the women to talk about it. The tendency would be to move away from the subject, and speak about relationships in general terms, and this is the feeling I often got while talking to the women close to him. In that sense, he was the archetypal playboy, who had them under his romantic spell.

Information about delicate matters such as these, whenever it came my way, did so from other quarters. I must admit that my informants were invariably male, never women, and to the extent, we are susceptible to the charge of chauvinism. My 'secret source', let me call him Mr X now, actually provided me with an inventory of the names of all the women Nissim was 'involved' with. He said: 'Nissim's gentleness, musk odour of fame and man-about-town adventures gave him a kind of aura in his best years.' He suggested it was this aura that made him so attractive to all the women listed above. He also pointed out that while his male friends were those that did not challenge him, his women friends were ones that did.

Mr X particularly zeroes in on one of these women, Eunice de Souza. Like Nissim, de Souza too is a poet and Professor of English. Their association, I was told, dates back to the years 1970-71. Together, they put up 'Nalini' but the relationship fizzled out soon after they were done with the play, as Nissim called de Souza an 'intensely irritating person'. That was when they broke up.

Once she fell out with him, de Souza had her revenge by writing a poem about Nissim, entitled 'Poem for a Poet'. It reads as follows:

It pays to be a poet
You don't have to pay prostitutes.

Marie has spiritual thingummies.
Write her a poem about the
Holy Ghost. Say:
'Marie, my frequent sexual encounters
represent more than an attempt
to find mere physical fulfillment.
They are a poet's struggle to
transcend the self
and enter into
communion with the world.'

Marie's eyes will glow.
Pentecostal flames will descend.
The Holy Ghost will tremble inside her.
She will babble in strange tongues:
'O Universal Lover
in a state of perpetual erection
Let me too enter into
communion with the world
through thee.'[2]

If Nissim was hurt or angered by the poem, he did not show it. On the contrary, he maintained a stoical silence. Though on his part, Nissim too, as we have observed, frequently wrote poems on women, and although he never named any of them, the portraits he etched were often based on women he intimately knew. In fact, 'Virginal' in *The Exact Name* is supposed to be about de Souza, so in a way she was only getting even. I asked Mr X what he thought of these poems, from an ethical point of view. He described them as 'a product of voyeurism' and said the subject called for a full-fledged study: 'It's a cultural thing–this fascination for other people's sexual lives.' Mr X is also certain that Nissim never showed the poems to the women on whom they were based. They were written after he was finished with the women, and then they were free to chance upon them on their own. I asked him, further, if he felt women made themselves available to Nissim because he was in a position to promote their careers. Mr X did not think so. Women of the calibre of de Souza and others were not opportunists. 'If anything, there's been opportunism on Nissim's side, as there is in any man-woman situation,' he said. After that, Mr X proceeded to describe Nissim as 'a normal horny man.'

Ronita Torcato was a student at Bombay University's English Department in the late '70s (probably around the same time I studied there, and Nissim and Nabar were our professors). She had heard rumours about Nissim's affair with Nabar, but dismissed it as vile gossip. 'After all, they worked together and when people work together, it's usual for such things to come up,' she remarked. She belives that all said and done, Nissim is innocent.

Likewise, as already stated, Gauri Deshpande hints at the 'platonic' relationship that she and Nissim had. This kind of relationship she says, 'I have found . . . to be true, often in my friendships with women . . . but rarely with men. Nissim is the exception.' But exactly what kind of relationship does she have in mind? 'A comfort in each other's just being there. A non-necessity of doing or saying anything special. Just a few casual questions and remarks that may set the other thinking.'

To women like Deshpande who appeared mannish to him, Nissim never came across as a womanizer. The reference to friendship between two women or two men is apt. There were several men to whom Nissim was close, minus the expectations that heterosexuals have in their dealings with persons of the opposite sex. Because there are no expectations of a sexual kind, the friendships tend to last. Deshpande boasts that her association with Nissim is thirty years old:

'There has been only one break in this "friendship", which is now thirty years old. When I wrote a scathing review of his translation of Indira Sant's poems, he stopped talking to me. Since I was out of the country for about three years after that review, and since Nissim and I have hardly ever written to each other, I hardly noticed the break. When I met him after the long break . . . he was again as I had always known him. A friend, but with a comfortable distance between us which neither had . . . ever wanted to cross.'

Yet it is hard to come by opinions such as Deshpande's when one views his track record with women. Mr X argues that if Nissim was indeed innocent, Daisy wouldn't have been 'one of the most bitter people in the world.' According to him, not only did Nissim have the audacity to have extra-marital affairs, but he also flaunted them by writing about them. In order to corroborate his allegations, Mr X cites the example of the poem 'Jewish Wedding in Bombay' which, of course, is about Nissim's own marriage. He says: 'If I were Daisy, I would never forgive Nissim [for writing this poem]. I would tear out his entrails.'

Mr X's experiences with Daisy and other members of Nissim's family are diametrically opposed to mine. Where I found them reticent, reluctant to open their hearts out and talk, he finds Daisy 'all too willing to talk about her husband for hours together.' Mr X, of course, bases his views on personal observation. A young woman he was friendly with and whom he would later marry, once happened to pick up the phone at the PEN when Daisy rang. Instead of disconnecting the line on being told that Nissim was out, Daisy, it seems, went on and on about how cruel Nissim was to her and the children, how he never was a good father who was around when the kids were growing up, and so on. It amazes Mr X that she didn't even bother to find out who the young woman was, before venturing to speak her heart out. As it turned out, the young woman had never met her before, but this didn't deter Daisy. Mr X uses the incident to gauge how hurt Daisy was by her husband's wayward ways. This was no ordinary wound; it was causing her to go over the brink.

In marital squabbles, it is always difficult to pinpoint who exactly is at fault. In the case of the Ezekiel couple, it may seem, on the face of it, that the responsibility to save their marriage was Nissim's more than Daisy's, for it was he who went out of the house and met people, he it was who had name and fame. And although in truth, matters may not have been simple, even his closest friends believe that, assuming someone was wronged, that person wasn't Nissim. Toni Patel says matter-of-factly: 'I don't believe he's wronged. His lifestyle was entirely of his own choice and making. So Daisy cannot be blamed for deserting him.'

The upshot of the quarrel between them, of course, was that their wedding ended in a separation. Daisy continued to live in Kala Niketan with the children, while Nissim moved back to the Retreat. As time went by, their house at The Retreat would witness fewer and fewer occupants. After the death of Moses Ezekiel, the only people who lived in the house were his wife, Nissim, and two of Nissim's aunts and uncles. Eventually, the aunt and uncle decided to settle down in Israel, and left. Nissim describes the 'last stages' at The Retreat as those when only he and his mother lived there. This was until her death in 1974. At the time of writing, Nissim remains the sole occupant of the house. It has been like that for a long time now.

Ever since he began living by himself in the large flat, Nissim began to slip increasingly into the mould of a recluse and an ascetic. It was as if he was done with *Grihasthashram* and had entered *Vanaprastha*. As a general rule, he forbade people from visiting him at home. The PEN was the preferred place for meetings, even with intimate friends. The number of persons who managed to defy the 'ban' and sneak into The Retreat can be counted on one's fingers. I was curious to meet as many of these people as I could, for I wasn't as lucky as them. The maximum I managed was to get as far as his front door on a Sunday morning. But he was out, the door was locked, and I spent half my day waiting in vain. The neighbours did not know where he had gone or when he would return. Sometimes, I suspect he'd seen me from a distance, as he approached the house, and had deliberately gone away, in order to avoid letting me into the flat! 'Over my dead body,' he once said to me, when I demanded that he let me visit him at The Retreat.

Toni, as stated earlier, is one of the handful of persons who has been to the house. Not just once, but a couple of times. Of course, these were casual visits, to pick up a book, say; it's not as if Nissim ever invited her to come and see him at home. She uses just one word to describe the state of the house as she remembers it: unkempt. The house reflected Nissim's personal habits, which again can be expressed in a word: neglect. Toni says: 'I don't know why he neglected himself, but whenever I've asked him, he's said he could use that time writing a poem or thinking about one.' Whenever Nissim visited Toni's flat, he'd be surprised to see her slogging away at the housework. He felt it was a waste of precious time that could be utilized to read, write. Toni compares him to Gieve here, who tends to be a bit like that, but only a bit. 'Gieve is immaculate about his work things,' she says, 'paints, brushes, books. With Nissim, even his desk goes to hell.' Toni also defends her husband by pointing out that he's a much busier man than Nissim, what with his flourishing medical practice.

On the credit side of the balance sheet, he never made a fuss about food, especially when he made it out with friends. To quote Toni, 'He ate whatever he was given.' She remembers once taking a photograph of his at the breakfast table at Malabar Apartments. He had spent the night at their flat, and had left the next morning, after breakfast.

Over the years, he did this again and again, giving Toni close insights into his personality and character. One of the things that she immediately noticed was his ascetic streak. This has always existed in his psychological make-up, but as the decades passed, it tended to be on the increase. Speaking about the early '90s, when Nissim stayed with them to recuperate after his hernia operation, she tells me the story of the ladoos. A plate of ladoos, all rich and sugary, is placed on the table before Nissim, the man with the sweet tooth, he has one, his host asks him out of politeness to have another. He says to her: 'I went three times to that plate, then decided not to pick up another ladoo.' He sticks to his resolve, not giving in to temptation. Toni feels 'asceticism' is in Nissim's blood. It is there in his family, on his father's side, who practised simplicity for generations. She refers, in this connection, to his grandfather's participation in the war. Once again she compares the family to Gieve's, her own (late) father-in-law being thrifty to the point of absurdity. To her way of thinking, some of this rubbed off on Nissim. Why, otherwise, would a man keep old envelopes and reuse them as he frequently did?

Nissim himself does not use words like 'asceticism' to describe his lifestyle. He finds them too pompous. To him, all he tried to do was lead a simple, natural life, keeping his wants down to the minimum. This is how naturopaths advise their patients to live, and there is no gainsaying that he was deeply influenced by the work of the late Dr J.M. Jussawalla, a pioneer in naturopathy. The association began when Dr Jussawalla sought his editorial help on a manuscript that was being readied for publication. Even as he read through the manuscript for incorrect or inelegant use of language, he learnt much about the art of nature cure. On Dr Jussawalla's recommendation, he then spent a week at his clinic at Kemp's Corner as an observer, hoping to learn a little about naturopathy. He saw this as complementary to his interest in health, which dated back to the years he spent in London in the late '40s. Of course this does not mean he practised naturopathy all the time. When circumstances demanded it, he gave himself (up) to modern allopathic medicine. I distinctly remember the time he was hospitalized for a week (I was a student in the Department of English), and we were all worried.

It would be unfair to portray Nissim as straightforward human being, obsessed with health, but not very healthy himself. We're talking about the '70s when he was in his prime, at his peak. Even if he didn't dress ostentatiously, there was a charm and an appeal about him that made him attractive to the world. In short, he had personality. But who says he wasn't fashion-conscious? The well-fitting guru kurtas in pleasing pastel shades, the not-too-short hair, the gold-rimmed spectacles, if these are not a fashion statement he was making at the time, I don't know what is. Nissim had certain role models when it came to matters of dress and physical appearance. Although he denies it, one of them was the American poet Wallace Stevens, who tried to maintain complete anonymity in dress, so that he wouldn't be proclaiming to the world that he was a poet. The other was T. S. Eliot, who dressed well, but not necessarily as poets are supposed to. While Nissim 'wouldn't go that far' just in order to externally seem as little of the poet as possible, these attitudes were closer to his heart than those of, say, Walt Whitman, where one had to physically look the part, before one actually wrote a poem. While discussing the subject, he said to me: 'There is such a thing as temperament, and if one goes against his temperament, he pays the price for it.'

I find the attitude incongruous. True, clothes can make a man look flashy, and this was what he tried very consciously to guard against. But such behaviour is manifest in other ways as well. Flirting with women, going to bed with them, in spite of the fact that one is married and has grown-up children, can be equally outrageous. And what about getting drunk? Nissim wasn't the kind who boozed at parties until he was sozzled, but it's not as if this never happened at all. Mr X reports that once, sometime between 1972 and 1975, he fell into a ditch on his way home. Mr X cannot tell whether it was alcohol that caused it, or let us say bad street lighting, but speculates it was alcohol. 'He's had his accidents, which he doesn't talk about,' says Mr X.

I returned to another source, a more 'reliable narrator' than Mr X, to find out more about Nissim's relations with his immediate family in the '70s–Vrinda Nabar. But there wasn't much luck. Nabar denied any knowledge about them, insisting Nissim was only a colleague with whom she did not discuss his family. She let me know, of course, that his younger daughter, Kavita, was a student in the Department of English, when she joined in 1973. I did not make much headway with Nabar when I asked her to tell me something about Kavita, as she perceived her. What she said was: 'I only saw a fair bit of Kavita. I never discussed Nissim with her, but from what little he said in those days, [I gathered] they were temperamentally very much alike. One doesn't know how children react to parents–there are all kinds of undercurrents.' As for Daisy and the rest of the family, Nabar only met them when Nissim brought them along to readings and shows. On these occasions, conversation did not go beyond the mandatory hello and goodbye.

Another woman who has met the family is Tara. 'I've met Daisy on a couple of occasions, Elkana on one occasion, Kavita on one occasion,' Tara said. 'I didn't talk to them much–we never discussed Nissim.' Here Tara finds it imperative to say: 'I'm not an intimate friend of Nissim's.'

Like Toni, the other Patel, Tara too managed to make forays into The Retreat once in a while. These visits were not necessarily restricted to the '70s about which we are talking. From the way she portrays Nissim in his domestic den, it is clear she is referring to a much later period. Tara comes to the conclusion that he 'is a man who likes to punish himself.' In other words, he's a masochist. She founds this opinion on what she observed during one of her visits. This was the time Kavita was married and lived in Mussoorie, and came with her husband to Bombay once a year to stay with Nissim. The house was a 'functioning house' as long as Kavita was around, but once she left all hell broke loose. Nissim, apparently, left the milk on the stove, it spilled over, and he punished himself by not drinking tea at home for three months after that. When Tara asked him what purpose it served, he said it would remind him not to ever leave the milk on the stove in the future. Tara felt, as anyone else in her senses would, that it was needless punishment he was inflicting on himself. Like going out of his way to buy vegetables for Daisy after they separated, a practice that continued until very recently.

Nissim made two short trips to the Western hemisphere in the '70s. The first was in 1974, when he went to America on a Cultural Exchange Programme of the Government of the United States. He was required to give readings from his work, as well as seminars. The second was in 1976, to Hawaii. He was invited to a conference on Inter-Cultural Encounters in Literature at the East-West Centre. On home ground, he received an award known as the Excellence Award for his contribution to poetry on 30 April 1976.

Apart from teaching at the university and writing poetry, there was the *Indian PEN* that kept him busy. The *PEN* had a large editorial staff at that time, so Nissim didn't really have to do much. In his words, he merely 'dropped in at the office for a few hours, gave instructions to the editorial staff and then disappeared to the university to take my lectures.' The poems and articles that appeared in the journal were selected by him.

The poems in the issues of that time are, on the whole, of a higher standard than those in the decades that followed. Was it because Nissim himself was a more discriminating editor then (as opposed to now)? He doesn't agree. He also denies that he has had to compromise the quality of poems published in the journal over the years. He says it is natural for editors of poetry magazines to receive good poems at times, bad poems at others. When that happened, he published fewer poems in some issues, or sometimes even no poems at all. As for asking poets to revise their poems, he came to the conclusion that the situation differed from individual to individual. 'I tried never to say anything that amounted to putting the person down,' he told me. I asked Nissim whether it was true that more women came to see him with their poems than men? He replied that there were people of both genders who wanted him to read their poems on the spot and give them an opinion. When he explained to them that that was not how it was done, they were put off. Some of them left the office grumpily, never to return again. Behaviour of this kind, however, did not upset him. He realized it happened everywhere in the world, not just in India.

What did Rameshchandra Sirkar think of the journal Nissim edited? He felt that compared to the time Madame Sophiya Wadia edited it, it had improved. For one thing, it carried more original poetry and less by way of surveys and reports. The poems that Nissim sometimes published were positively experimental. They were written by a new and upcoming generation of poets that Sirkar had no contact with. 'We began to see that, as in the case of his students, here too he was very open to a new writer making experiments with writing–he would encourage it, though at times he would return it with suggestions for improvement.' Sirkar said that once in a while, there was a general feeling among the 'big shots' of the Theosophy Lodge that Nissim spent too much time 'tinkering with the manuscripts' of poets. He himself does not share this view. Observing the man for decades, however, he has noticed a kind of transformation in him. In those days, when Nissim was in his fifties, he worked hard on the journal and gave the impression of being driven, as if the time he devoted to it was at the expense of his own poetry. What mattered, when a poem was placed before him for consideration, was literary merit. Today, in his seventies, he is more concerned with helping the person who has come to him for advice. And if publishing the poem is the only way in which he can offer help, he will do so.

A new poetry magazine was started in Bombay in the mid '70s by four young poets, some of whom were Nissim's students at the university. It was called *Kavi* (later *Kavi India*), and the four who published and edited it were Santan Rodrigues, the late Rajiv Rao, Ivan Kostka and Aroop Mitra. Nissim's name appeared as 'consultant' or 'advisor' in all the issues. If my memory isn't failing me, I remember copies of *Kavi* being stocked and sold at his office at the Department in 1977, when Mitra and I were classmates. The magazine had his 'blessings' from the word go, and this cannot be ruled out as one of the factors responsible for its success. *Kavi* had a longer shelf-life than *Poetry India*, and to several people, this alone indicated that Rodrigues and his friends had greater organizational abilities than Nissim. When I spoke to Nissim about his association with *Kavi,* he said he 'had a hand in its publication, in a sense.' What he liked about this work was that 'someone else was taking the initiative and the responsibility for editing it, arranging the finance, and so on.' This was 'ideal' from his point of view, because there was no commitment he made to anyone. The situation, thus, was very different from *Poetry India,* where he had to look after everything single-handed. Moreover, *Kavi* was ultimately Rodrigues' journal, it reflected his taste and judgement, although he regularly consulted Nissim about the material received. But Nissim was happy with the journal the way it was brought out; he was sure it was run as he would have run it.

Following the example of *Kavi,* a number of literary and academic journals (including some abroad with an interest in Commonwealth Literature) began to use Nissim's name as 'consultant' or 'advisor' for the prestige it involved. While talking to me, he especially singled out *Ariel*, a journal published by the University of Calgary, Canada, and said he found the practice a 'bit embarrassing' because he virtually did nothing.

Editing a literary journal and being on the advisory board of others, was not, of course, the only thing that kept him occupied, besides teaching and poetry. There was a large quantity of prose that he turned out, in the form of reviews, and columns for newspapers and magazines. Of this voluminous body of writing, much of which is of scant or no value today, one essay that stands out and proves that he was a perceptive critic, is

'Naipaul's India and Mine'. The essay was a rejoinder to Naipaul's *An Area of Darkness* (1964), based on his first visit to India in the early '60s. I find the essay thought-provoking because it reveals more about Nissim, his obsessions and his hang-ups, his dogmas and his biases, than it does about Naipaul.

He begins the essay by informing us that his quarrel with Naipaul is that 'he writes exclusively from the point of view of his own dilemma, his temperamental alienation from his mixed background, his choice and his escape.' A few lines later, he defines Naipaul's perspectives as 'wholly subjective and wholly self-righteous.' Towards the end of the essay, he accuses Naipaul of coming 'dangerously close' to denying human beings their humanity. The methodology that Nissim follows in the essay is to take up specific incidents that Naipaul refers to in his book, and respond to them. This is how he proceeds: 'What is to be thought of a man who writes, "I stood in the shade of Churchgate station and debated whether I had it in me to cross the exposed street to the Tourist office?"'

Nissim charges Naipaul with making the truth of India seem simple. He faults his book for having 'the moral authority of hysteria, the interest and value of a suffering impotence.' But he is not interested in merely condemning the man for his short-sightedness; he offers his own alternatives, and this is where the essay becomes at least as much about Nissim as about Naipaul:

'But I see India in my own way, a way I would like to take this opportunity of clarifying and developing by contrasting it with Mr Naipaul's.' What follows, is his defence of clerks, stenos, engineers and other members of the community of common men, whom Naipaul systematically dismantles. Nissim tells Naipaul: 'In my India, a clerk will do virtually anything for you if he is treated humanely. I know those clerks, their background, their problems, their conditions of work, their income, how they are transported to and from their places of work, their educational and cultural limitations, their sense of dignity and worth, their humanity, in short.'

I get the feeling that, once again, he is here playing the devil's advocate and criticizing Naipaul for the sake of criticism. This is because Nissim himself has never displayed patience and understanding in his dealings with the average Indian; there are any number of poems, articles and speeches where he has scoffed at them, directly or indirectly. One is therefore somewhat suspicious, when he says: 'It is often the arrogance of the whites in India, and of those "educated at an English university" that makes me despair, not the intelligence of clerks, stenos, and subs.'

Yet he betrays his own snobbery when he finds a Jamini Roy painting hung beside a Picasso in Bunty's home 'infuriating'. Moreover, he concedes to much of Naipaul's reasoning as the essay advances. For example, he says at one point:

'Let me pause to explain again that I see India in most ways as Naipaul sees her. All that he says against the grossness and squalor of Indian life, the routine ritualism, the lip-service to high ideals, the petrified and distorted sense of cleanliness, and a thousand other things, all this is true.' The remark that follows ('My dissatisfaction is with his mode of argument, his falsifying examples') doesn't really take away from the fact that he admits to seeing things the way Naipaul does. This happens at two other places. Once, when he writes: 'In the India which I have presumed to call mine, I acknowledge without hesitation the existence of all the darkness Mr Naipaul discovered.' And again, when he tells us: 'Mr Naipaul is right to see us as we are in the streets, in buses and trains, in our kitchens and lavatories.'

Of course, as compared to Naipaul, it is his optimism that comes through, and ultimately this is what redeems him.

There are two things about Nissim I learned from the essay. The first concerns his Indianness, and the way he views it. He argues that as he is not a Hindu, he cannot identify with India's past, and at the same time cannot reject it. The only solution left to him, as it were, is to identify with modern India, an India 'with more things in it than are dreamt of in Mr Naipaul's philosophy.' He also proclaims he is neither proud nor ashamed of being an Indian, and of being Westernized.

The second is the problem he encounters in trains:

'"The top bunk in a railway sleeper is avoided in India," Mr Naipaul writes, because it "involves physical effort, and physical effort is to be avoided as a degradation." Well, I avoid the top bunk because it brings me too close to the fan that is attached to the ceiling. Turning the fan away causes the bunk to be rather airless; in the heat of India this makes it very uncomfortable . . . The top bunk in Indian railways often has no ladder up to it. One has to swing up, placing the feet on the arm-rest of the lower bunk. So I have sometimes given up my reserved lower bunk to a lady or an elderly person.'

There are a couple of critical articles he wrote in the '70s that stand out. His combined review of A.K Ramanujan's *Relations* and Keki Daruwalla's *Apparitions,* which appeared in the *Illustrated Weekly of India*[3] is one such. He uses the phrases 'sophistication of the rootless' and 'parochialism of the native', which suddenly gave me a perspective on nativism. When I asked him for the meaning and implication of these expressions, he said all he meant was that nativism could be parochial, and rootlessness sophisticated, depending on the attitude of the person. He was right. It is an 'attitude problem', and he was also right in emphasizing that it was especially to be found in multicultural countries like India. However, he vehemently denied the suggestion that he was privileging, or at least validating, his own rootlessness. On the contrary, he believed that a rootless person was more likely to be sophisticated in his responses 'because he knows that his behaviour and attitudes in any matter are not conditioned by or dependent on his roots.' Unlike a rooted person, the rootless human being is also searching for something–his roots. Our discussion brought us right back to Naipaul, and other diaspora writers, like David Dabydeen. Nissim was of the opinion that the fault was theirs if they felt their roots were irretrievably lost. He defined 'diaspora' as being away from the centre, and argued that such writers had a special responsibility to rediscover their past.

I was eager to find out what other people thought of Nissim's criticism. Jussawalla remarked bluntly that for all his talk about painting, Nissim was not really interested in the image, as his own poems so overpoweringly reaffirmed. He called his art and TV reviews 'culture criticism', for they purported to talk about the squalor of life. 'It can be petty, dry, full of sobriety, why-can't-they-put-a-comma-here sort of thing.'

A stronger and more condemnatory view came from Ranjit Hoskote. 'As an art critic he was a failure,' he declared, and then poured his heart out, recollecting all that he found unpalatable about Nissim's art criticism. His principal objections were: Nissim didn't have an eye for visuals; his criticism consisted of moral ideas and textbook categories, like form, line, colour, 'a do-it- yourself kit' of art criticism. Since it is Hoskote we're discussing here (a formidable art critic himself), it's best that I switch my tape-recorder on and let him speak for himself.

'Nissim has always tried to look for literal meaning in a work of art. For a long time he was on an indigenous trip, trying to work out an aesthetic that was purely indigenous. It had its value for a time, but in the end was a limiting factor. He's never been able to formulate his arguments historically–they've always been didactic, literary and literal. His pet phrases in all his art criticism are: "is this justified", "is this necessary" etc. The history of image-making practices are a closed book to him. They have never been something in which he is really interested.

'His view of the arts has suffered from what you may call the English Department view of history–a position which often leads students of Eng. Lit. into the nominalist fallacy, that is to say, if two things are called the same, they are the same (like the English Renaissance). Nissim similarly applies literary concepts to art historical problems. But his formulations often go awry because there's no connection between the two things.

'He's never been able to tackle the materiality of the image. It hasn't occurred to him that the image in painting creates expectations and effects which have to be apprehended in a completely different way from the word. He begins and ends with the word–a non-discursive experience is always something he's had problems with. All his poems which deal with non-discursive things like spirit, knowledge etc. are thus a failure. Likewise, his writing on art which is born of non-discursive experience, is a complete zero.

'One suspects that self-destruction of romantic life is what he aspired to always. He's a romantic manque who aspired to become romantic, but failed to make the grade. What you have is a book-keeper counting his pennies regularly.'

The Hoskote-Nissim association, is a complex one. It was Nissim who 'discovered' Hoskote, gave him his first break, and then wrote a fulsome blurb to *Zones of Assault* (1991). Why then does Nissim rile him? Perhaps what American critic Harold Bloom has to say about 'anxiety of influence' is true after all. Hoskote is Bloom's 'belated poet', who wants to castrate Nissim, the 'precursor poet'. Nissim stunts him, prevents him from being original, has already said all or most of the things that Hoskote wants to say. And when one realizes that both men did dangerously similar things in life, the theory falls into place.

Rameshchandra Sirkar, too, has many things to say about Nissim as an art critic, but specifies that these are not based on expertise of any kind. On the contrary, he admits it was a side of him he couldn't enter, since it was outside his field of specialization. Sirkar approaches the issue subjectively. Mihir, his son (who died tragically in a mountain-climbing accident at the age of eighteen), got interested in painting, and Sirkar's wife Ambika took him to Nissim with some of his work. Nissim looked at the paintings carefully, and said that at that stage one could either ask a person to go on, or tell him politely that it was not his scene. To Mihir, he would say 'continue', and see what happens. That certainly made Mihir's parents glad.

As hinted earlier, much of Nissim's criticism amounted to dismantling whatever was placed before him, whether it deserved such treatment or not. A case in point is his review of Jehangir Sabavala's exhibition, sometime in 1973. Nissim was then art critic of the *Times,* and he took full advantage of his position by demolishing Sabavala's work, arguing that a man who had never seen poverty at close quarters had no right to depict it on canvas. Twenty-two years later, as he, Hoskote and Minakshi Raja were sitting one morning at Sanman, sipping their tea, he denied he had ever written such a piece. Later that year (1995) it suddenly came back to him, and he admitted it to Raja; but Hoskote, who was writing a book on Sabavala, had by then left for the International Writing Program at Iowa.

In his curriculum vitae, Nissim calls himself a 'radio and TV columnist' between the years 1973 and 1978. The work he did for radio mainly consisted of talks that he gave on literary subjects, usually in a late evening slot. TV was still in its infancy in India in those days, and he did much the same thing here as well. For example, he often participated in book-discussion programmes, either as a moderator or as an invitee. Occasionally, it would be a discussion on art. In some of these programmes, one also saw the familiar (and striking) face of Vrinda Nabar, who had a stronger television presence than Nissim. This is not, of course, to undermine Nissim's charm, which unquestionably came through as he articulated a point.

As I was researching the various things he did in the '70s, I was in for surprises. Take his review of an exhibition held by Vivian Sundaram, which appeared in the November 1976 issue of *Z* magazine. No, I was not astonished by Nissim's pontificating remarks in the opening paragraph, or by the artificial distinction he makes between art and politics, or that he calls Sundaram both 'naive' and 'intelligent', in almost the same breath. All this was more or less expected, and I realized that Hoskote does indeed have a point when he denigrates Nissim's art criticism. What surprised me was a far more trivial matter. It was that Nissim, for all his snobbishness, should have chosen to write for *Z*, edited by maverick culture-vulture Arun Sachdev, and that too in an issue which had the words 'Verbal Masturbation by Satyadev Dubey' prominently displayed on its cover. And this was not the only review he wrote for *Z*- there were a handful of them. But then, perhaps I'm not seeing things in the right perspective. In the '70s, Nissim tried hard to be 'offbeat'; writing for magazines like *Z* was only an extension of his love for LSD. Between 1969 and 1972, Nissim also conducted a course in art appreciation at the J. J. School of Art in Bombay and was a member of the General Council of the Lalit Kala Akademi as well as the Sahitya Akademi.

In 1976, Nissim published his sixth book of poems, *Hymns in Darkness*,[4] dedicated to Keku and Khorshed Gandhy. It was brought out by Oxford University Press (OUP), marking his entry, thereby, into the world of mainstream publishing. The switch from Writers Workshop (that had brought out his previous collections) to OUP seems to have partly happened on account of poet R. Parthasarathy's intervention. Parthasarathy was working then for OUP, first in Bombay and later in Madras. His own anthology of Indian English poetry, *Ten Twentieth Century Indian Poets* was published that year by OUP, and it included poems by Nissim. The initial suggestion was Nissim's–he approached Partha, as his friends affectionately called him, and asked if he would recommend his manuscript to OUP. Parthasarathy, it must be recalled, was for a while Nissim's colleague in the English Department of Mithibai College. Nissim and he had a mutual respect for each other's work, and for each other as human beings. Parthasarathy had no hesitation in recommending his friend's manuscript to his company. The company accepted his recommendation, signed a contract with Nissim, and within a year the book was out.

The volume *Hymns in Darkness* consists of twenty-seven poems, the last four being in several sections each. The book gets its title from the last poem, 'Hymns in Darkness', which has sixteen sections in all. A title such as 'Hymns in Darkness', complete with all that it paradoxes, the prayers of a secular man or a 'sceptical seeker'[5] as Bruce King calls it, is symbolic of the kinds of transformations we witness in the book. Broadly, these are of two kinds. At one level, the poems begin to take on religious themes, marking Nissim's passage from atheist to believer in his post-LSD years. On another level, their form becomes more open than it was in *The Unfinished Man* and *The Exact Name*. The sixteen 'Hymns' simulate a form used in the Old Testament; it is for this reason that they are so special to Nissim. He emphasizes that he did not change to free verse simply because it was being used all over the world. He is of the opinion that (as the New Critics in America said), form and content had a bearing on each other: in any case, this is how he would characterize his poems in *Hymns in Darkness*.

Nevertheless, as in the case of his previous collections, the poems in *Hymns in Darkness* can be classified in the usual ways. There are religious poems, love poems, Bombay poems and poems about the artistic process. In addition, there are, for the first time, a couple of 'Very Indian Poems in Indian English', for which Nissim achieved much notoriety. There is also the autobiographical poem, 'Background, Casually'. Apart from these, there are a few poems that we may classify as miscellaneous. The form varies from the extreme formality of the opening poem 'Subject of Change', to the extreme informality of the two Indian English poems, 'The Railway Clerk' and 'Goodbye Party for Miss Pushpa T.S.', to the minimalism of the final 'Poster Poems', 'Passion Poems' and 'The Egoist's Prayers'. Lastly there's 'Hymns in Darkness' which, as pointed out above, ambitiously tries to experiment with a form of verse used in the Old Testament.

In terms of number, the poems with a religious theme dominate.[6] I would include in this category, besides, the sixteen 'Hymns in Darkness', 'Guru', 'Rural Suite', 'Tribute to the Upanishads' and 'How the English Lesson Ended'. Both 'The Egoist's Prayers' and 'Passion Poems' contain sections that may be construed religious. Of course, religion is worked into the poems in different ways. 'Guru' and 'Rural Suite' are deceptive, because while they appear to be irreverent on the surface, anti-religious even, they manage to draw enough attention to religion. The personae they invoke are, after all, religious figures–saints in the one case and bhikshus in the other. 'Background, Casually', together with 'How the English Lesson Ended', crudely harps on cultural differences between Hindus, Muslims, Roman Catholics and Jews, giving the poems a communal air. In the latter poem, we are almost led to the conclusion that the English lesson wouldn't have ended, had the neighbour's daughter not been Muslim! 'Tribute to the Upanishads', and three 'Passion Poems' ('The Sanskrit Poets', 'A Marriage' and 'The Loss') are religious–Hindu–in a self-conscious sort of way. Once again, the poems deceive us because outwardly they seem to poke fun at mythical and mythological figures. In truth, however, they betray Nissim's desire to assimilate into Hindu India, a desire that possessed him strongly in his post-LSD years. 'The Egoist's

Prayers' and 'Hymns in Darkness' are unconventional prayer-poems; but they are 'prayers' all the same, in which Nissim accepts the existence of God, and prays to Him the way ordinary people do, asking for favours. What makes them unconventional is that unlike the prayers of the masses, who at least feign humility, Nissim goes out of his way to flaunt his ego:

> O well, if you insist,
> I will do your will.
> Please try to make it coincide with mine.
> ('The Egoist's Prayers, IV')

The trouble with 'The Egoist's Prayers' and 'Hymns in Darkness' is that Nissim wants to have his cake and eat it too. This leaves us dissatisfied, although the 'Hymns' successfully imitate the form of Vedic and Old Testament verses.

The genesis of 'Hymns in Darkness' is best explained by Bruce King. 'The sixteen "Hymns . . ." were written during a period after Ezekiel's mother and father had died, and when living in a room alone, he would turn out the lights and compose poetry in his head related to the Vedic hymns he was reading in English translation.'[7] Nissim thus wrote the poems as a therapeutic or cathartic exercise. This may have brought him relief; but it was still himself he was writing the poems for. The love poems provide little evidence of growth and maturity; they do not appear different from similar poems in previous collections. 'The Couple' is a spillover from poems in *The Unfinished Man, The Exact Name* and the three volumes before them, where the woman is projected as a shrew.

> Indolence and arrogance
> were rooted in her primal will,
> a woman to fear, not to love,
> yet he made love to her

'Poem of the Separation', though based on a specific incident–Nissim's break-up with Linda Hess–fares only slightly better, with the woman being credited with some intelligence and sensitivity. 'Ganga' treads on dangerous ground. It dares to appropriate the voice of a servant woman, on whose behalf the poet-narrator speaks. It's true it is the employing class that becomes the target of attack in the poem; yet there are enough stereotypical ways in which Ganga, the maid, is seen. For example, she is suspected of being a prostitute. She expects the usual cup of tea, stale chapati, annual sari and blouse, and money for paan from her employers. Above all,

> She brings a smell with her
> and leaves it behind her

In 'Tone Poem', the woman fails to appear as anything but a sex object. 'Your breasts are small /tender like your feelings', Nissim writes in the opening stanza.

There are two Bombay poems in *Hymns in Darkness:* 'Island' and 'On Bellasis Road'.[8] The former poem contains the important lines 'I cannot leave the island, /I was born here and belong'. These echo the famous concluding lines of 'Background, Casually', the previous poem in the book, where Nissim expresses his commitments:

> I have made my commitments now.
> This is one: to stay where I am,
> As others choose to give themselves
> In some remote and backward place.
> My backward place is where I am.

As I have argued elsewhere,[9] the word 'backward' here is ironic and deceptive. Nissim does not imply that India–Bombay–is essentially backward, and leave it at that, in a spirit of resignation. Instead, he chooses to inhabit backward Bombay, and by doing so, rids it of some of its backwardness. This happens in two ways: one, he writes his poems in English; two, he sees Bombay in much the same way that Yeats sees Dublin or Eliot sees London. Both these amount to modernizing acts. 'Island' similarly displays a creative tension and ambivalence: in general, it is undesirable to be an 'island'; it is necessary for Nissim, however, to be on this one (Bombay).

On the other hand, 'On Bellasis Road' is unique in its attempt to evoke a specific local reality–this is not something that Nissim, self-absorbed as he is, had the time for earlier. What's especially delightful about the poem is the details about the street that he provides, though perhaps these are by no means sufficient to bring it entirely to life. Even so, the poem marks a certain development in his style.

'Background, Casually', apart from swearing life-long allegiance to Bombay, movingly tells the 'story' of Nissim's life in all of fifteen five-line stanzas. It begins with his childhood, of which we get to learn the following: he was weak and timid; ate and slept little; couldn't fly a kite or spin a top; went to a Roman Catholic school, where, as a Jew, he felt intimidated and threatened by Christian, Muslim and Hindu boys; participated in Friday-night prayers at home, without making much of them; grew to the age of twenty-two and took off for London, where he lived in a basement with three companions–Philosophy, Poverty and Poetry. (The basement room, incidentally, became a motif in his consciousness, and he would return to it again and again. In *Hymns in Darkness,* there is another reference to it in the first stanza of 'London'.) The second section of 'Background, Casually' tells us of how he lived in the basement room, first alone, and then with a woman who informed him he was 'the Son of Man'; how he earned his passage to India scrubbing decks in an English cargo ship taking French guns to Indo-China; and how, after his return, he felt estranged in India by the crudity and vulgarity of the Hindu herd. It also informs us that he got married, changed jobs, and even that he saw himself as a fool. The third and last section of the poem is reflective: it speaks of his grandfather who fought in the Boer War, and of his own realization that poetry is his vocation. The last-but-one stanza has the line 'The Indian landscape sears my eyes'. Considering this, the last stanza, in which he declares his resolve to stay on in India, no matter what, may come as a surprise. However, like the line 'My backward place is where I am', the above line too is not without its share of irony; it is the irony, in fact, that brings wholeness and consistency to the vision. There are two other things about the poem that stand out. One, Nissim, in a deft stroke of self-parody, describes himself as 'poet-rascal-clown' in the very opening line. Two, he uses the third-person mask in the opening stanza, only to get rid of it from the second stanza onwards, and reveal his true self.

The most experimental poems in *Hymns In Darkness* are the two 'Very Indian Poems in Indian English', 'Goodbye Party for Miss Pushpa T. S.' and 'The Railway Clerk'. Here Nissim attempts to distinguish standard or regular English from the English Indians who have had their education in the regional languages speak. As pointed out earlier, it was at Mithibai

College that the idea to write such poems germinated in his mind. Because his sample consisted mainly of Gujarati-speaking Indians, some commentators feel he should call the poems Gujarati English, rather than Indian English poems. But Nissim dislikes phrases like Gujarati English and Bengali English–he thinks it amounts to a lot of hair-splitting. If it came to that, he would prefer to call it Indian English as spoken in Bombay, and Indian English as spoken in Calcutta. After leaving Mithibai College and joining Bombay University, he had more opportunities to observe how Indians spoke English, which he calls 'direct experiences'. His sample here included Maharashtrian clerks at the university, among other people, and he discovered that by using English the way they used it, he could get things done more quickly, than when he spoke to them in 'correct' English. What struck him was that at such times, no one laughed–neither the clerks, nor other teachers who may have been around; whereas the Indian English poems have, on the whole, been thought to be funny or humorous. Nissim is intrigued by the way his audiences at poetry readings laugh on first hearing the poems, and then say, 'It's not funny'. This, however, happens only in India; abroad, people listen to the poems, laugh, but do not ask questions like 'Do you thinks it's right to makes fun of Indians?' Even so, he is aware that the humour in his poetry is restricted to the handful of Indian English poems he has written; the ones written in standard English are, without exception, serious. He is even prepared to see this as a limitation.

Sunita Sharma, daughter of writer Vera Sharma, recalls how once, when Nissim and she were travelling together in a taxi in the mid-'80s, he told her he kept notes on the way people spoke. When she asked him to share some of his observations with her, he told her of the man who said to him: 'I shall see you when I'm empty and you are vacant.' Nissim wasn't exaggerating; Sharma is inclined to believe what he reported to her. However, Vanashree Joshi, a lecturer in English at Somaiya College in Bombay, is less sure. She takes the title of 'Goodbye Party for Miss Pushpa T.S.' as an example to prove how inaccurate Nissim's observations are. She points out, with the precision of a scholar, that in a name like 'Pushpa T.S.', one would normally expect 'Pushpa' to represent the person's surname. Everyone in India knows, however, that 'Pushpa' cannot be a surname–it's a first name. Joshi calls this a 'distortion'.

My own reading of the Indian English poems leads me to believe that, in writing these poems, Nissim was vicariously satisfying a desire to be bilingual. 'I always felt unhappy that I did not succeed in becoming bilingual,' he told me. 'I would certainly encourage anyone who wanted to be bilingual. It's a good thing for the country's culture as a whole.' The language of the Indian English poems, insofar as it tried to approximate the Creole of the West Indies, or be its equivalent, performed the role of a 'dialect'. And if he was able to write in both standard English and 'dialect', that was reason enough for him to consider himself bilingual. It may not have been the bilingualism of a Ramanujan or a Chitre, but then as a non-Hindu, that was perhaps the maximum he could aspire to.

One of the biggest surprises of *Hymns in Darkness* is 'The Truth About the Floods'. A parenthetical note at the beginning of the poem informs us that it is 'a found poem based on a report by V. K. Dixit in the Indian Express, Bombay, 25 September 1967.' As I have already noted, Nissim had disdain for poems of social realism, made out of real-life events. There is thus no explanation as to why he suddenly chose to write a poem about a journalist's visit to 'the flood-affected areas' of North Bihar and Orissa. The poem is written in the form of a journal. It is postmodern in the way it sticks to a flat idiom and abounds in commonplaces of speech, like some of the early work of Arun Kolatkar.

> I went to the village
> to find out the truth.
> All the houses had collapsed.
> Many were washed away.
> The men, women and children
> were silent.
> They gazed at the sky.

In addition to the diarist's voice, we hear the voices of some of the villagers. One of them says:

> 'I have eleven children.
> Two I have left to the mercy of God.
> The rest are begging, somewhere.'

The poem has similarities with A.K. Ramanujan's well known 'A River'. It's purpose is satirical; it seems to be saying that all the effort and expense involved in travelling to far out places to file a news report is a waste, because in the end, the villagers are going to be as wretched as they always have been. Journalists should not, therefore, have an exalted idea of their worth.

> The district authorities
> at Balasore
> admitted they had failed,
> but they claimed they could not have done better.
> Nature, they said,
> had conspired against them.
> 'Write the truth' they said,
> in your report.'
> And so I did.

However, Nissim's lack of faith in investigative reporting and socialist realism, his belief that poetry must keep away from subjects too immediate, betrays his own failure to keep abreast of changing trends all over the world. The notion of the personal-as-political is virtually unknown to him; in that sense, he has remained stuck in the narrow groove of modernism.

That is why he is much more at ease with two poems about the artistic process, 'For Satish Gujral' and 'Advice to a Painter', although the tone of the latter poem is again satirical. Both poems are a throwback to 'Jamini Roy' in *The Unfinished Man*. In 'For Satish Gujral', he says:

> Deaf artists all,
> all of us who martyr the meaning
> in the flux to lonely
> and heated visions whoring after truth.

'Advice to a Painter', needless to say, is advice to a woman painter; the perspective is coloured by her gender. She is portrayed as someone who is more interested in the idea of being a painter, a pseudo-painter at best, than in painting itself.

> Buy lots of paint, I'll send you some from here.
> Plan a trip abroad, all the artists do.
> Plan publicity, all the artists do.
> A woman has her hopes and dreams.
> Announce yours to *Eve's Weekly* and feel fulfilled.

As in his other poems with woman as subject, Nissim's sexism is manifest here. It is almost as if he sets out to prove that only men can be real painters; women can be no more than pseudo-painters and poetasters.

Hymns in Darkness came out in 1976. This was a significant year for Indian English poetry, with a large number of critically acclaimed first collections making their appearance. Vilas Sarang calls the year the 'annus mirabilis'[10] of Indian English poetry. When we survey the poetry scene in 1976, we find that *Hymns in Darkness* was competing with Adil Jussawalla's *Missing Person,* Arun Kolatkar's *Jejuri,* Gieve Patel's *How Do You Withstand, Body,* Arvind Krishna Mehrotra's *Nine Enclosures,* R. Parthasarathy's *Rough Passage* and Jayanta Mahapatra's *A Rain of Rites,* all of which appeared that year. This surfeit of poetry was evident to everyone; M. Sivaramakrishna published an article in the *Sunday Times* the following year, in which he called 1976 'a year marked by creative opulence of undoubted maturity.'[11]

In a way, it is surprising that the year should have witnessed such an upsurge of creativity. This is because the previous year, 1975, was notorious for the Emergency imposed by Indira Gandhi, which put curbs on artistic freedom. The Emergency was still on in 1976–it was lifted in 1977. But then, writers are perhaps at their best when they perceive a threat to their freedom. It wasn't just Indian poets in English who wrote prolifically during the Emergency; poets in other languages did too. This is what prompted American scholar John Oliver Perry to compile an anthology of 'Emergency' poems a few years later.'[12]

Of course Nissim, like most other Indian English poets, was not the one to write a political poem about the ills of the Emergency. One of the criticisms sometimes levelled against Indian English poets by their fellow-poets in the regional languages, is that they have failed to respond to socio-political events such as the Emergency, or the Bhopal gas leak of 1984. However, when *Kavi India* decided to bring out a special issue on the Emergency,'[13] Nissim gave them a poem called 'Toast'. This poem isn't to be found in the *Collected Poems.* It is rare, by all accounts, and I reproduce it in full:

> To those in power
> beyond the law,

and those in prison
with no recourse to it,
I drink a glass
of this or that–
it tastes
like poisoned mud.
A cheerful company
downs the drink with me:
it doesn't complain.
Its testament
is silence: the new creeds,
faces, voices serve
the old cause of self
as well as the older lot.

Another drink,
the same toast,
Let others fight
for you know what.

Hymns in Darkness was reviewed by Anita Desai in the *Indian PEN.*'[14] It is somewhat unusual for a novelist of Desai's stature to review a book for a little Indian magazine, a book of poems at that. Desai concedes that, as a volume, *Hymns in Darkness* is an experiment. She then says: 'However, I cannot help thinking these experiments have not the theme or the form in which Ezekiel is most at home or at his best. A "found" poem like "The Truth About the Floods" is simply too easy for a poet who has always been so meticulous, such a perfectionist in his craft. As for the poems in "Indian English", I find it difficult to grasp the purpose–is it to create hilarity? Or to prove that poetry can be written in pidgin? It could be both, and yet neither purpose contains the inner compulsion that underlines every true poem.'

Another review was John Beston's in the *Sydney Morning Herald.* '[15] Beston spends most of his time explaining and justifying Nissim's need to write in English. In the bargain, he ends up saying very little about the book itself. This was perhaps expected, considering he was writing the review for an Australian readership.

According to him, 'the most ambitious and successful poems in the volume is the title poem 'Hymns in Darkness'. However, he doesn't mince words telling us why the poem is ambitious or successful. The only reason he offers is that 'it is his [Ezekiel's] most sustained investigation of the nature of man's search for the great truths.'

Twenty years after *Hymns in Darkness* was published and reviewed, several writers and scholars, Nissim's peers, continue to have strong opinions about it. Jussawalla informed me: 'In the '70s everyone was making posters. In writing "Poster Poems", Nissim thought he had found an ideal amalgam, that he was working among artists. It was the surfacing of a man who was trying to be a popular figure, not just a well-known one. This was also the time he started to write his Indian English poems, which is the only thing about him as a stand-up comic that has remained.'

To Jussawalla, 'posters' is a politically-loaded word. It is a leftist term that Nissim appropriated. In truth, he was anti-left once he fell out with M.N. Roy, and took to LSD. He thus felt betrayed by Jussawalla and Eunice de Souza, whose political ideology continued to remain strongly left-wing, and who were concerned, for example, with what was happening to the Naxalites. During a Bombay University workshop entitled 'Why I Write', held in the early '70s (at which Shiva Naipaul was also present), Nissim even accused Jussawalla and his friend Cyrus Mistry of heckling him.

Anthony Burge, a British poet who spends time in India, told me he bought a copy of *Hymns in Darkness* from the OUP showroom in Bombay in October 1994, soon after he had met Nissim for the first time. Upon reading it, he decided he preferred the 'objective' poems to the introspective, self-questioning ones. He calls this self-questioning 'typically Jewish' and attributes his dislike for such poems to personal taste—'as a poet myself, I don't like self-questioning poems.' Commenting specifically on the 'Hymns', he feels some of them have good lines, 'but the tortured self-examination is bit too much.' Among the 'Hymns', he likes those poems that tell him something about Nissim's school days and his surroundings, rather than about his inner gropings.

The other group of poems that Burge comments on is the Indian English poems. He likes both 'The Railway Clerk' and 'Goodbye Party for Miss Pushpa T. S.' for their humour. Having said that, however, he is quick to add: 'I'm careful to avoid orientalism. I'm more of a realistic than a romantic writer.' Burge is also of the opinion that 'Nissim's distancing himself from fellow-Indians in the Indian English poems smacks of disdain and a patronizing attitude.'

And Vrinda Nabar says: 'I agree there was a decline in his poetry in the '70s, but *Hymns in Darkness* still has some fine poems. It is affected by a sense of his trying-to-do-everything, which enters the poems. What Nissim had to say reached its end in the mid-'70s, and after that the poetry didn't have further inputs to live itself out, for all the more significant stuff was written by then. I can't understand, however, why this should have been the case, why there was no nourishment from within.'

Verse, Versatility

Two years after it was first published, *Hymns in Darkness* continued to be discussed. As late as 25 July 1978, *The Hindu*[1] ran a combined review of the more important volumes of poetry published in 1976, as well as of the books that followed. These included, besides *Hymns in Darkness,* R. Parthasarathy's *Rough Passage* and his anthology *Ten Twentieth-Century Indian Poets,* Keki Daruwalla's *Crossing of Rivers,* Shiv K. Kumar's *Subterfuges* and A.K. Ramanujan's *Selected Poems.* Kamala Das, Jayanta Mahapatra and Arvind Krishna Mehrotra were also referred to in the article. *Hymns in Darkness* gets all of a paragraph, in which the reviewer, S. Krishnan, admits that 'it is difficult to say anything new or different about him [Ezekiel].' Having said that, he goes on to describe Nissim's style as 'lean and spare . . . which manages to pack in tremendous substance and profundity.'

Nissim, in the late '70s, was a star. He had a well-received and widely-reviewed book of poems from OUP, wrote for the *Times of India* and other high circulation newspapers and magazines, and was promoted from Reader to Professor at Bombay University. Yet on the personal front, his life cannot be described as happy. The 'separation' with Daisy had taken effect by this time, and he lived by himself at The Retreat, without being physically, mentally, spiritually and psychologically equipped to do so. Like most heterosexual men, Nissim needed women around him to look after him, do the cooking, washing and housekeeping. With both his mother and wife now removed from the scene, he was lost. This helplessness, which at first he successfully masked, had over the years begun to assert itself. In the '90s, it has reached its pinnacle, with old age contributing to take him close to 'destitution'. But more of this later. Back in the late '70s and early '80s, things were still not so bad, or if they were, he still had the fortitude and presence of mind to put on an act before the world. One of the strategies that he evolved, as pointed out earlier, was to completely forbid people–including his closest friends–from visiting him at home. His privacy was protected in this way, and the embargo also guaranteed that nobody saw him in his most vulnerable and powerless of moments, he who was intellectual king in India's cultural universe. However, from time to time, some of his friends did manage to sneak into the hallowed precincts of The Retreat, under one pretext or another. Tara Patel has already been mentioned in this context. She told me that sometime in the very late '70s or very early '80s, she went to The Retreat and was shocked by what she saw.

'He was living like a recluse, with no one to look after him. There were dirty bed sheets on the floor. There were hundreds of books all over the place. I picked up a couple and took them away–Nissim is not possessive when it comes to books, and this is something about him that I appreciate very much. The kitchen was filthy. I offered to help him, to clean up the place for him. I did so once or twice, and then I stopped going. Whenever I asked him if he wanted me at The Retreat, he said no. I came to love him in a daughterly sort of way, and I would tell myself that if I were his daughter, I wouldn't let him live like that. I found it very strange that his wife and children did not come to help him. He has a very insensitive family.'

Tara was not the only one who was sympathetic to Nissim's 'plight'. A number of young men, and especially women, entered his life in the post-*Hymns in Darkness* period, and became his companions. It may have had to do with the fact that after *Hymns in Darkness,* he had arrived. Several of these youngsters started out as students at Bombay University or Elphinstone College, where he still taught the evening MA classes, and then went on to become his friends after passing out. Ronita Torcato is one such woman, who has, over the years, stood by him unfalteringly. In the late '90s, she remains one of the few people who still visited him at the PEN with strict regularity. 'I first met him while doing my MA in English Literature at Bombay University,' Torcato said. 'I was in the evening batch. The year was 1976–the year in which I enrolled. I do not remember my first meeting with him, but I distinctly remember a subsequent one. I knocked at his door and he welcomed me with open arms. I was taken aback by his enthusiasm.' After she completed her MA, there was a break in the association for a while. A couple of years later, however, Torcato became a 'Friend' (a category of membership) of the PEN, and this gave her an opportunity to renew her contacts with Nissim. 'There came a time in the '80s when I used to drop in to see him everyday. We would chat, I would browse through the journals lying about, which he was very generous in lending, or giving away as a present. We went for tea to the Sanman, for which he paid sometimes, and sometimes I. I found him to be a very good listener. He encourages you to talk. One of the first things he would say on seeing me is: "so what's the gossip?" I talked to him about my personal problems, and he acted as a sort of counsellor. I suspect he felt honoured to be privy to my affairs. I didn't mind too. But I don't think I was the only one who went to his office to talk things of this kind to him. I had a feeling there were others too, though I can't really say if the women outnumbered the men.'

Torcato is not a feminist. She sees nothing wrong in the connection Nissim made between women and gossip. I was curious to know what she thought of him as a teacher.

'As a student, I used to attend most of his classes, though this is not to say I never bunked. As a teacher, he seemed somewhat dry to me, but he tried hard to make his classes lively by cracking jokes once in a while. Maybe it was the texts that he was teaching that made him sound like that. It wasn't his fault. He had this dispassionate way of lecturing. He never got emotional, unlike, say, Nisha da Cunha [former Head of the English Department, St Xavier's College, Bombay] who often would cry in class while teaching a moving poem. There is a view that New Yorkers and Jews are supposed to be loud and pushy. But Nissim is just the opposite. He's quiet.'

The late '70s and early '80s were also a time when Nissim continued to travel. He went on annual lecture tours to Goa and Hyderabad. The Hyderabad trips were to conduct an advanced course for college teachers, perhaps the equivalent of today's refresher courses. To Goa he would go as a visiting professor, for Goa was then within the ambit of Bombay University. But his travels were by no means restricted to the shores of India. There were several foreign trips that followed in quick succession. For example, he was invited to Hawaii in 1976, Australia in 1977 and Rotterdam and West Berlin in 1978–three trips to three very different parts of the world in three successive years!

There is an interesting story that surrounds his visit to Australia in 1977. He was invited to attend a cultural-cum-literary festival, in which he was expected to participate by reading his poems. The Australian consulate sent him a first-class air ticket, which instead of flattering him, made him worry about the money that was wastefully spent. He contacted the consulate and told them that a first-class air ticket was okay if he was habitually accustomed to travelling in such luxury. But as this was not the case, as he was no company director, would they please take the ticket back and send him an economy ticket instead? The consulate people were equally stubborn. They replied that they would convey his feelings to the Australian government, but at the moment there was nothing they could possibly do, for there were rules, which had to be abided by. And the rules of the Australian government were that for travel within Australia, delegates were paid the economy fare, but for international travel it was always the first-class fare. And so Nissim went to Australia like a maharaja, in first class.

Sometime later, Nissim also went to Canada, where he stayed with Frank Birbalsingh, scholar in Caribbean literature, cricket enthusiast and Professor at York University, Toronto. I could not establish the exact date of his visit, as there are no records available. One possibility is that it was in 1976, the year he went to Hawaii. He could have broken journey at Toronto, either on his way to the Pacific Island, or on his way back.[2] Frank Birbalsingh and I became good friends ever since we got acquainted with each other as postdoctoral fellows at the University of Warwick (UK) in 1990. When I told him I was writing this biography, he tried to recall as much as he could about the time Nissim stayed with him and his family in Toronto. One of the things he vividly remembered was that Nissim was mortally afraid of their pet dog. He was distinctly uneasy whenever the animal came anywhere near him, and no amount of guarantees and reassurances from his host put his fears to rest. Apart from that, he remembers Nissim as a 'decent' house guest who made his own bed, and did not make unreasonable demands on his host. Birbalsingh came to respect Nissim, and called on him whenever he got the opportunity.

Like Torcato and Birbalsingh, another of Nissim's associations that originated in the late '70s /early '80s and went to become permanent, was with Jerry Pinto, who eventually became a journalist with the *Times of India*, and one of its more (if not most) prolific writers. Pinto says he first met Nissim in 1982 at the age of sixteen as a First Year BA student at Elphinstone College. Nissim had come to his college to conduct a poetry workshop for members of the English Association, and Pinto participated in the workshop. He recounts: 'I had read "Night of the Scorpion" as a schoolboy, and some of his poems that appeared in old issues of the *Illustrated Weekly.* I enlisted for his workshop and read two poems. I found it charming that he did not hand down opinions but drew them out of us. He was to do a series of six workshops, and in the second session he talked of rhythm, scansion and meter. He said he liked a poem of mine, entitled "Loneliness". I've since found the poem juvenile and thrown it away. But he was sympathetic and encouraging.'

Pinto did not follow up that first encounter with visits to the PEN. At any rate, not until much later. I asked him why. 'I didn't go to the PEN to see him because he was a busy man and asked people to make an appointment before coming. This puts me off. So for a long time [after the workshop] there was no contact.'

However, as he was to soon discover, Nissim had a good memory for faces, and whenever they bumped into each other at bus-stops–Pinto especially mentions the bus-stops at Kalina and Breach Candy–or at the Fort campus or Elphinstone College, Nissim would smile at him without being able to place him. This attracted Pinto to him. Although he had opted for Sociology and Psychology as special subjects for BA, he started reading Nissim's poems with seriousness. He picked up a copy of *Hymns in Darkness* at a sale organized by OUP, where he acquired it at a substantial discount. *Hymns in Darkness* automatically led him to Nissim's previous volumes, and then to *Latter-Day Psalms.* Gradually, Pinto started attending literary functions at the PEN; this brought him face to face with Nissim more often.

Meanwhile, Nissim continued to charm, and be charming to members of the opposite sex. But there was a conservatism (prudishness?) about him that made him reluctant to write about love and sex, except in the most general terms. Toni Patel claims that it was only after she nagged him for lacking the courage to write about his love life, that he wrote 'Nudes 1978', which was later included in *Latter-Day Psalms.* This, according to her, happened sometime in the mid-'70s. In 1980, *Youth Times,* a magazine published by the *Times of India* group (the magazine has since closed down) brought out a special issue on the Poetry of Love. An interview with Nissim[3] appears in the magazine in which he says certain things about love (and his own married life) that he had never said before. For example, he admits in reply to the question whether he is cynical about marriage, that he has experienced difficulties in his own marriage, although he is not cynical about marriage as a whole. Another question that was put to him was: 'Have you written any love poems in Indian English?' His reply: 'To write love poems in Indian English, I would have to overhear some typical wooing conversations and other amorous jeu d'esprit.'

A month before the *Youth Times* interview, Nissim gave another interview to *Eve's Weekly*[4] (like *Youth Times* this magazine too is now defunct). Being a woman's magazine, the editors were interested in his views on women and literature. His answers are amongst the most chauvinistic, conservative, politically incorrect, and offensive of statements he has ever made. The magazine reports:

'So far as the well-known women writers are concerned, he [Ezekiel] felt that their success was often because of their themes rather than their abilities.' Furthermore, 'Indian women poets seem to Ezekiel very weak in technique and form.'

As if this is not enough, they then begin to quote him directly:

'One sympathizes with that element in their lives and the way they insist on expressing it. But the literary values achieved are not really impressive. A woman emphasizes her special problems as a woman. A man may express anger or frustration, but he goes beyond the male element in it.'

To the question, what in his opinion was the general attitude of Indian men to writing by women, his reply was:

'I'm afraid it is usually one of male chauvinism [hear, hear!]. There is definitely a feeling of superiority to women deep in the male subconscious. It is so in most countries of the world, but dying out slowly in a few Western nations.'

Finally, his 'last word' on poetry by women: 'Well, it has to be judged ultimately as poetry, not as women's poetry.'

As pointed out earlier, and as all the above statements demonstrate, the notion of the 'personal-as-political' was unknown to Nissim at the time. Perhaps, because it was the end of the '70s and the beginning of the '80s, he could get away with the statements he made. Had it been today, such an interview would perhaps never have found its way into print.

What is most revealing about the *Eve's Weekly* interview, is that Nissim was genuinely of the belief that women were fundamentally different from, and inferior to, men. Jussawalla put the issue in perspective when he said: 'Nissim's male friends, unlike his women friends, are those who don't challenge him' (Hoskote has expressed the same view.)

The *Youth Times* and *Eve's Weekly* interviews notwithstanding, the year 1979 saw Nissim give one of his most intelligent interviews to a serious literary periodical. The periodical in question was the Indian *Literary Review*[5] edited by Suresh Kohli, and the interviewers were poet Imtiaz Dharker and her journalist-husband Anil Dharker. There are several opinions that Nissim expresses in this interview for the first time. Or almost. In their introduction, the Dharkers speak of his approachability, and say: '. . . Nissim Ezekiel's approachability does not come from any sense of false modesty. He is firmly aware (though he never says so) of his place in Indian letters. And that place has for so long been in the forefront of English poetry and critical writing in India, that it is difficult to imagine a time when he was not there.'

The first issue that the Dharkers take up is Indianness. What Nissim has to say on the subject is something we have never heard him say before so forthrightly. If anything, he has in the past said things that are contradictory to what he says now; to me, this indicates growth and maturity on his part. The relevant paragraph in the interview is as follows:

'Now, I think that the attempt of thirty years [to become a Hindu] has been a failure. I see a great difference between a real Indian and my Indianness. A major Scottish poet recently said to me . . . "You're not a real Indian", and my response was, "No, we've lived in India only 2000 years." A Jew can never be a "real" Indian or a "real" Chinaman. I'd say Parthasarathy and Ramanunjan are "real" Indians.' The question that immediately follows is: 'Are you saying one has to be a Hindu to be a real Indian?' And Nissim's answer is: 'I'm aware of identity problems among non-Hindus: Muslims, Parsis, Christians. I think the problem of identity is important in all literary and cultural activity. I don't believe it's possible to be a universal man without some specific roots which are strengthened, accepted or revolted against . . . Of late I've found myself more deliberately turning to Jewish sources and themes as though some inner movement has required it.'

The next important thing that the Dharkers touch upon is the Indian English poems. Their questions cover diverse ground: why are the Indian English poems more widely known than Nissim's other work; what kind of effect was he aiming at in the Indian English poems; was he making fun of the speakers in these poems. Nissim speaks on the poems at some length, providing information and opinions: 'I've written only eight Indian English poems. Five are published, of which only three are known. They are sensational in the conventional sense. Khushwant Singh read out these poems during his lectures in various cities of India and told me that they brought the house down every time . . . What happened [in the poems] was a form of typecasting . . . I was identified as their creator, the poet who writes in Indian English. My other poems were overlooked. If people are amused by a poem, they remember it . . . Even if I were only making fun of him [the speaker in the poems], it would be valid from the literary point of view. A taxi driver might smile when I speak Hindi. If it is mocking, it survives only as long as the social situation lasts. American Jews used to say their types didn't find a proper place in American literature. In due course they were represented. The reaction was of shock and some resentment. So, I hear a person talking in a certain way. I catch the idiom, his attitudes in a poem. Should this be interpreted as lack of respect, a colonial snobbishness? I take the risk. With the passage of time, the emphasis will change . . . The Indian English poems I'm writing now use the language, not for pathos, but for tragedy in the Greek sense . . . I've never written tragedy–my normal preference is for comedy, serious emotions and ideas, with irony. I don't write to entertain, but if I do I am not displeased.'

Conversation shifts to 'Latter-Day Psalms'.[6] Nissim speaks of the genesis of the poem. '. . . The idea is an accident. In response to an invitation, I travel to that poetry festival in Rotterdam, mentioned earlier, taking no books with me, so as to give myself a chance to see and hear. I arrive at my hotel, and am immediately struck by the total silence of the place. We're so accustomed to noise in India. I sleep for a few hours, get up, and it's too early for a meal. I need something to read. The only thing to read in the hotel room is the Gideon Bible . . . I read something from the Old Testament. I turn to Job . . . Still plenty of time for dinner, and I read the first Psalm.

'I think I realized suddenly that I had never accepted the Psalms, and this crystallized into an answer to the first one. Within ten minutes I'd written the first 'Latter-Day Psalm' and formed the idea of writing ten. I completed nine 'Latter-Day Psalms' in Rotterdam (June '78). The tenth is a commentary on the other nine, written in English.

'The idiom is important. It had to be a very special kind of English, not old-fashioned and dead, but also not ultra-modern and sparkling either. The characters had to speak functional, idiomatic, non-dated English.'

From here, Nissim moves on to talk of his other writing: the early poems, the poster poems, the plays, his critical writing.

About his early poems, he says: 'I don't repudiate them. In a sense they provide the continuity with my later work. The themes are not so different, from the earliest to the most recent. But I would now retain fewer poems from each book–I do find weaknesses–weak lines, throwaway images, careless construction. In those days I was anxious to complete the poem. I don't know why I was in such a hurry. I suppose everyone is, at that stage. Now I've more patience. I'm willing to revise more thoroughly. The poem has to grow. I give it plenty of time.'

About the poster poems, he supplies much information:

'Several things worked together: posters with poems on them had already made their way on the scene internationally. I had seen them in New York in 1957 . . . Then again when I did regular reviewing of art exhibitions, I used to enjoy the occasion for which the poet has no equivalent. The exhibition is opened, and the artist's friends come along, discuss it. I wanted that experience. In 1971 -72 I was looking for new sources of inspiration in life and literature. I read a book of American Indian songs in translation. All of them were short, compressed, highly poetic. There was a kind of communal feeling in them. The poet is a member of the tribe, capable of embodying its feelings. All these things came together in my mind with the idea of an exhibition of poster poems. One tends to stumble on the next development. It's a turn of events . . . you rely on the fact that you are talking, listening, reacting. A recent unexpected development for me was Zen telegrams. While recovering from a surgical operation, I read a book called *Poetry as Therapeutic Experience.* One of the articles described a therapist's use of Zen telegrams to help his patients. I took a ballpoint pen and paper and did nine telegrams in the spirit of the original Zen telegram, as a spontaneous expression. The next day was a Sunday. I saw no reason to follow the traditional format of the Zen telegram. So I lay in bed the whole day, thinking about the form, completing each in my mind, and wrote/drew twenty-four that day. I had both the visual and verbal very clearly in mind when I did each. A number of them reflect the after-illness state of mind.'

The Dharkers ask Nissim whether he plans to write more plays. He deflects the question. 'When I started, I planned to write as many plays as Shakespeare!' he says.

Their next question is: 'Would you find it constructive to spend more time on writing poetry and less on critical writing?'

To which he replies:

'Yes, I expect, now, to spend more time writing poetry and less on evaluating the work of others. It isn't always a question of time but of need. I'm the kind of writer who needs to evaluate the work of others all the time. I do it in any case, in my mind.'

Yet he adds:

'My critical articles and reviews must remain uncollected. I've always done different kinds of writing–criticism, novels [?], short stories. I have never completed a novel, and though I published my early short stories in magazines, I never brought them together in a book and don't plan to. I stand only by my poetry.'

Sixteen years after this interview was published, I asked Nissim why he made the remark that he stood only by his poetry. He said: 'For me to say [for example] that I'm a playwright, as opposed to one who writes plays, would be like going up a hill and saying I'm a mountain climber . . . That way, I've written songs too, but can I be called a songwriter? For me, poetry goes on non-stop–writing, revising, thinking up new poems. Therefore I wouldn't object to my being called a poet.'

Coming back to the interview, however, there is something biographically significant about the way he sees his interest in literature. He reveals this for the first time.

'I don't belong to a literary family, but literature was part of the mix, so to speak. One of my sisters [Asha] has been on the Marathi stage for over thirty years now . . . But the real source of my literary sensibility was my mother. I always knew it came straight from her to me. She reacted intuitively to my writing. With the rest of the family it was conscious encouragement; with her it was a primal assurance.'

The last questions are about his place in Indian literature and world literature. Locating his work in a global context, he says:

'It belongs to the Indo-English tradition of writing, through that to Commonwealth Literature, and finally to world literature written in English . . . In addition, it hopes for a place in the Indian literary scene through translation into Indian languages. That too is some kind of text . . .'

Finally, a word about his place in world literature. He is honest enough to admit:

'I don't make it on the international scene, nor on the Commonwealth scene in a big way. Most Indian writers don't. We're just not good enough.' Obviously, Nissim was speaking before the phenomenon of expatriate or immigrant novelists, beginning with Salman Rushdie, became the rage of the day!

The late '70s and early '80s were also a time when Nissim wrote some of his most perceptive criticism. He was, so to speak, at his critical best. By criticism, I do not merely mean art or literary criticism in a narrow specialized sense; rather, it was all-encompassing social and cultural criticism. These writings appeared in forums ranging from serious journals to popular evening newspapers. I propose to discuss some of these articles for the ideas they represent, and through the ideas, for the man they portray at this juncture.

In the article 'Cross Cultural Encounter in Literature',[7] based on the paper Nissim presented at the Hawaii International Colloquium 1976, he uses Ruth Prawer Jhabvala's Booker Prize-winning novel *Heat and Dust* as an excuse for scrutinizing the power relations that exist between cultures. The paper continually oscillates between a highly-traditional viewpoint and a futuristic and forward-looking one, as if he is afraid of being too revolutionary. Already he displays some intuitive (if not intellectual) understanding of post-structuralism, when he says: 'The purely literary values it [a work] implies are less important than the critical ones in relation to the reader's culture. He broods over these as though they are aimed at him personally. He is right to do so. His response is rarely to the complete and complex artistic product. Acknowledging the fact that its full meaning is larger than the more limited one expressed in its cross-cultural theme, he still focuses on that theme . . . And the cultures cannot be "equal"–one is in some ways more powerful.'

At the same time, he also says: 'I found *Heat and Dust* worthless as literature, contrived in its narrative structure, obtrusive in its authorial point of view, weak in style, stereotyped in its characters and viciously prejudiced in its vision of the Indian scene.' There is no doubt that Nissim makes this remark as an Indian reader of the novel, for whom 'there could be no separation between these [the Indian aspects] and the quality of the novel, its authenticity, its literary substance.' It will be recalled that in recent times, the same criticism was levelled against *The God of Small Things,* another Booker Prize-winning novel, by Indian readers. But then, the inconsistency in Nissim's viewpoint surfaces once again, a few paragraphs later:

'The multicultural viewpoint is rare in the contemporary literary scene. Its emergence would help greatly to clarify those scenes and characters in a literary work that were obviously created with cross-cultural insights in mind . . . How would an English reader respond to a novel set in England, entitled in the same spirit by an Indian writer as *Cold and Fog?*'

Nissim is absolutely right in asking this question, which, among other things, displays a desire for equality. However, before he can fully realize the implications of the stand he has just taken, he slips back into a highly orthodox mode of thinking:

'I would not seem to be on the side of those who habitually think of literature in non-literary ways, not even when these ways are sufficiently intellectual and disciplined to merit respect. I refer to the political and philosophical modes of confrontation, which reduce fiction, drama or poetry to ideas and ideologies.'

His intention here is to criticize Ruth Prawer Jhabvala for essentializing the Indian experience. However, he goes off the mark by mistaking all ideology for some kind of essentialism, and dismissing it as reductive. Yet, in the last paragraph of his article, we once again encounter the following statement: 'The cultural perspective, I suggest, is likely to displace the literary one.' This is confusion at its worst.

In the aftermath of Mrs Indira Gandhi's Emergency, which saw severe curbs on the freedom of the government-owned All India Radio (AIR) and Doordarshan, a committee known as the Verghese Committee was constituted. Nissim was one of the people to whom the Verghese Committee sent out its questionnaire. He later wrote an article entitled 'AIR and Doordarshan: How Should They Function?' based on his replies to the questionnaire, and published it in the Pune-based *New Quest*.[8] The authority and knowledge with which he speaks about Indian radio and TV in the article is impressive. It proves he has done his homework well, has thought about these issues in great detail. His position, however, is on the whole conservative: he is simply not in favour of complete autonomy for radio and television. As is his wont, Nissim tries to give readers the impression of objectivity by representing both points of view in the debate; the scales, of course, are insidiously tipped in favour of control. In one paragraph he writes:

'There cannot be absolute freedom for a public organization. But this should not be used as an argument for arbitrary interference when personal beliefs are opposed or when government policy is freely discussed. The responsibility of AIR and Doordarshan is confined to striking a balance in these matters in a reasonable way. AIR/ Doordarshan on the one hand and Government on the other must first of all learn to exercise self-restraint. The relationship has of course to be statutorily defined.'

If Nissim attacks Jhabvala in the 'Cross Cultural Encounters' article, he becomes the target of attack for his piece, co-authored with Vrinda Nabar, in *Vagartha*.[9] The piece is really a note on the translated poems of Marathi poet Indira Sant,[10] jointly undertaken by Nissim and Nabar. The attack is in the form of a 'reaction' by scholar and poet Vinay Dharwadker.

In their note, Nissim and Nabar claim: 'Marathi is the mother tongue of both the translators. For one of them [Nissim] it is a lost mother tongue, with no hope of recovering it;'

They then explain their strategy, how they went about translating the poems from Marathi into English:

'He [Nissim] relied on his collaborator to select the poem, and to read it aloud. They then worked at providing a literal version in English, followed by an attempt to describe, to interpret, and to consider possible English equivalents for every Marathi phrase.'

Nissim and Nabar begin to tread on dangerous ground when they make provocative or controversial statements, such as the following:

'For both translators, fidelity to the word or the spirit of the originals was death; freedom tempered by critical judgement was life.' (Having said this, they, in the very next sentence also run 'transcreations' down.) At times, the reasoning seems specious:

'The *same* is abandoned and the *similar* is sought to avoid jarring verbal effects, incongruous images, any mode of expression that is natural in one language and unnatural in another' (emphasis mine).

As is to be expected, in his 'reactions' to the above note, Dharwadker forcefully criticizes the authors for their 'inconsistency, evasiveness, vagueness and inexperience.' For him, 'the original text is the only "absolute" frame of reference one can adopt while translating or while evaluating translation.'

Therefore, the most objectionable statement in the note, from his point of view, is that where Nissim and Nabar argue that fidelity to the original is death, freedom is life. He counters this claim by quoting from Ramanujan's

Note to *Speaking of Siva:* 'In the act of translating, "the spirit killeth and the letter giveth life".' Dharwadker then makes several allegations that amount to doubting the very integrity of the translators. For example, at one point he writes: 'Nabar and Ezekiel undoubtedly have English at their command; but their ability with Marathi, the language of their original text, seems suspect.' Later, he says: 'It seems to me that most translators of verse begin with a "literal translation" of the original, which they then work into the finished version. But very few realize the implications of the term "literal", and Nabar and Ezekiel unfortunately fall in with the majority.'

At the end of his article, he makes the 'unkindest cut' of all: '. . . Indira Sant's poems in their English translations are undifferentiated from Ezekiel's own poems in English. From Sant, as from Mangesh Padgaonkar and B.B. Borkar, Ezekiel seems only to select, prune and transplant, and thus appropriate these poets rather than let them speak in their own voices.'

Nissim and Nabar, whatever the problems with their translations, are victims of nativism here. Dharwadker is not the first and only litterateur to condemn them. Others such as Gauri Deshpande and P. N. Paranjape (former Head of the Department of Journalism, University of Pune), have launched vituperative attacks on them for their translations. It is no accident that Dharwadker cites as authoritative a figure as Ramanujan to pooh-pooh Nissim and Nabar. The pattern of the polarization is clear; it is caste-Hindu versus 'untouchable' minority. Vrinda Nabar, despite her Hindu origins, was for long written off as 'anglicized' by the nativist lobby. Presumably this was because of her Oxford education, her extremely sophisticated use of English, and her defence of Indian Writing in English. The fact that she was personally close to Nissim, and that her name was romantically linked to his, only worsened matters.

Towards the end of 1978, Nissim published another article in the *Indian PEN* based on a paper he had read the previous year at Hyderabad.[11] He called the article 'American Poet and Critic Today: An Indian Viewpoint.' His thesis here is that since the social, political, economic and cultural context of American poets is vastly different from that of poets in India, comparisons of the two are futile. In one of the more aggressive paragraphs of the article, he writes:

'Poverty in an affluent society is not related to poverty in a society where it is the rule rather than the exception. The word is the same, but the experience is not. The surface similarities such as unemployment or shortage of cash conceal the realities of the two situations and make all comparisons misleading. That is why when comparisons are made, it is better to relate them to the realities than to the words, the experiences than to the concepts.'

Nissim refers to the American poet Randall Jarrell, who at a seminar at Harvard 'accused his audience of being philistine for treating poetry as "the concern of the few". The point is, neglect is relative. Stephen Spender is quoted to inform readers that the seminar in question saw Jarrell speak 'to an adulatory audience of about two thousand deeply interested colleagues, teachers, students and autograph hunters.' Yet he felt neglected. Nissim tries to compare his situation to that of poets in India. For some reason, he speaks not of Indian English but of Marathi poets, both traditional and offbeat. The hypothetical event he creates is a poetry reading in a village or small town in Maharashtra, where, in terms of number, the audience exceeds that which Jarrell was addressing at Harvard. 'These people are familiar with the forms of the poetry because those forms have been used for hundreds of years,' he says. At the same time, 'The Marathi poets are not paid for their public readings, their books are not bought by even a handful of those who listen to them reading their poems and there are no rewards except those of communicating and belonging.'

As for the offbeat Marathi poets, ('modernists, experimenters, innovators') Nissim believes they do not have the advantage of their mainstream counterparts. However, . . . 'these Indian poets also accept the situation and mildly hope it will improve, taking whatever attention comes their way, and astonished at the rewards the American poets enjoy, but not, I think, enviously.'

Nissim's use of the word 'envy' gives me the cue. There are two kinds of envy that exist in his own essay; that of financial gain as the American poets know it, and of large attendance at poetry readings by Marathi poets. Indian poets in English, sadly, are not a party to either of these benefits; they are (to use a cliche) neither here nor there.

The late '70s was a period when Nissim's writing diversified to the maximum extent he was capable of. Poetry, plays, criticism, journalism, he had by this time tried his hand at them all.

If there was anything that was still left, he attempted to fill in the gaps without delay. As a university professor of English, one of the things that gave him an inferiority complex was that he had not produced a student's edition of a canonical text, as other scholarly academics did. This desire was fulfilled when OUP invited him to write a 'special introduction and notes' to Ibsen's widely-prescribed *A Doll's House*. Nissim jumped at the offer and wrote a sixteen-page introduction, followed by seven pages of notes on the text. It was important for him to do work of this kind to justify his existence as a teacher at one of India's oldest and most prestigious universities. As it is, by the late '70s, the U.G.C. had already come into the picture in respect of determining the qualifications and experience of university teachers. One of Nissim's 'weak points' (as I have already noted) was that he did not possess a Ph.D. Preparing student editions of literary texts was one way of dealing with the problem, and in the years to come, there was more such work that he did.

In 1978, he also published an article entitled 'How a Poem is Written', which is one of his better critical pieces. When OUP asked him, in the early '90s, to help them put together a volume of his selected prose, this article was unanimously chosen for inclusion by both Nissim and his publishers.[12] I used the article as recommended reading for my MA course in Creative Writing at the University of Pune. Like T.S. Eliot's 'Tradition and the Individual Talent', albeit on a smaller scale, this is an article that is bound to have a prolonged shelf-life. Early in the article, Nissim says: 'In biology we say: for the perpetuation of the species. In poetry, virtually the same phrase would be used. Poetry begets poetry. Reading poems, some people write them.' The simile from biology seems like a throwback to days when Nissim lived with his scientist-father Moses, some of whose passion for the discipline rubbed off on him. If the above sentence thus has some kind of biographical relevance, the one I quote below, which occurs a few pages later, is even more directly related to his personal life. The significant part is in parentheses.

'The poet, particularly if he belongs to the twentieth century, may be tempted to manufacture a highly esoteric theory, out of the despair of isolation, to raise the prestige of his profession and also with a secret desire for cultish disciples. (There are always people waiting in the wings to acclaim the propounders of such theories and to build cults around them so as to satisfy their own need for a father-figure and for doctrinal warmth).' Although Nissim was a poet rather than a critic, what he has to say about 'people waiting in the wings' and about their need 'for a father-figure and for doctrinal warmth,' applies to him, more than to anyone else in Bombay. While a cult may not exactly have been built around him, he comes pretty close to becoming a cult figure, what with his reputation as post-Independence India's first modern poet, who had the willingness to entertain emerging poets.

In another statement, he runs 'vanity, ambition [and] all those worldly qualities which are the enemies of poetry' down. This is characteristically Nissim, wearing his unworldliness on his sleeve, which according to me, is one of the factors responsible for his ongoing sense of failure. The unworldliness is counterbalanced by an intuitive belief in the irrational-–'an obscure and undeniable force'–that (Nissim believes) guides poets in the act of creation. 'A stage arrives in the composition of a poem, beginning perhaps with clear self-conscious decisions, where decisions are taken out of the poet's hands. He reads his own poem with surprise and eventually discovers it to be more true than the poem he set out to write.' Things get progressively mystical. At one stage, Nissim's poet 'walks on this tightrope fearfully as well as confidently, and gets to the other side *by the grace of God*, that is by faith, patience and persistence' (emphasis mine). The high standards that Nissim sets in his article for poets, are often standards to which his own verse fails to measure up. One of my students in Creative Writing class was quick to point out, somewhat arrogantly, that the following sentence in the article could be said to apply to Nissim himself–'Every poet knows what it is to be delighted with the poem he has written, while at the same time undergo the misery at the thought that a better poem was sacrificed to it.'

What I have tried to demonstrate is how a critical article can be especially studied from a biographer's point of view. This, of course, is not to undermine the value of the article as criticism. Since Nissim largely writes on the basis of personal experience, it helps the reader to probe the mystique of creativity and the creative process, at least to some small extent. The examples that he provides of other poets, such as T. S. Eliot, W. B. Yeats and the Russian poet Mandelstam, are equally insightful. Perhaps, when all is said and done, the poetic process cannot be explained without resorting to abstractions, as Nissim occasionally does: 'The circle is complete. The rhythm of the poetic process from subconscious to conscious and back again is the rhythm of life itself.'

In the '80s, Nissim became associated with *Freedom First,* a journal devoted to serious political issues in India, published by a group that called itself Democratic Research Service. His name appears on the masthead as 'Editor' in all the issues brought out between 1980 and 1983, directly below the name of founder M.R. Masani. The editorials on the front page bear his byline. Scanning a handful of issues of this monthly magazine, I came across editorials on topics as varied as: the 1979 elections, Sanjay Gandhi's death, communalism, communism, Brezhnev's visit to India, non-alignment, the US and the Soviet Union as superpowers, the judiciary and Mrs Gandhi, Bulgaria, Poland, martyrs of Maharashtra and Rajiv Gandhi in politics. What is a poet doing writing on such topics, one is at first induced to ask, with some justification. For these are about the most political articles Nissim has ever written. While the editorials cannot be said to display the expertise of a political pundit, they are still distinguished by thoroughgoing analysis. Nissim cannot be accused of lacking a basic understanding of the issues he chooses to write on. That understanding, complemented by his ability to be objective, scientific, rational, makes the editorials balanced pieces of composition, on the whole.

According to Nissim, the reason why he took up the assignment was because 'I was deeply involved in politics for a long time. So when I was asked to edit [*Freedom First*], I thought I would come to grips with it again. All my editorials are a result of that.'

The Gandhi family, he states in an editorial entitled 'Rajiv in Politics', is as fascist and dictatorial as Hitler and Stalin: 'What was Sanjay . . .? What is Rajiv? As for seriousness, sincerity, dedication and commitment, do Hitler and Stalin fall short of Mrs Gandhi's ideals?' he asks. (If one finds him going over the top here, one might relate it to his well-known dislike of the Nehru family and of Nehruvian politics, especially in the post-Emergency period.) His conclusion is: 'Only slaves follow the movements of their master's eyes and interpret the expression on his face, moving in the required direction. Free men want argument and evidence for trusting a man to tackle their problems, not the kind of testimonials Mrs Gandhi has given Rajiv. Even if he is not the disaster . . . that Sanjay proved to be, he is the artificial creation of his mothers devious politicking.'

In another editorial written exactly a year later,[13] Nissim takes a different stand on the Soviet Union's nuclear arms policy from the familiar Nehruvian one, where the Soviet Union is perceived as a friend of India. He is scathing in his criticism of the superpower's double standards, its deviousness.

By 1986, *Freedom First* had changed its format. There were more pages now, the journal had a slicker get-up, as it got ready to meet the

A more elaborate version of the essay 'How a Poem is Written' appears in a memorial volume of essays for C. A. Sheppard. Entitled 'The Writing of Poetry',[20] it is concerned with defining the creative process, which Nissim believed only a poet could do. As he says, the reader, the critic, the teacher and the student are, after all, concerned with the finished product. We come by some details of his life here, which earlier we had no way of knowing. For example, he speaks of how he began writing poetry back in the late '30s and early '40s. 'The earliest remembrances are all of quiet, unexpected, spontaneous and direct compositions expressing a single sentiment of a confessional nature . . . Those early and natural delusions persist for a good ten years or more.' We may identify these ten years as the ten years immediately prior to India's Independence, that is to say, the years between 1937 and 1947. It is interesting that he should use the word 'delusions' to describe his juvenile attempts to write poetry. For in the next paragraph, he suggests that a poet who is not careful may continue to be under these delusions throughout his life, and may even 'die without knowing, literally, what his poetry is worth in his own third eye.'

Nissim attributes the meagre output of poets to these delusions, and it struck me on reading the passage, that what R. Parthasarathy has to say about the 'aphasia'[21] that grips Indian English poets, and prevents them from writing, may be another way of describing the delusions that Nissim has in mind.

The metaphors that Nissim uses to explain the business of writing (or not writing) poetry are startling. Some of them bear a psychoanalytical relation to the things he tried to do in his life, and failed. Driving, for instance, and other mechanical pursuits of various kinds. Why, otherwise, would he think of saying: 'The sense in which a man knows how to drive a car or an engineer knows how build a bridge is never the sense of knowing what works for the poet.'

One thing that Nissim seriously believed enabled a poet to progress from an early, immature draft of his poem to a final, mature one was 'the response of knowledgeable friends.' This belief is based on personal experience. In an essay written the following year (1983),[22] he reveals that in his own case, it was the late A.K. Ramanujan who was such a friend. 'I once had an experience with the help of A.K. Ramanujan which taught me to cope with such poems [uninspired ones]. It was in 1967 in Chicago, where I was his guest, using part of the available time preparing a few lectures and the rest to revise a batch of poems I had taken along. I was very pleased when Ramanujan picked up one of my poems from the batch on my table and said it was inspired. Immediately afterwards he shocked me by saying, "If you cut out the first nine lines and the last fourteen lines, this will be a good poem." I stammered something to the effect that since the poem had only thirty-five lines in it, cutting out twenty-three would leave only twelve. "Yes," he replied, "but those twelve lines are the inspired ones. If you want it to be a longer poem you can revise some or all of the other twenty-three." Nissim discloses, for our benefit, that 'Eventually, I cut some [lines] and revised others, making it a poem of nineteen lines.'

The other ideas expressed in the essay are either ideas that we have heard before, or that have, over the years, become obsolete and old-fashioned. The familiar comparison he is fond of making between Rilke's and Yeats' method of composing a poem recurs, with the Russian poet Mandelstam thrown in for good measure. That a poem 'cannot be demanded or forced, though it may be waited for with patience and hope' is a truism, that was more skillfully dished out for us in 'Poet, Lover, Birdwatcher'.

.Another truism is the facile distinction he tries to make between 'thinking' and 'intuition', which he calls 'two well-known mental processes.' He then contrasts them with poetic inspiration. In any case, this inspiration, at a later stage in the essay, takes the form of Robert Grave's 'White Goddess', both metaphors being repugnant. Why can't 'inspiration' be a man for a change he asks. The view that, 'Many poets take to the study of philosophy, but from Coleridge onwards; philosophy has destroyed as many poets as it has helped in the writing of poetry,' is about as dated as the gramophone record. Before taking his leave of readers, Nissim cannot but help debunking domestic stability, the very stability that could have saved his marriage, had he paid more attention to it.

In the early '80s, in his desire to diversify and do different things, Nissim even managed to get beyond the written word, and enter the enticing world of visuals. Here he was once again treading a path traversed by masters like Tagore. His drawings, of course, were nowhere near those of Tagore. But the impulse was the same–a man who had achieved fame and renown as a poet, now wanted to give wholeness to his vision by perfecting the art of pictorial communication. The best example of his efforts is a series of what he calls 'Zen Telegrams' (see his interview with the Dharkers). There are over a dozen of these 'telegrams' that comprise a pen-and-ink illustration, followed by a sort of caption beneath the illustration. The drawings and captions cover varied aspects of life, but the prevalent note is one of irony. The underlying theme of many of the illustrations is pretension and the need to expose it. However, there are an equal number of drawings that deal with more metaphysical themes such as old age, youth, ambition, the conflict between the mind and the spirit, and so on. If the drawings had to be critically commented upon, I would have to say, much against my will, that they are amateurish. Yet the overall effort succeeds as an experiment.

In 1985, Nissim managed to get most of his 'Zen Telegrams' photographed and mounted. Their visual appeal was thus enhanced. The photographing (in black and white) together with the mounting must have cost him quite a packet. It is clear, though, that he did not shell out any money from his own pocket. One of his numerous admirers took the task on his (her?) shoulders, and presented him with the final product. Nissim did not resist–he took maximum advantage of the generosity of his admirers, convinced that they were, after all, his admirers. All the mounted 'telegrams' bear the rubber stamp of New Sagar Studio, Chowpatty, Bombay-7, with the date 20 August 1985 stamped below the name of the studio.

His other attempt at non-verbal communication is a collaborative one and dates back to a much earlier period. A sequence of short poems written by him, prosaically entitled 'Child Psychology', are accompanied by the pen-and-ink sketches of Bombay-based Kavita Sahni. In all, there are thirty-one poems in the sequence, which Nissim may have hoped to someday publish, of course without success. The child in question, on whom the poems are based, and to whom they are, in a sense, addressed, is his own son Elkana. Poem No. 19, which informs us that the son is seven years old, is the only clue we have as to when the poems were written– sometime in the mid-'60s. The poems are an ironic comment on child-rearing in an average Indian household. They satirize the way parents lay down a random set of do's and don'ts for their offspring, and then expect them to comply. For example, Poem No. 2 says:

> Don't hum all the time,
> we tell him, so he stops humming.
> Don't be noisy, sit up straight

so he is silent, sits up straight,
a solemn, vertical child.

In Poem No. 16, the son is told–

Read your lessons,
Study your Marathi,
Study your Gujarati, Tamil, Telugu,
Malayalam, Panjabi [sic], Oriya, Bengali, Assamese,
Pushtu.

Even in the '60s, Nissim was aware of the manner in which parents, teachers and society in general cruelly contributed towards adding to the burdens of children. There was no scientific awareness of the niceties of parenting. In writing these poems, he was, in a way, empathizing with Elkana and extending his sympathies to him. Among other things, it proves that Nissim loved his children; he was not as callous and indifferent as he is sometimes made out to be.

Like the 'Zen Telegrams', the 'Child Psychology' drawings too were mounted on card-paper, some of them redone in colour. I interviewed Kavita Sahni to find out all about the genesis of the project, and why she agreed to team up with Nissim. It just so happens that Sahni did the cover illustration of one of my own books,[23] this contributing in no small measure to the excellent rapport that exists between us. She spoke to me at length.

'I first heard of Nissim when I was a student at the J. J. School of Art. I attended a talk by him on the History of Art, in which he spoke about the Expressionists, Cubism etc. It was a public lecture with a fee. It must have been sometime in the early '60s. Afterwards, at some stage, I began to make books for my son. I went to show them to Nissim. I met him at the University Club House on C Road, Churchagate, where he had a room.

'If Nissim saw talent in anyone, he built a link between that person and himself. He did not expect anything to come out of it, but if it did, well and good. He was enthusiastic about my work, found promise in it, though he didn't say so openly. I gave him the books I did for my son. I wanted to know what to do with them. My problem is that I didn't study commercial art.

'On a subsequent meeting, Nissim gave me carbon-copies of many of his poems, and these included "The Actor". He asked me if I could make it into a children's book. I worked on it at home. When I showed it to him, he didn't say if it was good or bad, but accepted it. (I know my work is good). Both "The Actor" and "Child Psychology" are one poem, which I broke up and complemented with several drawings (as they exist in their present form). "The Actor" was published by IBH in 1974, when Nira Benegal was in charge. It was published in a limited edition and wasn't well distributed, but it got at least two reviews, one of them in the *Times of India*. "Child Psychology" never got published.

'Later, I tried to do "The Actor" for TV. It's meant for animation, I realized. But it didn't come about, because they didn't know where to slot it. It's not really a children's book–it's too sad for children.

'When I showed Nira the original of "The Actor", she asked me to do it in black and white. My original illustrations were in colour. Nira also changed the format. I didn't find it hard to redo the drawings in pen-and-ink–I have a feel for line. The original was in paint.'

Here I interrupted, to ask Sahni what kind of rapport she had with Nissim.

'Curiosity,' she replied. 'He was a well-known writer. Till today, I'm curious about writers, how their mind works, how they behave etc. I was very young then, less than thirty.

"Child Psychology" is about Nissim's son. I didn't really talk to him about his family. The moods in the poem were crystal clear, full of meaning. That's all I needed.

'I can't tell whether Nissim felt intimate towards me or not. There was this other woman who worked with ceramics, who illustrated his poster poems for the exhibition he had at Chemould. I was too innocent, naive even. Even if he had designs about me, I wouldn't have known. I wouldn't have been able to respond to it even if I tried, because it would be alien to me.'

The last book of poems that Nissim published was *Latter-Day Psalms*,[24] that appeared from OUP in 1982. While all his earlier books had been dedicated to mistresses or friends, this one, surprisingly, was dedicated to his wife and children–Daisy, Kavita, Kalpana, Elkana.

The time-lag between the publication of *Hymns in Darkness* and *Latter-Day Psalms* was almost half of what it was in the case of *The Exact Name* and *Hymns in Darkness*. Nissim himself attributes this to the nature of the job he held at Bombay University; the workload was less than it is at undergraduate colleges. As he wasn't the Head of the Department, there wasn't much administrative work to be done. Above all, he had his own room at the Department, where he worked on his poems.

The book acquired its title from a sequence of ten poems, written seemingly in the manner of traditional Biblical psalms, but actually a take-off on them. He was thus repeating the 'experiment' he first carried out in 'Hymns in Darkness'. The story of how he came to write these poems is well known and has been told often.[25] A footnote at the end of the poem informs us: 'The first nine 'Latter-Day Psalms' correspond to numbers 1, 3, 8, 23, 60, 78, 95, 102 and 127. They are chosen as representative of the 150 psalms.' What he was attempting was a rejoinder to the Bible, just as many years ago he had written a rejoinder to *An Area of Darkness*. While the first nine psalms make their point by simulating the manner of the original psalms, the tenth one is written in a more contemporary style. It thus serves as a counterpoint to and a commentary on the other nine.

Bruce King painstakingly compares the first verse of the first psalm in the King James Version of the Old Testament, with that of Nissim's first stanza in 'Latter-Day Psalm I', to show how he departed from the original and thereby parodied it.[26] Since I cannot better his efforts, I shall merely reproduce what he has done.

Psalm I, Verse I, in the King James Version:

> Blessed is the man that walketh
> not in the counsel of the ungodly,
> nor standeth in the way of sinners,
> nor sitteth in the seat of the scornful.

Psalm I, Verse I, in Nissim's 'Latter-Day Psalms':

> Blessed is the man that walketh
> not in the counsel of the con-
> ventional, and is at home with
> sin as with a wife. He shall
> listen patiently to the scorn-
> ful, and understand the sources
> of their scorn.

King then repeats the exercise with Verse II of Psalm I. As in the first 'Latter-Day Psalm', Nissim was making a departure from accepted moral codes in all the other nine as well. He was 'heretically' questioning God and His authority. In 'Latter-Day Psalm III', he asks:

What are we doing to the sheep and the
oxen and the beasts of the field,
the fowl of the air and the fish
of the sea?

In 'IV', he says:

I shall not expect goodness
and mercy all the days of
my life, even if I dwell
in the house of the Lord.

And in 'VI' he wants to know:

How long are we to rely
on those marvellous things
in ancient Egypt? Tell me of the
marvellous things in Nazi Germany.
Even with manna in our mouths,
we are not estranged from our lust.

The reference to Nazi Germany acquires a sharper perspective in 'X', where Nissim directly refers to his 'Jewish consciousness'. It becomes clear that he is responding to the Old Testament as a modern-day secular Jew, rather than as any common liberal humanist. As Bruce King aptly points out, the 'Latter-Day Psalms' 'reflect Ezekiel's struggle with his own Jewish heritage . . .'

The problem with the position Nissim takes, however, is that it isn't consistent. Some of his 'Latter-Day Psalms' ('X', for example), are written from an entirely secular, rational and humanist point of view; but then there are other poems where he goes back to his old dithering attitude. 'Counsel', *'Healers' and 'Family'* (which are part of the series of 'Songs for Nandu Bhende') are such poems. They simultaneously try to be and not be, very much like 'Guru' in Hymns in Darkness. Upon reading these poems, we are confirmed in our belief that Nissim is never quite sure about his stand in relation to religion. That is why he constantly wavers between the serious and the ironic. One part of him wants to be spiritual (in an assimilationist sort of way), because he knows that that is what it means to be Indian; another part wants to critique and question the stereotype. The poems are thus an exercise in fence-sitting.

Then, there are poems that traverse ground already covered. 'Poverty Poem' returns to beggars, and to a portrayal of women as mindless.

> She didn't know beggars in India
> smile only at white foreigners.
> 'Indians are a friendly people anyway,'
> she said. 'So they are,' I agree,
> 'so they are.' She stares at me
> dubiously. I listen to the buzzing air.

There is one Bombay poem in *Latter-Day Psalms*. It is 'Hangover'. I prefer the poem to most of Nissim's other Bombay poems, because it's one of the few with an indoor setting–a restaurant at the Taj Mahal Hotel. As I argue in my article for the festschrift volume, this gives it a concreteness, found earlier only in poems like 'Night of the Scorpion'. The poem moves in staccato fashion, and we are provided with striking word-pictures. Nissim is able to achieve this almost with the confidence of a photographer; for the first time he almost completely dispenses with comment. Perhaps the reason is that the poet-narrator is himself in an inebriated state. 'Half the day hazy with the previous night,' as he puts it in both the opening and the concluding lines, leaving us with the feeling that he should have allowed himself to get drunk more often.

Very different from 'Hangover' are the introspective, self-scrutinizing poems, where he looks inward and tries to assuage his guilt. 'Warning: Two Sonnets' invokes the image of the clown ('They know the sage is probably a clown'); it is a throwback to the 'poet-rascal-clown' of 'Background, Casually'. The autobiographical element is veiled here, though there is no doubt that it exists. The poet-narrator wears the third-person mask to start with, but unlike other poems where he eventually returns to the first-person, here it is the second-person:

How much love do you expect from whores?
How much truth from failures
who cannot hold on to a wife or job?

Come, confess, and do not talk of God.
Your vanity is not as wretched as your style.

In 'Minority Poem' the narrator chides himself for not trying to be like Mother Teresa, and overcome the cultural barriers that keep people apart. We get an interesting insight into what Nissim at that point perceived as cultural barriers (that kept him aloof from fellow-Indians):

I lack the means to change
their amiable ways,
although I love their gods.
It's the language really
Separates, whatever else
Is shared.

These are sad lines because he is admitting to yet another kind of failure–the failure to assimilate into the Indian mainstream, an obsession that seized him ever since he returned from his first trip to England. The poem is also more honest than most of his other poems; as a document that gives us a peek into what he really thought about his life in India, it must he placed alongside the interview he gave to the Dharkers.

The 'Postcard Poems' too belong to this category. In a way, they counterbalance the 'Poster Poems' of *Hymns in Darkness*. They have titles like 'Dilemma', 'Credo' and 'Furies'. The first six lines of 'Dilemma' disclose that:

The further I move
away from madness
towards stability
and a measure of sense,
the closer I seem
to the verge of madness.

The mood here is as downbeat as in 'Minority Poem', and Nissim comes across as thoroughly demoralized.

'The Patriot' and 'The Professor', together with 'Irani Restaurant Instructions', are the three 'Very Indian Poems in Indian English' in Latter-Day Psalms. The last poem is quite different from all the other Indian English poems. For one thing, it is shorter. Then, Nissim is not saying his own thing about the people he's talking about, but is faithfully reporting what is written (or rather painted) on a wooden signboard in an Irani restaurant:

> Do not write letter
> Without order refreshment
> Do not comb
> Hair is spoiling floor
> Do not make mischiefs in cabin
> Our waiter is reporting.
> Come again
> All are welcome whatever caste
> If not satisfied tell us
> Otherwise tell others
> God is great.

On Saturday evenings in Bombay, my friend Rakesh and I have a beer at Bastani's and an omelette at Kyani's, right opposite. I can swear that if I haven't actually seen a signboard with the above instructions in one of the restaurants, I've at least seen something very similar. Twenty years is a long time, and the managements probably had their signboards redone (with only slight improvements) since the time Nissim used to frequent these places!

The 'Songs for Nandu Bhende' strike me as evidence, once again, of Nissim's constantly wanting to do new things. Nandu Bhende, incidentally, is his nephew who is active in theatre and advertising. That Nissim should want to dedicate his 'songs' to him is thus understandable. It is as if he's cheekily saying to his sister's son that songs are your domain, poetry is mine. However, except for 'Undertrial Prisoners' where he skillfully plays on the rhyming words 'jail' and 'bail', the 'songs' mostly fail to come off. In 'Touching', Nissim just can't keep away from a moralizing tone. 'Song to be Shouted Out' is less important for its musical properties, than it is for the insight it gives us into what was happening on the home front:

I come home in the evening
and my wife shouts at me:
Did you post that letter?
Did you make that telephone call?
Did you pay that bill?
What do you do all day?
I come home in the evening
And my wife shouts at me:
Did you bank that cheque?
Did you buy those tickets?
Did you ask if cheese is in stock or not?
What do you do all day?

This is probably another reason why the 'songs' are dedicated to Nandu Bhende. Being 'tyrannized' at home by wife Daisy, Nissim was seeking the sympathy and understanding of another man, a younger one and a relative at that, who was also in the arts. Nandu Bhende, on his part, had nothing to lose and everything to gain; for it ensured that if his own wife Usha, say, ever made life hell for him, he could turn to his uncle for support, in whom he would find an ally.

The most weighty poems in *Latter-Day Psalms*, from a biographer's point of view are 'Jewish Wedding in Bombay' and 'Nudes 1978'. There is a great deal of personal information that can be culled from the poems. 'Jewish Wedding in Bombay', for instance, can help us put our finger on what exactly went wrong between Nissim and Daisy. As pointed out in an earlier chapter, the wedding in question is Nissim's own. The poem is made up of eleven stanzas (an odd number of stanzas to have in a poem), of unequal length. The first five stanzas describe the wedding rituals, but they also do more than that: they make fun of the wife's family for taking the ceremonies so seriously. Clearly, Nissim was being insensitive to Daisy's feelings here.

There was no brass band outside the synagogue
but I remember a chanting procession or two, some rituals,
Lots of skull-caps, felt hats, decorated shawls,
And grape juice from a common glass for bride and bridegroom.

In the seventh stanza, some autobiographical information is provided about Nissim's own family vis-a-vis the marriage. Their progressiveness has made them snobbish; we distinctly get the feeling that Nissim was marrying beneath him, or at least that is how all of them perceived it:

> Nothing extravagant, mind you, all in a low key,
> and very decently kept in check. My father used to say,
> these orthodox chaps certainly know how to draw the line
> in their own crude way. He himself had drifted into the liberal
> creed but without much conviction, taking us all with him.
> My mother was very proud of being 'progressive'.

But the most offending stanzas are the last three. Nissim has no qualms about exposing his wife by talking about the very private things that went on between them. He is as confessional as he can get here, and may be compared to Kamala Das, who similarly exposes her husband. The difference, of course, is that Kamala Das, as a woman, belongs to a de-centred category, unlike Nissim; she can therefore do what she does with some degree of impunity.

This is what Nissim tells us in the final stanzas of 'Jewish Wedding in Bombay':

> Anyway, as I was saying, there was that clapping, and later
> we went into the photographic studio of Lobo and Fernandes,
> world-famous specialists in wedding portraits. Still later,
> we lay on a floor-mattress in the kitchen of my wife's
> family apartment and though it was past midnight, she
> kept saying let's do it darling let's do it darling so we did it.
> More than ten years passed before she told me that
> she remembered being very disappointed. Is that all
> there is to it? she had wondered. Back from London
> eighteen months earlier, I was horribly out of practice.
>
> During our first serious marriage quarrel she said why did
> you take my virginity from me? I would gladly have
> returned it, but not one of the books I had read instructed me how.

Needless to say, the lines 'Back from London/eighteen months earlier, I was horribly out of practice' are revealing. They obviously indicate that while it was Nissim who was taking his wife's virginity from her, the reverse was not true. This was yet another way, then, in which the relationship was an unequal one.

To know just what he was up to in London, we only have to follow up a reading of 'Jewish Wedding Bombay' with 'Nudes 1978', which once again has an autobiographical basis. Before I dissect the poems, let me attempt a brief description of them. They are a sequence of fourteen numbered poems, each fourteen lines long. This may give the impression that they are sonnets, love sonnets, which in a sense they are, without the formal metres and rhyme schemes of the traditional sonnet. In content, more than in form, they remind me of a cycle of poems by Walt Whitman, entitled 'Calamus'. These poems, named after a certain leafy American plant, were explicitly about love, homosexual or 'adhesive' love as Whitman called it. 'Nudes' on the other hand, is about heterosexual love, this being the principal difference.

The reference to the 'basement room' in 'III' suggests that the sexual encounters Nissim is speaking of, happened in England in the late '40s and early '50s, when he visited the country for the first time. But he held on to them all this while, not quite sure whether to write about them or not.

As usual, the statements and remarks he puts into the mouths of his women personae in the poems (especially 'II', 'III' and 'XII') depict them as lustful and fickle. 'Now . . . /you are within me. Aren't you /within me?' one of them asks him, during intercourse. There is no doubt that to Nissim, despite all the progressiveness of his upbringing, Woman is always the temptress, the seductress. I cannot help commenting that, fundamentally, this stems from a mindset that is Judeo-Christian.

In 'V', it's almost as if it is Daisy who is the speaking voice:

It's inconceivable
that he's not sleeping with
someone these days, so why
shouldn't I, too, have my
fling? Yes, I suppose I
do still love him, for all

the things I've always loved
in him. He has as sense
of humour, almost yours.
I'm sure he would be quite
amused to know that I
am here with a stranger,
free, frank, and in his words,
nakedly beautiful.

But we know that it isn't Daisy. She was far too much of the traditional Indian wife to give her husband a tooth for a tooth, or an eye for an eye. Like any Indian wife, she accepted that there was one standard for men and another for women, even though it brought her pain and unhappiness.

While 'VI' plays on the familiar distinction between nakedness and nudity (which Nissim first discovered in 'A Woman Observed' in *The Exact Name*), 'VII' is fairly representative of the manner in which every one of his extra-marital affairs began:

Beginning as a possible
love of art, theatre, writing,
the contact–or whatever
you call it–ripened into
the art of love

'VII', together with 'XI', may shock us, simply because we didn't know (nothing that ever happened before prepared us for it) that Nissim had it in him to be that graphic:

And I, amazed, 'You mean you miss
orgasm?' Then she, once again,
'With you, it does not matter.'
('VII')
I counted two hundred thrusts
then fell asleep upon you. Waking,
when you called, 'I want to sleep too,
and can't with your weight on me.'
('XI')

'XIII' discloses Nissim's dressing (or undressing or under-dressing) habits, which, if it were not for this poem, we would have never known:

> The richest of them all
> who spent the money, once bought
> expensive underclothes
> for me, and sent them with
> a letter: 'These are for
> the women of Bombay
> to see you sporting, not
> the worn-out ones I find
> so funny on a man
> of such implacable
> dignity. All the same
> please wear the older pieces
> when you come to me. It
> makes you more desirable.'

Informal comments on *Latter-Day Psalms* come from some of Nissim's friends. Hoskote, giving me his impressions of 'Nudes 1978', says: 'The finest poets can wait for words but they can also force the pace. "Nudes 1978" is a classic example of this kind of work.' Conversely, Toni is willing to stand by Nissim. When I ask her whether she thinks there is a decline in the quality of his verse in the '70s and '80s, she agrees. However, she qualifies her statement by referring to A.K. Ramanujan, and his brand of Hinduism, and comparing Nissim to him.

'May be the content of *Hymns in Darkness* and *Latter-Day Psalms* doesn't appeal to many people here because it's not Hindu. So Nissim wouldn't receive the cult following of Ramanujan. But personally there are things about Ramanujan's English poems that I find difficult to relate to. You have to read the poems again and again, and yet they don't stay in the mind. I don't see why someone has to go on and on about being a Hindu in New York. May be Nissim's Judeo-Christian poems put people off, as the Islamic element [in literature] would do in this country.'

On a more formal note, Shyamala A. Narayan critiqued the book for the *Journal of Indian Writing in English*.[27] While she maintains a firm neutrality throughout her review, and desists from saying whether she likes the book or not, she quotes two statements from a letter written to her by Nissim. These are of interest to us. In the first statement, Nissim is quoted as saying: 'I intend them [the Latter-Day Psalms] to be only post-Judaic-Christian.' At the same time, 'there may be a touch or two of the Hindu in my Psalms.' The second statement is paradoxical. Nissim claims: 'Obviously, I wasn't working on them [the Latter-Day Psalms] for very long, from one viewpoint, and on my life from another.'

Latter-Day Psalms brought Nissim the Sahitya Akademi Award in 1983. In order to confer these awards, the Akademi sends out a shortlist of books published during that year in the language concerned, to selected people. A sub-committee then prepares a smaller shortlist on the basis of the recommendations received. This may contain up to three, five, six, or on occasion even ten books. Nissim himself had an opportunity to be on one such sub-committee, ten years after he had won the award. That year, it was G.N. Devy's *After Amnesia* that won the prize.

I did a short interview with Nissim to find out his reactions to the award. Would he admit to being happy on receiving it, or would he, modestly or snobbishly, say it was not important. Luckily for me it, was the former: 'I was glad on getting the award, as anyone else would be. People, libraries etc. would be more interested in an award-winning book, than in others. I, for one, would always make it a point to read an award-winning book first, and decide how good it is later. All over the world, an award does help to increase the sales of a book.'

To my question whether he felt the Sahitya Akademi Award consolidated his reputation as a poet, his answer was:

'I don't think I gave much thought to all that. But most people in the field know that it makes a difference. There is an all-India scale to it, as compared to a book that doesn't win an award, of which only a handful of copies are printed, reviewed here and there, and then forgotten. *Latter-Day Psalms* and *Hymns in Darkness* are in their tenth edition. How many books of poetry would go into so many editions?'

(The Sahitya Akademi, incidentally, also ensures that an award-winning book is translated into all the languages recognized by the Akademi. I was chatting with Nissim once at the PEN in 1995, when the Assamese version of *Latter-Day Psalms* suddenly arrived, much to his delight.)

Did the members of the Jewish community in Bombay feel proud of Nissim's achievement? 'They did take the line that I had brought credit to the community by winning the award. I would have felt the same way [about any one else in the community]; it's not unusual.'

Where are Nissim's awards–the Sahitya Akademi Award and the Padma Shri (which he won in 1988) right now? Has he decorated his study with them? He calls the suggestion 'childish'. Then, he adds: 'I would never do that. The certificate must be somewhere, the metal thing elsewhere. Anyone who buys a copy of *Latter-Day Psalms* would know that I have received the award for it. So where is the need to put it up on the wall?'

Yet, modest as he tries to be about his awards, there is no doubt that he values them. They go a long way towards restoring his self-esteem and self-confidence, and obliterating some of that sense of failure that haunted him throughout his life. After the 'Able Seaman' award that he received more than thirty years ago, which doubtless had the same effect on his morale, this was only the second time that someone was telling him that they believed in his abilities; that he was a cut above the rest.

Nissim's certificates also include relatively unimportant ones, like the Certificate of Appreciation he received from the 'Gate of Mercy' Synagogue in Bombay on 6 December 1981, for his 'Outstanding Performance as a Poet, Journalist, Author.' (On 2 September 1988, Nissim scribbled out a note to Persis Anklesaria in which he wrote: 'Can we keep this [certificate] in a large envelope so that it doesn't degenerate over the years?' This is proof enough that his honours, howsoever small, were important to him.)

In this respect, the books and articles on his work that began to get published around this time, were only slightly less important than the awards and certificates. Some of these articles, such as Vrinda Nabar's 'A Perspective on Indo-English Poetry'[28] and R. A. Malagi's 'Indian Poetry in English Today: Some Observations'[29] were only indirectly about Nissim, but they mentioned him prominently. Nabar, for example, speaks of him as 'The only poet . . . who can be described as self-consciously seeking to evolve a "philosophy".' Others, like 'The Indianness of Ezekiel's Indian English Poems: An Analysis' by Vinod and Shiva Kumar[30] (which, incidentally, is the only thorough-going analysis of the Indian English poems) and 'Nissim Ezekiel: The Most Recent Poems' by Carlo Coppola[31] were exclusively devoted to his work. Then, there was a profile on him in the Ahmedabad edition of the *Times of India* on 30 September 1981.[32] In his lead to the article, the author, S. D. Desai, a lecturer in English at a local college, is prompted to say: 'Perhaps we in Ahmedabad have yet to learn how to have a purposive dialogue on purely an intellectual plane.'

Two book-level studies appeared in the late '70s and early '80s. The first, special number of the Osmania Journal of English Studies[33] on Contemporary Indian Poetry in English, was edited by the late Vasant A. Shanane and M. Sivaramkrishna, both Hyderabad-based professors of English. There are scholarly articles on Keki Daruwalla, Kamala Das, Adil Jussawalla, Shiv K. Kumar, P. Lal, Jayanta Mahapatra, A.K. Mehrotra, R. Parthasarathy, Gieve Patel, A.K. Ramanujan and Arun Kolatkar, besides Nissim. This makes it the first and one of the most comprehensive studies of all the major canonical poets. *Form and Value in the Poetry of Nissim Ezekiel*[34] by Anisur Rahman, like Chetan Karnani's book, is a monograph. It is based on the author's academic research, with the emphasis placed entirely on the formal aspects of the poet's craft, such as imagery, symbolism, language, diction and rhythm.

Padma Shri Shri Ezekiel

Latter-Day Psalms made it to the *Times Literary Supplement*.[1] It was a review of three OUP books by Anne Stevenson, the other two books being *The Keeper of the Dead* by Daruwalla and *Middle Earth* by Mehrotra. The reviewer's response was lukewarm. Of Nissim's work she says: 'So, despite the cleverness and wit, a desolation pervades these poems. Professor Ezekiel is teaching, but whom? Not the English, not the Jews, not, apparently the Indians either.' Earlier, she describes his talent as 'overstrung' and feels that his verse is inhibited by 'frantic intellectualizing'. To which Bruce King, taking up cudgels for Nissim and the other two poets, writes to the *TLS* pointing out: 'To describe Ezekiel as an "overstrung talent", "inhibited occasionally by frantic intellectualizing" is genteel attitudinizing.'[2] Stevenson asked for it.

Another significant review appeared in the London-based *Jewish Chronicle*.[3] The reviewer, Iris Kalka, attempts a Jewish reading of the poem. This is what she discovers in the process: 'Ezekiel, the person, emerges as an Indian-Jew, aware of his Jewish origins but equally influenced by the Indian heritage . . . He is painfully aware that his own, and others' "Westernisation" (Jews and non-Jews alike) is only skin-deep. He hovers between a feeling of guilt, which is a consequence of his own successful "Westernisation" and sheer enjoyment of the freedom that it allows him.' Except that what Kalka tells us is hardly a discovery. She is unable to penetrate the poems deeply enough to bring out what is essentially Jewish about them, if at all such a thing really exists.

Nearer home, there was a review of the book by fellow-poet Kersy Katrak.[4] Nissim's poems are seen from the point of view of Eliot's theory of impersonality, to which Nissim himself subscribed. No new or original ideas from Katrak there. And yet Nissim attaches a note to the review, dated 27 July 1988, addressed to Persis (Anklesaria). It reads: 'To be preserved among the more notable reviews of my books.' Perhaps only because the review is by Katrak, a well-known name.

On a more academic note, there was Darshan Singh Maini's review in *Indian Book Chronicle*[5] ('Ezekiel's achievement finally makes him out as a minor poet in the great Anglo-Saxon tradition'); and Ajit Khullar's in *Indian Literature*[6] ('Ezekiel's basic humanity has performed the eighth wonder [sic] tailoring feat on some of the selected Psalms and has made them new and serviceable'). Of such fulsome statements and exaggerated claims is Indian literary criticism made!

Like all celebrities, Nissim spent some energy trying to cope with his celebrity status. He agrees that the recognition, the adulation, the acceptance by his readers that made him a literary star, gave him a sense of security. But it did not answer the larger question: how was he to come to grips with the poems he was writing?

'I don't tell myself all the time that I'm a celebrity,' he said to me. 'I just go on with my daily activity.' One of Bombay's 'prominent citizens'– he refuses to say who–attributes his (Nissim's) fame to the fact that he is a widely-read columnist, and that his poetry is accessible. 'But the writer doesn't need the kind of celebrity status that film stars or politicians do. It's a question of values ultimately–if a writer or philosopher or historian doesn't have values, he's going to be very unhappy.' Nissim is not flattered by too much media attention, not upset by the lack of it either. An absence of attention from his reading public doesn't embitter him. What about the fact that, as in the case of several writers all over the world, people know him rather than his work? 'I just laugh,' Nissim says, as stoically as he can.

In 1984, Nissim retired from the University of Bombay at age sixty. Here was a man who had earned his living doing what he liked best– teaching. But right until the end he never saw himself as a typical English teacher. While they were closed in their approach, he was open to influences of different kinds. Chinese literature, Japanese literature, world literature in the widest sense of the term, this is what he went for, provided it could be made available to him in 'reasonable' English translations. At the same time, as pointed out in Chapter Nine, he is not in favour of views propounded by the radical postcolonial lobby that wants to dispense with Eng. Lit. altogether. He calls this 'short-sighted'. His thinking on these issues appears muddled: 'You have to take wise decisions in relation to the past, present and prospective future, so that you don't have a generation that finds you are putting them down through your decisions, which I agree, may be a form of nationalism. But I can't imagine my life without all the translations into English of world literatures.'

I discovered that at the end of his career as a professor of English, Nissim was still somewhat opposed to giving a political context to literature. 'It's true you can't avoid questions of race and gender in literature today. At one time it was called Commonwealth Literature. Today you can simply call it World Literature in English [not postcolonial literature, please note]. Whether it is Hong Kong, China, India, Singapore or Malaysia, any one in these countries who chooses to write in English will be part of the world literary scene.'

Simplistic? Perhaps. But then that is what universalisms of any kind are. As is to be expected, Nissim is still caught in the trap of formalism. 'Anyone who is connected with educational studies shouldn't take ideological stances,' he asserts, without any remorse. At the same time, when I prod him on the subject, he has no hesitation in admitting that literature by traditionally oppressed groups, even if it's not of the 'highest' quality, helps to set right the imbalance of years, gives voice to people who have been denied it. 'What's the harm if all these literatures are studied alongside English literature?' he asks. Then adds: 'However, the quality of writing has always mattered to everybody, everywhere.' So we're back to square one. I try to make Nissim see that belief in only the aesthetic merit of a poem amounts to a sort of dogmatism. But he refuses to see the point. We talk about I.A. Richards' *Practical Criticism*. Does Nissim believe that a poem can be evaluated without any knowledge of the author's identity and cultural background? He replies by referring to *Practical Criticism*, first of all, as 'one of those processes that everyone can benefit from at a certain stage, and then move away from.' Having said that, however, he is still unwilling to discard what is old and proven, and blindly rush into an acceptance of maverick ideas. He then throws up his hands in despair: 'One can only relate to any problem in relation to one's total situation,' he says. It is clear he is in a dilemma, unable to decide between older and newer approaches. To stubbornly cling to the old, would earn him the charge of being reactionary; on the other hand, his inherent conservatism will not permit him to be too radical. The most practical solution, in the circumstances, is to sit on the fence and preach an elusive neutrality; which is what Nissim more or less did from the time of his retirement as a professor of English.

The best account of the kind of man Nissim was during the time of his retirement, and in the years that immediately preceded it, comes from Freya Barua, his one-time student and PEN secretary. Freya was a colleague on the English faculty at Pune University for a while, and even after the completion of her assignment, continued to be associated with the department as a visiting lecturer. One Saturday morning she and I had a long chat about Nissim in my office. Barua's association with Nissim was at two levels–first as a student and then as his secretary. Freya Taraporewala (as she was then known) always found Nissim, her teacher, to be 'open, welcoming, generous with his time.' (She places the emphasis on 'time'. I soon discover that this is in order to contrast it with money–she can't say good things about his generosity with money.) She continues: 'He was humble to the point of never refusing to do tasks he thought were low, like writing addresses on PEN notices and posting them. Hierarchical divisions did not exist in his mind. He always spoke to people, including students, as equals. He was appalled at the thought of being called "sir" and preferred to be addressed as "Nissim".

'As a teacher, he would take you for what you were–if you were reverent to him as a person, he took it; if you sidled up to him flirtatiously, it was all right; if you were informed, it was fine. Meeting all these different types of students at the same time in a classroom situation can create social difficulties. Sometimes Nissim's method of coping with the problem was a little more stuffy than he usually is. But there was always a peculiarity about this.'

Barua told me a little about what she thought of his teaching methods: 'They were formal, old-fashioned. He would write out his whole lecture, must be spending quite a lot of time doing so. The lectures were traditional, historical, biographical, factually based . . . and yet, not stimulating enough. He taught us American literature. The transcendentalists–Thoreau, Emerson–were a matter of deep personal interest to him. But there was something that destroyed the quality of these lectures. On the other hand, he taught us Donne brilliantly, responding to his poem 'The Litany' as one poet would respond to another, almost as if it were a creative writing class, where there was no room for conventional criticism. Because his lectures on Donne were not "heavy duty" like his America literature lectures, the bulk of the students in the class enjoyed them.'

Barua's older sister Soonoo Taraporewala was also taught by Nissim. She was in the same batch as his daughter Kavita, who was her classmate.

Barua remembers her sister being fascinated by Keats' odes and the way Nissim dealt with them in the classroom. 'It's remained in her memory for long.'

In Barua's opinion, Nissim was not attuned to pedagogical issues at all, though he tried to give the impression of being well-read. 'Throughout my MA years, I never once encountered in his lectures mention of structuralism, postmodernism, postcolonialism etc. Criticism-wise, he was stuck in Eliot and Leavis. He was well-read in a limited way in the classical and Romantic tradition.'

In the running feud between Nissim and R.B. Patankar at the Department of English, Barua and her friend Nandini Dhuldhoya 'were always a part of Nissim's circle, for he always thought of himself as an individual, never a Reader, Professor etc.'

So much for Nissim, the teacher. What about Nissim the boss, the employer?

'I joined the PEN as Honorary Secretary in 1983 while I was in my final year of BA at Elphinstone College,' Barua clarifies. 'This is when I first met Nissim. Dr Homai Shroff (the then principal of Elphinstone) was appalled that I should be working directly under him, and asked me to be careful. He certainly had a reputation of that kind [as a womanizer] in the past. But throughout my time at the PEN, I never got any improper vibes from him.'

Barua spoke of the nature of her work at the PEN and the way Nissim got his tasks done. She managed to recount a couple of anecdotes.

'I remember how he would send his peon with a flask to get tea for all of us from Sanman. Usually it was he who suggested what functions would be held at the PEN. He was autocratic in that respect. May be he thought we were inexperienced and immature, and wouldn't be able to come up with valuable suggestions. But I didn't get the feeling he was imposing his ideas on us.'

The two events Barua distinctly remembers both concern women professors of English in Bombay colleges.

'Once there was something happening in the area of *Indian Writing in English* and I mentioned Eunice de Souza's name. He vehemently opposed it, saying he had had a major battle with her and would have nothing to do with her. It's the only time I know he actually refused to invite someone.

'Another time [the late] Dr Mehroo Jussawalla was giving a talk on Elizabeth the Virgin Queen. Nissim raised his hand at the end of the talk, and mischievously asked: "Excuse me, one cultural issue has not been discussed–how can you prove Elizabeth was a virgin?" Everyone laughed. Dr Jussawalla was very upset.'

What does Barua think of this kind of playfulness?

'I used to enjoy it then. But I now see it as patriarchy. Now I would think of this type of humour as patriarchal. What Nissim did to Dr Jussawalla that evening, would he do it to a male speaker?'

There are other programmes that she talks about.

'At Elphinstone College during our undergraduate years, we frequently invited him to speak at our literary society meetings. The first time he came, he spoke on his attitude to religion. The year was 1982, and it was soon after the publication of *Latter-Day Psalms*. He very clearly came out as a theist, though not necessarily rooted in Judaism. He was fascinated a lot by Hinduism. Yet there was a lot of "aestheticising"–looking at religion from the aesthetic and the rational point of view. I was impressed by the fact that he was a compelling speaker, and not a fuddy-duddy one.

'Then I remember a programme of the PEN where Linda Hess was to read out her translations of Kabir. Nissim was very excited about the programme. He shared his excitement with us, irrespective of the fact that we were only students.'

Barua's overall estimate of the man:

'He definitely was one of the more influential teachers in my life. I got to know him when he was nearly sixty (although I've been seeing him from the time I was eight or nine). I don't think of him as macho. I think of him as paternal. He never imposed himself on you sexually. But that may be because he was much older by then. His poems were erotic, but as a human being he wasn't. He wasn't very good with practical things such as fund-raising and general administration. The PEN was ramshackle during the time I worked there. Nissim was unconventional, but not bohemian. He was unconventional in the more human sense. He basically treated you as you treated him. He was woolly-headed and yet clever, making that woolly-headedness a pose.'

What's the most personal trait about Nissim that she observed?

'When he was my teacher at Elphinstone, I noticed he was very close to his grandson–daughter Kalpana's son. He would go into raptures at the thought of him. He would write letters and draw for him everyday. He also loved his daughters very much.'

Finally, how does Barua evaluate his poetry?

'There is a Jewish mother syndrome in some of his work. Freud's Oedipus complex too comes from this. His autobiographical and confessional poems are neo-classical in their declamatory, formal style. This is a new blend he's trying out. It reverses his modernist aesthetics. A kind of paternalism or patriarchy pervades all his early poems. His later free verse poems are still formal: they never entirely lapse into slang or colloquialisms. His explicitly sexual poems are voyeuristic and exhibitionistic.'

As in previous decades, foreign travel continued to be a part of Nissim's busy itinerary in the '80s as well. In 1983, it was to the Edinburgh Arts Festival, where, apart from participating in the general fanfare, he also read his own poems at one or two of the many poetry readings that form a part of this annual event. In 1985, he went to Salzburg, Germany. A year later he went to Germany again, to the Frankfurt Book Fair, and managed to tour the country with a visit to five cities, where he did readings and took active part in the discussions that followed. In 1987 he went to Hong Kong. And in 1988, he travelled abroad once again, this time to the southern hemisphere, where he read his poems at the Adelaide Book Fair and the New Zealand International Festival of Arts.

The most important journey that he undertook in the '80s, however, was to the relatively close-by Singapore. He had already visited the country in 1985. This second visit, however, was a longer one that covered all of three months, beginning December 1988. Nissim was invited to be poet-in-residence at the National University of Singapore (NUS), where some notable Indian expatriates (such as Professor Kirpal Singh) hold senior faculty positions. Like any writer-in-residence fellowship in the West (after which it is designed), the Singapore fellowship gives writers plenty of leeway to do as they please. They can shut themselves up in a room and not see the face of the world till they have completed a book; or, conversely, they can socialize and spend their time addressing students, faculty and the general public. This Nissim thinks of as extremely 'kind and thoughtful' on their part, unaccustomed as he is to such freedom in India. In his case, he realized as soon as he landed in Singapore, that he couldn't imagine shutting himself up in a room; couldn't imagine not taking an interest in the manifold activities that were going on all around him. As is his wont, he ultimately settled for the Middle Path. He decided to fulfill the expectations of the NUS by giving a public reading of his poetry upon arrival, and then retreating into his room to write more poetry. When he would become tired of that, he would get back to the public sphere and do another round of readings at schools and colleges. The arrangement worked very well. The principal of one of the schools where he read told him on the last day of his stay in Singapore that for the first time in the history of the school, the students had signed a petition to have more poetry included in the syllabus. The NUS, wealthy as it is, gave him a well-furnished apartment to live in, with a lot of teakwood furniture. Furthermore, it had 'every amenity under the sun.' As if this was not enough, they also provided him with an office on campus, giving him the impression of extreme generosity. He did not have to 'lift a finger' (to use one of his favourite phrases) to decide the venues at which he would read: all that was taken care of by the English faculty at NUS. An air-conditioned car would drive him to the institution he was performing at, and then drive him back.

The easygoing life that he had at Singapore gave him sufficient time to observe this city-state and compare it with India, virtually at the other end of a very vast scale. But it was not nations he was really comparing, as much as forms of government; dictatorship versus democracy.

'Everyone knows there is a dictatorship in Singapore, although nobody actually uses that word,' Nissim said. 'If you're the guest of a government which is a dictatorship, the situation is obvious, you can't say anything that you like, you can only do what you're expected to do.'

Did Singapore's dictatorship personally affect him while he was there?

'During my stay there, without accepting the general principles of a dictatorship, I became aware of how a dictatorship functions in positive terms. For example, one of the aims of the NUS was that it should match the standards of any university in the West. I don't think they really came anywhere near it. Yet the intention was laudable.'

What did he observe of life outside the university campus, its civic aspects, let us say?

'If you spit, you're fined. After you come out of a public toilet, an inspector immediately goes in to check whether you've flushed. There are scores and scores of similar procedures that are meant to improve standards. I observed them, I knew I was going to be in the country only for three months. I wouldn't want to be there for three years. Personally, I prefer a democratically-elected government that can maintain the same standards. I wouldn't want to live in a dictatorship forever.'

The standards, though, are important to him.

'If you're walking down the street and you see even one house in bad condition, you are entitled to write to the government and they will rush to the spot and repair it at their own cost. Can one ever imagine that happening in India?'

Yet, given a choice between squalor on the one hand, and a dictatorship on the other, Nissim would opt for the former. To him, solving the problems of poverty through dictatorship is the easy way out; the real challenge is to deal with it democratically.

Accustomed as he was to noting down the way people spoke Indian English, Nissim made notes on the use of Singapore English. One outstanding trait, according to him, is to suffix every other word with 'la'. 'I'm telling you, la', a native of Singapore is most likely to say. In the twenty-two poems he wrote during his three-month stint at the NUS (known as the 'Singapore Sequence'), one is in Singapore English. Soon after his return, he gave one of his first readings of these poems at a Bombay English Association meeting.

Some of Nissim's sojourns abroad led to prestigious literary assignments that kept him busy once he was back in Bombay. Three years after he participated in the Edinburgh Arts Festival, the contacts he had established there paid off, and he was asked to serve as advisory editor to *Inter Arts*, an Edinburgh-based quarterly of cultural connections. Of course, as everyone knows, work of this kind is hardly very demanding. It is only when an issue is being put together that an advisory editor may be sent manuscripts of poems and stories for his opinion, or might be asked to solicit new writing from his region on behalf of the journal. Nissim enjoyed every bit of this work. And, although he denies it, he loved seeing his name on the masthead of the journal, especially when it was published from an advanced country.

Republic Day, 1988, saw Nissim receive his second major award for 'contribution to Indian literature in English.' It was the Padma Shri, and he had to go to New Delhi to formally receive it from the President of India. He went. Although Nsim considers his Padma Shri less important than the Sahitya Akademi award, it's not as if he isn't proud of it. I asked him how the whole thing came about. After all, there is a mystique that surrounds these awards, especially as they are given away by the union government. He said it all began with visits by a certain government official, who wanted him to provide data about himself and his work. The data, this government official clarified, was being sought with the express intention of recommending Nissim's name for a Padma Shri. However, he also made it clear that he could give Nissim no guarantee that he would actually win the award. More rounds of questions followed, both from this government official and from others who represented the central government. He dutifully answered all these questions, and the next thing he knew was that it had been announced in the newspapers that he was one of the recipients of the Padma Shri. Ironically, the government official who had recommended his name got to hear from Nissim that he had won–he didn't know of it before-hand.

A year after he had won the Padma Shri, almost as if he now felt obliged to stand by the union government in all its decisions relating to culture, Nissim supported the ban that was imposed on Rushdie's *The Satanic Verses*. Even the reasons he offered were more or less similar to those put forward by the government: artistic freedom notwithstanding, no one had the right to hurt the feelings of others. He even managed to gather a handful of fellow writers and academics who were able to see things from his point of view, Vrinda Nabar being one of them. Together they signed petitions and wrote letters to the editors of newspapers, explaining why they felt the ban on *The Satanic Verses* was justified. The literary world was shocked. Was this the same man who, a little over a decade ago had been so vocal in his criticism of Mrs Indira Gandhi's Emergency in his *Freedom First* editorials? A Bombay-based magazine invited Nissim and Dom Moraes to debate the issue, with Moraes condemning the ban on the book outright. When they published the proceedings in one of their issues, Nissim somehow sounded more convincing than Moraes. But that was because, by this time, he had thought about the matter a great deal, and had a well-defined position on it. Moraes on the other hand, had been roped into the debate at the last minute, regardless of the fact that he himself is no great admirer of Salman Rushdie.

I learned, during my interview with Sirkar, that the PEN's own official line was that the ban on the *The Satanic Verses* was justified. Members were unwilling to pass a resolution opposing the union government's decision to ban the book, because they felt that whatever Prime Minister Rajiv Gandhi did, was done in the interest of law and order. It was the loss of life that was witnessed in the rioting in Bombay that led Rajiv Gandhi to pass an order that would ensure that the book was quickly withdrawn from the bookstores, though not without an eye on the Muslim vote, as many educated Indians believed. Sirkar feels that Nissim's stand may have been related to that of the PEN, since he was an important office-bearer. Sirkar's own view is that the PEN's upholding of the ban did not contradict the general principles of intellectual and cultural freedom in which the organization strongly believed. The American poet Donald Hall was in Bombay soon after *The Satanic Verses* was officially declared to be illegal. He was against the banning of the book, and against all those who said the government was right. But he began to see things from the PEN's point of view after he had a talk with Sirkar during his next visit, a few months later.

To emphasize that the PEN did not behave high-handedly, Sirkar pointed out to me that the resolution in support of the ban was only an official one. Another resolution granted individual members the freedom to publicly say what they wanted on the issue, regardless of the PEN's views. Coming back to Nissim, Sirkar recalls something that once happened during a literary meet of the PEN in the late '70s, with Nissim in the chair. A certain book (he can't remember which) was being critiqued, and at the end of the talk, an elderly lady raised her hand, stood up, and asked why so much fuss was being made about the book when it was obscene. Nissim answered her. He said: 'In literature we try to tell the whole truth.' Sirkar was so impressed by this, that he quoted it in a meeting of the Lodge of Theosophists, calling it 'an important factor in deciding what to say and how.' He was also reproducing it for me now, to prove that Nissim's opinions on *The Satanic Verses* couldn't be taken as a general indicator of his views on censorship, artistic freedom etc.

Jussawalla, on the other hand, attributes Nissim's 'hostility' to Rushdie to the sense of moderation he always tried to practice. Excesses of any kind were anathema to him. Jussawalla, too, calls it his 'Middle Path', and points out that whether it was love poems he was writing, or personal feelings he was expressing, moderation was his watchword. Even if a certain social cause moved him deeply, he was careful to disguise his emotions. This sometimes went to 'an unimaginable and unsympathetic extent from my point of view,' says Jussawalla. But the anxiety is familiar; many modern heterosexual men in the West are seized by exactly this kind of anxiety, which prevents them from showing too much closeness to parents, children and spouses. The theory is that feelings take a man's manliness out of him; they pose a direct threat to his masculinity. Therefore, a man must try to appear as dispassionate as he can in public. I am certain that Nissim's moderation originated in the association that he saw between moderation and rationality. A lack of moderation would, to him, seem as if he were going over the top; it would seem womanly. I also gathered from Jussawalla that Nissim's dislike of Rushdie did not begin with *The Satanic Verses*. It commenced much earlier, when *Midnight's Children* was out. From that time onward, Nissim and he had 'frequent eruptions' over Rushdie. Says Jussawalla: 'I never could agree with his opinion of *Midnight's Children*. One will have to threaten him with bowel washes and enemas to make him read *Midnight's Children*.'

On the domestic front, it was quite some time now since Nissim had been living on his own at The Retreat. But it's not as if he and Daisy never saw each other. In Minakshi Raja's opinion, he started to have a 'guilt complex' about his wife. Apparently, some lawyers whom he consulted told him he would have to frame false charges against her if he really wanted a legal separation. This he simply couldn't do. On the contrary, he tried to make it up to her for the ugly turn their married life had taken, by bringing her to parties. To Raja, Daisy always seemed a misfit at such dos. Nissim felt morally responsible for her; he felt obliged to spend all his time looking after her, as a result of which he couldn't really move about among the guests. Sometimes his hosts, foreseeing this, invited only Nissim (making it clear to him they wanted him to come alone), and he plainly said so to Daisy. But Daisy had grown accustomed to the attention he bestowed on her after the separation. Raja distinctly remembers a couple of occasions when Daisy accosted her, and said something like: 'You invited Nissim to the party, not me.'

Nissim tried to fill the emotional void in his life by encouraging some of his women acquaintances to be dependent on him. This especially bore fruit if the woman in question was also without an emotional anchor. Towards the end of the decade, he started coaxing Tara Patel to put her poems together for a book. A major Delhi publisher was about to launch a new series of poetry titles, and Nissim was one of their consulting editors. The assignment gave him power over authors far less successful than himself. (Later, in the early '90s, there would be other women poets, such as Menka Shivdasani and especially Charmayne D'Souza, with whom he would attempt to establish a similar equation.) Tara herself was surprised that Nissim should be asking her for a manuscript, rather than some others who had better reputations (as poets) than she. This is because 'I am an erratic writer, I'm moody, it's painful for me to put things together.' However, opportunity was everywhere in the air; no one was silly enough to let it go untapped. Tara worked on her poems, sometimes in Nissim's presence, but mostly on her own, and in 1993 *Single Woman*[7] was published. 'The credit for the book must go to Nissim,' Tara says.

I egged Tara on to tell me why she chose to revise her poems on her own, rather than, as would have been thought natural, in Nissim's presence. She said she thought she could manage things on her own. Then, more intriguingly: 'After I got to know him better, I stopped showing my poems to him, except sometimes when I had a doubt about something.' I further wanted to know why, after *Single Woman,* she more or less stopped writing poetry. 'Because my own poems started to upset me, the way I was writing them, she very frankly confessed. There are other writers who would agree with Tara here, in her estimate of her own work. Jerry Pinto, for one, strongly believes that Nissim should have put pressure on her to rework her poems before he okayed her manuscript. '*Single Woman,* in that case, would have been a much better book.' I reflected on Pinto's remark, and tried to correlate it to Tara's statement about how, she readied her manuscript for publication. Could her revising her poems herself (in her Juhu apartment) mean that she ended up turning out stuff that was not as good as it might have been, had she laboured on them under Nissim's watchful eye?

Tara, of course, brushes off the suggestion that Nissim was partial to women writers (as compared to men). 'He's a very kind person, and when someone's need is obvious, he responds,' she says. After a short pause, she continues: 'Nissim takes a lot of nonsense and arrogance from others. There are so many other well-known poets in Bombay with airs, but Nissim isn't like that. He's very approachable and accessible, he's never rude. He's received even obnoxious people with patience and charity.'

Tara's subsequent inclusion in Eunice de Souza's *Nine Indian Women Poets*[8] proves that her poems in *Single Woman* were not completely ephemeral in value. This is especially borne out by the fact that all the five poems selected by de Souza are from Single Woman. Her views about her own work, therefore, are either the outcome of excessive modesty, or are a slight and purposeful distortion of the truth, to misguide her readers.

Distortion of the truth is a phrase that also comes to mind when we place her remarks about Nissim's virtuousness side by side with an interview that she herself did with him in 1984.[9] This idiosyncratic interview begins in the usual way, with Tara faithfully reporting on all his accomplishments up to that time. Then, all of a sudden, something takes hold of her and she writes:

'So much about Nissim Ezekiel the poet. I stretch my luck and return to the *Imprint* write-up (the one mentioned earlier)[10] wherein the writer had questioned his relations with young women . . .'

Nissim's reactions to Tara's transgressions are equally startling. As she puts it, 'the interview suddenly collapsed like a pack of cards in the face of his distress.' This causes her to repent having raised the subject: 'I should have known better than to have asked the question, at least I could have framed my question more discreetly.' But it is too late. Tara is left with no option but to transcribe this part of the interview (along with the rest of it) and send it for publication. She writes: 'I quote from my tape-recorder for whatever it is worth.' And this is what appears:

TP: Is this a personal dilemma, or fetish, or weakness, according to the *Imprint* allegation you have 'roving fingers' . . . do you deny it?

NE (angrily): Now you are falling into a trap which is exactly what some journalists want you to do. I don't think it's fair or right. You're catering to the *Celebrity* readership, you're selling your soul . . .

TP: But it's a very human question to ask.

NE: No, it's a circulation question and you know it. It's not a literary question, it's not a human question. It's like asking me to ask you how many men you've slept with! A deliberate attempt to try and create a sensation or scandal. I don't like your spirit of mentioning the word 'allegation' ten times in fifteen minutes, it's a bad sign. As if you're the judge. I want to stop this interview.

TP: But I'm only quoting from hearsay and a published allegation . . .

NE: I think you are delighted that the interview is going this way.

TP: But you haven't said anything so how can I be delighted? To make a profile of a person you have to ask him about himself, his work as a human being, a man, my question is valid. Why would I have the guts to ask you otherwise . . .?

NE: Guts! ALL journalists these days have the guts, they feel it's some vocation of theirs.

TP: But you yourself in your poetry have disclosed that your marriage was a failure. 'Nudes 1976' [sic] in your latest publication [sic] is obviously about your relationship with women.

NE: So you want to tell *Celebrity* readers all about it. What rubbish! I'm not a filmstar. Just forget it. Go and ask someone else who loves to talk about his or her private life.

'So be it, I fumed quietly, as with a polite smile he escorted me out of his room. May the fascinating personal life of Nissim Ezekiel continue to remain a rumour-ridden mystery! He has, of course, answered the question by making an issue out of it,' is Tara's concluding remark.

The Nissim Tara exposes in her *Celebrity* interview seems a bit more familiar than the one she invents for me during my research. I asked Nissim whether he ever forgave Tara completely for her audacious piece. He couldn't remember.

The year 1984 when the above interview was recorded, may have been the year Nissim retired from service. But he was still middle-aged. Old age was nowhere on the horizon. He continued to be in full command of all his faculties, physical, mental and spiritual. He wrote as extensively as before. The most significant new poems that he turned out were a sequence called 'The Edinburgh Interlude' based on his 1983 visit to the Edinburgh Arts Festival. In all, there are thirty poems in the sequence, although it is doubtful whether all the thirty have ever been published. The *Illustrated Weekly of India*[11] ran the first fourteen in January 1984, when Pritish Nandy had just taken over as editor. (An even smaller number of them–eleven–are included in *Collected Poems,* which came out in 1988.) Nissim was so prolific at this time, that he readily responded to requests for new poems by the editors of journals-some of them obscure and short–lived–by writing them to order. This poses grave difficulties for Ezekiel scholars, who often have to track down back numbers of long-forgotten journals published from godforsaken towns, to lay their hands on an uncollected poem. I speak here from personal experience, for when I was commissioned to edit the special anthology number of the *Literary Endeavour* (referred to earlier), Nissim especially wrote three poems for me, which today can be found nowhere, except in the *Literary Endeavour.* The best of the three is titled 'The Local', and it goes as follows:

> A slow train, perhaps,
> or is it fast?
> No one knows for certain,
> and we ask one another.

It's generally slow, sometimes fast.
To Andheri? Yes, as a rule,
but may be to Bandra only.

When does it start?
In a few minutes–in ten–in twenty.
A daily lesson in life's uncertainties.
There is a lighted sign-board
but it often changes
just before the train starts.
Now it does, someone shouts it has . . .
passengers on the platform rush in,
those in the train rush out.

The card-playing groups begin their game.
A blind beggar and his son
chant their song.
Hawkers raise their voices,
offer nuts and chikki, ballpoint pens,
funny toys for children and mothers.

All conversation now is for all to hear,
in Marathi, Gujarati, Hindi, Tamil, Punjabi.
The silent ones turn their heads
and listen, smile or even laugh.
They stare at me and others,
scrutinize the women,
open a book or newspaper
which those without books or newspapers
also read.
We are, after all, in the same boat, i.e. train.

My neighbour says, you are Parsi?
No, I say genially, acknowledging his interest,
Zoroastrian.
He leaves the subject alone.

The train has stopped between stations.

It was something of a humbling experience for me when I discovered that I was not the only editor whom he had thus favoured. An uncritical anthology, unoriginally and mindlessly entitled *Indian English Poetry,*[12] edited by one I.H. Rizvi, carries two uncollected poems. One of these is called 'Literary Career', the other 'Dilemma'.

It's the extremes I wonder about,
the advice some give,
that drunk or mad
You find the truth, beyond
the marriage-vows of moderation.

How shall I learn to dance
among the gigolos of fate?
This is the time and place, they say,
abandon sense and soul
to find your real voice.

There's no salvation, though,
in the academic life.
Almost everyone is more moderate
than you are–so go on,
feel superior, drunk and mad!

Similarly, a supplement issued by the daily newspaper *Nagpur Times,*[13] runs 'Futile Protest Against Poetry' and 'A Dubious Art', both uncollected.

Whatever the poets say
the moon is only the moon,
it cannot change.
It is the metaphors that change
and those who make them
reeling under their own words.
Then the critics come
to recreate the poems,
until the moon is wholly lost:
pig, lotus, nude lovely lady,

large abstraction, tiny torch
or candle
replace the moon.
But the moon remains,
indifferent, desirable bitch–
there, I've done it too,
resorted, after all,
to the lure of language,
battered the clarity of prose
for an image or delusion,
lost the thing, the object,
the sheer itness,
the absolute hereness or thereness
of the mere moon
behind a cloud of words.
See how it makes the clouds shine,
like the bright radiation
in and around poetry.

The self-reflexivity of this poem, pointing towards a postmodernist aesthetic, is unlike anything Nissim has done before. It therefore surprises me that he chose not to include it in *Collected Poems.*

I asked Nissim why he staked his reputation by obliging the editors of low-grade journals and anthologies with poems. After all, no established poet anywhere in the world would do such a thing, no matter how compassionate he (or she) was. His answer: 'If I can submit a poem to the editor of an international journal when he asks for one, what harm is there if I help a struggling editor in a small town in India?' So it was 'patriotism' of a kind that motivated him here.

As pointed out earlier, Nissim has stated several times in his curriculum vitae that he has written over 500 bookreviews in his lifetime. This is no exaggeration. It was mostly work by contemporary authors that he took up for review, especially if they were Indian. In the late '80s, after Penguin commenced operations in India, he got an opportunity to review books by writers who were not just his contemporaries, but his rivals. He tried hard to retain his objectivity and balance (often unsuccessfully), although his belief that a bookreview had to be fundamentally critical (rather than gushing) remained unchanged. Perhaps this is best demonstrated by his review of Dom Moraes' *Collected Poems*.[14] In the first paragraph of his review, Nissim praises Moraes for his 'impressive collection' and expresses the hope that his poems will be widely read in India, now that they are available in a single volume. This is because Nissim is convinced that although everyone has heard of Dom Moraes, few people are really acquainted with his work. 'This is a pity because much may be learnt from it, in the Indo-English context, about the art,' he says condescendingly. The little generosity that is displayed in the first paragraph, vanishes in the second. Nissim writes:

'It may be argued that Dom has nothing special to offer those Indians who use English for creative purposes. He writes like an English poet, and does not reflect any significant aspect of Indian life. There are allusions to his life in India but they are personal, with no social and cultural implications.

'There is, for example, a poem on the Kanheri caves . . . Though the scene is imaginatively described and its historic background projected, the poem could have been written by a "stranger".'

That year (1988), Nissim reviewed books by two other Indian writers. One of them was Upamanyu Chatterjee and the other Satyajit Ray. Chatterjee's *English, August: An Indian Story*[15] was bound to scandalize him. Nissim begins by calling the novel 'highly provocative . . . the word fucked appears seven times [on the first page]. Marijuana is mentioned, and so is shit.' As in the case of the Moraes review, here too he quickly gets personal: 'One guesses that he [the protagonist] is, has to be, a projection of the author's obsessions, no less.'

As is to be expected, of his three contemporaries we are talking about, it is Satyajit Ray that he was least likely to mess around with. Ray, after all, was an institution by himself, and a Bengali, and the flak Nissim would have received had he dared to 'bitch' about him, would have been unbearable. He therefore studiously avoids references to Ray's films; nor does he attempt to make connections between the stories in *The Adventures of Feluda*[16] and the films. Feluda was marketed by Penguin India as a book for young adults, and the one critical comment that Nissim manages to slip in, is: 'I must add that I cannot imagine these novellas, at least in their English translation, as appealing to readers of a children's magazine.'

The most surprising of all columns in *Mid-Day* was 'TV Time'. The tone of these pieces is not very different from those that he did ten years ago, for 'Sight and Sound'. Yet what intrigues me is that he should have spent so much time before the idiot-box viewing programmes in Hindi, Marathi and Gujarati, only because he had to comment on them. If ten years ago, Nissim surprised us by writing about a Dilraj Kaur concert on TV,[17] he now does the same by critiquing 'Yuvadarshan' in Gujarati, or 'Samuhan Gaan' in Marathi. I was also very curious to know where he watched TV—since he never owned a TV set at The Retreat. But by 1994, Nissim couldn't remember. My guess is that he viewed it at Kala Niketan, when he went to see Daisy with the bazaar (shopping). However, ten years ago, when he did TV reviews for *The Times of India*, *The Times* lent him a TV set at The Retreat.

Yet, we must give him the benefit of doubt. Perhaps he saw a connection between the TV reviews that he wrote, and the larger issue of autonomy for the mass media, with which he was deeply concerned. This is proved by his article 'Arts and the State' written in 1986 for *Indian Horizons*.[18] The article itself is based on a paper he presented at Goa that same year, at a seminar on 'The Arts and Letters and the State'. The issue that preoccupies him is whether AIR and Doodarshan should be given autonomy. Nissim doesn't quite know the answer. He presents arguments both in favour of and against autonomy, and ends the article inconclusively, hinting at a Buddhist Middle Path.

I want to relate Nissim's rejection of total freedom for the mass media with his view that books like *The Satanic Verses* are justifiably banned in India. As late as 1993, he held on to this view in an article on Taslima Nasreen that wrote for the *Independent* (Bombay).[19] He makes a fundamental, if far-fetched distinction between 'criticism' and 'contempt', and suggests that with authors like Rushdie and Nasreen, it is the latter. In other words, it is not serious, dispassionate criticism that is to be found in *The Satanic Verses* and *Lajja*, but a contempt for the feelings and sentiments of ordinary people. If we apply the theory to radio and especially to television in India in the '90s, we shall come up with horrifying results. We shall discover that Nissim's reasoning is not far removed from that of the BJP, which holds that the programmes aired on private channels like MTV, reveal a contempt for Indian culture and are morally corrupting. While we were discussing the matter, Nissim personally said to me: 'Freedom of speech must always be within limits. A person who does not maintain these limits is not being critical, he's being offensive and abusive.'

Sometimes, it is tricky trying to tie all the loose ends of the man called Nissim together. Okay, he is opposed to writers who show contempt for fellow human beings by treading on their corns. But is he himself completely free of this quality. In 1988, Adil Jussawalla who was literary editor of *Debonair*, requested Nissim to contribute a piece to 'Printed Matter', a column he was in charge of.[20] Nissim decided to write on the naivete of average Indians. In the process he was utterly contemptuous of three of them. The first was a 'well-known Indian novelist' who allegedly asked him after a public lecture, what the difference between poetry and prose was. The second was a Ph.D. student who planned to read only one book before writing his dissertation, that book being the biography of the author he was working on. The third was a poet who declared that 'though he writes poetry he feels no obligation to read it.'

Whether or not these actually happened (it's most likely they did), it is difficult for Nissim to hide his snobbishness. And he isn't even talking of average Indians in the real sense; a poet, a novelist and a Ph.D. scholar, howsoever incompetent, are by no means a part of the common citizenry. I dread to think, then, what opinions he has of, say, Indian housewives or door-to-door salesmen.

Of the various articles he wrote in the '80s, the one that stands out is in *Science Age*.[21] The magazine ran a column called 'Science and I' to which they invited people from different walks of life to contribute. Nissim's piece is both analytical and informative, and is probably the only article of its kind he has ever written. This, is in spite of the fact, that the article has a fair amount of truisms. One of these is: '. . . science cannot supply all the necessary values. They need to be supplemented by values which have no relation to science, on the surface, but which may well turn out to have the same human roots.' Another is: 'Science is not an end itself, as religion and the spiritual too are not.' Yet the article is starkly honest. Nissim says, 'I reject all anti-scientific attitudes and anti-technological attitudes. I believe that life without science and technology is not even conceivable on the scale that matters.' The irony in this statement, as far as his own life is concerned, does not upset him. Here was someone who, in principle, believed in the importance of technology in modern living, but whose own life remained untouched by too much of it. It is also significant that Nissim should confess that he has not been able to incorporate science into his verse on a scale that matters; this is similar to his professed inability to write, say, a political poem or a travel poem.

According to me, one of the most important articles Nissim wrote in the '80s was 'To Revise or not to Revise', based on a talk he gave at C.D. Narsimhaiah's *Dhvanyaloka* in Mysore, during a Resident Fellowship at the centre in May 1983. The article was included by Narsimhaiah in the *Literary Criterion*,[22] the journal that he edited. It was also later reprinted in Nissim's *Selected Prose*. I consider the article valuable because it is among the few that gives us an insight into his creative processes, the way a poem came to his mind, and what happened between that time and the time it was finally put down on paper. It also provides us with vivid accounts of his own experiences at poetry workshops, which he narrates with a view to helping his readers understand the intricacies of the poetic craft. Not all poets feel the necessity to do this. A poet is like a chef; he is possessive about his 'recipes' and is not in a hurry to give them away. To that extent, Nissim was being generous by sharing his secrets.

One of the first admissions he makes in the article is: 'I've never relied entirely on inspiration . . .' To this he quickly adds: '. . . but [I] feel no need to discount it altogether.' Over the years, he has grown 'so suspicious of inspiration that I will not allow it to "dictate" a poem to me. I tell "inspiration", to go to hell but overlook the fact that it may actually do so, taking me along.' There are several personal anecdotes that Nissim garnishes his article with. The first of these happened in Leeds in January 1964, and concerns 'Night of the Scorpion'. While I have referred to it in an earlier chapter, I reproduce it here in full.

'. . . I had to read a few of my poems at a party. That morning, when I made the selection, I was dissatisfied with it because there were not enough recent poems with an Indian ethos. I felt it was essential to pick recent ones and not those from my earlier books, and also to read some poems which would interest a non-Indian audience by their Indian themes. I decided to spend the day in my university room, waiting in Rilke's sense, for a poem, with only one proviso: it had to be Indian. My wife and I settled down in that room around 10 a.m.; by lunch-time I had no luck, by tea-time none either. Eventually, when my wife warned me that it was approaching 6 p.m., and that we would soon have to leave for the party, I wrote down in a fit of desperation, and after making a joke about the words "I remember", the joke being "I remember the house where I was born", suddenly I wrote, "the night my mother was stung by a scorpion" and, in as much time as it would take to make a copy of the poem, I had completed it. That night at the party I read it out. Later I sent a copy to a friend, anticipating his criticism by informing him that it was a first draft and I would in due course revise it. "Leave it alone" was his response. Other friends said the same, all of whom had won my affection by their ability to tear my poems to pieces. Eventually, when I was sending the poem for publication I made one small change: I allowed for extra space between the body of the poem and the last three lines. That was all the revision I made in "Night of the Scorpion".'

The second anecdote took place in London that same year, 1964. Some smart aleck suggested to Nissim that he could make money by selling preliminary drafts of his poems to an American library for $20 per draft. When he replied that he was not in the habit of preserving his drafts, he was told: 'That's all right, you can write those earlier drafts now, making changes in each as you go along.' Says Nissim, ironically: 'That was a kind of reverse creative method which I've never learnt. But I was assured that several of my English contemporaries had done it.' The smart aleck, or one of his friends, added: 'Poets are justified in making money so long as it is by creative means . . . even manufacturing earlier versions of a poem requires imagination after all.'

The third anecdote, which has already been quoted earlier, is about how A.K. Ramanujan reduced a thirty-five line poem by Nissim to a twelve-line poem.

Nissim ends his essay with a fourth anecdote. He talks about an 'Indian-English poet who claims that she doesn't even read other poets any more because she doesn't want to be influenced by them.' He remarks: 'That way lies the death of poetry as an art.' Everyone knows who the poet in question is.

Critics are parasitical insofar as their existence demands that they feed on the work of others. Poet-critics, on the other hand, atone for some of this by producing a body of work that other critics can consume for their livelihood. This is exactly what happened to Nissim in the '80s. Apart from providing opportunities to aspiring book reviewers and seminar-hoppers, not to speak of M. Phil and Ph.D. scholars who wrote on his poems, he also paved the way for a full-fledged study of post-Independence Indian English poetry, with himself as the starting point; for a special Ezekiel number of a university journal; and for a twenty-seven minute video film on his development as a poet. The last three events occurred within the span of a year, beginning 1986.

The special Ezekiel number came out first. The journal was the *Journal of Indian Writing in English (JIWE)*,[23] not exactly the official mouthpiece of the English Department of Gulbarga University (Karnataka), but taken as such, since its editor, G.S. Balarama Gupta, was on the faculty. The guest-editor of the special number was Havovi Anklesaria, who later went to Cambridge to do a PhD. In a way, Anklesaria was an odd choice for a guest-editor of a journal such as *JIWE*. This was because her milieu is Bombay, whereas the people who wrote for (and read) JIWE were usually teachers of English in rural or semi-urban areas. But the Anklesarias have always been dear to Nissim and know him sufficiently well; so in all probability, it was he who suggested her name to Balarama Gupta. The issue has an assortment of contributors and is critically uneven, with perceptive and shoddy articles coexisting side by side. One wonders how much editing Anklesaria really did. It is unlikely she had a personal rapport with contributors like D. Ramakrishna, A.S. Gupta, P.M. Chako, M.K. Naik, G. Damodar, A.N. Dwivedi, N.D. Dani and B.N. Prasad. What is much more plausible is that articles by these scholars were either already lying with Balarama Gupta for consideration, or that he especially commissioned them. He then probably passed on the articles to Anklesaria for minimal editing, and to Nissim for his final approval, before going to the press. Balarama Gupta's intentions in starting *JIWE* were no doubt noble. However, there came a time when he was swamped with financial constraints, and had to bluntly tell potential contributors that he would consider their submissions only if they took out a subscription! Could this have dictated the choice of writers for the special number? I can't say. What is clear to me is that the only contributors with whom Anklesaria seems to have personally interacted are the Bombay-based ones: Toni Patel, Santan Rodrigues, and to a lesser extent, N. P. Acharya. She also may have been familiar with the abilities of Charu Bhagwat, who although not based in Bombay at the time, did his MA from Bombay University in the '70s.

Bruce King's *Modern Indian Poetry in English* is the first serious and thoroughly researched book on the subject. But as an American, King wouldn't have been able to conduct his research as indefatigably as he did, had he not had the support of the poets. Of all the poets King spent time talking to, it was Nissim's opinions that he regarded as the most worthwhile. There could be several reasons for this. Where other Bombay poets (Arun Kolatkar and Gieve Patel for instance) are known for their reticence,

Nissim loved discussing things with visitors; unlike the others, he was used to lecturing in the classroom. Also, not completely inconsequential is the fact that Nissim, like King, is a Jew. The result is that Bruce King's book somehow gives readers the impression that modern Indian English poetry wouldn't have existed, if Nissim wasn't present on the scene. This, of course, is a highly contestable view, that is bound to invite controversy.

King devotes a whole chapter (Chapter Six) to what he calls 'Ezekiel and his Influence'. In addition, Chapter Seven ('The Poet's India I') also evaluates Nissim's work, together with that of A.K. Ramanujan, Gieve Patel, Keki Daruwalla and Shiv K. Kumar. As if this were not enough, the first five chapters of his book, which are concerned with introducing modern Indian English poetry to readers, and with its publishing history, its market, and its poetics and criticism, duly acknowledge Nissim's importance in all these areas of inquiry.

Reviewers of *Modern Indian Poetry in English* were quick to sense King's partiality towards Nissim. Dinyar Godrej, reviewing the book for the *Indian Post* wrote: 'For King, Ezekiel is the Big Daddy of Indian Poetry, not only in terms of pioneering work (in which case he is), but also in an area of influence (in which case he isn't). Most admirers of disciplined poetry that is mentally and morally agile will find much that is excellent in Ezekiel. But even they will, perhaps, be annoyed by the constant refrain that attributes to almost every poet only an extension of ground covered by Ezekiel.'[24]

Four years later, when King wrote his second book on Indian English poetry, he still accorded the pride of place to Nissim. But this time, he elevated two other poets to Nissim's level: A. K. Ramanujan and Dom Moraes.

Picture a Poet (1981) was scripted and directed by Jane Swamy. It begins with a voice-over of 'Background, Casually', the voice being Nissim's itself. As the film progresses, we find that the voice-over technique is used throughout, and in the process Swamy manages to pack in as many of his poems as she can. We get the distinct feeling that it is because she doesn't know her subject well, that she provides so much footage of Nissim's poetry, excellently rendered in his own voice. In fact, it is for the first time that Nissim moves away from the flat tone that he usually adopted at poetry readings (his admirers hated him for it), and reads his poems in an emotionally-charged voice. The stills that accompany the poems are somewhat hackneyed. We see him against the backdrop of the Antonio

D'Souza High School, Wilson College, the Magen David Synagogue and the Bombay skyline. We see him at his desk in the PEN, in London, taking a walk in the snow, in an Irani restaurant, on the beach. We also see him at the Hanging Gardens, amidst hedges cut to the shape of animals (which he refers to in one of his poems) and in the Jehangir Art Gallery. The things he says about his life and his work–answers to questions by Jane Swamy–are not things we haven't heard before. He talks, for example, of how he came to write poetry, enjoying it from an early age, and trying to find more poems by the poets represented in his school textbooks. 'At fourteen or fifteen, I realized I wanted to write poetry,' he tells the camera. At the same time, he believes that 'you can't talk much about poetry, can't communicate with the general public about poetry.' Then he proceeds to speak about LSD, about his atheism and agnosticism that were cured by the drug, and were replaced instead by religious and mystical experiences. The one profound question that Swamy, quoting one of his own phrases, asks him is: 'Do you see poetry as a way to honesty?' To which, Nissim replies: 'I can't imagine any one writing a good poem which is also a dishonest one.'

There is no talk any where in the film about the nature and quality of his poetry, his aesthetics etc. Swamy's research is imperfect; at one point she claims that he ended up being the Head of the English Department at Bombay University, which, of course, he never was. The background score is, in the main, appealing, except towards the end where the 'sare jahan se achha' tune grotesquely takes over, even as the last stanza of 'Background, Casually' is being rendered on the screen.

Picture a Poet was premiered at the Alliance Francaise in Bombay soon after it was made. It is a sincere, if amateur, effort by the students and faculty of Bombay's Xavier Institute of Communication (where Nissim took part-time lectures) to document the work of India's premier Indian English poet.

Whatever their shortcomings, it cannot be denied that the efforts of Balarama Gupta, Havovi Anklesaria, Bruce King and Jane Swamy enhanced Nissim's prestige. But this was now beginning to soar in other, unexpected ways. Two refereed journals abroad published articles on him, and although the articles, by Inder Nath Kher[25] and S.C.Narula[26] respectively, did not offer fresh perspectives on him or his work, the fact that they were written augured well for him, and for Indian English poetry.

Even more surprising was an article from Germany by Klaus H. Borner.[27] Who would have thought that German readers would be interested in an English-language poet from one of Britain's former colonies? (Borner takes care to play Nissim's Jewishness down, except for a brief and passing reference to it at the beginning of his article.)

In India, younger scholars joined the bandwagon of Ezekiel criticism, and began to compete with older ones for a toehold. If Dnyaneshwar Nadkarni, whose scholarship he has often ridiculed, still continued to feed on Nissim's poetry, he was joined now by more sophisticated poet-critics of the next generation, such as the late Dhiren Bhagat and Makarand Paranjape. Nadkarni is condescending. He writes: 'Nissim Ezekiel is one of the very few Indo-Anglian [sic] poets I have read with some care.'[28] By contrast, Bhagat and Paranjape are reverent. Bhagat, although he is pooh-poohing what he calls 'the limited club' of Indian English poets, nevertheless has a good word for Nissim: 'For the first time an Indian poet writing in English had consciously forsaken the easy elegance of the English tradition and had resolved to look with as honest an eye as he could summon at his world, limited as it might be to the environs of his body and self. Modern Indian English poetry began then.'[29] Paranjape, in keeping with Indian traditions that he upholds, assumes that one must always be respectful towards one's elders. He therefore refrains from anything but the most objective (and cold) analysis:

'Ezekiel's poetry reveals his primary concern with understanding the meaning of his life and attaining self-realization. Poetry seems to be the means to this goal. In the process of pursuing this quest, he is acutely conscious of his own failings and self-deceptions, yet he finds himself preserved again and again. Somewhere along the way, he stumbles upon his Truth in its pristine form; the secret principles that govern the universe are divulged to him and he finds the answer to the mystery of his life. Having once grasped this secret, be it for a single moment, his life is changed completely. This appears to be the essence of the poet's mysticism.'[30]

Even the Marathi press, not normally known for its generosity towards the English lobby, sat up and took notice. *Kesari,* the Pune-based newspaper first started by Bal Gangadhar Tilak, commissioned Shirish Chindhade to do a survey of Nissim's poetry.[31] *Navshakti,* reporting on the Frankfurt Book Fair of 1986, preferred to carry his picture, rather than that of a Marathi writer.[32]

Most articles that appeared on Nissim–scholarly or journalistic– focused on his poetry. This is because he chose to project himself as principally a poet. However, by the mid-'80s, he had become a 'saleable commodity'; anything that he did was bound to interest the public. At least that was the assumption of the scores of people who wrote on him, and desperately tried to find new things to say about him. A revival of Nalini in 1985, led to a four-column write up in the *Sunday Observer*.[33] The writer, Radhika Ramaseshan, said typically: 'A little-known facet of his literary career is that Ezekiel is also a playwright, although his output in this form has not been as sustained and prolific as his poetry.' Don't Call it a Suicide, a less substantial play than 'Nalini', was published by Macmillan in the late '80s as a student edition.[34] While the book did not get many reviews, a reading of the play in June 1988, followed by another one at the British Council Auditorium, Bombay, in August, provided the necessary opportunities to critics. Indu Saraiya, who reviewed the first reading, still referred to the play by its old name, 'Soft and Sad Music'.[35] She spent most of the space allotted to her giving away the plot. The British Council reading was reviewed by Rochelle D'Souza,[36] who taught English at the fashionable Jai Hind College. Her review, though short, was critically sound, with comments on all the varied aspects of theatre, such as lights, music and acting. Very little was said about Nissim as playwright, though– the one thing that D'Souza did say was that his Indian English dialogue was convincing.

One of the most unusual things that Nissim did in the late '80s, was to team up with his nephew Nandu Bhende, and produce an album of songs, that were written by him and set to music by Bhende. Just how unexpected a project of this kind was, can be judged from the introduction to Ajith Pillai's preview article in the *Indian Post*.[37] The introduction says: 'It sounds incredible, but it's true: respected poet Nissim Ezekiel has been providing the words for many of his rock-musician nephew Nandu Bhende's songs.' Pillai asks Nissim how the whole thing came about. Nissim explains that it all began when his sister Asha asked him to talk to her son Nandu, who was always singing songs. He did so, and advised Nandu to write his own songs, which he could then set to music. But Nandu wasn't confident about writing. That's when Nissim stepped in and offered to write for him. Pillai then gets to the heart of the matter, and inquires whether Nissim felt foolish writing pop lyrics. He did not. 'I don't think there is anything wrong with it. And I personally don't mind composing songs even though it means I have to structure my lines to fit into the format into which songs are normally written.'

We also get to know that Nissim was accustomed to listening to classical music, but after pairing up with Bhende, started listening to pop music, his favourites being the Beatles. To me, however, the veracity of these claims is doubtful.

Pillai betrays his own prejudices, when he writes, 'One cannot help feeling slightly disoriented watching Ezekiel pull out a little book which is an assorted collection of the lyrics and chords of pop hits.' Nissim himself is not unduly worried about the fact that he has had no formal training in music to attempt an experiment of this kind. 'Well I don't bother about the chords because I know little about music, but what I am interested in is the structure of the songs which are different from the poems.' We are told that of the twenty songs Nissim has written, Bhende has selected five for his album. The reason he chose them is: 'Nissim is a well-known name all over the country and the curiosity of a certain class of people would certainly be aroused because he has written the songs for me.' Pillai further discloses that HMV, which is bringing out the album, 'is pumping in Rs 1 lakh for the production.'

Assignments of different kinds always came Nissim's way. In the late '80s, the Sahitya Akademi invited him to guest-edit a special issue of their journal, *Indian Literature*[38] with poems by Bombay poets. E.V. Ramakrishnan reviewed the special number,[39] together with the other similar (if more exhaustive) one, edited by me. It is evident, from the following paragraph in Nissim's preface, which Ramakrishnan quotes, that he is looking for a school, a Bombay school, which he can take the credit of forming:

'None is experimental, and none is traditional in form. There is a certain kind of middle path in free verse which characterizes them. They can be assessed only in terms of the qualities which that path implies. Within that limitation, I consider them authentic. Most of them are also substantial in content, personal statements with a wide appeal. They communicate easily, which I believe is a virtue, and their imagery is not extravagant.'

These are exactly the qualities that are to be found in Nissim's own later verse!

In the '80s, my own personal contact with Nissim increased. We began to find ourselves together at poetry readings and seminars more often.

Frequently, we shared the same platform, both of us being invited by the organizers of the event to lecture or read poems. Possibly, the seeds of this biography were sown then, as I was slowly beginning to form impressions about the man. Some of the occasions at which we came together should be of interest to readers.

It began in 1984, when in December, the English Department of Pune University (which I would later join as faculty) hosted the All India English Teachers' Conference. Sudhakar Pandey was then the Head. I was a lecturer at Bombay's SIES College, and on the spur of the moment decided to apply for leave and go to the conference. It was a jamboree, to say the least, but Nissim was prominently present, having a good time. There are two things that I distinctly remember. A leaking faucet that refused to be turned off, upset him no end. He noticed it during a tea-break, and after that nothing but the tap seized his attention. If anyone came up to him to say hello–he was after all the most famous person at the conference–he immediately showed him (or her) the tap. Nobody other than Nissim seemed to bother about it. People laughed his concern off as a poet's eccentricity, before moving on. At such out-of-town conferences, Nissim tended to hang around with the Bombay contingent. At this one– and this brings me to my second observation–he identified Shakuntala Bharvani and me. Bharvani was teasing him about something or the other, and Nissim was playfully retaliating by punning on her surname. 'Bore-wani', he was calling her, and we were all having a hearty laugh.

Two years later, in 1986, we met at the University of Pune again. This time it was for a U.G.C. seminar on the 'Image of India in the Indian Novel in English', a more serious event than the 1984 conference. Nissim however, was bent on being the court jester. In my introduction to the conference volume[40] (it fell to my lot to co-edit it with Sudhakar Pandey after I joined the Department of English in 1988) I point out how he annoyed every paper reader by asking him during question time, whether the novel (on which he had read his paper) was a good one! The implication of the question was, of course, that the paper had not addressed this most vital issue. It had not told him why the theme that the author was tackling needed the novel as a form of expression, rather than a series of newspaper articles. Makarand Paranjape, who was present at the seminar, freshly returned from the US, gave it back to Nissim by asking him the same question after his paper on Shourie Daniels' *The Salt Doll*.

And Nissim didn't have a satisfactory answer! I was sitting next to Nissim during a session, and I remember him openly making fun of up-country participants like S. C. Dwivedi of Allahabad, mimicking their gestures and facial expressions. All this, while the session was in progress! I had to put a hand to my mouth to prevent myself from bursting out laughing.

In June 1987, after a severe bout of malaria, I walked one morning from my mother's house near Liberty Cinema to the PEN, about a kilometre away. Reason? I wanted Nissim to organize a reading from the Special Number of the *Literary Endeavour* on Bombay poetry, that I had just guest-edited. Nisim readily agreed, and we decided on a date, some three weeks later, so that he would have enough time to send out invitations. For some reason, however, Nissim kept calling it the 'Bombay Poets on Bombay' issue, which of course was not my title. When the circular was printed, I found that it had his title. I was too exhausted (after the malaria) to protest. When the event finally took place, it was well-attended. Nissim was the charming host who pointed out in his introductory remarks, how ten years ago such an issue would have been unthinkable. But he continued to refer to it as the 'Bombay Poets on Bombay' issue. Such was his arrogance.

Most Bombay-raised and Bombay-based poets of my generation have received some kind of encouragement from Nissim whenever they have gone to him with their poems. My experience, however, has been slightly different. He was plainly baffled by my aesthetics and did not know what to make of them. The few times he published me in the *Indian PEN* he did so with great reluctance. At the same time, he was uncertain whether he was right in his estimate of my work. I received unqualified support from Gieve Patel, and Nissim must have read Gieve's favourable reviews of my poems. In the early '90s, he rejected a short story I submitted to him, with a little note explaining that he did not think it worked, but he could be wrong. As it turned out, he was. The story eventually found its way to Vrinda Nabar's page in the *Independent*. More significantly, it was picked up by Welcomgroup's in-house magazine, *Namaste*. I made a total of Rs 3000 on the story, whereas if it had been accepted by Nissim for the *Indian PEN*, I would have got nothing!

In 1988, OUP finally decided to publish all of Nissim's work in a single volume. *Collected Poems*,[41] with an Introduction by Gieve Pate!, came out that year in hardback. A few years later, it was also issued in paperback. The volume included all his seven individual collections, beginning with *A Time to Change*. In addition, it carried seventeen new poems that were written after the publication of *Latter-Day Psalms*. The 'Edinburgh Interlude' sequence was a part of this. It's not as if all the poems in individual collections were included: in each collection, a couple of poems were left out by mutual consent of Nissim and his editors. Then, there were revisions of old poems, sometimes for the better, sometimes for the worse: 'Enterprise' in *The Unfinished Man* provides a good example of the latter kind of revision. I remember Nissim tediously trying to explain to his friends why changes of this kind were effected. Apparently, they had to do among other things, with accuracy of meaning. His arguments, however, did not convince anybody. But Nissim is not alone in this. The history of poetry is full of examples of poets who destroy the spontaneity of their poems by labouring over them too much.

Patel's *Introduction* is as transparent as a glass of water. The only point on which I differ with him is whether Nissim can be called a religious poet. Patel concedes *Hymns in Darkness* and *Latter-Day Psalms* provide the evidence of religiosity, yet refrains from calling him a religious poet. I am less circumspect. If one has to apply a label of this type to distinguish the later Ezekiel from the earlier, I am not unwilling to do so, merely in the interest of moderation. Precisely this question comes up in the interview Nissim gives to V.C. Harris in Cochin, in 1994.[42] Harris, referring to Patel's unwillingness in his Introduction to describe Nissim's poetry as religious, points out that Bruce King, by contrast, has no qualms about suggesting that the poetry is Jewish. He wants to have Nissim's views on the matter. And Nissim gives him a 'guarded reply'. This is what he tells him: 'I can't say Gieve is right and Bruce wrong, or the other way round. I can't quite explain it. There are of course the critic's own needs and perceptions. Yes, I've seen some people in London, for instance, read my poems and exclaim: "Oh how Jewish!" It's not of course intended, but that element is there. And hearing a lot of very knowledgeable readers responding to it in these terms, I have come to accept it. It has to do with my experiences as a child, prayers, synagogues, and so on, though I have never consciously tried to capture that kind of tone or feeling. Apart from that, I really don't know if my poems are religious or not.'

There are seventeen new poems in the book, written after the publication of *Latter-Day Pslams*. They are simply called 'Poems 1983-88'. Thematically, the most significant of these are the poems in which

Nissim speaks in the first person, and writes of his own life. 'The Way it Went', like 'Jewish Wedding in Bombay', is about his marriage, the raising of a family and suddenly discovering that he has become a grandfather. Throughout, Nissim is the spectator, watching in amazement his own 'foolish' actions. His final remark is:

> O well, I'll be damned,
> is all that I can say.

'A Different Way' and 'At 62' give us an insight into his state of mind, after crossing sixty. In the former poem, he complains:

> Now I feel driven to the wall
> by age and circumstance:
> holiness matters
> Sceptical as always,
> I cannot go in search of it
> to an ashram, or settle down alone
> on the top of a mountain
> with an assured income of some sort
> and a servant to do the cooking.

In the latter, we are provided with a sort of inventory of his concerns at sixty-two. One of the things he has become aware of suddenly, is:

> Death,
> in the distance
> and near,
> is my only halo.

In 'Blessings II', it is the familiar water-tap that distracts him once again:

> When your water-tap
> leaks, may you care
> as if you are paying
> for every drop
> needed by the city's source.

I have already related the tale of his obsession with a leaking water-tap at Pune University! But this, certainly, was not the only instance of its kind. Apparently, in the past while bathing at Daisy's house in Kala Niketan, Nissim would turn on the water-taps only very slightly, so that the water came down in a trickle. Why? The poor of the city did not have the luxury of flowing water, so why should he? Daisy would be justifiably furious.

'Cleaning Up' is a classic case of dramatic irony. Nissim depicts himself living among ants, cockroaches, lizards, crows, pigeons and sparrows, that freely roam his kitchen and bedroom. There would come a time–in the late '90s–when this would actually be the case, and there would be no one to do the cleaning up for him. 'An Atheist Speaks' is a throwback to Nissim's halcyon days, one last time.

> It's is all quite plain.
> If you look into a mirror,
> it's the Devil reflected
> and God remote.

Then there are poems where Nissim is again out to expose, satirize, ridicule. What? Pretension in 'Torso of a Woman': he prefers a real-life woman with arms and legs, to a torso that passes for art with 'arms cut off / just below the shoulders, /legs cut off /just below the knees'; the bureaucracy in 'Poem VIII' of 'Ten Poems in the Greek Anthology Mode'; film-makers and crusaders in 'A Film Fable' (which, incidentally, is written for Aruna. Aruna who?), art in 'Edinburgh Interlude IV', where he skillfully contrasts the use of colour by the artist, with his colour-prejudice, giving the poem a racial dimension.

Of the three or four Bombay poems in the present batch, 'Woman and Child', like 'On Bellasis Road' in *Latter-Day Psalms*, attempts to explore local reality. 'Occasion' brings to life the nondescript Indian clerks whom Nissim has always claimed to know well and be in sympathy with. In 'Edinburgh Interlude XXI' and 'Edinburgh Interlude XXVIII', he grows nostalgic for Bombay while he is away in foreign lands. In the former poem, the city is seen in terms of its mangoes:

> Perhaps it is not the mangoes
> that my eyes and tongue long for,

but Bombay as the fruit
on which I've lived
winning and losing
my little life.

In the latter, with astute observation that is unusual for him, Nissim uses 'the grass that grows / between Bombay's pavement tiles' as a simile for the commonplaces of speech. Whitmanesque, that.

The number of girlie poems in this batch is lesser than in previous volumes. It is as if, at last, in his old age Nissim has begun to tire of the theme, which is confined here mainly to 'Ten Poems in the Greek Anthology Mode'. In 'Poem I', he writes:

From the age of 20 to 30
She waited passionately for a lover.
From 30 to 40
She tried actively to catch one
Now she is known
As the lively virgin
Of the National Centre for the Performing Arts.

'Poem V' is about the woman's lover sending her Tik-20 instead of flowers (ostensibly to deal with the bugs in her bed). 'Poem VIII' has already been referred to above as a satirical piece. However, even when his aim is to ridicule the bureaucracy, he solicits the services of a 'female railway clerk' to accomplish his objective!

Three other 'Greek Anthology Mode' poems (IV, VI, X,) together with 'Subconscious' are self-reflexive poems, which deal with poetry itself. In 'Subconscious', Nissim, who has never had any real use for surrealism, pictures his subconscious complaining to him of neglect. In 'G.A.M. VI', he says, succinctly:

Here lies a poet whose theme was human failure,
For which he was praised in a dozen famous obituaries.

Then there are poems on miscellaneous subjects, mostly dealt with before. Thus 'Soap' is an Indian English poem (the last Indian English poem he would write); 'Blessings' recalls the earlier poster and postcard poems; 'More Songs for Nandu Bhende' are lyrics he wrote for his nephew to set to music (see earlier); and 'Death of a Hen' is a kind of animal-rights poem, where he laments the destruction of 'a hen / . . . swept aside by a passing car.'

In terms of sheer craft and finesse, the three top poems, amongst this new set, are to my mind, 'The Fence', 'To the Sun' and 'Edinburgh Interlude XXVIII'. In 'The Fence', a fence is personified, and it speaks in its own voice. The poem displays the maximum use of metaphor, making creative use of the expression 'to sit on the fence'. Likewise, in 'To the Sun', he playfully talks to the sun as an equal, demonstrating how the sun doesn't possess the freedom that he does.

> Try to rise, sunny boy,
> rise before I rise–
> you'll never succeed!
>
> . . .
>
> I've got an alarm clock,
> you don't have one.
> you can't beat me.
>
> . . .
>
> I don't have to follow
> a fixed pattern
> on when to rise early.
> and when to rise late.

As pointed out above, I would rate 'Edinburgh Interlude XXVIII' highly, for its minuscule observation of 'the grass that grows / between Bombay's pavement tiles.'

Collected Poems was the last volume of Nissim's verse that would be published. It was therefore apt to ask him to take stock of his work. How did he feel, at the end of his career, about being remembered as a poet of ideas rather than images? He said it was a question of going (or not going) into extremes. Poems with a surfeit of images (but no ideas to link the images) seemed to him contrived. It was far better if some of those images said something, or at least provided a context to the poem. Hence he never cared for poetry–or wrote poetry, for that matter-where the emphasis from start to finish was only on imagery. At the same time, he agreed that the absence of imagery could be construed as a weakness in the poem, unless of course, it specifically required it. A moral statement in a poem could simultaneously possess other attributes, such as sound and rhythmic effects. Nissim, for one, has never believed that a poem has to be morally uplifting and educating, although willy-nilly some of his own poems fulfil this criterion. He also points out that poems can include moral statements without necessarily being moralistic. The statements may pertain to a poet's views about religion or politics, for example, and may really be personal statements. I asked him whether personal statements, too, could have an air of preachiness about them. He rejected the word 'preachiness', and said it was rather a matter of conviction. I probed further, and inquired whether he thought, Indians being Indians, they needed a poetry that was not pure form. He vehemently denied that such a thought had ever crossed his mind. 'I never went through such a phase,' he said. Did simple poetry also amount to popular poetry? 'Popular poetry is another thing altogether,' Nissim replied, 'but everyone who writes simple poems is not necessarily being popular.'

(Adil Jussawalla, when posed with the question of Nissim's tendency to moralize, says: 'I certainly don't find him ponderous . . . Can any artist prevent his art from being a part of his life's concerns? People want unformed emotions. So however undisciplined Kamala Das is, they like her. Nissim loses out on that count, because he's not like that.')

A final, more hard-hitting question: what did Nissim see as the principal failure in his poetry? It would be hard for even a monk to be more honest. 'Originality [the lack of it],' Nissim said, and startled me. And where, according to him, does the reason for this failure lie? Within, or without? 'I wouldn't blame the environment,' Nissim replied. 'I'm critical of myself–as critical as I am of others, without allowing self-criticism to undermine my worth and my work.'

Nissim disagrees that in evaluating himself thus, he is being harsh, and applying too strict standards that can only end in pessimism and dejection.

Totem Pole

When poets publish their collected poems, it may be a way of telling the outside world that they have reached the end of their tether; their best work is behind them. What new poems they may now write, may or may not be published as a volume, or may be appended to the collected poems in later editions. However, even if these poems remain unpublished, they will not be any the worse for it. This is exactly what happened to Nissim. It isn't as if he did not write new poems after 1988; but he wasn't very successful in getting them published, even in journals, let alone as a book. Nor did this seem to bother him. At one stage, there was some talk of OUP bringing out a volume of his new and unpublished poems, written mainly in the '90s. But eventually this did not come about. What OUP did bring out, somewhat half-heartedly, was a volume of his *Selected Prose*, and Nissim also managed to convince Macmillan to publish his play, *Don't Call it a Suicide*. The poems, on the other hand, remain scattered among his papers at the PEN, and face the danger of being mislaid or lost without a trace, given the fact that Nissim will now probably never return to his one-time citadel, and the Theosophical Society which owns the place will soon order it to be cleaned up.

Ruthless as it may sound, the ten years between the publication of *Collected Poems* and now (we are nearly at the end of 1998 as I write this) provide a sort of countdown to the final moment, zero hour, when the soul takes leave of the body, and perhaps transmigrates.

. . . But will there ever be another Nissim Ezekiel?

Yet there is a deeper and more ideological explanation for his decline as a poet in the '90s. In this last decade of the twentieth century, postmodernism was fast pushing modernism into oblivion. Postmodernism came with its own baggage, with a different set of imperatives as it were, and Nissim's aesthetics were clearly unequipped to deal with this. The artificial barriers that existed between 'high culture' and 'low culture' (or popular culture) were being dismantled. Poetry was no longer merely about form, imagery, symbolism, moral values and elegant language. Instead, it began to reflect more crucial concerns, such as the divide that existed between homo sapiens, on the basis of race, gender, class, caste, and even sexual orientation. English departments in colleges and universities throughout the country were losing some of their Victorian character. Their bases began to broaden, as like their counterparts on Western campuses, they made room for the allied arts, and for inter-disciplinary critical approaches in the syllabus. Everywhere, literary theory came to replace literary criticism. Plato, Aristotle, Coleridge, Mathew Arnold and T.S. Eliot began to rub shoulders with (or be sidelined by) Foucault, Derrida, Barthes, Bakhtin, Gayatri Spivak and Homi Bhabha wherever serious cultural debates were taking place. Perhaps, as far as Nissim was concerned, the most debilitating effect of the onslaught of 'theory' was its insistence that all judgement of literary value be deferred or shelved. For someone whose literary education was founded on the belief that all poems were either good poems or bad poems, this was indeed perplexing. Thus it is that Nissim found himself increasingly alienated from the cultural and literary climate of the '90s. Although he continued to attend poetry readings and seminars, he opened his mouth less and less to ask a question or make a comment. Youngsters like Ashley Tellis and Ranjit Hoskote took full advantage of his helplessness and openly ridiculed him for what they called his ignorance. In doing so, they were getting back at a man who for years had wielded unlimited patriarchal power, and whimsically used it to promote his favourites and crush dissenters.

The hapless situation in which Nissim found himself was only intensified by the fact that a crippling disease–Alzheimer's–was slowly engulfing his once hyperactive brain, leading to embarrassing memory lapses in public. At first, these 'treacheries' of memory were under control. As late as 1994, when I began work on this biography, Nissim was able to recall all the major events of his life. However, during the last couple of years, the disease has tightened its stranglehold. The highpoint was reached in 1998, when he collapsed at an American Jewish Joint Distribution Committee (AJJDC) meeting and had to be hospitalized. It was only then that the doctors formally pronounced his condition as Alzheimer's. This unexpectedly triggered off a new controversy, with his friends, admirers, well-wishers and the intelligentsia of Bombay more or less unanimously accusing his family of neglect. Articles began to appear in the newspapers, some of them by well-known columnists such as Vimla Patil and Shobha De, suggesting that it was the duty of his family to look after him, that it was because of their indifference that he was in his present sorry state. Elkana, who in fact had arranged for his treatment (his company, Johnson & Johnson, had agreed to foot part of the bills) was visibly upset. He rightly felt that it was irresponsible on the part of the Bombay press to comment on a matter about which they had little or no knowledge, and certainly did not possess a perspective. It was only Nissim's very close friends and associates, like Adil Jussawalla and Gieve Patel, who knew the truth. And the truth plainly was that it was Nissim himself who continually resisted hospitalization, still believing there was nothing irreparably wrong with his health. He also reacted badly to the suggestion that he wasn't eating properly, and that if this was because he did not have the money, his friends were willing to come to his aid. It was true, however, that his intake of food had greatly reduced, and undernourishment was one of the reasons why he collapsed that afternoon at the AJJDC meeting.

What follows, is a year-by-year account of all the little events in Nissim's life during the last ten years.

1989

'Don't Call it a Suicide' was published in the *Bombay Review*[1] (later called the *Bombay Literary Review*). This journal, issued by the Department English, University of Bombay, where Nissim was once a professor, was edited by Vilas Sarang, himself no great admirer of Nissim's work. So it is a bit surprising that Sarang agreed to include the play in the very first issue. It isn't one of Nissim's best or even better plays. It tells the story of a family in which the eldest son commits suicide at the age of twenty-five, and by the end of the two-act play, his father follows suit. There is much talk and little action. The son hangs himself from the ceiling fan, but this is merely reported rather than enacted for us. We do, however, see the father, Mr Nanda, ending his life by consuming an overdose of sleeping pills. The character of Mr Sathe is sketchy. We never quite know why Mr Nanda has such implicit faith in his judgement—after all, he is only a casual visitor to their house.

As pointed out in an earlier chapter, Nissim got the title of the play (and possibly even the plot) during a visit to Professor Sudhakar Pandey's house at the University of Pune. I was curious to know whether Sudhakar

Pandey had read the play once it was published, or at least realized that it was a chance remark by his wife during a casual conversation that gave Nissim his title. So one morning, almost ten years after the play was written, I telephoned him to ask. The incident had completely slipped his mind. Not only was Professor Pandey unaware of the play, but he couldn't remember the circumstances in which he had invited Nissim to his bungalow at the Pune University campus, and chatted to him about his domestic life. However, he did not rule out the possibility of its having taken place in 1984, when Nissim had accepted his invitation to attend the All India English Teachers' Conference at the university. This was only two years after his son's tragic death; it is possible, Professor Pandey said to me, that the subject figured in their conversation.

That same year, a radio talk that Nissim had given five years previously (in the Orwellian year, 1984) appeared in an anthology of Indian English prose, especially prepared for students.[2] Here he is ambivalent about the question of assimilating into the Indian mainstream, as he speaks of the complications involved in attempting to define attitudes (his and everyone else's) to the heritage of India. He says, 'I have experienced those complications and have found it necessary from time to time to define my attitude, either publicly or to myself.' What we get is a frank set of personal statements about the dilemmas he has faced. For example, he says at one point: 'Marathi was my mother tongue but I never really learnt it; Judaism was my religion but I not only rejected it in early youth but all religions with it. That I am today back into Judaism in a small way and accept the core of all historical religions is a different story. I lived in a literary world and still do, in the world of ideas, art and human relations, as I still do, and in India as my environment, which it continues to be. I cannot imagine living permanently outside India but it does not follow that I live within the Indian heritage.' The reference to Marathi as his mother tongue leads him to make a confession a few paragraphs later: 'To try and relate to the country as a whole without relating to any particular regional culture seems to me an unavoidable consequence of not having mastered one's regional mother tongue. I have always regretted this greatly but am now reconciled to it. I have dreamt of compensating for the limitation by collaborating in translations from Marathi poetry or seeking opportunities to promote Marathi literature.'

One of the implications of the essay is that, for Nissim, art has always provided the securities that real life has denied. Art, thus, becomes a way out of the tangle, the continual conflict as it were, 'between my Jewish racial soul and my Indian choices.' Having convincingly made out a case for his dependence on art and literature, however, he ends the talk with a sentimental one-liner: 'I need India even if India does not need me.'

Nissim's Singapore stint between December 1988 and March 1989 earned him many admirers. One of these was a Singapore-based poet, Lin Hsin Hsin, who on 21 February 1989 actually wrote what she thought was a poem addressed to him. I reproduce it in part:

> Professor Ezekiel
> you're one of the many few
> to whom I owe my gratitude
> you've a heart to heal
> may be, you never knew.
>
> Professor Ezekiel
> your poems have revealed
> more than a great deal   .
> you've reached beyond your zeal
> . . .
> Professor Ezekiel
> your words
> in my heart are retained
> your lines
> in my mind they refrain [sic]
> . . .
> Professor Ezekiel
> T'is my wish to you
> may your voice stay in tune
> may god bless you & your kin
> now and evermore.[3]

While no one in their senses would call this a poem, Nissim happily displayed it when the volume in which it appears arrived at his office by post. His own critical standards were declining, or at least becoming more lenient, as the poems that he accepted for publication in the *Indian PEN* showed; so it is possible that he was willing to forgive Lin Hsin Hsin her lapses. It is also true that what he was flaunting was not the poem itself, or a poet who had learnt something about poetry under his tutelage, but rather a young woman's total devotion to him. And Lin Hsin Hsin, as we know, wasn't the first such woman.

On 25 November 1989, Nissim received an enthusiastic letter form Adil Tyabji of OUP (dated 15 November), who on behalf of OUP expressed his willingness to publish Nissim's prose in book form. Initially, Tyabji speaks of the prose in glowing terms: 'Rukun [Advani] made my return to the desk painless and indeed very enjoyable by giving me the collection of prose writings you had sent (at our request) [for us] to look at. The uniform excellence and thought that goes into your writing . . . is an object lesson for any aspiring writer. The output has . . . been small and will make a slimmer volume than one would ideally have liked. We would, nevertheless, like very much to go ahead with a 125-140 pp. volume.'

Having praised the writing, Tyabji then goes on to express subtle criticisms of it. He suggests that the opening paragraphs of 'Uncertain Uncertainties' [sic] should be rephrased. He also thinks that 'Art and the Indian Environment' as it presently exists is superficial and must be fleshed out 'into a more substantial essay.' He wants the Introduction to the book to be written by someone other than Nissim himself. While he asks Nissim to name someone for the task, on his part he hints at Adil Jussawalla. In a post-script, Tyabji lets Nissim know that Rukun Advani's favoured title for the book is *Ezekiel's India: The Selected Prose of Nissim Ezekiel*. This, he claims, is 'a clear allusion to your brilliant "Naipaul's India" essay.' Finally, Tyabji offers Nissim a ten per cent royalty on all copies sold.

Correspondence on the publication of the volume would continue, and it would be another three years before the book actually came out.

1990

Jerry Pinto remembers 1990 as the year he went back to see Nissim (after his first meeting with him at Elphinstone College in 1982). Pinto was a freelance journalist by now, and wanted to interview him for a column on celebrities. The interview took place at Sanman; Hutokshi Doctor and Persis Anklesaria also accompanied them to the restaurant. Pinto remembers Nissim answering his questions with a 'literal exactness' that annoyed him, because he expected Nissim to be, like most other poets, tangential in his replies. At the same time, he realized that by being 'painstakingly literal', Nissim made delightful copy to most journalists. But this is not how Pinto personally saw it. Nissim's tendency to balance everything with everything else prevented Pinto from eliciting the violent, earth-shaking responses he was looking for.

Yet it was this very quality of level-headedness that endeared Nissim to Pinto. Pinto says he was lucky that the first poet in Bombay he got to know was Nissim–'remarkably sane, not agonized, depressed or on drugs.' This was reassuring. 'I wouldn't have survived if I had met Dom or Adil first,' he remarks.

Pinto was beginning to take his own poems seriously, and he tried showing some of them to Nissim; but, as in the case of all emerging poets he did not wish to mollycoddle, Nissim conveniently mislaid them. In marked contrast to the vibes Pinto got from Nissim, he saw Hoskote shaping up as his blue-eyed boy. This, he stoically claims, did not make him feel envious, because he was convinced there was no one quite like Hoskote. But, as pointed out earlier, the friendship between Hoskote and Nissim was complex, complicated. Pinto was a regular spectator to their relationship that swung between cordiality and contempt. Nissim's over-generous words on the blurb of *Zones of Assault* did have an impact on the book and the kind of attention Hoskote got. But much to Hoskote's irritation, Nissim had positioned himself as his literary father who needed to be beheaded. Pinto was a witness to strange goings-on at Sanman, such as a daily squabble about who would foot the bill!

In 1990, Nissim was still a man of clout. He was a consultant to major publishing houses such as Rupa & Co and Orient Longman, who were suddenly keen on bringing out first volumes of poetry. Pinto was aware of this and knew it was difficult to talk to Nissim without appearing to impose himself on him. But as he did not have enough poems then to think in terms of a book, he wasn't as vulnerable as some of his seniors.

Two such 'seniors' were Charmayne D'Souza and Sanjiv Bhatla. Orient Longman had just launched their new literary series, Disha Books, and had appointed Nissim as poetry editor. It was his job to select manuscripts, help the poets to revise their poems, and then pass them on to Priya Adarkar, publishing director at Orient Longman. Both D'Souza and Bhatla were old friends of Nissim who visited him often and showed him their poems. They were obedient poets who took his advice seriously when he pointed out weaknesses in a poem, and they carefully revised their poems till he was satisfied. This helped. D'Souza's *A Spelling Guide to Woman*[4] and Bhatla's *Looking Back*[5] were the very first books with which Orient Longman launched their series. To other poets of their generation, they seemed to be the chosen ones, on whom Nissim had bestowed a singular honour. Several poets at the time, such as Prabhanjan Mishra, Menka Shivdasani and myself (all part of Bombay's Poetry Circle) had a manuscript ready for publication, but it was not us that Nissim had approached. The 'preferential' treatment that D'Souza and Bhatla got led to the usual bitchiness. People wondered what Nissim saw in Bhatla's work, which wasn't extraordinary. As for D'Souza, Nissim frequently spent long hours of the evening with her, ensconced in his room at the PEN, as they sat together revising her poems. I distinctly remember an evening at the British Council auditorium at Mittal Tower, Nariman Point, around this time. We were invited to a talk by some visiting writer, and I walked Nissim from the PEN to Mittal Tower. A few minutes after we had taken our seats, D'Souza walked in and sat next to me, so as to sandwich me between herself and Nissim. Nissim was greatly peeved at the lost opportunity of getting to sit next to D'Souza. 'Let me sit near her, please,' he kept nudging me throughout the talk, till I obliged him by exchanging places.

It is said a man of no enemies is a man of few friends. Nissim had many friends and many enemies, and the gulf between them was widening. What determined whether one was his friend or his enemy was, of course, fairly simple. If he had taken you under his wing, you were his friend. If he had cold-shouldered you, you were his enemy. He was Bombay's Poetic God or Poetic Devil, depending on how one saw him, which in turn was determined by the treatment one had received at his hands. Some of his enemies who saw him as the Devil were coming into their own as writers and critics, and were waiting to settle old scores. Orient Longman's third book in the Disha series was not a first collection of poems, but an anthology of Indian English poetry edited by Vilas Sarang, one of Nissim's old foes. Sarang hadn't forgotten the uncharitable review of his own collection of poems, *A Kind of Silence,* that Nissim had written in the '70s. Thus, even as he was preparing his anthology for publication, Bombay's literary world was rife with rumour that he had decided not to include Nissim's work. When the book finally came out, Nissim was there, but what Sarang had to say about him in the Introduction wasn't flattering.

'Rather than the first poet of the new era, he is among the last notable poets of the old era,'[6] he wrote. This, because like the Indian Romantics before him, Nissim revelled in a 'lack of concreteness'.

Be that as it may, Vilas Sarang was certainly the first critic of the new era who was initiating a new way of looking at Nissim's poetry. Sarang's adverse comments on Nissim's poems may also be traced to another source. He was a protege of R.B. Patankar with whom, it will be recalled, Nissim had a problem while they were colleagues at Bombay University's English Department in the '70s and '80s.

1992

Nissim decided to go to the international conference of the Association of Commonwealth Literature and Language Studies (ACLALS) at Jamaica. It was his first visit to the West Indies. It would also be the last time he was attending an ACLALS conference. The next conference of the Association, of which he was a member, would be in Colombo, Sri Lanka in 1995, to which he would be scheduled to go, but would back out at the last minute. Tejaswini Niranjana, feminist critic and scholar, was in Jamaica at the time for a research project. It is possible Nissim met her, for, the tendency in strange and foreign lands is for Indians to hang together, no matter how dissimilar they are, or how unlikely it is for them to engage in even casual conversation with each other back in India. Nissim, as usual, was pampered at the conference. His airfare was pre-paid, he was given the best accommodation, and delegates hovered around him.

OUP finally published Nissim's prose. The title they settled for was *Selected Prose*.[7] Nissim dedicated the book to his sisters Sarah and Lily (Asha) and their husbands Srini and Atmaram. Adil Tyabji had suggested that Adil Jussawalla be invited to write the introduction, and Jussawalla it was who wrote it. Jussawalla made four observations in his opening paragraph: that the selections were restricted to less than twenty years of Nissim's work (1965 to 1984); that they were not comprehensive; that the book reviews, which were Nissim's trademark, were mostly left out, except for four of them in a section entitled 'On Books'; and lastly, that it was not he, Jussawalla, who had made the selections. Somewhere in the text of his seven-page introduction, he was emboldened to actually use the word 'moralist' to describe Nissim. Few of Nissim's friends had dared to use the word before.

Selected Prose was divided into four sections, 'On Poetry', 'On Art and Culture', 'On Life and Thought', and 'On Books'. 'Naipaul's India and Mine' was included in the 'On Art and Culture' section. This was undoubtedly the most 'famous' piece in the whole volume. The four books whose reviews comprised the last section were *Two Virgins* by Kamala Markandaya, *Relations* by A. K. Ramanujan, *Apparitions* by Keki Daruwalla and *Scholar Extraordinary* by Nirad C. Chaudhuri. The choice, in this case, seemed fairly arbitrary.

The Appendix to *Selected Prose* consisted of an interview with Nissim by Frank Birbalsingh, the York University professor with whom he had stayed during a visit to Toronto. It is a long interview that goes on for eleven-and-a-half pages, and is thorough, as Birbalsingh's work mostly is. It was recorded in Bombay on 30 June 1986, when Birbalsingh was visiting India. There are, from our point of view, several informative responses that Birbalsingh was able to draw out of Nissim. I outline some of these below:

On Nissim's interest in Indian philosophy and religion: 'That started for me at a very early age. I was, after all, in a Roman Catholic school, and the Fathers used to say to the students that there was nothing at all in Hinduism. The Hindus, Parsis, Muslims, all said, "What? There is nothing in Hinduism?" So we started reading the Gita and the Upanishads at school, which I may not have done in the next ten years had the Fathers not said there was nothing in it.'

On writing an obscure poem (or what Makarand Paranjape calls an esoteric poem in the high modernist tradition)[8]: 'I think all I can say is that whenever I wrote, from my point of view, a successfully obscure poem, and then studied it, I would say "What game am I playing? How did I fall into this trap? Is it impossible to rewrite this poem and clarify it?" So I would rewrite it and I invariably found that I could clarify it.

On the view that in his Indian English poems, he makes fun of ordinary people: 'I regret it very much when I hear that kind of response. There is a linguistic, political and social nationalism in India which can also be very strong in the various regions.'

On Dom Moraes: '. . . if I were writing a history of Indo-English literature, I would not hesitate to include Dom Moraes. Then I would explain his circumstances and decisions. His starting point is India; he goes out and comes back to India. That's different from someone born outside India who comes here and then leaves.'

Nissim's last remark gives me the cue; I am suddenly able to see what is wrong with Birbalsingh's own interview. He is writing as a diasporic Indian, and is attributing political motives to Nissim that are somewhat irrelevant, given the fact that Nissim has always lived in his own country. His comparison of Nissim to Naipaul further strengthens this view; it is a comparison that Nissim instantly rejects: 'I think [the belief that it is impossible for postcolonial people to achieve identity in the modern world] suits Naipaul, because it is his answer to his own problems. But I can think of almost any regional Indian writer–a Bengali or a Tamil– ultimately deciding . . . that he is a Tamil or whatever, and nothing can shake him out of that.' What Nissim is saying here is what I have, over the years, personally come to believe in: that the Indian writer in English who lives in India has more in common with the regional writer than he/she does with writers of the Indian diaspora.[9]

There was a longish review of *Selected Prose* by Jerry Pinto in the *Sunday Free Press Journal*.[10] After discussing each article in detail, Pinto comes to the Appendix, and suggests that instead of the Frank Birbalsingh interview, OUP should have used excerpts from Eunice de Souza's interview of Nissim, published in the *Bombay Literary Review*.[11] He is right: de Souza, like Nissim, lives in India, and comprehends the problems Indian writers face from the inside. Significantly, she is also a poet.

In 1992, OUP issued its second anthology of post-Independence Indian English poetry, edited this time by Arvind Krishna Mehotra.[12] OUP's first anthology was, of course, edited by R. Parthasarathy sixteen years earlier. Mehrotra had serious disagreements with Parthasarathy over some of the statements he had made in his Introduction and elsewhere.[13] The battle became personal, and Parthasarathy's poems did not find a place in Mehrotra's selections. Mehrotra included Nissim's work, but like Sarang, took a critical view of his poetry. In an introductory note on Nissim, he described him as an 'heir to Sarojini Naidu's mellifluous drivel.' He also charged him with using language that was under no pressure. When Nissim read the Introduction, he was so upset, that he reportedly chucked the complimentary copy of the anthology that OUP had sent him, into the dustbin. At any rate, that was where Ranjit Hoskote recovered it from.

I allowed Nissim to react to the opinions expressed by Sarang and Mehrotra by giving me his side of the story. He started by pooh-poohing Sarang's suggestion that he was the last of the Romantic poets. 'It is ridiculous,' he said, without losing his equanimity. 'There is nothing

Romantic about my poems. There are psychological, descriptive, realistic statements in the poems, but you can't call them Romantic. Romance is a specific state of mind, with its own values, and is often in conflict with what is "real". Aurobindo was a Romantic poet, but as I've never used his kind of terminology or sound effects, I don't find anything in common between his verse and mine.' Nor did he agree with the comparison Mehrotra made between his verse and Sarojini Naidu's. 'These are merely opinions,' he said to me, 'which are not sustained by even one paragraph of writing. If someone did a serious critical analysis of individual poems, and then came to this conclusion, it's okay. But Mehrotra and Sarang express only opinions without evidence.'

Once again, Nissim gave me in his defence the example of Robert Frost, whom many academic critics had denounced as old-fashioned, for writing in rhyme (as compared to, say, Wallace Stevens). Yet no one could claim that Stevens was better than Frost. Both were great poets who moved in different directions.

And once again he expressed what was inmost in his mind: that the criticism of Sarang and Mehrotra was motivated by personal considerations. I have already referred to Nisism's hostile review of Sarang's *A Kind of Silence* which he believes was enough to turn Sarang against him. Mehrotra, on the other hand, was a MA student at Bombay University's English Department, when Nissim joined the department in the early '70s. He wasn't exactly one of Nissim's favourite front-benchers, and it is likely that he felt rejected by Nissim, in whom everyone looked for a sugar daddy. He thus declared war on Nissim. Jussawalla, who is a friend of both Nissim and Mehrotra, once reported to Nissim that Mehrotra did not think he was a poet at all! Nissim himself got the impression that Mehrotra was very critical of him in the classroom; the seeds of Mehrotra's hatred were probably sown then. Nissim was able to take a dispassionate view of the affair: 'Prejudices of this kind are possible in the world of Indian English poetry, because it's a small world with no definite or objective standards of criticism,' he told me, with a wave of the hand.

If Nissim were to edit an anthology of Indian English poetry, would he include or exclude the poems of Vilas Sarang and Arvind Krishna Mehrotra? About Mehrotra, he replied in a roundabout manner: 'If I were editing an anthology and decided that Mehrotra's poems could not be left out, I would include them, without bringing personal prejudices in.' About

Sarang, he was more direct: 'I would exclude Vilas Sarang because I don't think his poems come up to any standard at all.'

While Mehrotra and Sarang demolished Nissim, two young writers of a much later generation, penned affectionate tributes to him. Poet Sudeep Sen, describing a reading he did at the PEN, where as usual, he was introduced by Nissim to the assembled audience, wrote: 'I didn't quite know what to say when I first walked into his office . . . at the Theosophy Hall. He walked towards me carrying himself within a lean posture, wearing a bluish long-sleeved shirt which was not tucked in, a style which seems to work practically to alleviate the oppressive air of humidity around. His steel-rimmed rectangular frame showed behind the lenses his studied eyes, and his hair was greyish-silver curling at his nape with wisdom. Before I could say anything, he welcomed me warmly, and introduced me to the group of people who had already arrived there before me. He said many kind things about my work and offered me tea.'[14]

Playwright Zubin Driver, on the other hand, tried to assess his plays: 'What makes Ezekiel interesting as a dramatist, is his decision to tackle the normal, everyday experience of living in urban India. Unlike in his poetry, however, one detects a certain tentativeness with regard to his control over form. His plays never reach any shattering heights in terms of dramatic experience.'[15]

Talking about the plays, *Debonair* for some reason published the old 'Song of Deprivation' that year.[16] It seemed quite unnecessary to publish a play that was over twenty years old, without any reference to its origins. And it is not as if Nissim revised or improved the play, which depicts a telephonic conversation between a man and woman, referred to as 'He' and 'She'. Magazines, it seems, will publish anything by a well-known author, just to fill up their pages!

On 22 January, Nissim gave a talk on Russian writer Dostoevsky, and read from his novels, at the Cultural Centre of Russia at Peddar Road, Bombay. On 4 April, he performed at a 'Meet the Author' session organized by the Sahitya Akademi, New Delhi, with the winners of its literary awards. By the end of the year, he had resigned as a trustee of Sanjiv Bhatla's Society for the Promotion of Poetry, which published the journal *Poetry Chronicle*.

1993

The Retreat being located where it is, Nissim was gravely affected by the riots that broke out in Bombay after the demolition of the Babri Masjid. Either he was unable to reach home, or then if he had managed to, he couldn't get out because of the curfew. For a man who depended on restaurants for all his meals, this was indeed bothersome. On days he couldn't go home, he spent the night at the place of a friend. Gieve and Toni gave him shelter on more than one occasion during the riots. Another time, I took him to my mother's flat at Barrack Road, and whisked him away to Pune the next morning, where he gave a talk at my department, and spent the night at my place. When I reached him to the railway station the following day, he was virtually the only passenger on a deserted Pragati Express to Bombay. Obviously, no one wanted to risk their lives travelling to the metropolis.

It was on days that he was trapped inside The Retreat that he witnessed the carnage at close quarters, and was shocked. He saw hoodlums from the Shiv Sena looting shops owned by Muslims, with the police as silent bystanders. He felt anger rising within him, and experienced a sense of helplessness at not being able to do anything about events that were literally happening in his backyard. His natural sense of justice and fairplay were violated. It is not as if Nissim had never seen a 'communal' riot earlier. In fact, there is a tradition of rioting in his neighbourhood, which is communally sensitive, with a police chowki just outside his house. Right from the days of his boyhood, such occurrences took place from time to time, but never on the scale on which they were taking place now.

Several Muslim families live in The Retreat. The mobs, at one point, managed to get past the compound wall, and throw stones at their houses. Some residents wanted to retaliate by flinging the stones back at the mobs. Nissim dissuaded them, pointing out that the stones would land not on the culprits, but on innocent people who would be injured. He feels he is lucky that they listened to his advice.

To Nissim who has never had a soft spot for Muslims, that day was an eye-opener. The police had imposed a twenty-four-hour curfew for three days in a row; he would have starved had it not been for his Muslim neighbours who brought him hot meals twice or thrice a day.

Many years ago, V. S. Naipaul was so angry with Nissim for his essay 'Naipaul's India and Mine', that he reportedly didn't want any of his interviewers to even refer to him. Now it was Nissim's turn to be furious with Naipaul for publicly saying that the riots in Bombay amounted to a kind of resurgence on the part of the Hindus, who felt that enough was enough, that they should not take it lying down any more. 'Naipaul is going mad in the head,' he exclaimed. 'His view of Hindu resurgence is going from one extreme to another.' Then he gave me his own position on the matter:

'Resurgence is all right, but it need not be in the form of a counter-attack 450 years later. Research should have been done into the scores of temples destroyed by Islamic forces in their zeal to convert. However, the answer to that is not revenge in the tooth-for-tooth, eye-for-eye manner. Resurgence can happen in more positive, constructive ways. Otherwise you are not going to get the support of anyone except the extremists. We should think more in terms of a real resurgence.'

By 'real resurgence', what Nissim meant was a progressivism that was not necessarily Hindu or Muslim. For, if one spoke only in terms of a Hindu resurgence, then there was bound to be a Muslim response to that resurgence, which eventually would lead to riots. 'What is gained by extreme steps like demolishing a mosque,' he asked me, as straightforwardly as possible.

But suddenly, Nissim compared the Hindu-Muslim problem here to the Arab-Jew quarrel in Palestine. As a Jew, it was impossible for him to be neutral in that war. Now it seemed to me that no matter how catholic he tried to be, his real sympathy was for the Hindus, with whom he identified. In this, he was no different from Naipaul. He did not agree with me, but what he said in his defence was unconvincing. It did not matter to him, for example, that the Muslims (as per the findings of the Sri Krishna Commission Report)[17] suffered more during the riots than the Hindus. 'The scale will naturally differ,' he said, to my astonishment. 'But you can't say that minority suffering is more important than majority suffering.' Then he added, as a concession: 'If you want to understand the India of the Upanishads and Vedas, it automatically brings you close to Hinduism—there's no other way you can do it.' Going back to the Upanishads and Vedas is of course a familiar tactic employed by the fundamentalists, nativists and Sanskritists, to discourage debate.

In February 1993, Nissim undertook a sixteen-day tour of England as a guest of the Arts Council of Great Britain. The Arts Council called it the 'Writers from India Tour', with two other writers, novelist Nayantara

Sahgal and poet Meena Alexander also participating. In a letter to Nissim dated 28 January 1993, lain Stewart, literature touring officer at the Arts Council, said: 'You will be staying in very comfortable hotels throughout the tour and will be well looked after'.

Nissim left Bombay for London on 9 February, and was put up at the St Ermins Hotel, Caxton Street, where Sahgal and Alexander joined him the next day. After a reception at the Nehru Centre, all three writers spent an hour with journalists who asked them about their work. On the 11th, they did a reading at the Royal Festival Hall in London. Two days later, they travelled to Brighton by a morning train, and checked in at the Oak Hotel on West Street. The reading was at 2.15 p.m. the same afternoon, at the Friends Centre on Ship Street. It was hosted by the Montpelier Society.

On 15 February, Nissim and Alexander went to Portsmouth, stayed at the Forte Post-house on Pembroke Road, and attended a civic reception given in their honour by the Mayor of Portsmouth. Sahgal arrived at Portsmouth on her own shortly before the reception. They did a reading at the Portsmouth Grammar School on High Street at 7.30 p.m. On 16 February, Nissim, Sahgal and Alexander were taken by lain Stewart to Bradford. Here they were housed at the Novotel on Merrydale Road, and, as usual, read at 7.30 p.m., this time at the Bradford Playhouse and Film Theatre on Chapel Street.

On 17 February, the three writers took a British Rail train to Leeds, and then another connecting train to Liverpool. Here they met Alastair Niven, director of the Arts Council. They checked in at the Atlantic Tower on Chapel Street, freshened up, and proceeded to Toxeth Library on Windsor Street, where their reading was scheduled for 7 p.m. The following day, Niven and the three writers went to Leeds. They were booked at the Hilton International on Neville Street. For some reason, they did not do a reading here. Instead, Nayantara Sahgal delivered her Ravenscroft Memorial Lecture. Niven took their leave on the morning of the 19th, and once again they were in the care of Stewart. They quickly proceeded to Huddersfield, found rooms at The George on St George's Square, and readied themselves for a reading at 7.30 p.m. at the Huddersfield Arts Gallery. The next day, the group started out for their final destination, Slough. They stayed at the Copthorne Hotel, and did a reading that evening at the Rotunda.

All the readings were well-attended, with an audience of at least hundred people on an average. In spite of the hectic schedule that wore him out, Nissim spent five extra days in London, going back to some of the haunts of his youth, where he had hung out forty-five years ago. He finally departed for Bombay by British Airways flight BA 19 on the 25th.

What were Nissim's reactions to the tour? To use his favourite phrase one more time, the Arts Council made all arrangements for them, 'from A to Z'. Their airfare to and from London was pre-paid. Everywhere they were lodged at expensive hotels. Even train travel was often by first class. Some of this lavishness, however, pricked his conscience. Although he never opposed any of Alastair Niven's decisions, he felt in his heart of hearts, that he could easily have travelled standard class on British Rail, and stayed at bed-and-breakfast places in some of the cities. Here was an Indian, a Jew and an ascetic speaking.

Nissim began the year 1993 with a tour of England, and ended it with a tour of America. In December, he spent two weeks in the States for an AJJDC event. In between, he was operated upon for hernia, which he saw as a problem of old age. He was also on the Sahitya Akademi's panel of judges, to decide the winner of the best English language book. The award that year went to G. N. Devy's *After Amnesia,*[18] a work of criticism, and there was a widespread feeling in literary and academic circles that Nissim had simply gone along with the decision of the other judges, without really understanding Devy's thesis, which was reactionary in the extreme.

Poets and academics continued to write about him. Raji Narasimhan, feminist critic and scholar, reviewed *Selected Prose* for the Sunday *Economic Times.*[19] She lambasted him for 'the low awareness in the writing of an, or any, India prior to Nehru.' She dismissed him as a liberal humanist, and claimed that 'the persona of the essays emerges as a practitioner of poetry, a committed one but nothing more.' Narasimhan, of course, is a leftist who was bound to see Nissim in this way; her review, which was negative on the whole, did not come as a surprise.

What was surprising was an article on him by poet Vijay Nambisan in the *Hindu.*[20] One would have expected Nambisan to write about Moraes or Jussawalla, rather than Nissim. This is because as poets they are a stronger influence on him than Nissim. But the occasion was a lecture that Nissim was invited to deliver at ITT, Madras, as a part of their series called 'Extra-Mural Lecturers'. Nambisan attended the lecture, and also met him for an interview at the bar of the Madras Club the next morning, where Nissim 'indulged without fuss in one drink and one cigarette.' He said the usual things about his life and writing to Nambisan over his drink, providing no new insights. However, he did say something about his poems that he hadn't said before: 'When my *Collected Poems* appeared, I read my earlier poems and compared them with my present ones . . . I couldn't help noticing the repetition: there was nothing new. Not that they're bad, but there's nothing special. So I've turned to writing plays.'

By observing Nissim closely, both at the talk and during the interview, Nambisan was able to zero in on some of his character traits. For example, he was struck by the fact that, when after the lecture, a shy girl approached him and asked him, 'Sir, what do you think of Dostoevsky?' Nissim did not burst out laughing (as Nambisan himself might have done in the circumstances). Instead, he replied as gently as he could, that Dostoevsky was indeed a very great writer!

On his part, Nissim wrote about fellow-authors who were his friends or contemporaries. In July, painful as it must have been, he managed to write a tribute to A. K. Ramanujan, who passed away in the United States that month, at the early age of sixty-four.[21] Nissim refrained from personal anecdote, and spent most of his time talking about Ramanujan's poetry and translations.

As stated in Chapter Eleven, he wrote the piece justifying the fatwa that had been imposed on Bangladeshi writer Taslima Nasreen.[22] His stand here was no different from what it had been in the case of Rushdie. Nissim described Nasreen's work as writing that promoted civil war. He criticized her for not making people rethink their beliefs, for not promoting any new debate or dialogue. 'All you have done is provoked some extremists within the community to attack you,' he said. In 1989, when Nissim had posed the same questions to Rushdie, people took him seriously, and there was some discussion on his views. By 1993, no one was interested. Here was a poet who was advocating, rather than opposing censorship; it was best that he be left alone.

On a lighter vein, Nissim gave an interview to Ronita Torcato, in which he talked about his ideal weekend.[23] No, his idea of a weekend wasn't to sit at home doing nothing–that 'doesn't satisfy me.' His ideal weekend was when he could write a letter on which he could spend hours, put his feet up, dip into this and dip into that. Nothing less, nothing more.

1994

It was now six years since *Collected Poems* had appeared. Nissim was getting a little anxious about the fact that he hadn't published another book of poems yet. One day, towards the end of May, he told me he had completed a new collection (comprising mainly poems in the 'Singapore Sequence' and poems from the 'Edinburgh Interlude'). He would be dispatching his manuscript to OUP in a week's time. The book however, did not materialize.

The first signs of Alzheimer's disease began to make their appearance. Friends frequently complained that Nissim failed to remember things that were said to him even the previous day. He was also growing repetitive, repeating to people what he had said to them only a while ago. But he was fully aware of this. He had always regarded himself as absent-minded, but this was more than an innocent absent-mindedness. He knew that his memory was playing tricks.

In 1994, Nissim's average day still began with exercise, followed by breakfast, which comprised half a glass of milk, a couple of slices of bread, lightly buttered, or with thin slices of cheese on them, and a couple of bananas, of which he was very fond. Sometimes he also munched the groundnuts that were left over from the previous evening. Occasionally, he pampered himself with fruit such as chikoos, apples and mangoes. This he especially did when he was shopping for his 'wife's family', and felt tempted to pick up a few extra items for himself. There was a fridge at The Retreat, which he was still able to maintain all by himself, defrosting it periodically. The newspaper came 7.30 a.m., by which time he was done with breakfast. He often had to tell the newsboy to ring the doorbell when he brought the newspaper, instead of leaving it on the floor by the door. He subscribed to the *Indian Express* at The Retreat, because Daisy and Elkana subscribed to the *Times* at Kala Niketan, which he got to read whenever he went there. He did not read the newspaper in great detail–spent no more than fifteen to twenty minutes on it. Then he shaved, had a cold shower if he felt like it, and by 8.15 a.m. readied himself to leave the house. Sometimes, on his way out, he visited the neighbourhood laundry with clothes to wash or iron. (Yes, they opened that early.)

As usual, Nissim walked to Bombay Central station and caught a train to Churchgate to get to the *PEN*. Here he spent time reading submissions that had arrived for the *Indian PEN*, glancing through literary magazines that came in the post, and above all, chatting with visitors who popped in at regular intervals. Lunch was at Sanman, often in the company of one or more of these visitors. After lunch, he developed the habit of dozing off on an armchair in his office. He was woken up by a telephone call from Daisy, dictating the list of items she wanted. So by 4 p.m. Nissim was on his way to the Grant Road market, where he shopped, and by 6 p.m. he was at Kala Niketan where he sat for a while, and then left without dinner. He usually ate his dinner at two Muslim restaurants close to The Retreat, alternating between them for the sake of variety. On getting home, he washed the dishes he had used for his breakfast, before going to bed.

The pattern would be broken if Nissim was invited to a programme in the evening. On such days, he would linger on at the PEN until it was time to leave for the event. Daisy dreaded such days and kept nagging him with repeated phone calls. I recall one such afternoon when the phone kept ringing, and Nissim prevented people in the office from picking it up because he knew it was his wife. Nissim's lifestyle would also undergo a change whenever Kavita and her husband came down from Mussoorie, each year during the winter. Kavita took over the management of her father's house and his kitchen, and for two months Nissim would be able to move around with relative ease. It is significant that Kavita chose to spend her annual sojourn in Bombay at The Retreat with her father, rather than at Kala Niketan with her mother, which was more of a 'home' in the regular sense. This clearly indicates that she has a soft corner for her father, and doesn't share the feelings of resentment that his wife and son have towards him. Kavita even contemplated a permanent shift to Bombay, so that she could be close to her father. This, however, wasn't practical, as both she and her husband held full-time teaching jobs at Mussoorie.

In spite of the fact that he lived by himself, and had virtually nothing by way of 'family life', Nissim never gave his friends the impression that he was lonely. If there was pain or self-pity about his condition, he successfully disguised it. He liked to show people that he was at peace with himself and with the world around him. In any case, emotions were not meant for display. Sirkar, as we have seen, attributes this to the cultural influence of the British on people like himself and Nissim. But it is also true that, in this respect, Nissim continually sacrificed the poet in him to the philosopher. Whereas poets thrive on personal conflict, philosophers aspire to be hermits. This kind of heroism immediately appealed to him.

Heroism, of course, is an elusive ideal, even if it is the heroism of the common man. What rescued Nissim was the attendant sense of failure that was always prevalent. Nissim felt he was a failure in the psychological, spiritual and moral sphere; no amount of success that he attained as a poet could neutralize that. He did not think he had managed human relations very well, especially when it came to his family. Surprisingly, he also felt he had failed as a poet. I have already quoted his famous words: 'When high standards are applied, one can say that one hasn't arrived anywhere, except at the point where one stagnates.' Nor did he believe he had revolutionized Indian English poetry after Independence. 'Revolution? I'm not within a thousand miles of it,' he said to me. And he attributed the reasons for this failure only to himself, not to his environment. 'I'm critical of myself, without of course allowing criticism to undermine me and my work.'

Hoskote calls Nissim's claim that he was a failure a 'pose'. He elaborates: 'It is the last vestige of that very romanticism which he deplores, but of which he's the unintended victim.' To Hoskote, no matter how hard Nissim tried to get away from heroism, it relentlessly pursued him. This is because deep inside, he was fascinated by it.

If heroism goes hand-in-hand with youth, old age is possibly its antithesis. By 1994, when Nissim was in his seventieth year, he was at last ready to accept the fact that he had grown old. Some of his earlier arrogance had disappeared, and he was more accessible to 'ordinary mortals' than he had been in the past. Through his visits to old age homes run by the AJJDC, he became sensitive to the problems of the aged, and began to think in terms of rights for senior citizens. He realized how important it was for people like him to 'face the reality of old age,' and not behave as they did when they were young or middle-aged. 'Something may otherwise go wrong,' he felt. The mind too slowed down in old age, so he knew he wouldn't be writing any more new poems. He rejected the Hindu idea that people became wiser as they grew older.

Elkana's marriage posed some problems. Nissim's liberalism did not go as far as to allow him to willingly give his son the permission to marry outside the Bene Israel community. As he, and his brothers Joe and Hannan had done, he wanted Elkana to marry a Bene Israel, even if she was not ideally suited to him. He therefore took him to see a girl that Elkana immediately rejected, because she was not the kind of girl he wanted to marry. Although Nissim was disappointed, he realized there was not much he could do. Eventually, Elkana married a Hindu.

For Nissim, his relationship to members of his family was a private affair, and it was best that things were allowed to stay that way. On 27

May, as I was interviewing him, Hannan unexpectedly dropped in at the PEN. Unlike every other visitor, to whom he introduced me, Hannan was not told who I was or what I was working on. Nissim excused himself, moved to another part of the large room, and chatted with his brother in English, somewhat formally. They kept their voices low, as if he was afraid that I would eavesdrop. Their conversation, from their gestures and body language, seemed so formal, that but for the resemblance in features, one wouldn't have been able to tell they were brothers. Hannan, who is an economist in Washington, was visiting Bombay. He was dressed in a shirt and tie, and his attire marked him out from his elder brother, who rarely, if ever, wore a tie. After a while, Hannan asked Nissim out to tea at Sanman. I thought I would be invited to join them, but no! Nissim walked up to me, apologized for the 'intrusion', and left the room with Hannan, while I waited.

After Hannan left, our discussion veered towards economics. I asked Nissim whether he understood concepts like 'free economy', 'market forces', and so on. He said he couldn't, of course, deliver a lecture on any of these topics. However, he often discussed them with Hannan, and did have some ideas. For example, he was as critical now of capitalism, as he had been in his youth. 'Free economy shouldn't degenerate into chaos,' he said. He was also concerned with the moral and ethical questions that arose. He was opposed to the principle of competitiveness, for it meant 'winning at any cost'. He did not support free trade 'in the sense of anyone coming and starting anything in India, say a chocolate-manufacturing company. You have to face who the beneficiaries are–they can't only be the people at the top.'

We went on to talk about consumerism, materialism, and so on. Suddenly, I asked Nissim whether he had even thought of charging poets a small fee for all the literary advice he provided. He was horrified–even disgusted–at the question.

We arrived at the topic of beggars. Why did Nissim think more of them, than he seemed to think of himself? I mean, here he was, shabbily dressed, and yet made it a point to give money to every beggar who approached him. He blamed his appearance on his family, and suggested it was the wife's duty to see to a man's wardrobe. Since that was not possible in his case, he couldn't care less. In this context, he pointed out that Elkana had recently insisted that he should buy a first-class season ticket for his journey from Bombay Central to Churchgate, rather than a second-class one as he had been doing all these years. It was only on Elkana's insistence that he agreed.

As if to round off the issues we had been talking about, he referred to the Russian writer Solzhenitsyn. 'Solzhenitsyn was not at all happy in America,' he reminded me. 'Perhaps, America to him was not as bad as Stalinist Russia where thousands were being killed. At the same time, values that emphasized only money and success were not acceptable to him.'

1994 was the year when I started this biography. This was the year when, during my sessions with him on Saturday afternoons, I was able to talk to him on a wide range of subjects. One such, was this business of Indian English poets being famous (infamous?) for writing little: one-book wonders, as several of them were. Why did this happen? Was it because, as R. Parthasarathy claimed, English wasn't a 'living language' in India? Nissim's reply to this question was formal, somewhat like a lecture he might have given to postgraduate students. But it indicated he had thought about the matter.

'As long as one is not inhibited by the language one uses, and tries to make the best use of it,' he began, 'it's enough. If one has a real alternative between English and the mother tongue, then one has to decide whether to drop one and take up the other. But finally we are left with a large number of poets writing in English, whether they've written in another language or not. Once they write in English, you have to assess their work on the basis of its merit, that's all.'

After this 'general' speech, Nissim got personal, and actually named some of his fellow contemporaries. 'The puzzling thing about R. Parthasarathy is that in spite of all the conflicts he talks about, he goes to America and settles down there for life. Everything then collapses. Now Saleem Peeradina is doing the same thing.'

Next, was the turn of the one-book wonders: 'It is sad that Dilip Chitre decided not to write in English, after the publication of his first book, *Travelling in a Cage*. But at least he continues to write in Marathi. By contrast, Arun Kolatkar has not written anything new, either in English or Marathi. Tara Patel also says the same thing: that she's not going to write any more poetry. This is sad, tragic.'

Nissim dismissed the suggestion that poets wrote little in India because they did not have enough subjects on which to write. They were not involved in the political, social and cultural life of India in a big way. 'I don't think a concern with the national life of India would really enable them to write more,' he said. 'And so what if there's alienation? That itself can become the subject of their verse.'

Although Nissim has travelled around the world, he is unused to the idea of the world as a small, shrunken place. He is still conscious of the distances between places. A long-distance call surprises him, even if it's only from Pune to Bombay. On his seventieth birthday on 16 December, he was surprised that I made an STD call from Pune to greet him.

On 11 and 12 June, Nissim was in Kerala for a Poetry Workshop organized by the Society for Literary Insight and Creative English (sic) at Ernakulam. Kamala Das, too, was present. He read poems and participated in a discussion entitled 'Poetry Today'. Not only was he paid the airfare to attend the workshop, the president of the Society, Mrs Bina Menon and her husband, took him home and looked after him with traditional Indian hospitality. I wanted to know why he was always successful in being received warmly, wherever he went. Was it because he was a famous poet? That, according to him, wasn't the reason. It was because he related to the audience well. He freely allowed them to ask questions, and unlike, some other poets, did not make them feel ludicrous even if they asked silly questions.

'Maybe I was more arrogant when I was younger,' Nissim said, 'but everyone goes through that phase, and sooner or later one has to learn.' In this case, 'learning' for him was made up of the realization that at any seminar, anywhere in the world, there were always two types of participants–the experts and the laymen. It was best that one learned to accept this fact as quickly as possible, so that, when one was faced with an unintelligent question or comment, one turned it around and tried to. make sense of it.

In 1994, I spent so much time with Nissim, that for the first time I noticed the little things that made up his day. Naturally, these gave me valuable insights into his character. I list some of my observations below:

On 13 May, two good-looking young women entered the office as I was interviewing him. One of them had left a manuscript containing some eighty-three poems with him, which he now could not find. What was worse, she had given him her originals, without retaining a copy. Nissim was happy that the girls were in his office (his demeanour changed the moment he set eyes on them), but embarrassed that he had mislaid the poems. He advised the disappointed girl to 'start working with whatever poems you have ten, twelve, fifteen,' while he looked for the manuscript. After a while, the girls abruptly left.

On 3 June, I found Nissim presiding over a cleaning-up operation, as I entered. Pinto, Hoskote and his girlfriend Nancy Adjania were trying to rearrange the books in his office, to bring some semblance of order. Nissim reminded me of a pet animal who couldn't actually help his 'masters' in their task, but was happy to simply be around.

On 9 July, Nissim, Minakshi Raja and I went to Sanman for coffee. As we were coming out of the restaurant, I noticed that his shirt was in tatters at the back. I said half-seriously, that I would take him to Fashion Street, nearby, and buy him a new shirt. Nissim flatly refused to accept a new shirt. Suddenly, I found him covering the torn part of his shirt with his hands. 'I didn't notice it at the time of leaving home,' he said.

Finally, an observation made by Hoskote. On 8 and 9 October, both Nissim and he attended a seminar organized by the Sahitya Akademi at an auditorium in South Bombay. More than the papers and talks, it was the food that Nissim enjoyed. Hoskote was appalled that all Nissim should be able to comment on was the food, saying it was the best he had had in years. And no, he was not being ironic: it was not his way of saying that the proceedings of the seminar were worthless.

Yet Nissim kept doing the seminar circuit. Before the October seminar in Bombay, he went to the Banaras Hindu University at Varanasi to give a memorial lecture on 'The Infinite Aspects of Critical Writing' on 6 and 7 September. His policy was not to refuse an invitation when it came his way. He still liked travelling, even if it was by train. Outstation travel also provided him an opportunity to get away, and be free of Daisy's afternoon phone calls. His lectures themselves were nothing to write home about. The fire had gone out of him, and he often struggled to keep talking for forty-five or sixty minutes, camouflaging his lack of knowledge with empty words and phrases. But the organizers of these events who invited him were so taken in by his one-time glory, and were so overwhelmed by the fact that a celebrity poet had 'condescended' to grace the occasion, that they rarely, if ever, noticed his discomfiture. He cashed in on this subservience. It suited everyone: Nissim was pleased to be taken care of, and provided with sumptuous meals; the organizers felt triumphant at being able to state on paper that India's most famous IndoEnglish poet was present for their seminar.

There was an exhibition called 'Excavation' by one Pushpamala N. at the Chemould Gallery in Bombay in November. The artist's exhibits were all made from scrap. Nissim went to the exhibition and thought it brilliant. Hoskote, on the other hand, thought it was pretentious. One day as I walked into the PEN, I found Hoskote and Nissim arguing over this, each refusing to budge from the position he had taken.

On 16 December 1994, Nissim was seventy. Jussawalla decided to organize a small birthday party for him at the *PEN*. Four or five days before the 16th he telephoned friends like Jerry Pinto and Hoskote to inform them of his plan. All of them welcomed the idea. The 'guests', no more than eight or ten in number, started arriving around mid-day, some of them bringing an item or two of food as their contribution. Jussawalla wanted to have the party at the PEN rather than at a restaurant, because there would be more freedom here. Although liquor cannot be consumed in the Theosophy Hall, Sirkar made an exception that day, and allowed them to drink wine. And what did they all do? They wished Nissim, cut the birthday cake, gave him presents, engaged in banter. It was a nice, informal gathering of kindred souls, minus the poetry, minus speeches. Fun and games all along, although Pinto was peeved that when he went to hug Nissim, Nissim impolitely walked way. Pinto's observations here coincide with mine: there is an element of homophobia in Nissim; he's uncomfortable when another man touches him.

This is how the *Metropolis* reported the event:

'Last fortnight a birthday was celebrated. No, not that 2000-year-old one, but one of slightly more recent vintage–a Jew nonetheless [sic]. Nissim Ezekiel turned seventy and friends and well-wishers gathered around the Grand Old Poet of Indo-English Writing. They decked him with laurel wreaths made of bougainvillea and sang Hindi film songs pastiched to suit the occasion. Wine from Vashi flowed and pizza from Altamount Road sizzled on the tongues of all.

'Through it all, the GOPIEW sat, comfortable, calm and smiling. Age does not wither him nor custom stale his infinite variety. However, when mention was made of Dom Moraes' Sahitya Akademi award, he perked up. "I'm very glad for him," he said, and added, "I got my Padma Shri eight years ago."[24]

Santan Rodrigues paid a personal tribute to Nissim in the *Sunday Observer*. He began his article with the following anecdote: 'Recently my school-going nephew accompanied me when I called on Nissim Ezekiel. I introduced Nissim to my nephew as a poet whose poems he had probably studied in his school textbooks. At that, Nissim narrated an incident. He was walking along a street near his home when he found that a group of schoolboys had focused their attention on him. Aware that they had recognized him, he expected that they would either greet him or ask for an autograph. As he approached them, he heard to his amazement [sic] one of the boys pointing out to him, 'Look, there goes the scorpion.' The scorpion obviously referred to Nissim's better-known poem 'The Night of the Scorpion' which finds a place in many textbooks.[25]

In marked contrast to Rodrigues' admiration, is Hoskote's scepticism. In 1994, all that Hoskote could say in praise of Nissim was that he had indeed supported emerging poets in Bombay, including himself. He was also grateful to him for writing the generous blurb to *Zones of Assault*[26] and for publishing him, from time to time, in the *Indian PEN* or featuring him in an AIR programme. Other than that, Hoskote, referring to Nissim's tendency to look at punctuation marks in the poems he was commenting on, thought of him as a 'grammar machine', nothing more. 'Apart from simple humour, other finer things in a poem are lost to him,' Hoskote felt. He was also critical of the manner in which Nissim hurriedly looked up digests and guides whenever he was called upon to chair a literary event. As evidence, he cited the example of the Amichai reading of Hebrew poetry at the NCPA Bombay, sometime in 1991 or 1992, when Nissim frantically searched for material for his introductory remarks. He also recalled an afternoon at Sanman, when Nissim asked Hoskote and Pinto to give him a couple of 'points' for his lecture on post-structuralism at the Xavier Institute of Communication that evening. These things made Nissim appear like a 'Jurassic figure' to Hoskote.

'His two deepest impulses are to belong, and to be popular,' Hoskote continued. 'In order to belong, he finds it necessary to go along with shared prejudices. In order to be popular, he finds it necessary to play up the Vidhushak aspect of himself–the entertainer, the buffoon.' To furnish the proof for these observations, Hoskote told me about a multilingual poetry reading at the NCPA that year, where each poet was paid a thousand rupees to read just two poems to an audience of 'banias'. Nissim smartly made it a point to read his 'Indianized' poems at the event, i.e. those poems 'which represented some form of engagement with what is often called "mainstream Indianness".' This made Hoskote realize that the man truly had many personae–the one at the PEN was quite different from the one here at the NCPA, among 'typical' Indians.

Hoskote sees Nissim's involvement with the Bene Israel of Bombay as social rather than spiritual. 'His philosophical attitudes were frozen in the '50s and '60s,' he said. I asked him again whether he ever felt like a son to Nissim.

'I don't think I ever felt like son to him,' he replied. 'I'm genuinely fond of him, except when he goes out of his way to be objectionable. But these small meannesses are natural to someone going senile' Hoskote narrated how betrayed Nissim felt when, some months ago, he had read a paper on him at a seminar at the SNDT Women's University, Bombay, and taken a critical view. 'For days afterwards, he kept taunting me, calling me Judas.' But Hoskote wasn't repentant. 'The plain truth is that Nissim couldn't follow my argument, since it was in a post-structuralist idiom. My analysis would have left him cold, since he's never heard of Foucault.'

Hoskote had once again got into the mood; there was little I could do to restrain him. 'The major impetus of Nissim's life is to programme himself in a certain way, breaking away from history. He can be located, in that sense, in a post World War II context. But he doesn't have the other thing that sustains the modernist self-replenishment from the culture. For example, he completely missed the surrealist boat. His rationality side is his book-keeper. His lack of understanding of the avant garde comes across in the silly joke he keeps telling of the artist who has long hair, and after a few months cuts it because he says he's no longer an artist.'

Hoskote likes very little of Nissim's work. He mentioned *A Time to Change, The Unfinished Man* and *The Exact Name,* when I asked him to specify what appealed 'to him. The rest of it he dismissed as 'lacking in imagination, it's almost as if the man is incapable of delving into the subconscious for images.' Nissim's 'decline', according to Hoskote, began with and continued through *Latter-Day Psalms,* and the 'Edinburgh Interlude' poems. It worries him that 'Nissim's sort of cheap irony becomes an end in itself, and is taken up by so many poets and poetasters.' On his part, he is convinced that it is a grave mistake to derive from Nissim's poetic experience a model for all Indian English poetry since Independence.

Then Hoskote went on to outline the intellectual reasons for the rift between his mentor and himself. He prefaced these with the remark that 'unlike Gieve Patel, the son, and Toni, the daughter-in-law, I didn't quite keep to the terms of the spiritual sonship.' The reasons themselves are as follows:

(i) Nissim's public support of the fatwa on Rushdie, and the ban on his work in India.

(ii) His pro-American stance in the Gulf War of 1990.

(iii) His sympathy for the Israelis in Palestine (even though they are white settlers), and his condemnation of the Arabs.

(iv) The role of Judaism in India. Hoskote believes that the Indian Jew in Israel cannot expect the same sympathy as a white Jew. This is because the Indian Jew has little to do with anti-semitism. 'The decisive moment in Judaic history is Auschwitz and the Israel problem is a direct outcome of that. This is not part of the Indian Jew's baggage.'

(v) Nissim's view that decisions and circumstances bind him to India, suggesting that there is choice involved. Hoskote disagrees. He thinks that Indian Jews were, in the first place, hardly aware of their distinctiveness, until it was brought to their notice.

The title for this chapter comes from a phrase Jussawalla once privately applied to Nissim in his seventieth year. What Jussawalla had in mind, when he invoked the image of the totem pole, was a poet who frittered away his time giving useless TV and newspaper interviews; performed 'roles' that did not fit him because he was too small for them; and combined in himself characteristics of a schoolmaster, family man and a poet, that, in the end, severely limited his criticism. He also saw Nissim as lacking in the human touch, self-conscious of his role as a poet, and negligent about his personal hygiene. In short, he was a totem pole around whom everyone had to dance. It all happened during a party at Jussawalla's place in October, at which Nissim, Eunice de Souza, Dilip Chitre and Arun Kolatkar were present. Eunice said of Nissim at the party: 'Oh, leave him alone.' The poets stayed the night over, and the next morning Nissim opened the *Sunday Times* which carried Jussawalla's review of Rushdie's *East, West,* thinking, for some reason, that the review was by Chitre.

Chitre is critical of Nissim. Jussawalla, coming to Nissim's rescue, agrees that Hindu poets like Chitre could be opposed to him because he's non-Hindu. It's about time that people saw himself and Nissim as poets who were responsible for the 'Europeanization of Bombay'. Jussawalla said: 'It's okay if Nissim is the Father of modern Indian poetry in English. Others didn't have it in them to be Fathers.'

Gauri Deshpande was staying with the Sirkars on Nissim's seventieth birthday. She didn't of course remember that it was his birthday, and was taken by surprise when she got out of the lift in the Theosophy Hall, and saw all the 'guys' there. This is how she described what happened:

'I was surrounded by children and grandchildren, we were rushing off as usual to this, that or the other spot on earth . . . I was delighted to see Gieve, Adil and Imtiaz [with Nissim]. They brought to my mind those that were absent. As I kissed Nissim, wishing him a happy birthday, I think the "old times" were in both our minds. I said, "Nissim, Raj wants me to write about our friendship for his book on you." And he said, "Well, write on, then!" He was confident, just as I was, that we were friends after all!'

In early 1994, while Nissim was briefly in New York for an AJJDC meeting, his one-time student, Rochelle D'Souza, organized a poetry reading by him at her house. It was well-attended, and when Rochelle D'Souza was invited to write about the event for the *International Indian*, she was graphic in her reportage:

'Not even the sudden snowstorm that enveloped the city (weather forecasts had predicted "a few snow flurries" in a classic example of understatement) and made visibility nil, could stop most people from driving into Queens, where I live, from Long Island and New Jersey. Ezekiel himself, at sixty-nine, appeared none the worse for his first arduous drive in a blizzard, and was his gracious, smiling self as he exchanged frozen handshakes with members of his audience. With his shoulder-length wispy white hair [sic] and thick granny glasses (currently enjoying a fashion revival), Ezekiel looked every inch the poet-professor he is! If the audience expected to see an erudite, philosophical character with a faraway look in his eyes as he read his verse, they were not disappointed. What they were unprepared for was Ezekiel's benign, almost avuncular manner, his utterly lovable unassuming stance and his irrepressible sense of humour. As he began reading his first poem, "Night of the Scorpion", with its mantra-like chants and marvellous use of repetition, a mantle of respectful silence descended over the room.'[27]

Speaking of New York, and the AJJDC, the city-based Jewish Week, did a feature on it in one of its issues.[28] Needless to say, Nissim was prominently mentioned. In another classic instance of wanting to have his cake and eat it too, he projected himself as an unlikely candidate to represent an organization 'which dispenses food and aid to struggling Jewish communities around the world.' The journal wrote: 'By his own admission, Ezekiel is a strange man to oversee the JDC's expanding operations in Bombay. One of India's highest regarded English poets . . . , he has spent much of his life exploring the literature and thought of other religions. But seven years ago he agreed to be a kind of lay leader for the Bombay Jewish community, a position that converged with his increasing interest in things Jewish.' It further reported: 'Despite his admission, he [Ezekiel] still finds it a little unsettling to be so actively involved in the community's financial and policy issues. But he said the work was greatly satisfying, and that with the JDC's continued help, poor Jews could not only eat better but send their children to Jewish schools.'

1994 was the year when Nissim gave a large number of interviews to newspapers. He had of course been giving interviews all his life, but these would be among the very last: journalists would, after this, leave him alone. During his visit to Kerala in June, the Kochi edition of *Indian Express*[29] spoke to him. One of the questions they asked him was why *Poetry Review* had left him out in their special number on India, 'In Search of Kavita'.[30] The question was somewhat imprecise, for the journal had not 'left him out' completely. It had published an article on him by Peter Forbes (the editor) himself.

But it had not used any of his poems. Nissim fielded the humiliating question with poise: 'I don't think the magazine was hostile to me, and I even know its editor. Let's say it just happened.'

Other interviews included Behram Contractor's personalized piece in his own newspaper, the *Afternoon Despatch & Courier*,[31] and an interview in *Weekend* (*Mid-Day's* supplement) by my former student Neema Kamdar.[32] These interviews contain information and opinions that have been quoted elsewhere in this book.

The most significant of all the interviews he gave in 1994, however, was the one that appeared in *Health and Nutrition*.[33] The magazine, anxious to portray that even at seventy, he was in sprightly health, asked him to pose for a photograph in a red T-shirt. This reportedly annoyed Elkana, for the truth was his father's health was on the decline. Pradhan (the interviewer) asked Nissim whether he had resisted the idea of growing old. He replied: 'No, that would be absurd. Aging is one of the facts of life and it should be faced. Not that there is a great deal of change. I mean, all your faculties are still there, you just slow down a bit. A task that would take you half an hour before may now take slightly longer to complete. And, there is a certain amount of memory loss. My friends have been pointing this out in the last two to three years that I'm forgetting things. But these are not great drawbacks. It simply means you have to be more methodical and careful about details, you take the precaution of jotting down things so you won't forget. But other things remain. You still want to work, to write, to do all the things you set out to do. You certainly don't lose interest in life.

1995

As my Saturday afternoon sessions with him continued, Nissim revealed more and more about himself. One day he surprised me by declaring that he dreamt of writing his autobiography. Long ago, he had already chosen a title for the book–as stated earlier, 'A Thousand Failures'. This was based of course on his persistent belief that he was a failure in life on most counts. It was the kind of self-deprecation that in the end perhaps amounted to heroism.

I didn't take him seriously then. But three years later, as Pinto would clean up the cupboards at the PEN during Nissim's last days there, he would actually stumble upon four-handwritten pages in Nissim's hand, scribbled at the back of American Centre notices. Nissim's name did not appear anywhere on the sheets, but the handwriting was unmistakably his, and the pages bore the title 'My Story'.

He talked of the usual things: his childhood conflicts with his father about Judaism; his role as a teacher; his tendency to give advice. There was a frankness about the way he saw himself. For example, writing about his days as a professor at Bombay University, he said: 'It began badly in the postgraduate department because the students were from the best as well as other colleges. Those from the best were not at all satisfied with my lectures because they found them rather simple. When their views reached me through some of my friends, I was able to raise the intellectual level for them in every lecture, after explaining each time that the preliminary statements were for those in the class who needed them. From that stage, till my unavoidable resignation [sic] at age sixty, I won increasing praise from my students.'

Elkana, who was until now staying with his mother at Kala Niketan, moved into his own apartment at Prabhadevi in September. The flat was given to him by Johnson & Johnson Limited, the multinational for which he worked. The company also provided him with a car for his personal use, and he drove his parents to his flat a couple of times.

Daisy was now alone at Kala Niketan and not in the best of health. As her physical dependence on her husband increased, so did her afternoon telephone calls to him at the PEN. The calls were mainly in connection with her shopping. She did not spare him even on his birthday! On 16 December 1995, she dictated the following list of items required by her: (1) 3 lemons (2) ½ kilo cucumber (3) ½ kilo tomatoes, hard and round (4) ½ kilo capsicum (5) a small bundle of methi for Rs 2 (6) oranges (7) Vijaya or Amul cheese (8) two matchboxes.

A fortnight later, on New Year's eve, I was at the PEN again when Daisy called. Nissim gradually began to lose his temper as he spoke to her, seeming to answer her 'unreasonable' demands, till finally, he slammed the phone down.

I recalled an afternoon six months ago, in June, when he called Daisy at home to ask her for her shopping list. She replied that there was no shopping to be done, as Elkana and she were invited to a ceremony of some kind, and would be having their dinner there. Nissim felt as relieved as a schoolboy who has just been told by his teacher that there was no homework for the day.

Having missed his seventieth birthday, I made it a point to be in Bombay for his seventy-first. But this time there was no party. Poet Sanjiv Sethi took him for lunch to Sanman. Earlier in the day, Minakshi Raja came to wish him, and in the afternoon it was Torcato and myself. Roma his secretary was also there. Torcato brought a cake and some mutton patties along. There was no knife at the PEN with which to cut the cake, so we used the black paper knife with the African head. Roma, Torcato and I sang as Nissim cut the cake. Then Nissim picked up Daisy's shopping list and headed for the Grant Road market. Torcato accompanied him. They took a train to Grant Road, and after doing the bazaar caught a bus to Warden Road. As they approached Kala Niketan, Nissim told Torcato to leave. Under no circumstances did he want Daisy to see them together.

Amrit Dhillon, the then book-reviews editor of *India Today* sent Nissim A.K. Ramanujan's *Collected Poems*[34] for review. Why? Because Nissim told him on the phone that he had written over 500 book reviews in his life. Once Nissim received the book, he developed cold feet. He doubted whether he would be able to turn out a 'good' review, as it had been very long since he last reviewed a book. However, he accepted the book and did indeed write the review, which was eventually published. It was one of his last book reviews that we would see in print.

One day early in 1995, as we came out of Sanman after having had tea, Nissim and I saw a couple of street children outside the restaurant. The youngest of them, a girl, was crying bitterly, while two slightly older male children were trying to pacify her. Nissim went up to the the boys and asked them why the girl was crying. They were too startled to answer. They merely looked at us and beamed.

On 8 April, Nissim was in a foul mood when I went to see him. I soon found out the reason. He had brought along a black closed-collar coat from home, which Daisy had insisted that he should wear to the wedding reception of her sister's relative in the evening. April in Bombay is no time to be wearing a coat! But more than the heat, it was his wife's 'bossiness' that irritated him. 'I don't mind talking to people at the reception,' he told me,' although it's possible that every word I utter is faithfully reported to her [Daisy]. But to be told what to wear!'

In August, both he and I were supposed to go to Sri Lanka for an ACLALS conference. I offered to be his travelling escort, but he declined my offer. Either Professor Anniah Gowda or Professor C.D. Narasimhaiah (I cannot remember who) had invited him to Mysore, and had promised to accompany him to Sri Lanka from there. Eventually, neither Nissim nor Narasimhaiah nor Anniah Gowda were seen at the conference.

Many people I interviewed in 1995 talked not only of past associations with Nissim, but also of how they perceived him in the present. Sirkar was impressed by the fact that he still travelled everywhere alone. He recalled how, only a year ago, Nissim sat in for two whole days on a Mahesh Elkunchwar workshop organized by Toni Patel. Sometime before that, he once fell sick in the office, Gieve Patel came to see him, and thought he might have had a heart attack. But it wasn't a heart attack. At seventy, his mind was still continuously occupied. He believed there were always worthwhile things to do, and he detested a heavy atmosphere.

Toni Patel was honest enough to point out that friendship required a lot of time, and over the years, her closeness to Nissim had 'suffered' for want of time. 'I would be busy for months together, and not be able to see him,' she said. Yet she was aware of so many of his idiosyncracies. For example, he genuinely regarded not The Retreat but the PEN as home.

He was hospitable to visitors at the PEN, but never so at The Retreat, if anyone broke his sacred rule and went there to see him.

Jussawalla, too, felt that although he was close to Nissim, the intimacy had not reached a point where he could, say, discuss his personal life with him. In one of his own not-too-happy moods, Jussawalla remarked: 'Sometimes I think of him as a character in a Narayan novel, not loving his wife, staying separate from her, yet doing her shopping, attending to her shares and stocks, and so on.'

By 1995, Jussawalla saw Nissim as virtually living the life of a tramp: 'Most of us like to wear at least a fresh shirt every day, if not fresh trousers. I'm not sure he's like that.' If some of these opinions seem too strong, Jussawalla may have even been provoked into forming them. He was very upset by the fact that Nissim had borrowed from his father (the late Dr J. M. Jussawalla) a book recently authored by him, and had conveniently mislaid it. 'The book was expressly lent to him for review, but he says he cannot trace it,' Jussawalla complained. 'Probably someone has borrowed it from him, and he can't remember who.' Apparently, Dr J. M. Jussawalla was so annoyed at Nissim's negligence, that he asked him on the phone if he was losing his mind. Jussawalla was pained that Nissim should have so ruffled his father.

However, when it comes to Nissim's contribution as a poet, Jussawalla is willing to defend him at any cost from the harsh (and somewhat personal) criticism of Sarang and Mehrotra. 'If Nissim's poems are Judeo-Christian, as Sarang claims, so what? Do we object to the "Hindu" context of Kalidas or any other more contemporary poet?' Although Sarang is a friend of Jussawalla, and has dedicated one of his books to him, Jussawalla is unsparing in his condemnation of the man here. 'I don't take Sarang seriously as a critic. He's fond of giving labels like "Able Seaman" which are too pat.' He also refutes Sarang's claim that Nissim is the last notable exponent of the Sarojini Naidu-Aurobindo Ghose school of verse. 'This is shaky. If you are going to put the birth of modern Indian English poetry so close to us, you're bringing the knife so close that there is the risk of slitting our throats. No one says that Nissim's poems are all that great, but certainly a beginning was made.' Jussawalla is only slightly less vituperative when it comes to Mehrotra, though he feels Mehrotra is correct in saying that in several of Nissim's poems, the language is under no pressure.[35]

This, of course, doesn't mean that Jussawalla is willing to condone each of Nissim's decisions concerning poetry. He is critical of some of the poets he published (such as Aneela Mirchandani). He finds it surprising that he is so critical of Hoskote's work, and yet wrote a generous blurb to *Zones of Assault*. Jussawalla once recommended to Nissim that he publish the poems of Tapas Chakravarty, a young poet, whom he himself had published in *Debonair* while he was literary editor. But Nissim failed to heed his advice.

Moving from poetry to administration, Jussawalla quotes Carmel Berkson of the AJJDC, who said she had 'unpleasant experiences' working with Nissim on one of the organization's projects. She complained that Nissim merely made her do clerical work, and treated her as a secretary rather than as a colleague.

And then we come to the ancecdotes. Nissim once reported to Jussawalla that in the course of a bus journey from Bombay to Pune, a fellow-passenger in front of him spat, and the spit landed on his face, presumably in the form of a shower. But he didn't wipe it off. He let it be as it is, till it naturally dried up in the breeze. The 'asceticism' of his act reminded me of how, according to Toni Patel, despite the heat and humidity, he slept with the fan off whenever he spent the night at their house. 'What's he trying to prove?' Jussawalla asks. 'That he's a Gandhian?'

Another time, about a year ago, Nissim and Jussawalla went down for a morning walk. (Nissim had stayed over with the Jussawallas the previous night.) On their return, Nissim spotted two street kids fighting, and as usual, intervened. He said to Jussawalla that every time he saw such a thing, it affected him badly.

It was New Year's eve, 1995, when Jussawalla narrated this incident to me. Just two days earlier, I myself witnessed a spectacle in which Nissim, Jerry Pinto, and an old and sick beggar woman were involved. She was spotted outside the PEN by Nissim, and he wanted Pinto to 'rescue' her. Pinto, the practical man, contacted a home for the destitute that promised to send an ambulance to pick the sick woman up. Nissim the poet could do nothing except display his restlessness while they waited for the vehicle to arrive. Eventually, it did arrive. When Nissim accidentally bumped into Jussawalla at Warden Road that evening (as he was on his way to Kala Niketan), he repeated the whole story verbatim to him. He said he was amazed they had actually been able to 'rescue' her. It also surprised him that the woman offered no resistance, but merely gave her two arms to Pinto and allowed him to put her into the ambulance.

Then there was the time, Nissim, after another overnight stay at the Jussawallas, was asked if he would like to have a shower. He replied, characteristically (Jussawalla mimicked him perfectly here): 'I don't quite feel like it.'

Finally, Jussawalla told me that after Elkana moved out, Daisy thought of disposing off her Kala Niketan flat because it was crumbling. She seemed to be totally out of touch with real-estate prices in Bombay. Well-wishers pointed out to her that she would have to spend anything up to a crore of rupees to buy a similar flat in the Warden Road area, or for that matter, anywhere in South Bombay.

Gieve Patel had views on Nissim's dressing. While he appreciated that there was no affectation in his personal mannerisms, he regretted Nissim's inattention to hygiene, his sloppiness which, according to Gieve, had increased in the last five to eight years, and his carelessness about his appearance. 'He used to dress better when he was younger, though he was never a dandy,' Gieve said. And then elaborated: 'People become careless about their appearance either when they are too happy or too sad. In Nissim's case it has a simpler explanation—he lives alone. Some men, when they live alone, tend to get slack in the day-to-day looking after [of themselves]. It's a certain kind of depression—not being part of a home, and so on. It's also a cussedness. A mistaken notion on his part that dress is not important, that when there are all kinds of other things to think about, who has the time to think about clothes. But why this attitude should have more markedly developed over the last eight years, I can't say.'

Gieve narrated how one day, about five years ago, he found Nissim looking extraordinarily despondent when he dropped in to see him. He tried to find out the reason, but Nissim was in no mood to talk. He simply said to Gieve in a whisper: 'That thought has come to me again . . . the thought that the universe is controlled by the Devil.' Gieve burst out laughing. 'To me, this idea that the universe is controlled by the Devil would be an interesting idea,' he told me. 'But to Nissim it came across as a horrifying fact. This easily explains why he came so close to the notion of self-destruction and suicide at this point, as he has done from time to time.'

I asked Gieve whether, as a doctor, he believed that Nissim was justified in priding himself on his health.

'This is full of contradictions,' he said. 'For, in truth, Nissim has been as ill as anyone else. But he has this comical notion that he knows how to look after himself. He is no doubt a health buff–reads all kinds of health magazines, is interested in diets, etc. But I have found nothing particularly consistent in his approach to the health question. I know health buffs who make a systematic study of their subject, and their whole life revolves around it. Take the example of people who practice yoga–you see health radiating from their faces. Nissim, on the other hand, plunges into the area, but it is never fully thought through. Today he'll say he won't eat this because he read about it somewhere, tomorrow it's gone.'

How did Gieve Patel find Nissim at the age of seventy?

'Not strikingly healthy. Merely like any average human being at that age. He's only reasonably active for his age, not exceptionally so.'

1996

Another anecdote from Jussawalla, in July. He said, of late Nissim walked in a strange way. It was because his toenails had grown inward, and they hurt. He needed a pedicure, but of course his family would hear none of it. Speaking of the family, it seems Nissim recently admitted to Jussawalla that he found it a bother to buy vegetables for Daisy, and to attend to her stocks and shares.

I interviewed Minakshi Raja in 1996. She felt she got closer to Nissim as the years went by. This was because he had given her so much, and now he was 'disintegrating'. His mind was slowing. A few days ago she said to him: 'At seventy-one, Nissim, you look and behave as if you were eighty-eight.' This was partly reflected in the way he alarmed people at dinner parties by insisting, after the party was over, that he be allowed to spend the night at one of their houses. There was some party recently at which the cartoonist Mario Miranda and his wife were present. They were forced to take him home with them, as they left. (Not everyone realized that Nissim did this because he had grown afraid of the dark.) When Raja met him the next day, she scolded him for imposing himself on the Mirandas. Nissim, according to her, did not like to be criticized. He also did not like his friends to be criticized. Raja said: 'He did not like my piece on Shakuntala Bharvani's *Lost Directions,* because I found fault with her for sneering at lower middle-class people who don't speak English the way she does.'

If I gave Raja one last chance to point out a couple of other flaws in Nissim's character, what would she say?

'His plays are disastrous, and yet he wants to write more plays,' she said. 'He looks nice in a suit and tie, as he did at an Israeli consulate meeting the other night. Yet he neglects his appearance.'

Vrinda Nabar spoke of Nissim's deterioration as a critic: 'I don't know if this is because he's out of touch with current happenings, or simply because his interests have grown narrower. His world outlook always had very little patience with what was not direct. So maybe "theory" seemed like subterfuge to him.' Then she added: 'He is dilettant-ish to some extent. But the word doesn't seem to sit on him very easily. He isn't a superficial person who lacks a sense of seriousness. He only lacks discipline.'

On Vilas Sarang's views of Nissim as a poet, she said: 'The question one needs to ask is, in the "incestuous" world of Indian English criticism, how much of the criticism is subjective, based on personal prejudices? I agree Nissim certainly isn't a modernist in the way Sarang likes to call himself a modernist. So his poetry is bound to appear dated and decadent to someone like that. Yet it has a certain validity and significance, and I wouldn't discount that merely because fashions or ways of looking at things have changed.'

Tara Patel said: 'I like his poetry very much. I still tell people that if they want to read poetry, they can't do better than to start with Nissim Ezekiel. Sometimes, when his poems move me, I even write about them in my column "On My Own". Although Nissim doesn't read my column, he often asks me what I'm writing about. I still go to him when I'm emotionally disturbed. He makes me feel comfortable. Talking to him is always soothing for he makes me see the sheer unimportance of things.'

Jerry Pinto felt that Nissim had suddenly become a lonely man in the last two years. Some of his friends had died, he was estranged from his family. 'He has seen too many of the good fruit from the poetry tree.' Like Minakshi Raja, he too thought that Nissim was unbearable at parties, as he kept asking the guests by turn whether he could stay with them for the night.

There were occurrences that were centred on his Jewishness. Pinto related some of these to me in order to prove his contention that over the last few years, Nissim had grown increasingly conscious of his Jewish identity. In the early '90s, when Ashley Tellis used to call him Plasmodious and Hoskote Rabbi, Nissim took it as a joke. Now he had grown touchy. Two people were having sugarcane juice at a roadside stall, and Nissim overheard their conversation. One of them was explaining to the other that he always ordered two half-glasses rather than a full glass, because that way he got more juice. The other person replied that only a Sindhi and a Jew were capable of looking at it in those terms. When they left, Nissim was angry. Pinto pacified him, pointing out that it was only meant to be a joke, but Nissim was unconvinced. Yet Pinto, like Hoskote, was of the view that when it came to a more serious understanding of Jewish politics, Nissim failed to develop a perspective. 'He has a very minimal understanding of the Palestinian question,' Pinto said. 'He uses words like "anti-semitism" loosely.' Pinto also referred to a reading of Hebrew poetry in English translation at the NCPA, Bombay, at which Nissim, Hoskote and he were the readers. Nissim read out a couple of poems by the Israeli poet Amichai. After the reading, when a member of the audience asked him a question, Nissim 'missed the point entirely.' Pinto said: 'The Amichai poem that he read was actually an anti-war poem. But Nissim made it out to be some kind of sociological document.'

Pinto commented on Nissim's girlfriends: 'Lot of the women he met and made friends with, I thought, had large breasts.' At the same time, he was uncomfortable talking about love.

'During the last five years, there's also this intense fear of change,' said Pinto. 'If I tell him I'll clean up his office, and dispose off the old magazines and newspapers, he goes into paroxysms of fear.'

As someone who went to the PEN every other day, and who was in charge of the cupboard of books that constituted the Poetry Circle library, Jerry Pinto was obviously in a position to observe Nissim at very close quarters. Some things about Nissim, however, were common knowledge. For example, by 1996, all his friends knew that he left home very early, took a train to Churchgate, and whiled away his time on a bench on the platform, as he waited for the peons of the Theosophy Hall to unlock his office. He wanted Sirkar to give him a room to stay in the Theosophy Hall, which from Sirkar's point of view was out of the question, as Nissim was never a Theosophist. But only Pinto was able to see, for instance, how 'bureaucratic' Nissim had become. He frequently sent notes and memos to Sirkar, only three floors above. Perhaps he wasn't as official-minded as this even in his Bombay University days, although the set-up in any Indian university is bureaucratic.

There were other things Pinto noticed. When the Gujarati poet Prabodh Parikh organized a poetry reading at the Chemould Gallery, Bombay, Nissim was not one of the sixty poets invited to participate, although he was present at the reading. He was visibly upset. What made him all the more 'insecure', was that poets like Hoskote, born as late as 1969, were a part of the proceedings, whereas he was ignored. Pinto expanded on the 'insecurity' bit and related it to other discoveries he had been making. One of these was something that I myself had noticed on several occasions. Nissim clung on to visitors at the PEN, and simply did not allow them to go away. No matter who they were, he wanted their company: he had grown that lonely. 'One morning, in the middle of last year, I came to the PEN, and when it was time to leave, Nissim was quite surprised that I wasn't going to stay on and chat with him,' Pinto said.

He told me about the 'troubled relationship' his cousin Ashley Tellis had had with Nissim. Another case of 'anxiety of influence'. In Tellis' case, Nissim had nurtured him more directly. Got him a job at SNDT, which Tellis impulsively left, without informing anyone. Nissim lent him money to pay his M. Phil fees–had he not done so, Tellis would never have been able to do his M. Phil. Yet he kept accusing him of being a patriarch, phallocentric, etc.–all the curse words of feminism.

The beginning of Nissim's slow decline, in Jerry Pinto's estimate, was his prostate operation. This revived old tendencies in him, like the inability to take criticism, a loss of the sense of self-mockery, possessiveness about objects, loneliness.

Ronita Torcato found paper pins sticking to the hem of Nissim's trousers, when she went to the PEN one afternoon. It appalled her that he had reached a stage where he was incapable of looking after himself. A couple of years ago, it was she who had taken him to a cobbler outside the PEN, when his shoes came apart. 'It flusters me that he doesn't mind going about that way,' Torcato said. 'I feel men in general shouldn't be dependent on their mothers/wives for their personal needs.'

At the same time, she wonders why Nissim's family cannot provide the help that he needs. 'I talked to Daisy in April. She had telephoned Nissim, and I picked up. She screamed on the phone for ten whole minutes when I started to defend her husband. She said she didn't care if he was a poet. What mattered was that he had neglected his family. In her view, people made too much of him.'

After she put the phone down, the thought that crossed Torcato's mind was: a prophet is not honoured in his own country. However, she wanted to be fair to both parties. She knew that Nissim was often at fault. Take the time he was supposed to accompany Daisy to the house of a relative who had recently delivered a baby. Nissim conveniently forgot about the engagement, and went instead to the British Council to attend some programme or other. On the other hand, Torcato never quite understood why Daisy made Nissim go all the way to Kala Niketan every evening with her measly shopping. 'This is unreasonable. Why can't she or Elkana do it? Why do they insist that he must do it?'

Torcato is aware that it was Nissim's flirtations that drove a wedge between himself and his wife. Personally, she never found him to be a flirt. 'He has never made any sexual advances towards me ever. He only teases me and tells me Jewish Catholic jokes. But that doesn't lower him in my estimation.'

Did Torcato, who is unmarried and without a family of her own, ever see Nissim as a substitute father? 'No,' she replies. 'But I've always had this thing about having someone in my life with whom I can talk freely. In the past, they were Jesuit priests who are now dead. Today, maybe Nissim fulfils that void.'

Suddenly Torcato said: 'Sometimes when I come [to the PEN] and the lights are off, and the windows shut, I dread the thought of his passing away. What will I do when he's not there! It's not going to be the same when he's not around.

Torcato was now close to tears, and in order to shake herself out of her wistful mood, recalled the less ideal aspects of Nissim's personality. 'He's not very good at giving advice on practical things like jobs,' she told me. 'Whenever I've taken his advice on such things, I found it to be the wrong advice and suffered as a consequence. Of course, it was my fault for taking his advice in the first place. I don't hold it against him.'

1997

On 29 June, Nissim published one of his last articles in the *Sunday Times*.[36] The fact that Jerry Pinto, by then, had a full-time job in the newspaper, helped. In fact, it is possible that he wrote the autobiographical piece on Pinto's insistence. It is one of his finest articles, in which he looks back upon his life, and reviews all the major events in his own, and in India's history. Perhaps Pinto helped him to write it. About his early years, he said: 'As a child, I can remember how we moved from building to building in Bombay. My father had what could be described as a case of circumscribed wanderlust. He would tire of the view from one side of the street and move across to the other side. Or the old apartment would seem too small and we would move again. Every building had a "To Let" notice on it and each one seemed like an invitation to him. That meant a new address, a new set of neighbours, a new world almost every year.'

He went on to comment on Independence, the Emergency, the demolition of the Babri Masjid.

On Independence: 'Independence brought me a sense of happiness tempered with the questions that we didn't seem to be asking ourselves. Such as how we should use it and what part of independence we should internalize. I spent 15 August [1947] on my own, trying out that feeling.'

On the Emergency: 'During the Emergency . . . I realized that freedom could be lost by degrees, that it could leak away without the intellectual community being aware of it. "We need a dictatorship to run this country properly." How many times had I heard this said in passing, frivolously. And now a dictatorship was in position at last and perhaps the trains would run on time, but somewhere along the way we would also be derailed.'

On the Babri Masjid: 'How do I relate the threat of the stones that were hurled onto my roof in The Retreat to the riots that raged outside in 1992? And my Jewishness to what happened in the wake of Partition reprised in the horror that followed the demolition of the Babri Masjid? What connections have I made between what happened in my life and what went on in the abstract life of the country?

'In some ways I have come to the realization that such connections are not easily made, that they can be artificial when created out of some sense of artistic or political guilt . . .

'But in another sense, that can be the only answer that I find at all meaningful. That we must keep looking for these connections, that where we find them we build them so that we may revel in our differences and enjoy our plurality.'

1998

January

Joe's wife Khorshed Wadia Ezekiel is in Bombay. She gets talking about Nissim to friends. In the course of her conversation, it emerges that:

(i) Daisy is opposed to all the Ezekiels, including the late Joe. So much so, Khorshed once said in disgust that she would drop the 'Ezekiel' from her name.

(ii) Khorshed was not invited for Elkana's wedding. When she complained, all that Daisy told her was that they had sent her a card.

(iii) As per Khorshed's information, all the cheques that Nissim ever received (for his books, articles etc.) went to Daisy (alimony?). Nissim kept only the cash for himself.

(iv) Nissim was in Madras once. He stayed with Khorshed and Joe. They literally had to strip him and push him into the bathroom for a bath.

February

Nissim neglects his diet. His daily intake of food has come down drastically. Khorshed suggests to Elkana that they should leave a lump sum of money with the proprietor of Sanman (where he has his lunch every day) and instruct them to feed him on a regular basis. On his part, Elkana tells Gieve Patel that if his father has any major health problem, he is willing to pay for his treatment. However, he does not have the time to look after his father, this will have to be done by Nissim's friends.

March

Nissim says on impulse to Torcato that if Daisy is willing to have him back, he will move in with her without getting in her way. This, in response to Torcato's scolding. Daisy of course will hear none of this. She seems exceptionally indifferent to his plight, considering that her own sister Mozel suffers from Alzheimer's disease–the disease that will put an end to his working life in about four months' time.

April

Gauri Deshpande is in Bombay, living with the Sirkars. She walks into Nissim's office to greet him. It is more than three years since they had last met. However, Nissim fails to recognize her.

May

On a public holiday, when the Sanman is closed, Jussawalla goes to the PEN to see Nissim. He is quite content to stay without lunch. Like others, Jussawalla too is concerned about the fact that, of late, Nissim hasn't been eating properly. When he expresses his concern to Nissim, it boomerangs. He takes Jussawalla's offer of money as an insult, and retorts that it's all right, it's not as if he is without money; his friends needn't worry about him.

On 23 May, after a Poetry Circle meeting, Pinto offers to take Nissim to The Retreat. At 9 p.m. on being deposited at his door, Nissim, as usual tries to close the door on Pinto. But Pinto pushes his way in and enters the flat. The first thing that hits his nose is the smell of pigeon shit, cat shit and cockroaches. As he goes into Nissim's bedroom, he notices a three-foot pile of rubbish around his bed. Four cockroaches are dislodged from the bed when Nissim sits on it. Pinto leaves with three of Nissim's soiled shirts (which even the laundries refuse to accept because of their filth), and a determination to come back to The Retreat and clean up the place.

On 26 May, Pinto goes back to The Retreat with the shirts and a nail-cutter with which he trims Nissim's fingernails and toenails. Nissim is immensely afraid of having his nails cut, for he thinks he'll be hurt.

On 27 May, as per what is decided the previous day, Pinto lands at the Retreat at 8 a.m. He finds the house locked. He rushes to the PEN and waits for Nissim to arrive. Nissim arrives at 8.50 a.m., Pinto takes the keys from him and returns to The Retreat with four young men who volunteer to clean the house. As they commence cleaning, they stumble upon a dead rat under Nissim's pillow, and a scorpion in a corner of the room. The mattresses yield cockroaches and a dark-green lizard beneath their cozy warmth, and in the unused hall is a cat and several pigeons. Nissim's shirts have rat faeces on them. The books and papers in the house are so badly consumed by termites that they crumble to pieces the moment the boys lay hands on them. In one of the book-cases they find currency notes worth Rs 2000, all eaten up. There's more to come. The bathroom and the toilet apparently haven't been used for years. Pinto and his boys find excrement in the drain and have to use gloves to clean it up. In the kitchen, they discover a water container with dead cockroaches floating in the stagnant water. The latch on the front door is jammed, leading Pinto to suspect that Nissim habitually slept with the front door open.

The boys are joined by a cleaning woman who helps them to dispose off the sixty kilos of garbage they have collected from the flat. They pay her Rs 200. A neighbour, who thinks Pinto might be Nissim's nephew, watches with interest and tells them that 'this' has been going on for two years, ever since Kavita and her husband stopped visiting The Retreat.

Pinto begins his work around 9.30 in the morning and finishes only after 5.30 p.m. In eight hours they transform the house into a livable place.

All this while, Nissim waits restlessly at the PEN, aware only that his house keys are no longer with him, forgetting he has given them to Pinto. When Pinto finally returns with the keys, Nissim says that he even nurtured the hope that the peons would inadvertently lock him in at the PEN, so that he wouldn't have to go back to The Retreat for the night. Pinto takes Nissim out to buy him new pillow covers and bed sheets.

When Pinto and Nissim return to The Retreat, it takes Nissim a while to realize that he's back in his own house. He looks at the scrubbed floor and wonders whether Pinto has changed the tiles. He asks for his tissues and his Memory Plus tablets.

June

There is talk of Nissim being stripped of his duties at the AJJDC, on account of his deteriorating health. Mrs Elian Peters of the AJJDC wants to pay him an annual pension of $ 300 and ask him to retire. Nissim thinks this might amount to Rs 1000 a month, which he refuses to accept because 'there are more deserving Jewish people all over the world in need of the money.'

On 27 June, Nissim, Elkana and Jussawalla meet at the PEN. Elkana emphasizes that Nissim's family does not neglect him. It's just that they handle his finances because he is 'incompetent' with money. Elkana says Daisy is also of late behaving 'strangely'. He has to look after two ailing parents. He too wants to sell the Kala Niketan flat and find a place for his mother closç to his house at Prabhadevi.

July

After cleaning up Nissim's flat, Pinto attempts to bring some order into his office. It is while rearranging the books and papers in the cupboards that he comes across the four pages that contain Nissim's only attempt at autobiography.

Elkana decides to take matters into his own hands. He thinks of writing to Mrs Elian Peters to say that the Rs 1000 per month that they want to give his father as a pension is welcome, even though his father is opposed to the idea of taking any money from the AJJDC. He toys with the idea of using this money to find his father a place on rent, somewhere near his own apartment. Elkana wants the Jewish community to know that it is not as if the family has stopped taking care of Nissim.

August

Nissim collapses at an AJJDC meeting and has to be hospitalized at the Shushrusha Nursing Home at Dadar. He is diagnosed as suffering from Alzheimer's disease.

September

Articles start to appear in the Indian press, lamenting that a major poet who has given so much to the literary world now lies ailing, while his wife and children have no time for him. Some of them are by women journalists like Vimala Patil and Shobha De. Ms Patil goes to the extent of saying that according to Indian traditions, it is a son's sacred duty to look after his parents in their old age, and Elkana has failed in his duty.[37] The articles make Elkana and the rest of Nissim's family, including his sister Asha, her husband Atmaram and their son Nandu, very angry. They feel that people such as Ms Patil and Ms De, who do not know the facts, should refrain from commenting.

But it is not just the family that is annoyed. Friends such as Jussawalla and Pinto are equally outraged by the irresponsible reportage. Jussawalla, in a rejoinder to Ms Patil[38] sets the records straight by pointing out that several people (he mentions Elkana, Minakshi Raja and Asha Bhende) regularly visit Nissim in hospital. He also defends Elkana against Ms Patil's tirade. 'I would like to ask her [Ms Patil] who she thinks physically took care of Nissim and admitted him to a hospital when it was reported . . . that Nissim was on the point of collapse? Who does she think is paying the hospital bills and will pay for Nissim's needs in the future?'

And Pinto writes: 'His family? . . . There are no complete stories as far as families go. From the outside, it's easy to apportion blame and sit in judgement, easy to say, "He should have done something about this" and "she shouldn't have done that". But no one can know what goes on inside the family and so we should leave it to Nissim and his family.[39]

Nissim is suddenly in the news all over again and the media want to make the most of the opportunity. One Sunday afternoon, TVI, a private television channel, invites me to their recording studios at Nirmal Building, Nariman Point, to interview me before I can catch the Deccan Queen to Pune.

October

Nissim is shifted from the Shushrusha Nursing Home to the A. J. Dias Nursing Home at Turner Road, Bandra. I go to see him on the last day of the month. I find that the place is rather like an old people's home, in which most other inmates are deranged. Nissim is made to share the room with a man who constantly mutters something that he cannot understand, but for the sake of politeness, pretends that he does. From time to time he responds to the man, by speaking a word or two. He shows me around the place. The inmates of the home, men and women, are his new friends and the only company he has. He sees a pack of cigarettes in my pocket and asks for one. He says it is a long time since he smoked. The nurses in the room, who talk to all the inmates as if they are naughty children, overhear our conversation and firmly tell him they will report him to the doctor.

What is the state of his health? He seems okay externally, especially when compared to others at the home. Yet he asks me to write my name on a piece of paper because (apparently) he cannot remember who I am. Cannot remember, that for the past five years, I am his biographer. Does not know where I live or work. His speech is a throwback to the days when he was a professor at Bombay University. Or an organizer of events at the PEN, not so long ago. He keeps telling me of a 'performance in the next room' and the need for us to go in before the doors are closed. He uses his favourite phrases 'from A to Z' and 'from time to time' frequently. Obviously his brain is unwilling to accept that these things are no longer part of his life.

I stay with Nissim for exactly half an hour from 5 to 5.30 p.m. At the time of leaving, I shake his hand and promise that I will come back again. His hand trembles as I shake it. Suddenly he asks me if I am going back via Bombay Central–his station–and whether he can go with me. Then he says, it's all right, tomorrow he is leaving the nursing home anyway for Bombay. For Bombay? I learn afterwards that his family has told him that he is not in Bombay, but elsewhere in the country. This, so that he doesn't attempt to escape . . . . The cultural tzar of poetry is reduced to this.

November

A new book of essays in honour of Nissim Ezekiel is out.[40] It is edited by Vrinda Nabar and Nilufer Bharucha, and is intended as a festschrift volume. I receive a contributor's copy from the publishers (an essay of mine on Nissim's Bombay poems is included in the book). It is accompanied by a letter from Bharucha in which she announces that it is to be formally released on 16 December, Nissim's seventy-fourth birthday, at Bombay University's Kalina campus. Ms Bharucha also expresses the sentiment that while Nissim is ailing in hospital, and while they hope the hospital authorities will give him the permission to attend the function, he will continue to live immortally, in his poetry. Hence the launch function is to include a poetry reading by some of Bombay's leading poets who will read both Nissim's poems and their own.

Gieve Patel tells me on the telephone that he, along with Asha, Atmaram and Nandu Bhende, is trying to convince Elkana to shift Nissim from the Dias Nursing Home to some place else. It is true he is being looked after here. But since the other inmates are mentally disturbed, this impinges on him. I ask Gieve where they plan to shift Nissim. He replies that there are a couple of possibilities, but he doesn't want to talk about them until they are explored.

December
The festschrift volume is released as planned at the J.P. Naik Bhavan, Kalina campus. Ms Bharucha is a woman of contacts and is able to get both Dr Yehoyada Haim, the ambassador of Israel, and Mr Walid Mansour, consul general of Israel to attend the function. While Dr Haim releases the book, Mr Mansour is the guest of honour. As expected, Nissim is not given the permission to attend, although any number of his friends are willing to bring him from the A.J. Dias Nursing Home to the university in their cars. Nor are Daisy, Elkana or his daughters there. However Hannan, Asha, Atmaram and Nandu are present.

The afternoon opens with a round of speeches. In her welcome address, Yasmeen Lukmani, Chair of English, says that Nissim is 'sadly missing'. Ms Bharucha explains that doctors were against the idea of his attending the function, because they feared he might suffer a 'disorientation'. She also claims that the function is organized 'to celebrate Nissim, not mourn his absence.'

The speeches of the ambassador and the consul general are routine affairs, nothing to write home about. They are peppered with the usual bureaucratic comments. But after they are done, we are in for a surprise: Hannan Ezekiel and Nandu Bhende are invited to the stage to say a few words. Hannan has a sad look in his eyes as he says: 'It is very difficult to speak about my brother in his present condition.' Then, speaking on behalf of the whole family, he says that all of them are deeply concerned about Nissim, proud that the book is published. He also wonders why everyone refers only to Nissim's poetry, when in fact he has a sizable amount of prose to his credit. And he informs the audience that the ambassador of Israel has just proposed that his brother's poems be translated into Hebrew.

Nandu Bhende says he is lucky to have an uncle who was 'so cool'. He looked up to him with a sense of awe. He talks of the time Nissim, on sister Asha's advice, wrote songs for him to set to music. He also relates how Nissim was shocked when he once foolishly asked him to change some words in those songs. 'He merely looked at me, smiled and changed the topic.' Everyone in the audience laughs. Bhende rounds off his speech by saying it is impossible for him to talk about his uncle without getting emotional. Hence, all he wants to state is: 'Nissim is still very much with us, we still go and meet him, look forward to seeing him again.'

The poets who are invited to read are: Adil Jussawalla, Dom Moraes, Gieve Patel, Eunice de Souza, Imtiaz Dharkar, Menka Shivdasani, Ranjit Hoskote, Tara Patel, Jerry Pinto and myself. Of these, Gieve Patel, Dom Moraes and Eunice de Souza are absent. As the speeches have delayed us and we are running late, each of us reads only a couple of poems by Nissim and a couple of our own. Tara Patel reads a poem that she says 'Nissim would have liked.' To which Pinto who is seated in front of me, responds by muttering: 'Go and show him the poem and ask him if he likes it. Is he dead?'

Pinto has a point. As the last reader, he is the only one who introduces a measure of lightness to an evening laced with melancholy: he reads one of Nisim's Indian English poems, 'Soap'. All the other poets have opted for his more serious work. And Pinto is able to carry it off brilliantly. The tense atmosphere in the hall is suddenly transformed into mirth as he finishes his reading, and we are all invited to the lawns outside for batata vadas and tea.

But Pinto himself continues to be depressed. Somehow, the whole programme seemed to him like a condolence meeting. Although he lives at Mahim, he travels all the way to Cuffe Parade with Jussawalla for a drink. It is pretty late by the time he gets home.

All this while, Nissim lies in his hospital bed, blissfully unaware of what is happening. After the function, some poets and some members of the audience, too pained by his absence, dash off to the A.J. Dias Nursing Home with flowers. But he is unable to see what the fuss is all about.

The Bombay University function has actually served to drive a sharp wedge between Nissim's family and friends. The whole of his family, including Hannan, is of the view that Elkana should be allowed to stay in control of the situation. If Elkana doesn't want his father to be taken out of the Dias Nursing Home, even for a drive, that's how it should be. Gieve meets Elkana to explore the possibility of shifting Nissim out of the nursing home. Elkana is rude; he reiterates that it is he who is in the 'driver's seat', and he alone will decide whether or not to shift his father from the nursing home. Elkana reportedly says on the phone to one of Nissim's friends: 'Daddy will remain at the nursing home till he dies.'

1999

January

Roma, *PEN* Secretary, speaks to Usha, wife of Nandu Bhende on the phone. Apparently, there are three options before Elkana, as regards his father:

(i) Mr Pramod Navalkar, Maharashtra's cultural affairs' minister, has agreed to give Nissim a permanent room at the J.J. Hospital, with an attendant.

(ii) The Israeli Consulate has agreed to renovate Nissim's flat at The Retreat at their own expense, and provide him with a full-time helper.

(iii) The AJJDC has offered Nissim a room at their old people's Home at Thane.

However, Elkana rejects all these options. It transpires, during Roma's conversations with Usha, that deep down Elkana still bears a grudge against his father for walking out on them when he was just a boy.

February

Khorshed Wadia Ezekiel visits Nissim at the A. J. Dias Nursing Home. The old problem of his toenails has recurred. He has fungus under his toenails. Nissim will not allow the nurses and ayahs at the nursing home to cut his toenails. They manage to cut a few of them, wiping his feet with warm water each time. But Nissim does not allow them to continue. Jussawalla jokes about it. Khorshed's brother is a famous vet. She will possibly have to borrow a large pair of scissors, with which they cut the claws of animals, to use on her brother-in-law!

Khorshed goes all the way from Charni Road to Bandra four times to see Nissim. At first Nissim cannot recognize her. But when she says she's Joe's wife, he remembers. He tells her: 'Joe has done so much for me.' Khorshed tries to make Nissim walk. He has developed the habit of sitting down at one place. She is peeved that Nissim's friends aren't visiting him at the nursing home as often as they should. As Khorshed gets up to leave, Nissim kisses her hand.

March
Ronita Torcato visits Nissim and reports that his condition is deteriorating. She advises whoever she meets to go and see him.

April
The *Times of India* runs a story by Vidyadhar Date, the heading of which is: 'Unwell and Lonely, Ezekiel Yearns for Company'. Nilufer Bharucha is quoted in the article. She says: 'If he [Ezekiel] had a chair and a table he could at least start writing. What he needs is stimulus. He is not demented, he needs care. When I took some students of mine to see him, he read a poem to them, analysed it. That is the kind of environment he needs.'

Jussawalla and Imtiaz Dharker go to the A.J. Dias Nursing Home. Nissim recognizes Jussawalla, but not Dharker. They find him in good shape, physically. He looks well-fed. His bothersome roommate has been drugged, so he is quiet now. Contrary to Bharucha's claim they find that he has been provided with a table and a chair. Probably, it's Date's report that did the trick. It is Nissim who refuses to sit down and write. In his conversation with them Nissim keeps referring to 'mummy'. At first Jussawala thinks he has Daisy in mind. But then, after talking to Elkana on the phone, he realizes that Nissim has started to hallucinate about his own mother. Jussawalla is sympathetic to Elkana's point of view. It's not safe to let patients with Alzheimer's disease go out too often. Some of them are known to have jumped out of running cars. However, in Nissim's case, it is he now who is reluctant even to step out of the building for a walk with friends, relatives, or the nursing home staff.

After spending close to an hour with him, Jussawalla and Dharker take their leave. Jussawalla has carried a notebook and pen for Nissim as a present. But Nissim is unwilling to accept the present, not sure what he'll do with it.

May & June

Minakshi Raja visits Nissim and writes about her visit in her column ('Of Books and Things') in the *Afternoon on Sunday*.[41] She says:

'. . . I had the opportunity to visit him three times in a little over a month . . . and the last visit left me sad, and in a gloom that wouldn't leave me for a long while.

'This was the first time that he couldn't connect a name with a face. He remembered my name as his eyes lit up at the prospect of a visitor; he smiled as he put his hand out to shake mine and said, "Haven't we met before?"

'It was tea-time and the ayah brought him a cup of tea, with two Monaco and Glucose biscuits. He finished them in about a minute, and to me he still looked hungry. "Shall I get you some more biscuits," I asked him. He looked around uncertainly, and then said, "No, I suppose this will do."

'. . . Visitors are rare these days, shrugged the ayah indifferently, but it was a different story that Nissim told. "So many people come to visit me everyday," he said. "They come for advice for their university courses, and theses . . . we have meetings, we have discussions . . . students come with their essays and poems, and I read them all carefully, and make notes. I have a very busy schedule everyday."

'. . . Progressively, Nissim has begun to live in the past, and now the move is almost complete. This time . . . Nissim expressed an urgent desire to return to his flat near Bombay Central. "How long can I stay here?" he said. "I've been here long enough now, and I must go home. My parents are waiting for me there, and Daisy is also there . . . I must go to her."

'. . . As I watched him sink to the lower depths, I knew that he will never again return to the PEN and to Sanman. Few people ask after him now, after all . . . he is yesterday's story. For myself though, my affection and loyalty remain steadfast.'

December

Nissim is put on Exelon, the American wonder-drug for Alzheimer's disease, manufactured in India by Novartis. The medicine doesn't appear to have brought about any change in his condition. Jussawalla, Cyrus Mistry and I visit him. He has been given a prison crop that makes him look like a convict. Later, Jussawalla reports on the visit in the *Sunday Observer.* He writes:

'It's past four in the afternoon . . . and the day's drawing in, making the room darker than it was during my two previous visits. Nissim is roused from bed by Malti, one of the women who looks after him. He looks at us in wonder, his hand outstretched.

'. . . We have filed into the room awkwardly . . . We finally settle on a settee, one meant to be nearest to Nissim. If only we knew where he would settle. He prefers sitting on the edge of his bed; Malti insists he sit on a chair.

'. . . But no. He's suddenly there, right in front of me, sitting on a chair, his hands folded on his lap. Hair: close-cropped, grey-brown. Eyes: spectacled, greyish. Smile: gentle . . . Shirt: blue-grey . . . He asks: "Are all of you together?"

'. . . He asks: 'You are all from the same place?"

'. . . He looks at the book of poems I've brought him . . . He puts the book on his bed, folds his hands on his lap, and talks:

"I will read the book by and by. There's a lot to read. After I read them, the books are taken away. Otherwise there'd be no space. There's an institution next door. There's something happening there all the time. I was there before you came. There's something going on all the time. If you go there now, you might hear a discussion. I think they'll be stopping soon . . . I've been here a year, as you know. My son visits me. He has been very busy. He looks after things in my absence. I don't write too much but there's always something to do. Are you sure you won't go next door? They may be stopping soon." Then everyone gets up and goes home suddenly. Before you know it, things are over. Suddenly.'[42]

Interview with Khorshed Wadia Ezekiel

RRR: How close was Nissim to Joe?

KWE: Nissim was always the family's blue-eyed boy. My husband too admired him greatly. After Joe and I got married, Nissim used to stop by for a meal and Joe was always very proud and affectionate. As a matter of fact, while Nissim was in England and Joe was given the honour of naming his first-born nephew, he named him Nissim as a tribute to Nissim Sr. Must have been quite a burden for the young man growing up in a city that was used to feting Nissim Sr! The relationship between Joe and Nissim was cordial but in later years Joe perceived him as being selfish.

RRR: What are your earliest recollections of Daisy?

KWE: Daisy I remember from college days at St Xavier's but not with too definite a recollection. My one memory of her was the fact that she had told us (friends from Xavier's) that it was 'love at first sight' for her and Nissim. The facts behind this romantic notion were that Nissim had returned from England, love-lorn and desperate, and had told his mother that he wanted to get married and would marry the first girl that she introduced him to. His mother, in good faith, had lined up two or three suitably-educated girls. Daisy was an MA in English, I think. Within minutes of being introduced, Nissim said, 'Congratulate us, we are engaged.' I heard this story from Joe in '54. Some ten years ago, while talking to an Ezekiel relative who is lauded by the family for her amiable nature, I said, apropos of something—'One can't blame Daisy for her temperament, after all, she has been through a lot.' The lady's rejoinder was, 'Khorshed, Daisy has always been like that from the first day she stepped into the Ezekiel household.'

RRR: According to you, when did problems in their marriage first start to crop up?

KWE: In the '60s Joe's job took us to Germany. Nissim had an opportunity to visit England and managed to persuade Daisy to accompany him. Daisy went very reluctantly. Their two daughters stayed with my mother-in-law in the house that Nissim has been occupying. Joe had already left for Germany so I was also at The Retreat for a few weeks. I later moved to my parents' home before the children and I joined Joe in Germany. Daisy, if I remember correctly, came back pregnant with her third child, the son she had longed for and had said she would name him Elkana so that she could call him Elk–which was Alkazi's nickname. I think, soon after this, Elk fell from grace as far as Daisy was concerned and I don't recall Elkana ever being called Elk! Joe and I were away in Germany when Elkana was born. A young American Fulibright scholar (Linda Hess) was in India during that time. We heard that Nissim was in love with her, had asked Daisy for a divorce and she had refused. Last year someone told me that Daisy had complained to the US consulate about this girl destroying her marriage and they had cut short her stay in India. I was quite impressed (at Daisy's determination)!

A friend of mine told me that when she advised Daisy to let go of Nissim who did not want to go on with the marriage, she retorted that this was not the first time that he had been in love with someone and had asked her for a divorce.

RRR: Tell us something about Linda Hess.

KWE: She was Jewish. Later when we were in England Nissim wrote to us saying that this girl was going to England and since we were there at that time could we have her stay with us? I was reluctant. A certain feminine bonding with the wife, that too a 'wronged' woman, I suppose. But Joe prevailed upon me and we had her staying with us briefly. I have some photos somewhere in the home. As soon as I set my eyes on her, I was struck with the strong Ezekiel family resemblance–she was very young and looked even younger. As a matter of fact, she looked a lot like Nissim's older daughter Kavita. I had told her that I'd had my reservations about having her in my home and she sympathized. I also told her that as the other woman I'd expected her to be a long-legged, dark-suited, ciggy-smoking, femme fatale like in dozens of American movies! And here she was, fresh-faced, very easy to like, and all of us, as a family grew fond of her and close to her. By the way, she was also a scatterbrain who forgot to pack half a dozen dresses which she left hanging in a wardrobe she was using in our home. I recall that she had left her coat behind, so, I got the cab co. to radio the cab and she came back for it and even then did not check the wardrobe for her dresses, I remember it cost us a pretty penny to mail them back to her! In later years I remember reading some of her poems in some journal–could it have been an Indian publication?

RRR: Did Nissim ever talk to you about divorcing (or not divorcing) Daisy?

KWE: While we were in England, Nissim came to see us. He was teaching at Leeds. I used to tell my best friends that he had come there to teach English to the natives. He stayed with us for a while. One evening Sasthi Brata and his woman friend had come over and Sasthi told Nissim that he should have stuck to his American girlfriend since, according to Sasthi, Nissim wrote best during that period! Nissim broke down and said Daisy had said he would have to take the children with him. Nissim said, 'How can I deprive my children of their mother?' It didn't ring true then and does not now. I mean here was a man 'depriving' his children of a father, himself, but making a virtue out of not wanting to deprive them of their mother! Whenever Nissim did not want to face a certain situation, he used to hide behind Daisy's skirts. I got a bit impatient with him about this.

By the time I returned to India, Nissim had moved in with my mother-in-law and her elderly niece and was living at The Retreat. Nissim was cheerful, had taken to smoking. My mother-in-law told me that Nissim had wanted to move to a hotel after he left Daisy, but Mrs Ezekiel Sr felt that, left to himself, he might get into some other liaison or even do himself some harm–I suppose she meant suicide or something–so she asked him to move in. Then, while I was in the house at one time he had brought in a young woman. My mum-in-law said he was conducting some experiments with some drugs (probably LSD), and once again she had persuaded him not to use a hotel. She rather despairingly said 'You and I may understand but how do I explain this to the servant?' (Meaning Nissim being closeted in a room with some girl.) Some four years ago, when I visited Daisy she told me that she never forgave Mrs Ezekiel Sr for keeping Nissim with her. 'Otherwise he would have come back to me'–I doubt that. But I do wish he had moved in with someone else who could perhaps have looked after him as he grew older. But who can predict all that? When I defended my mom-in-law, Daisy said, 'I know what was going on then, I got reports from well-wishers.

I've also heard that when Nissim made demands about the divorce, Daisy said that she would keep the bank account, he could have the children. Most people were horrified but I thought there was a great lesson in that. Not many men looking for a divorce and a new life with a younger wife would be willing to take on the responsibility/burden of children. I think Daisy started women's lib as far as this was concerned. What I deplore is that she accepted his money–and I have this on good authority–made him run her errands but would not put out a hand to him when he needed it, or, in later years, invite him in. At the same time, Nissim is equally to blame. What he did he did most likely for himself–to salve his conscience or as a sop to his grown-up children–and eventually it became a habit.

To ask me or anyone else 'whose side?' is childish and unfair, or at best a badly-worded question; there are no sides in a situation like this. Nissim had no business marrying on the rebound and that too without any sort of attachment to the woman he was marrying. Nissim's mother and his cousin have both told me that within a few days of their wedding, they came home having a row since Daisy felt that Nissim would let his fame go to his head–anyway she could not accept his standing in the community and among his friends. If I remember correctly, F. Scott Fitzgerald's wife had this problem. So, how can you apportion blame? I don't think the children should be expected to sit in judgement in this situation. Nissim supported the family, visited regularly and once said, 'Oh we get on well now that we live apart.' They were often together on social occasions. I remember Nissim saying that Linda's father had said, 'How long can our daughter wait for you to get a divorce?' So, Nissim must have kind of released her from her promise or whatever. They were certainly living together when she was in Bombay. I do not know why he did not continue to do so. One thing I remember about Nissim is that he always considered India his home–and perhaps because of his parents' and his standing in the community, he could not openly live with another woman.

RRR: I believe there was some unpleasantness over the fact that Daisy had to repay the money Joe had sent to Nissim in England.

KWE: Yes, Daisy grumbled about the fact that after Joe and I were married, my mother-in-law requested /suggested to Nissim that he pay back to Joe what Joe had loaned /sent him while Nissim was in England. Daisy felt that that was Nissim's natal family's responsibility and there was no call for her to have to pay it back. 'Why did I have to return it?'

Mind you this was a couple of years after Joe had passed away and several years after his mother's death. I phoned Joe's sister after that and told her of this and resolved never to visit Daisy again. I then used to go to see Nissim at the PEN office.

RRR: Was Nissim a womanizer?

KWE: Another wonky question. I don't know what your definition of 'womanizer' is. I did not perceive Nissim as a womanizer. As a matter of fact, when Daisy started telling his mother and friends about her problems with him, I was very sceptical since I thought him singularly unattractive physically. 'As insipid as boiled doodhi', is how one of my friends described him. I have mentioned how a young friend admonished Daisy about selling those books, she was a very pretty girl. I heard later that Daisy said that this pretty girl was having an affair with Nissim. I really thought that it was a figment of her imagination. At another time, she made him leave a job because the lady-owner of the firm, according to Daisy, was demanding sexual favours from Nissim. I cannot vouch for any of this. What a partner in marriage notices in the nuances of his or her spouse is very different from what an outsider may see.

I have always felt surprise /amazement that any marriage built on so much mistrust should have lasted even as long as it did. I have sensed a sneaking growth of affection for each other on both sides, a kind of 'I've grown accustomed to her/his face' until say about seven years ago. Basically, Nissim's family's attitude to life's vicissitudes and Daisy's beliefs /attitudes were poles apart. When I visited Nissim this time he said, several times, about all sorts of unrelated things–'perhaps it was my fault.' I think perhaps he went through some kind of a guilt trip. His daily bazaar jog to Grant Road from Marine Lines and up the hill to Daisy's house was quite bizarre; probably some form of atonement.

Joe and I were away from Bombay from '56 onwards and out of the gossip circuit. I am not saying I haven't heard about Nissim's adventures and misadventures, but I never thought of it as philandering. I must have been particularly naive, or just plain stupid. Even Joe, I don't think, had any inkling except, of course, Nissim's poems, as I have said, are often 'kiss and tell'. As I have said, I knew Nissim and Sr Mrs Ezekiel long before I met Joe. There was always a bond of warm, affectionate camaraderie, humour that the five of us (Mrs Ezekiel, Nissim, Joe, Daisy, and I) as well as the rest of the family shared. Nissim had always been put on a pedestal by the family. It took some time before anyone noticed the toes crumbling. 'Even so, he was always the good-humoured brother-in-law /brother. From Daisy's point of view, he may seem the monster who destroyed her life, yet, if one looks back on it, he never physically harmed her or the children, starved them, or anything like that. He has always supported them financially, has visited them, been with them whenever he was needed–even at the cost of his own comfort. And one does feel one would want to help anyone–whatever the circumstances of his past–if his present circumstances were as Nissim's are today. Yet, how can anyone else gauge the hurt and pain he may have caused his wife? And how would another woman/wife have reacted to his present ills if she had been hurt in this manner? I do not sit in judgement over her or Nissim. I hope that whatever any of his children are doing or not doing has nothing to do with any form of pettiness. For Nissim's sake, as well as their's. If they are so badly hurt, it truly must have been bad for them in the past. If Nissim's wife and children do have some rankling ill-feeling towards him, I do not condone it but I do empathize. Human nature is a frail commodity . . .

RRR: Do you think Nissim was incapable of taking care of himself?

KWE: I have been fretting about his failing mind for years now. However I wept only when I heard that he had fainted from hunger. That at least could have been prevented had I done something instead of just talking. When I went to see him last in December '97 or January '98 I was distressed at his condition. I wrote to several people (wrote to you too!) about it. My letters did not seem to make any difference. It was only after he fainted from hunger and exhaustion–Hunger!–that things started to whirr. Whatever he may have done, no man deserves to go through so much. He was a good father and a good provider. His reaction to his turmoils with Daisy was always to harm himself physically. Perhaps if she had merely ignored him rather than verbally punishing him, he might have stayed on. What I am saying here is what I have heard long ago. I was not there as a witness. However the general consensus of opinion is that Daisy is a difficult person. In '93, Nissim visited Madras on some work–Joe died on 23 April and Nissim was here in October. He stayed in my home for a couple of days. He had then said to me that he gives all the cheques he receives to Daisy. 'Why?' Because she manages money better than I can. Even in '93, he was very shabbily dressed, reluctant to bathe, reluctant to change his clothes, have them washed etc. I had to talk him–trick him!–

into getting all this done. Also Ezekiel men have a pathological fear of doctors and dentists. Hannan has managed to get himself out of this grip but Joe too was MOST reluctant to visit a medico. Now, Nissim is even afraid of getting his nails cut and probably also frightened of the razor.

RRR: Are you happy with the way Elkana is in control of the situation at present and doesn't want his father discharged from the nursing home?

KWE: Well, I suppose someone has to be in charge. I believe the nursing home charges Rs 10,000 or Rs 11,000 for which Nissim's Jewish community and Elkana's firm jointly pick up tabs. If a whole lot of people 'take charge', there is sure to be chaos. Nissim has never been a good patient in any medical crisis.

This time when I met him at the A.J. Dias Nursing Home, I was greatly saddened. However I kept myself in check as I did not know how aware he was of his surroundings. Nissim talks about 'meetings', 'books' and 'publishing' in a rambling kind of a way. But he never steps into the realm of fantasy. He does not speak of talking to Shakespeare or Moliere, Frost or Spender. He does not commit himself to giving names—he neatly skirts around all kinds of issues. The place where he is, is in the physical sense, neat, pleasant, has good surroundings, a nice little garden. However I get the feeling Nissim is being sedated. He has that kind of a look in his eyes. Also, no one has visited him in a long time. He needs to have someone to talk to him, read to him, get him to read and to write. He is already fumbling over words. He must have company to stimulate his mind, to make him read and write or he will lose those skills. As I can see he stopped writing creatively more than seven years ago. Though I saw some newspapers and magazines on his bed when I visited him, they were all in their original folds. The nursing home is not the ideal place for Nissim. But then, what is the alternative? It's all very well for me to sit here and say 'why doesn't someone' etc. etc. I wish, of course, that his friends could have some roster and visit him once in three months (does he have a hundred people he can call friend?) Failing that, can't we all get together and pay some educated sensitive person to visit him twice a day, talk to him, walk with him and get him to talk of whatever he can recall? The patent tragedy of old age is that our peer group grows old with us. It would be totally unfair to expect the younger generation to pick up the threads of our lives. Neither Elkana, nor Nissim's daughters or sisters can take personal responsibility for him at this stage. I know for a fact that each of them has tried to persuade him to go and stay with them and that he did not want to do so. To take him on now needs more than just the will to do so. Mind you, when I saw him this time, I was strongly tempted to bring him away–it would be good for him to be with normal people. But I realize the impracticality of what I was contemplating. On the other hand Nissim does not 'belong' to any one person. He was the nation's pride, Bombay's pride, the Jewish community's pride and certainly for the last ten years and more his friends and admirers have done a lot for him–more than both his families. So I do feel strongly that he belongs to all of us and that is why everyone feels so concerned for him.

I know that since '93 Minakshi Raja has been telling me about her observations, which I could then see for myself. I told everyone in the family to look for these changes, to notice them and do something. But the general opinion was: 'But Nissim has always been like this.' Last year Alyque Padamsee met my son Gulu in Delhi and said he thought Nissim had Alzheimer's. Gulu called and told me. Alyque's mother had also suffered from Alzheimer's so I think he was the first one to put a name to it. I once again wrote to his sister Asha. I also wrote to Alyque and requested him to please call Usha/Nandu or Bapu/Asha and tell them of his fears. And dear Alyque, with all his tight schedule, did just that. Asha took some time to respond to my letter so that by the time she did, everything had come to a head with Nissim fainting from exhaustion and hunger. This is how she put it: 'Exhaustion and hunger.' Alyque later–no prodding from me this time–called Elkana and told him that Nissim should not have to share a room with a patient who was known to be inclined to violence. And, according to different people who told me of this, Elkana ticked him off. That was a pity, but then perhaps Elkana is in a stressful situation. Another person told me in '97, that Elkana was approached by a friend of Nissim's, about Nissim's welfare. Elkana said to him that he would pay whatever was required but he could not 'relate to his father.' The way I see this, a situation like this could arise even in a family that had not been fractured. Lots of adult children may have said the same thing about a parent. If you cannot relate to a parent, for whatever reason, it is better indeed to pay someone competent to look after this parent rather than grudgingly keep this person in the home and ill-treat them–that is ignore or scorn or whatever.

I was told by Nissim's sister that the home where he presently is was the only one willing to accept him. Heart-breaking and heart-wrenching as the situation is, the fact is that Nissim is not in pain. He is blissfully unaware of where he is and what his problem is. He likes to think and does think that he is 'in charge'. While I was there one evening, a woman in the next room was weeping loudly–Nissim said he would go out and check. I tried to dissuade him but he marched off purposefully and ticked them off with you are not to make her cry, stop it' and what is more, the woman stopped crying! Nissim strode in and continued his conversation with me. I think there is an area of his mind that is fairly shrewd. I remember that a year ago he tried to bluff his way out when he had forgotten something. When I met him this time, I said 'Nissim, I am Khorshed, I have come to see you. Let's go to your room.' When I first walked in, he was sitting in the room next to his. Not talking to anyone, just sitting and smiling benignly at everyone. After a while he said 'I've forgotten your name. Please put it down for me so that I can get in touch with you,' and produced a pen and paper (scrap, as usual!) so I wrote it for him. Now, that's a shrewd move. I also made him write down his name and address which he did–though he needed a little prompting. Also, his writing has changed a bit. He talked about his parents–could not recall his father's name and said, 'We always called him papa.' He also could not remember his younger sister Asha (Lily). Presently, his elder sister Dr Sarah Rao is in Bombay staying with Asha and Bapu. Do you know Asha and Bapu? If you want to know about Nissim's childhood and early years you really should talk to them.

RRR: You did not visit Daisy and the kids the last few times you were in Bombay . . .?

KWE: I just didn't want to spend one of the few evenings I have when I visit Bombay, with someone who was so insensitive as to complain to me about my long dead husband and longer dead mother-in-law. I decided I could do without that kind of aggro. I did call her, briefly, one time; that last time we met, it was really all attack-attack, and though I did put up some resistance, she was not having any of that!

I did not want to say anything I would regret later and didn't. But perhaps I should have! Ah well! Last year Kavita was in Bombay and I spoke to her about Nissim's condition and she said, 'We have told him so often to come and stay with us but he refuses to do so.' I can understand Nissim's attitude and K's as well. My children fret about me and keep saying I should go and stay with them but I just love my ramshackle old house, my independence, my solitude and all the joys of living on my own while I can still manage to do so. At the same time, I understand their concern.

RRR: Any other reminiscences?

KWE: I'd told you that Nissim kissed my hand the last time when I told him I was leaving and going away to Madras and so on. He said, rather wistfully I think, 'You won't be coming again?' I particularly mentioned this incident since the Ezekiel's (senior), other than my husband Joe and his mum, are all very emotionally undemonstrative. They shake hands when they meet even if it is after some years. My side of the family are more likely to get a little hysterical, to jump up and down, thump each other and exchange bear-hugs and kisses. Even Joe /Nissim's sisters are not comfortable if I greet them with a hug. I have looked after Nissim often. He used to stop by and have lunch with us when we lived in Bombay. He spent time with us in London. But never once was he demonstrative in his appreciation. And here he is, with his mind a clean slate, he has no memory of our past associations, but, because I spent (that's what I see of it) time with him and talked to him at his two levels (one, the Alzheimer's affected level and the other, the level he imagines he is at), he actually expressed his affection/gratitude in a way other than our usual bantering with each other. Also, as I recall, the Bene Israel's invest this gesture with something more than affection–respect, perhaps. Whatever it was, it came as a great surprise.

I recall calling on Nissim and Daisy–Elkana was there and perhaps Kavita also–soon after one of his awards (Sahitya or one of the Padma/s?). I was joshing along as usual–Nissim had come to Madras earlier and was confused about his new grandson's name (Kalpana's son had been named Vikram. Nissim remembered it as Vikrant and said, 'Sounds like a ship, whatever made them name him that?') So, I teased him–'Potay ka naam bhi nahin jantey ho aur Dliii kaise gaye–chikat (ticket!) kisne katwaee?' and giving him a couple of thwacks as I said it, Daisy said, 'He's just been given an award so watch what you say,' all in very good humour. That was a happy evening we spent with them. I don't know when it all deteriorated/degenerated, but it did and after some years I sensed a rift between Nissim and Daisy–I mean other than the main one.

Sometime, probably in 1990, Daisy and Nissim invited my son Gulu and me to lunch at an Irani restaurant on Warden road. Gulu was leaving on a trip to Israel and it wasn't exactly pleasant. That restaurant owner had once told Nissim that if Nissim would allow them to put up a plaque saying 'Nissim Ezekiel eats here,' then they would give him free lunch for life !!!

Notes

I. The Saturday Oil-Man

1. Shirley Berry Isenberg, India's Bene Israel : A Comprehensive Inquiry and Sourcebook, Bombay: Popular Prakashan, 1988, p. 49.
2. Behram Contractor, 'Nissim Ezekiel : Poet, Editor and Novelist', The Afternoon Des patch & Courier, 27 November 1994, p. 14.
3. Bharathi P.G., 'Secrets of Longevity', (Interview with Nissim Ezekiel), Health and Nutrition, November 1994, pp. 22-27.
4. Isenberg, p. 121.

II. 'I Was Born Here and Belong'

1. Isenberg, p. 122.
2. Ibid., p. 53.
3. The Afternoon Despatch & Courier, 27 November 1994.
4. John B. Beston, 'An Interview with Nissim Ezekiel' in Indian Writing in English ed. Krishna Nandan Sinha, New Delhi: Heritage Publishers, 1979, pp. 42-49.
5. Tara Patel, 'Wandering Lust', (interview with Nissim Ezekiel), Celebrity, May 1984, pp. 59-61.
6. The Afternoon Despatch & Courier, 27 November 1994.
7. Celebrity, May 1984.
8. Nissim Ezekiel, 'Science and I', Science Age, March 1984, p. 23.
9. Isenberg, p. 224.
10. Neema Kamdar, 'Towards Better Verse', (interview with Nissim Ezekiel) Mid-Day, 24 December 1994, Supplement, p. 3.
11. Quoted by G. Damodar in 'Search for Identity: An Estimate of Ezekiel's Poetry', The Journal of Indian Writing in English, Special Number on Nissim Ezekiel, Guest Editor, Havovi Anklesaria, July 1986, pp. 58-64.
12. Mid-Day, 24 December 1994.

13. Isenberg, p. 107.
14. Ibid., p. 224.
15. Ibid., p. 226.
16. Nissim Ezekiel, 'A Poet's Passage', Bombay, 22 May-6 June 1983, pp. 34-36.
17. The Literary Endeavour Vol. 8, Nos. 1-4, 1986-87. Special Number on Bombay Poetry: Poems on Bombay City, Guest Editor, R. Raj Rao.
18. Bruce King, Three Indian Poets, Madras: Oxford University Press, 1991, p. 53.

III. Freedom at Midnight

1. Bombay, 22 May-6 June 1983.
2. Ibid.
3. Celebrity, May 1984.
4. Jose Philip, 'I am a Natural Outsider' (Interview with Nissim Ezekiel) Indian Express (Kochi), 12 June 1994, p. 5.
5. Science Age, March 1984.
6. Ibid.
7. Bombay, 22 May-6 June 1983.
8. Ibid.
9. Isenberg, p. 253.
10. Ibid., p. 248.
11. Quoted by Isenberg, pp. 249-250.
12. See Gandhi's Letters on Indian Affairs, Madras: V. Narayan & Co., 1923, p. 164. Quoted by Isenberg, p. 249.
13. Visiting the Chowpatty sands for public lectures became one of Nissim's regular habits. The Wilson College is right opposite. On 15 August 1947, Independence Day, he remembers being at the Chowpatty sands to witness a celebration with flags.
14. N.V.K. Murthy, '1942: A Love Story', New Quest, 107, September-October 1994, p. 304.
15. M. N. Roy, Our Differences, Calcutta: Saraswaty Library, n.d., p. 27.
16. Quoted by V. B. Karnik in his Epilogue to M. N. Roy's Memoirs, Delhi: Ajanta Publications, 1984, p. 595.
17. Ibid., Introduction, p. viii.
18. Ibid.
19. Ibid., p. 601.
20. M. N. Roy, Reason, Romanticism and Rationalism, Renaissance

Publishers, Preface. Quoted by Karnik in M. N. Roy's Memoirs, p. 603.

21. Ibid., p. 601.
22. V.C. Harris, 'Breaking Patterns, Flowing', Indian Comminicator (Sunday Magazine), 26 June 1994, p. 1.
23. Science Age, March 1984.

IV. To Say Hello to the Queen

1. Bombay, 22 May-6 June 1983.
2. Celebrity, May 1984.
3. Indian Communicator, 26 June 1994.
4. Ibid.
5. Bombay, 22 May-6 June 1983.
6. Mid-Day, 24 December 1994.
7. The Afternoon Despatch & Courier, 27 November 1994.
8. Celebrity, May 1984.
9. Bombay, 22 May-6 June 1983.
10. Celebrity, May 1984.
11. Bombay, 22 May-6 June 1983.
12. To Bombay magazine (22 May-6 June 1983) Nissim gives a different version of the story. He says: 'Krishna Paigankar rang me up one afternoon informing me that two Calcutta crewmen of a British cargo boat carrying ammunition to Indo-China had absconded, and that the shipping company was looking for two substitute crewmen, and would I be able to join Krishna. We were to sail that very night.'
13. Eventually, Sarah got married to someone else, not to Solomon. They met each other at Hannan's son's wedding at the Radio Club, Bombay for the first time since 1952, when Sarah introduced her husband to Solomon. As they were based in Delhi by then, they invited Solomon to visit them in Delhi. But he had stopped going to Delhi.
14. As Sarah's name doesn't appear anywhere in the letter, nor does anything else indicate it is a letter from Nissim to his sister, we have to rely on the evidence of Abraham Solomon, in whose possession the letter is, to conclude it is to Sarah.

V. Jewish Wedding in Bombay

1. Isenberg, p. 103.
2. Ibid., p. 132.
3. Bombay, 22 May-6 June 1983.

4. The Afternoon Despatch & Courier, 27 November 1994.
5. Nissim Ezekiel, A Time to Change, London: Fortune Press, 1952.
6. Indian Communicator, 26 June 1994.
7. Three Indian Poets, p. 21.
8. Ibid., p.22.
9. Wiseman expresses this view, for instance in his article 'The Development of Technique in the Poetry of Nissim Ezekiel', in Contemporary Indian English Verse ed. Chirantan Kulshrestha, New Delhi : Arnold Heinemann, 1980, pp. 133-149.
10. Indian Express (Kochi), 12 June 1994.
11. See Bruce King, Modern Indian Poetry in English, New Delhi: Oxford University Press, 1987, p. 91.
12. The Afternoon Despatch & Courier, 27 November 1994.
13. Celebrity, May 1984.
14. P. Lal, 'An Arrival in Indo-Anglian Poetry', Thought, 28 June 1952.
15. Inder Nath Kher, 'A Time to Change: The Early Poetry of Nissim Ezekiel', South Asian Review, July 1978, pp. 4 1-55.
16. Nissim Ezekiel, Sixty Poems, Bombay 1953.
17. 'Beside the Final Void: Nissim Ezekiel's Sixty Poems', The Toronto South Asian Review, Vol. 4, No. 2 (Fall 1985), pp. 74-88.

VI. Everyman in His Humour

1. Health and Nutrition, November 1994.
2. Nissim Ezekiel, 'Souza: The Painter', Thought, 8 February 1958, pp. 10-11.
3. —, 'An Indian Dancer on Himself', Thought, 22 February 1958, p. 11.
4. —, The Third, Bombay: 1958.
5. Three Indian Poets, p. 30.
6. Ibid., p.28.
7. Ibid., p. 29.
8. Ibid.

VII. 'I'm a Poet and I Know It'

1. K. R. Srinivasa Iyengar, Indian Writing in English, Bombay: Asia Publishing House, 1962.
2. Bombay, 22 May-6 June 1983.
3. Gieve Patel, Poems (Published by Nissim Ezekiel, Bombay, 1966).
4. Nira Benegal is the wife of the well-known film director, Shyam

Benegal. Nissim and she once edited a journal together, and also attempted to collaborate on a film project, which ultimately did not work out.

5. R. Raj Rao, 'How Secular is Modern Indian Poetry in English?' New Quest, 103, January-February 1994, pp. 21-3 1.
6. Nissim Ezekiel, The Unfinished Man, Calcutta: Writers Workshop, 1960.
7. N. P. Acharya, 'Achievement and Failure in Ezekiel's Poetry', The Journal of Indian Writing in English, Vol. 14, No. 2, July 1986, pp. 73-90.
8. R. Raj Rao, 'Ezekiel's Bombay Poems: Some Opinions', in Postcolonial Indian Literature in English: Essays in Honour of Nissim Ezekiel eds. Nilufer E. Bharucha and Vrinda Nabar, New Delhi: Vision Books, 1998, pp. 132-143.
9. Ten Twentieth Century Indian Poets ed. R. Parthasarathy, New Delhi: Oxford University Press, 1976.
10. Three Indian Poets, p. 33.
11. Indian English Poetry Since 1950: An Anthology ed. Vilas Sarang, Bombay: Disha Books, 1990, Introduction, p. 16.
12. Three Indian Poets, p. 33.
13. Ibid., p. 34.

VIII. Flower Power

1. Isenberg, p. 228.
2. Health and Nutrition, November 1994.
3. Nissim Ezekiel, 'Drugs: A Personal Footnote', unpublished essay.
4. Science Age, March 1984
5. Indian Communicator, 26 June 1994
6. Eric Hobsbawm, Age of Extremes: The Short Twentieth Century, New York: Michael Joseph/Penguin, 1995, pp. 100-10 1.
7. Quoted in Neema Kamdar's interview with Nissim Ezekiel, Mid-Day, 24 December 1994. However, the name of Sudhakar Pandey is not mentioned.
8. R. Raj Rao, 'Theme of Alienation in Nissim Ezekiel's Plays', in Contemporary Indian Drama eds. Sudhakar Pandey and Freya Taraporewala, New Delhi: Prestige Books, 1990, PP. 82-91.
9. Nissim Ezekiel, Three Plays, Calcutta: Writers Workshop, 1969. The two other plays that are included in the book are The Sleepwalkers and Marriage Poem.

10. Quoted by Vrinda Nabar in 'Domesticity and Drama: An Analysis of Marriage Poem and Don't Call it a Suicide', Contemporary Indian Drama eds. Pandey and Taraporewala, pp. 75-8 1.
11. Ibid.
12. Ibid.
13. Nissim Ezekiel, The Exact Name, Calcutta: Writers Workshop, 1965.
14. Indian English Poetry Since 1950: An Anthology, Introduction, p. 15.

IX. Hymns and Fancies

1. Bombay, 22 May-6 June 1983.
2. Eunice de Souza, Fix, Bombay: Newground, 1979; p. 24.
3. Nissim Ezekiel, 'Two Poets', The Illustrated Weekly of India, 18 June 1972, p. 65.
4. Nissim Ezekiel, Hymns in Darkness, New Delhi: Oxford University Press, 1976.
5. Three Indian Poets, p. 40.
6. For a fuller discussion of the religious element in Hymns in Darkness, see my article 'How Secular is Modern Indian Poetry in English?' New Quest 103, January-February 1994.
7. Three Indian Poets, p. 45.
8. For a fuller discussion of the Bombay Poems, see my article, 'Ezekiel's Bombay Poems: Some Opinions', in Postcolonial Indian Literature in English: Essays in Honour of Nissim Ezekiel, eds. Bharucha and Nabar, New Delhi: Vision Books, 1998.
9. R. Raj Rao, 'The Real, the Imaginary, the Backward etc.: Negotiations with Indian Modernity' in Trends in Twentieth Century Literary Criticism ed. N. M. Aston, New Delhi: Prestige Books, 1998, pp. 103-106.
10. Indian English Poetry Since 1950 : An Anthology, Introduction, p. 5.
11. M. Sivaramkrishna, 'New Poetry in India', The Times of India, 6 March 1977, p. 4.
12. See Voices of Emergency: All India Protest Poetry, 1957-1977 ed. John Oliver Perry, Bombay: Popular Prakashan Pvt. Ltd., 1983.
13. Kavi India, Poems of the Emergency, No. 5, 1977.
14. The Indian PEN, March-April 1977, pp. 15-17.
15. The Sydney Morning Herald, 17 December 1977, p. 19.

X. Verse, Versatility

1. S. Krishnan, 'Poetic Moods and Postures', The Hindu, 25 July 1978, p. XI.
2. In the Appendix, Selected Prose has an interview with Nissim by Frank Birbalsingh (pp. 161-173). A footnote informs us that the interview was recorded in Bombay on 30 June 1986. Nissim's visit to Birbalsingh's home is supposed to have preceded the interview.
3. Santan Rodrigues, 'In Love with Poetry' (interview with Nissim Ezekiel), Youth Times, 1-14 February 1980, p. 17.
4. Mariana Pinto, 'Talking of Favourites' (interview with Nissim Ezekiel and five others), Eve's Weekly, 29 December-S January 1980, p. 29.
5. The Indian Literary Review, Vol. 1, No. 10, February 1979, pp. 2-8.
6. It is probable that although the date of the issue of ILR in which the interview appears is February 1979, the issue actually appeared much later, so as to facilitate a discussion of Latter-Day Psalms (1982).
7. The Indian PEN, Nos. 11-12, November-December 1977, pp. 4-8.
8. New Quest, 8, March-April 1978, pp. 132-134.
9. Vagartha, No. 22, July 1978, pp. 22-31.
10. Snake-Skin and Other Poems of Indira Sant, Trans. Nissim Ezekiel and Vrinda Nabar, Bombay: Nirmala Sadanand Publishers, 1975.
11. The Indian PEN, No. 11-12, November-December 1978, pp. 1-11. The paper was read at the American Bicentennial Interdisciplinary Seminar, Hyderabad, in January 1977.
12. The article was originally published in English and India, eds. M. Manuel and K. Ayyappa Panikar, Madras: Macmillan 1978, pp. 117-124. It was reprinted in Selected Prose, New Delhi: Oxford University Press, 1992, pp. 11-19.
13. Freedom First, No. 352, June 1982, p. 1.
14. Nissim Ezekiel, 'Caught in a Maze,' The Sunday Times, 15 June 1980, p. 2.
15. The Sunday Times, 15 February 1981.
16. Nissim Ezekiel, 'Why Live When You Can Have a Beautiful Funeral', The Sunday Times, 29 November 1981, p. 2.
17. - 'Full Marks for Nothing', The Sunday Times, 4 January 1981, p. 2.
18. 'Some Problems of Modern Indian Culture', New Quest, 28, July-August 1981, pp. 209-216.
19. '. . . And Thou Beside Me is Paradise Enow', The Sunday Times, 13 December 1981, p. 2.

20. 'The Writing of Poetry', in Focus on Literature: Essays in Memory of C. A. Sheppard, eds. C.T. Thomas, Sr. Cleopatra, S. Velayudhan and R. Viswanathan, Madras: Macmillan India Limited, 1982, pp. 135-142.
21. Ten Twentieth Century Indian Poets, p. 11.
22. Nissim Ezekiel, 'To Revise or not to Revise', The Literary Criterion, 1983. Rpt. in Selected Prose, pp. 20-28.
23. R. Raj Rao, The WisestFoolon Earth and Other Plays, Bombay: The Brown Critique, 1996.
24. Nissim Ezekiel, Latter-Day Psalms, New Delhi: Oxford University Press, 1982.
25. See The Indian Literary Review, Vol.1, No. 10, February 1979, p. 4.
26. Three Indian Poets, pp. 47-48.
27. Shyamala A. Narayan, 'Nissim Ezekiel's Latter-Day Psalms: A Study', JIWE, Vol.13, No. 1, January 1985, pp. 31-38.
28. Vrinda Nabar, 'A Perspective on Indo-English Poetry', Tenor, Vol. 4, 1980, pp. 10-17.
29. R. A. Malagi, 'Indian Poetry in English Today: Some Observations', Vidya: The Journal of Gujarat University, Vol. XXIII, No. 2, August 1980, pp. 61-66.
30. Vinod and Shiva Kumar, 'The Indianness of Ezekiels "Indian English" Poems: An Analysis,' in Perspectives on Nissim Ezekiel ed. S.C. Dwivedi, Allahabad: Kitab Mahal, 1989, pp. 78-97.
31. Paper presented at the Second Triennial Conference of the Canadian Association of Commonwealth Literature and Language Scholars, University of Winnipeg, Manitoba, 1-4 October 1981.
32. S. D. Desai, 'His Hymns in Darkness', The Times of India (Ahmedabad), 30 September 1981, p. 3.
33. Osmania Journal of English Studies Vol. XIII, No. 1, 1977. Special Number on Nissim Ezekiel eds. V.A. Shahane and M. Sivaramakrishna.
34. Anisur Rahman, Form and Value in the Poetry of Nissim Ezekiel, New Delhi: Abhinav Publications, 1981.

Xl. Padma Shri Shri Ezekiel

1. Anne Stevenson, 'Multiple Allegiances', The Times Literary Supplement, 19 April 1985, p. 449.
2. The Times Literary Supplement, 10 May 1985.
3. Iris Kalka, 'Under the Influence of Jewish and Indian Spirits', Jewish Chronicle, 27 September 1985, p. 9.
4. Kersy Katrak, 'Pater Familias', The Sunday Observer, 13 March 1983, p. 16.

5. Darshan Singh Maini, 'The Achievement of Nissim Ezekiel', Indian Book Chronicle, Vol. VIII. No. 9, 1 May 1983, pp. 161-163.
6. Ajit Khullar, 'Old Psalms for New Times' Indian Literature, September-October 1984, pp. 219-227.
7. Tara Patel, Single Woman, New Delhi: Rupa & Co, 1993.
8. Nine Indian Women Poets ed. Eunice de Souza, Bombay: Oxford University Press, 1997.
9. Celebrity, May 1984.
10. Tara Patel refers here to the July 1983 issue of Imprint.
11. The Illustrated Weekly of India, 22 January 1984, p. 44.
12. Indian English Poetry: An Anthology ed. I. H. Rizvi, Bareilly: Prakash Book Depot, 1988, pp. 2-3.
13. Nagpur Times Magazine, 28 June-4 July 1987, p. 4.
14. The review appeared in the now defunct newspaper The Indian Post. The photocopy that I managed to obtain, does not unfortunately bear the date. It is certain, however, that the year is 1988.
15. Nissim Ezekiel, 'The Comfortable Tiredness of Intoxication', The Sunday Observer, 31 July 1988, P. 17.
16. - 'An Indian Sherlock Holmes', The Indian Post, 30 October 1988, p. 6.
17. See The Times of India, 26 June 1975, p. 3.
18. Nissim Ezekiel, 'Arts and the State', Indian Horizons. Vol. XXXV, Nos 3-4, 1986, pp. 7-13.
19. - 'There's a Difference Between Criticism and Contempt', The Independent, 15 October 1993, p. 7.
20. 'The Naviete Disease', Debonair, June 1988, p. 93.
21. Science Age, March 1984.
22. Nissim Ezekiel, 'To Revise or Not to Revise', The Literary Criterion, October 1983, pp. 1-9.
23. The Journal of Indian Writing in English, Vol. 14, No. 2, July 1986.
24. Dinyar Godrej, 'A Seminal Status', The Indian Post. n.d.
25. Inder Nath Kher, 'The Creative Harmony: Introduction to the Poetic World of Nissim Ezekiel', South Asian Review, July 1983, pp. 52-58.
26. S.C. Narula, 'Negative Affirmations in Nissim Ezekiel's Hymns and Psalms', Ariel, Autumn 1983, pp. 52-71.
27. See Literature in English: New Territories, Band 33, Heidelberg, 1987.
28. Dnyaneshwar Nadkarni, 'Simplicity of Ezekiel's Poems', Financial Express, 23 September 1984, p. 5.

29. Dhiren Bhagat, 'The Limited Club', India Today, 31 July 1982, p. 131.

30. Makarand Paranjape, 'Nissim Ezekiel as a Mystical Poet', Commonwealth Quarterly, Vol. 13, December 1986-March 1987, No. 34, pp. 1-6.

31. See Kesari, 22 January 1984, p.S.

32. See Navshakti, 20 November 1986, p. 2.

33. Radhika Ramaseshan, 'Playwright Who Needs No Introduction', The Sunday Observer, 24 February 1985, p. 19.

34. Nissim Ezekiel, Don't Call it a Suicide, Madras: Macmillan, 1989.

35. Indu Saraiya, 'Traumatic End', The Sunday Free Press Journal, 19 June 1988, p. 14.

36. Rochelle D'Souza, 'A Quiet, Hard Hitting Tragedy', The Indian Post, 30 August 1988, p. 8.

37. Ajith Pillai, 'Presenting Nissim Ezekiel, Rock Lyricist,' The Indian Post, 29 August 1988, p. 7.

38. Indian Literature, No. 120, July-August 1987.

39. E.V. Ramakrishnan, 'Poets Bombay', Indian Express, 17 January 1988, p. 5.

40. Image of India in the Indian Novel in English eds. Sudhakar Pandey and R. Raj Rao, Bombay: Orient Longman, 1993.

41. Nissim Ezekiel, Collected Poems, New Delhi: Oxford University Press, 1988.

42. Indian Communicator, 26 June 1994.

XII. Totem Pole

1. See The Bombay Review (later called The Bombay Literary Review), 1989, No 1, pp. 99-120.

2. Nissim Ezekiel, 'The Heritage of India', in Links ed. G. S. Balarama Gupta, Madras: Macmillan India Limited, 1989, pp. 163-167.

3. Lin Hsin Hsin, 'Professor Nissim Ezekiel', in Take a Word for a Walk, Singapore: Select Books, 1989, p. 9.

4. Charmayne D'Souza, A Spelling Guide to Woman, Bombay: Disha Books, 1990.

5. Sanjeev Bhatla, Looking Back, Bombay: Disha Books, 1990.

6. Indian English Poetry Since 1950: An Anthology, Introduction, p. 17.

7. Nissim Ezekiel, Selected Prose, New Delhi: Oxford University Press, 1992.

8. Indian Poetry in English ed. Makarand Paranjape, Madras: Macmillan, 1993, Introduction, p. 24.
9. See, for example, my article 'And One Last Thing, Mr Rushdie', The Sunday Times of India (Review), 24 August, 1997, p. 7.
10. Jerry Pinto, 'Delightfully Dear', The Sunday Free Press Journal, 15 November 1992, p. 11.
11. Eunice de Souza, 'Interviews with Four Indian English Poets: Nissim Ezekiel, Adil Jussawalla, Gieve Patel and Arun Kolatkar', The Bombay Review, 1989, No 1, pp. 71-84.
12. The Oxford India Anthology of Twelve Modern Poets ed. Arvind Krishna Mehrotra, New Delhi: Oxford University Press, 1992.
13. See especially R. Parthasarathy, 'Whoring after English Gods', in Writers in East-West Encounter ed. Guy Amirthanayagam, London: Macmillan, 1980, pp. 64-84; and Arvind Krishna Mehrotra, 'The Emperor Has No Clothes', Chandrabhaga 3, 1980, pp. 17-27 and Chandrabhaga 7, 1982, pp. 1-32.
14. Sudeep Sen, 'Remembering The Night of the Scorpion,' Network, January 1992, p. 80.
15. Zubin Driver, 'The Poet as Playwright', Debonair, November 1992, p. 59.
16. See Debonair, September 1992, p. 138.
17. Damning Verdict (Report of the Sri Krishna Commission appointed for inquiry into the riots at Mumbai during December 1992-January 1993 and the 12 March 1993 bomb blasts), Bombay: Sabrang Communications and Publishing Pvt. Ltd., 1998.
18. G.N. Devy, After Amnesia: Tradition and Change in Indian Literary Criticism, Delhi: Orient Longman, 1992.
19. Raji Narasimhan, 'Critic in Search of a Context for Self', The Economic Times, 20 June 1993, p. 12.
20. Vijay Nambisan, 'Nissim Ezekiel: Foreground Casually', The Hindu (Magazine), 17 October 1993, p. XIV.
21. Nissim Ezekiel, 'Small-Scale Reflections on a Great Friend', The Deccan Herald, 24 July 1993, p. 4.
22. The Independent, 15 October 1993, p. 7.
23. Nissim Ezekiel, 'Working is Relaxation' (as told to Ronita Toracto), The Deccan Chronicle, 17 June 1993, p. 14.
24. See The Metropolis on Saturday, Bombay, 31 December 1994, p.6.
25. Santan Rodrigues, 'God Had Spoken to Us', The Sunday Observer, 17 December 1994, p. 6.

26. Ranjit Hoskote, Zones of Assault, Delhi: Rupa & Co., 1991.

27. Rochelle D'Souza 'Nissim in New York', The International Indian, Vol. 2. No. 3, Early Spring 1994, p. 52.

28. Daniel Schifrin, 'Beginnings of a Rebirth', Jewish Week, 1 June 1994, p. 10.

29. Indian Express (Kochi), 12 June 1994, p. 5.

30. 'In Search of Kavita: Poetry from the Indian Subcontinent and Beyond', Poetry Review, Vol. 82, No. 1, Spring 1993.

31. The Afternoon on Sunday, 27 November, 1994.

32. Mid-Day, 24 December 1994.

33. Health and Nutrition, November 1994.

34. A. K. Ramanujan, The Collected Poems, New Delhi: Oxford University Press, 1995.

35. Oxford Anthology of Twelve Modern Indian Poets, Introduction, p. 9.

36. Nissim Ezekiel, 'Poetry in the Time of Tempests', The Sunday Times of India (Review), 29 June, 199?, p. 3.

37. See The Free Press Journal, 2 September 1998, p. 3.

38. Adil Jussawalla, 'Vimala's Story on Nissim Makes My Blood Boil', The Free Press Journal, 4 September 1998, p. 3.

39. Jerry Pinto, 'The Poet of Small Things', The Sunday Times, 6 September 1998, p. 6.

40. Postcolonial Indian Literature in English: Essays in Honour of Nissim Ezekiel.

41. Minakshi Raja, 'Remembering Nissim Ezekiel', The Afternoon on Sunday, 20 June 1999, p. 13.

42. Adil Jussawalla, 'Notes Towards a Portrait of Nissim Ezekiel', The Sunday Observer, 12-18 December 1999, p. 3.

Index

A

Acharya, N.P., 176, 317
Adarkar, Priya, 337
Adjania, Nancy, 299, 355
Advani, Rukun, 336
Alexander, Meena, 345
Alkazi, Ebrahim, 43, 53, 67, 69, 70, 78, 106, 207,
Alkazi, Roshenara, 68, 71, 75
Alladin, Bilkees, 173
Amichai, Yehuda, 357
Anand, Mulk Raj, 168
Andrade, Br. Hector, 210-211
Anklesaria, Havovi, 300-01, 303
Anklesaria, Persis, 275, 292-293, 316-317
Antarkar, G.D., 155
Ashcroft, Peggy, 73
Auden, W.H., 114, 151, 176
Aurobindo, Sri, 273

B

Bakhtiar, Iqbal, 111
Bakhtin, 332
Balsara, Sabar, 111
Banerjee, G.D., 215
Barthes, Roland, 332
Bartholomew, R.L., 115
Barua, Freya, 296-299
Beck, Patrick, 202
Beckett, 104
Benegal, Nira, 174, 279
Benjamin, Joseph, 44

Berkson, Carmel, 336
Berry, Ana M., 117
Beston, John B., 26, 167, 236
Bhabha, Homi, 315
Bhagat, Dhiren, 303
Bhagwat, Charu, 207, 301
Bharucha, Nilufer, 361-62, 365
Bharvani, Shakuntala, 306, 351
Bhatla, Sanjiv, 320-21, 326
Bhattachary, Narendra, 49
Bhende, Asha, 305, 360, 362
Bhende, Atmaram, 360, 362
Bhende, Nandu, 270, 305, 360, 362-64
Bhende, Usha, 364
Birbalsingh, Frank, 242, 323-24
Barkar, B.B., 252
Borner, Klaus H., 303
Broker, Gulabdas, 105
Burge, Anthony, 237

C

Chako, P.M., 309
Chakravarty, Tapas, 359
Chatterjee, Upamanyu, 304
Chattopadhyaya, Harindranath, 53, 153-154
Chaudhuri, Nirad, 97, 198-199, 333
Chindhade, Shirish, 312
Chitre, Dilip, 240, 346, 352
Cochin Jews, 5-9, 42
Coelho, George, 51, 68
Cohen, S., 185
Contractor, Behram, 14, 24, 72, 111,

354, 389
Coppola, Carlo, 276
Cunha, Nisha da, 284

D

Dabydeen, David, 231
Dagli, Vadilal, 166, 190
Damodar, G., 309
Dandekar, Aaron, 99
Dandekar, Benjamin, 99
Dandekar, Isaac, 99
Dandekar, Ivy, 99
Dandekar, Joseph, 99
Dandekar, Lily, 99
Dandekar, Mozel, 99
Dandekar, Ruby, 99
Dandekar, Sarah, 99
Dandekar, Shalom, 99
Dani, N.D., 309
Daniels, Shourie, 315
Daruwalla, Keki, 159, 231, 246, 284, 286, 310, 333
Das, Kamala, 106, 141, 159, 246, 279, 284, 322, 341
Date, Vidyadhar, 375
De, Shobha, 326, 370
de Souza, Eunice, 37, 106, 159, 218-220, 244, 290, 298, 234, 352, 373, 394, 397, 400
Desai, Anita, 243
Desai, S.D., 284, 397
Deshpande, Gauri, 7, 158, 160, 182-183, 220, 259, 353, 367, 403
Devy, G.N., 283, 340, 400
Dharker, Anil, 252
Dharker, Imtiaz, 222, 252, 353, 373, 375
Dharwadker, Vinay, 258-59
Dhillon, Amrit, 356
Dhuldhoya, Nandini, 290
Dixit, V.K., 240

Driver, Zubin, 336
D'Souza, Charmayne, 106, 297, 330
D'Souza, Rochelle, 313, 353, 399
Dubey, Satyadev, 234
Dwivedi, A.N., 309
Dwivedi, S.C., 315

E

Eliot, T.S., 39, 40, 112, 171, 225, 237, 261, 262, 286, 290, 325
Erulkar, Abraham S., 44
Ezekiel (nee Dandekar), Daisy, 5, 11, 14, 27, 33, 73, 100-102, 115, 126, 130, 151, 154, 156-157, 161-163, 168, 173, 175-179, 182, 221, 226, 246, 272, 278, 342-343, 348, 356, 360, 369, 375, 378-381, 383, 387-388
Ezekiel, Diana, 1, 12, 19-20, 23-25, 32-33, 50, 221
Ezekiel, Elkana, 5, 16, 27, 33, 71-72, 163, 168, 226, 270, 326, 342, 344-346, 354, 354, 356, 360, 365-375, 384-385, 387
Ezekiel, Hannan, 2, 6, 8, 16, 22, 45, 55, 64-65, 86, 90, 157, 221, 344-345, 372, 384, 391
Ezekiel, Joe, 6, 10, 16, 22, 45, 55, 73, 76, 86, 93, 101, 221, 344, 366-367, 374, 378-384, 387
Ezekiel, Kalpana, 156, 177, 272, 291, 387
Ezekiel, Kavita, 6, 17, 156, 177, 226, 270-272, 289, 343, 354, 368, 379, 386-387, 401
Ezekiel, Khorshed Wadia, 6, 61, 106-107, 188, 210, 227, 366, 374, 378
Ezekiel, Lily, 2, 22, 99, 221, 332, 386
Ezekiel, Moses, 9, 11-12, 14, 16, 19, 20, 23, 28, 32, 33, 40, 43, 45, 50, 223, 261
Ezekiel, M.S., 43

Ezekiel, Nissim

Awards:
Certificate of Appreciation from Gate of Mercy Synagogue, 284
Excellence Award for Contribution to Poetry, 227
Padma Shri for Contribution to Indian Literature in English, 288, 294
R.K. Lagu Prize, 41
Sahitya Akademi Award for Latter-Day Psalms, 283

Foreign Travels:
as guest of Arts Council of Great Britain, 338
as poet-in-residence at National University of Singapore, 292
as visiting professor at University of Leeds, 152, 161, 162, 164, 199
for ACLALS conference in Jamaica, 322, 357
for Adelaide Book Fair, 292
for conference on Inter-Cultural Encounters in Literature, Hawaii, 227
for Edinburgh Arts Festival, 292, 294, 300
for Frankfurt Book Fair, 221, 292, 312
for New Zealand International Festival of Arts, 292
on Cultural Exchange Programme in USA, 227
other foreign travels, 241-42
to Hong Kong, 288, 292
to New York, 103, 104, 105, 186, 187
to Salburg, 248, 254, 282, 353, 394
voyage to England, 70-94

Jobs and Other Pursuits:
advisory board of Ariel, 237
art critic, 133, 136, 180, 197, 231, 232,
233
association with Kavi, 228
association with PEN, 55-56, 103-05, 204, 220-21
association with Theatre Unit, 98-99
at Bombay University, 220, 246, 265, 272, 311, 332, 335, 355, 371
at Chemould, 133, 272
at Design magazine, 134
at Hansraj Morarji School, 41
at India House, 71-74, 76, 80
at Khalsa College, 42, 50, 68, 69, 130
at Mithibai College, 149-152, 158, 161, 164, 168, 190, 170, 208, 210, 239
at Shilpi, 103-105, 121, 124, 130, 133, 151, 160
consultant to Rupa & Co;, and Orient Longman, 330, 331,
editor, Aryan Path, 106
editor, Disha, 330-331
editor, Freedom First, 52, 108, 262-264, 266, 295, 396
editor, Imprint, 137, 157, 158, 192, 198, 210, 214, 299
editor, Indian PEN, 106-108, 137, 181, 190, 231, 247, 259, 316, 328, 342, 350, 395
editor, Poetry India, 137, 166, 190-192
editor, Quest, 48, 100, 118, 119, 121, 122, 123, 124, 132
guest-editor, Indian Literature, 305-06
literary critic, 134, 256, 287, 325, 395, 400
sub-editor, Illustrated Weekly 98, 99, 121, 137, 153, 157
theatre critic, 184
tv and radio critic, 226, 296, 317

Personal
Alzhiemer's disease, 315, 332, 360-67
Bar Mitzvah, 15-16

birth, 3
education, 5, 9, 18, 19, 25, 52, 77, 80, 152
marriage, 117, 142, 209, 211, 216, 230, 239, 259
separation, 178, 256, 297, 288, 325

Views On:
AIR & Doordarshan, 257, 258
artistic process, 235, 241
ban on Rushdie's Satanic Verses, 253, 295-297, 305
ban on Taslima Nasreen's Shame, 53, 305, 341
cultural issues, 264
diet/health, 12, 13, 23, 44, 132, 154, 155, 181, 183, 186, 188, 225, 326, 354, 356, 360, 361
divorce, 177-180, 379, 381
domesticity, 90
failure, 22, 23, 27, 30, 39, 40, 110, 119, 131, 140, 179, 206, 231, 232, 241, 252, 262, 276, 284, 299, 320, 322, 343, 344, 355
Hindu-Muslim problem, 338
Indian English Poems, 160, 169, 235, 239, 240, 244, 254, 252, 253, 277, 284, 333, 373
Indianness, 8, 252, 284, 350, 397
Judaism, 45, 180, 291, 327, 352, 355
life and art, 86, 95
LSD, 178-84, 201, 226
marriage, 26, 55, 99, 100, 109, 115-117, 140, 142, 173-175, 178-179, 181, 196, 197, 221, 222, 236, 250, 251, 278, 279, 299, 302, 317, 344, 378, 379, 382
M. N. Roy and politics, 42, 43, 45-47, 51-54, 59, 62, 65, 67, 97, 120, 142, 164, 170, 211, 214, 234, 263, 266, 267, 322, 363
place in world literature, 255

poetry, 302, 312-13
poster poems, 247
religion, 7, 10, 11, 13, 15, 18, 32, 33, 38, 40, 43, 45, 46, 49, 54, 72, 127, 176, 183, 235, 274, 291, 306, 322, 327, 333, 354
science, 19, 23, 25, 40, 64, 75, 134, 150, 180, 186, 200, 306
teaching, 6, 9, 18-20, 31, 38, 41, 42, 149, 155, 162, 164, 183, 207, 209, 211, 212, 227, 248, 286-289, 343, 380
vegetarianism, 187-188
women, 176, 199, 244

Works of:
A Time to Change, 74, 76, 77, 86, 96, 101, 108-115, 138, 147, 316, 351
Collected Poems, 63, 172, 242, 300, 302, 304, 316, 321, 324, 341, 356
Don't Call it a Suicide, 193, 313, 324, 326, 394
Hymns in Darkness, 34, 36, 170-171, 234-240, 242-247, 250, 272-276, 282, 283, 317
Latter-Day Psalms, 100, 171, 250, 253, 272-276, 278, 282-284, 286, 291, 316, 317, 319, 351
Marriage Poems, 190, 192
Nalini, 192-197, 218, 313
Selected Prose, 261, 307, 324, 329, 332-334, 340
Sixty Poems, 96, 101, 112, 114, 116, 121, 137, 138, 147
The Exact Name, 35, 149, 170, 171, 199, 202, 204, 206, 219, 235, 236, 272, 281, 351
The Third, 21, 35, 83, 113, 127, 137-148, 161, 190, 191, 193, 238, 275, 306, 308
The Unfinished Man, 35, 149, 170-173, 199, 235, 236, 241, 317, 351

E

Ezekiel, Rahamim J., 43
Ezekiel, Sarah, 2, 22, 55, 65, 85, 88, 91-96, 221, 332, 386, 391, 392, 403

F

Forbes, Peter, 354
Fredericks, Leo, 111
Fromm, Erich, 93-94
Frost, Robert, 132, 335, 342, 384
Futehally, Laeeq, 170
Futehally, Shama, 212
Futehally, Zafar, 40, 170, 206

G

Gaikwad, Victor, 7, 150, 153-154
Gandhi, Indira, 242, 257, 266, 295
Gandhi, Mahatma, 42, 44, 46,
Gandhi, Rajiv, 263, 295
Gandhi, Sanjay, 263, 266
Gandhy, Kekoo, 133
Gandhy, Korshed, 227
Ghose, Aurobindo, 46, 53, 58, 265, 335, 358
Ginsberg, Allen, 177
Godrej, Dinyar, 310, 398
Gokhale, G.K., 89
Gopal, Ram, 134, 136
Gorawala, 159
Gowda, Anniah, 357
Grave, Robert, 269
Gupta, AS., 300
Gupta, G.S. Balarama, 300, 303

H

Haim, Yehoyada, 362
Hales, Authur, 153
Hales, Gloria, 153
Hall, Donald, 288
Harris, V.C., 53, 72, 186, 317
Hess, Linda, 104, 105, 167-168, 176-178, 237, 291, 379, 381
Hobsbawm, Eric, 189
Hoskote, Ranjit, 37, 106, 170, 176, 188, 218, 222, 231, 325, 334, 373
Huxley, Aldous, 185-186

I

Ibsen, 101, 261
Irwin, John, 124
Isenberg, Shirley Berry, 8, 14, 27, 32, 33, 42, 100
Israel, Haskelji, 4, 7, 18, 19
Israel, Jacob B., 43
Israel, Shalom B., 43
Iyengar, K.R. Srinivasa, 161

J

Jarrell, Randall, 260
Jeffares, Norman, 161
Jhabvala, Ruth Prawer, 256, 257
Jhaveri, M.M., 108
Joad, C.E.M., 71
Jones, James, 119
Joshi, Ram, 208
Joshi, Vanashree, 239
Jussawalla, Adil, 35, 37, 106, 156, 157, 159, 177, 192, 199, 206, 242, 285, 306, 322
Jussawalla, J.M., 224, 358
Jussawalla, Mehroo, 290

K

Kale, Pramod, 150, 153
Kalka, Iris, 286
Kamdar, Neema, 28, 72, 354
Kanitkar, Anand, 108
Kapoor, Prithviraj, 21
Kapoor, Raj, 21, 41
Karim, Mumtaz, 107
Karnani, Chetan, 172, 285
Karnik, V.B., 48, 50

Karve, R.D., 59
Katrak, Kersy, 156, 159, 165, 286
Kaur, Dilraj, 305
Kher, Inder Nath, 112, 114, 311
Khullar, Ajit, 287
King, Bruce, 37, 110, 138, 173, 234, 273, 274, 311
Koestler, Arthur, 108
Kohli, Suresh, 252
Kolatkar, Arun, 242, 285, 309, 346, 352
Kostka, Ivan, 228
Krishna Menon, 71
Krishnan, S., 246
Kumar, Shiv K., 246, 285, 310
Kutty, M.K., 150

L
Lakshman, Nikhil, 166
Lal, P., 111, 156, 157, 170, 194, 199, 285
Leavis, 290
Lin Hsin Hsin, 328
Lukmani, Yasmin, 214, 372
Lutendorf, Philip, 176

M
Mahapatra, Jayanta, 242, 246, 285
Maini, Darshan Singh, 287
Malagi, R.A., 284
Mandelstam, 262
Mandy, C.R., 98
Mansour, Walid, 372
Markandaya, Kamala, 333
Masani, M.R., 255
Mazgamkar, Samuel S., 43
Meganathan, R., 51
Mehrotra, Arvind Krishna, 285, 335, 358, 400
Mehta, Hare Krishna, 107
Menezes, Armando, 53
Menon, Bena, 337

Merchant, Norman A., 90
Miranda, Mario, 351
Mirchandani, Aneela, 359
Mishra, Prabhanjan, 331
Mistry, Cyrus, 366
Mitra, Aroop, 221
Montago, Edwin Samuel, 43-44
Moraes, Dom, 37, 70, 106, 157, 304, 373
Moraes, Frank, 106
Moses, Elijah, 43
Motiwalla, Mumtaz, 107
Munshi, K.M, 39
Murthy, N.V.K., 46

N
Nabar, Vrinda, 7, 196, 198, 213, 214, 220, 233, 258, 259, 284, 393-397
Nadira, 32
Nadkarni, Dnyaneshwar, 312
Naganikar, Elloji, 9
Naidu, Sarojini, 46, 53, 265, 334, 335, 358
Naik, M.K., 309
Naipaul, V.S., 43, 213, 229-231, 329, 333, 334, 337, 338
Nambsian, Vijay, 340
Nandy, Pritish, 300
Narsimhaiah, C.D., 307
Narasimhan, Raji, 340
Narayan, R.K., 162
Narayan, Shyamala, A., 282
Narula, S.C., 311
Nasreen, Taslima, 53, 305, 341
Navalkar, Pramod, 374
Nawgaonkar, Robenji, Isaji, 9
Nehru, Jawaharlal, 46, 49, 52, 71, 263, 265, 266, 340,
Niranjana, Tejaswini, 332
Niven, Alastair, 339-340
Nordan, Max, 61

O

Olivier, Lawrence, 71
Osbern, William C., 81

P

Padamsee, Alyque, 69, 101-102, 181, 385
Padgaonkar, Mangesh, 154, 259
Paigankar, Krishna, 73, 74-78, 82
Pal, R.M, 51
Pandey, Sudhakar, 193, 315, 326, 327
Paranjape, Makarand, 312, 315, 333
Paranjape, P.N., 259
Parikh, G.D., 49, 149, 150, 154
Parikh, Prabodh, 363
Parthasarathy, R., 106, 150, 157, 172, 191, 199, 234, 242, 246, 252, 268, 285, 334, 346
Patel, Avan, 181
Patel, Gieve, 37, 106, 159, 160, 163, 165-168, 180-181, 189, 191, 196, 224, 242, 285, 309-310, 316-317, 326, 337, 351, 353, 357, 360-361, 367, 371-373
Patel, Tara, 25, 73, 106, 146, 189, 215, 217-218, 247, 297, 346, 362, 373
Patel (nee Diniz), Toni, 102, 157, 163-165, 175, 180-182, 189, 194-196, 223-224, 226, 250, 282, 309, 337, 351, 357, 359
Patil, Vimala, 370
Patonkar, R.B., 290, 332
Peeradina, Saleem, 37, 106, 346
Perry, John Oliver, 242
Peters, Elian, 369
Pillai Ajith, 313
Pinto, Jerry, 222, 249-250, 298, 329-330, 334, 348-350, 355, 359, 360, 362-368, 373, 376
Pound, Ezra, 40, 171
Pradhan, 354
Prasad, B.N., 309

Pushpamala, N., 349

R

Radheylal, 64
Rahman, Anisure, 285
Raja, Minakshi, 102, 157, 168, 182, 233, 297, 348, 356, 361, 362, 370, 375, 385
Rajiv Rao, 235
Raju, S.V., 264
Rakesh, 277
Ramachandra Rao, P.R., 63
Ramkrishna, D., 309
Ramakrishnan, E.V., 314
Ramanujan, A.K., 196, 241, 246, 268, 282, 285, 308, 310, 356
Ramaseshan, Radhika, 313
Rao, L. Adinarayana, 37
Rao, Raja, 35, 162, 172
Rao, Srinivas, 150
Rao, Urmila, 107
Ray, Satyajit, 304
Ray, Shibnarayan, 64, 115
Richards, I.A., 288
Richardson, 71
Rilke, 68, 111, 132, 269, 307
Rizvi, I.H., 302
Rodrigues, Santan, 37, 106, 212, 228, 309, 349
Roy, M.N., 46, 49, 50, 52, 55, 69, 149, 244
Rushdie, Salman, 53, 256, 295-297, 305, 341, 352

S

Sabavala, Jehangir, 233
Sachdev, Arun, 234
Sahgal, Nayantara, 338-339
Sahni, Kavita, 270-271
Salesh, Carmes, 121
Samson, B.J., 43

Samson, I.J., 43, 44
Sant, Indira, 6, 220, 258-259
Sarabhai, Gira, 103, 124
Sarabhai, Vikram, 103
Saraiya, Indu, 313
Sarang, Vilas, 173, 203, 214 243, 326, 331-332, 335-336, 362, 393
Sen, Sudeep, 336
Sethi, Sanjiv, 356
Shah, A.B., 55, 127
Shakoor, 157, 182
Shanane, Vasant, A., 284
Shanbag, 117
Sharma, Sunita, 239
Sharma, Vera, 239
Shaw, Bernard, 195
Sheppard, C.A., 267
Shetty, Manohar, 145
Shivdasani, Menka, 106, 297, 331, 373
Shroff, Homai, 290
Simon, Oliver, 123
Singh, Iqbal, 82
Singh, Khushwant, 253
Singh, Patwant, 134
Sirkar, Ambika, 233
Sirkar, Mihir, 233
Sirkar, Rameschandra, 104-05, 151, 183, 206, 220, 225, 287-88, 333, 339, 343, 353
Sivaramakrishna, M., 242
Solomon, Abraham, 45, 51, 54, 59, 67, 69, 115, 125, 392
Solomon, Jacob, E., 43-44
Solomon, Ruby, 125
Solzhenitsyn, 346
Souza, Francis Newton, 134-135
Spender, Stephens 108, 260, 384
Spivak, Gayatri, 325

Srinivasan, R., 264
Stevens, Wallace, 225, 335
Stevenson, Anne, 286
Stewart, Iain, 339
Sundaram, Vivian, 233
Swamy, Jane, 330-331

T
Tagore, Rabindranath, 25, 46, 53, 110, 265-266, 269
Talkar, Aaron Daniel, 43
Talkar, Bahais Joseph, 9
Talkar, M.D., 9
Talkar, Moses Ezekiel, see Ezekiel, Moses, 1, 3, 223
Talkar, Shelomo Abraham, 5
Taraporewala, Barua, 289
Taraporewala, Soonoo, 289
Tarkunde, V.M., 50-51
Tellis, Ashley, 325, 362, 364
Tilak, Lokamanya, 43
Torcato, Ronita, 220, 247, 341, 364, 374
Tyabji, Adil, 329, 332

W
Wadia, Madame Sophiya, 53, 106-107, 210, 227
Whitman, Walt, 53, 225, 280
Wilde, Oscar, 56-57, 195
Wiseman, Christopher, 110
Wood, Kamal, 209

Y
Yajnik, A.B., 149-150, 169
Yeats, W.B., 110, 171